The Bullfighter

© Kelvin Robertson, 2021

Published by Keldaviain Publishing

All rights reserved. No part of this book may be reproduced, adapted, stored in a retrieval system, or transmitted by any means, electronic, mechanical, photocopying, or otherwise without the prior written permission of the author.

The rights of Kelvin Robertson to be identified as the author of this work have been asserted in accordance with the Copyright, Designs and Patents Act 1988.

This is a work of fiction. Names, characters, businesses, places, events and incidents are either the products of the author's imagination or used in a fictitious manner. Any resemblance to actual persons, living or dead, or actual events is purely coincidental.

ISBN-13: 9798740127286

Chapter 1

I was beginning to worry. News that the tribes were gathering had reached us and It seemed inevitable they would attack the town. I looked along the road towards the white buildings of Annual and then at my comrades. We were woefully unprepared to fight an enemy that was fierce and outnumbered us by perhaps three to one. We were not professional soldiers, just volunteers desperate to escape the poverty of home. We would be no match for a bunch of flamenco dancers never mind the fierce tribes streaming down from the Mountains of the Riff.

Then there were our officers, even I as a newly enlisted soldier could see that most were not of a very high calibre. Nervously I gripped my rifle, a thirty years old Mauser the sergeant said that in the right hands could do a lot of damage. Did we have the right hands and how far did the army think we could go on just twelve rounds of ammunition? I remember touching the rim of my chambergo and tilting it over my eyes to shade them for a better view of the town. We were convinced that any attack would come from that the direction and as if to reinforce our theory a car appeared from between the white washed buildings, a cloud of dust billowing in its wake.

'Who is that?' asked Miguel

'Officers, the rats are leaving us to fend for ourselves.' said a voice behind me.

Miguel and I turned to see our platoon sergeant, his eyes angry, his jaw set resolutely. Sergeant Pasqual was tough and uncompromising and the only one of us with any experience of real fighting. As young soldiers who had only been in the army a matter of weeks, we looked to him for the leadership our officers lacked but as the car sped past, he spat a great glob of spittle into the dry earth and his expression lost some of its edge.

'Typical of our officers, lazy good-for-nothings every one of them. All they ever do is strut about issuing nonsensical orders and now we have real trouble on our hands they are running away,' he said.

Was he right, were the officers really deserting us? Already I was aware some officers were taking outstanding leave and it was beginning to look as if their motive was not a chance to have some relaxation but the chance to escape what was beginning to appear a dangerous situation.

'What do you think is going on, sarge?' I asked.

'Isn't it obvious? We know the Riffians are heading our way and most likely they will try to take the town, the military camp and then they will head this way.'

'What will happen?' asked a young soldier barely out of his teens, his badly fitting uniform hanging loose on his skinny frame.

The sergeant tilted his head to one side and looked at the young soldier.

'I don't know, but considering our lack of arms and ammunition we will have a fight on our hands if they do decide to attack.'

Several Soldiers near us heard him and I could see a fear in their eyes, a fear I was beginning to feel. Most of them simply stared at the ground, others looked at the sky but none looked at the sergeant. Then a distraction, a movement on the road, several horsemen riding towards us from the town and, as one, we turned to watch them draw near. I could see they were officers from our regiment, the Infantry Regiment of Seville, and the lead rider I recognised as *Teniente* de la Gasca.

'Who's in charge here?' he said pulling up his horse.

'I am,' said the sergeant stepping forward.

'Ah, Sergeant Pasqual, yes, right, well as you are probably already aware the tribes of the Riff are on the move. My information is that they have overrun several outlying blockhouses and are heading this way. General Silvestre expects an attack on the camp at any time and is deciding what to do. At the right time you will receive your orders, but for now, you are to hold your position.'

'Yes, sir,' said the sergeant and then he asked about our lack of ammunition.

'Erm… you can hold out if you are careful,' said the officer. 'When we know the situation better, we will distribute more ammunition. The general intends to defend the town and with God's help we shall overcome these heathens.'

Brave words, but his eyes, his salute, they were uninspiring and I knew he did not believe what he was saying. I was not impressed and then he kicked at his horse's flanks to lead his subordinates away and the haste in which the group departed left me with a feeling of foreboding and as the sergeant turned, I could see worry etched on his ashen face.

'Right, you heard the officer, let's see what we can do to build some sort of defence. I can tell you now, lads, that when those natives turn up it will not be easy. They are a wild lot, but we can do it,' he said in a valiant attempt to lift our spirits.

But we were raw recruits, most of us not long arrived from Spain and our training was practically non-existent, our equipment was in poor condition, and the sergeant's words had little effect, even in the heat of the day I felt cold. I looked out across the dry Moroccan landscape in search of the enemy, wondering from where the Riffian horde might come. We were isolated, the road we were supposed to be guarding was not much more than a track of compressed mud, hardened by the summer sun, and there was little in the way of cover. I was not a military man, just a simple soldier, but common sense told me that the undulating terrain provided decent cover for an attack and looking at the sergeant I swear he was thinking the same.

'Corporal, take the men over there towards that building,' he said, 'it's the only place we can hope to defend,' he said pointing to a lone, single-storey structure. 'This position is too exposed for my liking. It is fine for checking traffic but not much good if those Riffians turn up. Okay, get moving, I will tell the other section to join us and then I will catch up with you.'

As he walked towards the rest of the platoon, I picked up my rifle, slung my water bottle over my shoulder, and followed the corporal towards the house.

'What do you think will happen?' asked Pablo for a second time as he caught us up.

'I don't know, Pablo, but at least we are setting up

some sort of defence and that has to be a good thing,' I said.

My explanation seemed to satisfy him though in reality, I knew no more than he did and we fell silent as we made our way towards the unimpressive stone structure. The walls looked solid enough but the roof of interlaced twigs and the flimsy wooden door had little to recommend them and just as the sergeant re-joined us that same door opened. A man, haggard-looking and dressed in traditional Moroccan clothes appeared his black headdress obscuring much of his face.

'*Salam alaykum*,' he said.

'Same to you,' said Sergeant Pasqual. 'Do you speak any Spanish?'

'A little.'

'The Riffians are on their way here and we need your house. I suggest you move out for the time being. If you stay you could be caught in any crossfire.'

'This my house, we stay,' he said, defiant eyes glaring out from his headscarf.

'Okay, but keep out of our way and stay where we can see you until this is over. Understand.'

The man nodded his head slowly before turning to speak to his wife who had appeared at his side.

'Right, Corporal Jimenez, get the men to take up defensive positions in the front of the house, Corporal Alvarez, take your men and set up at the rear. Martinez,' he said to me, 'there is a depression over there, go and make yourself invisible in it and keep an eye on the road for any sign of trouble.'

For several hours I lay in the depression, raising my head

frequently to scan the scrub and, with the sun still high overhead, I heard gunfire. Sporadic, still some distance away and no immediate threat but even so a feeling of fear grew inside me. No stranger to the feeling when I faced a full-grown fighting bull but this was different. At least in the bullring I had some control but out here, alone and facing an unseen foe I felt unsettled.

I decided that the sergeant must have heard the gunfire and I decided that it was time to retreat to the relative safety of the building and the rest of the platoon and with that thought in mind I began to scramble from the depression, my heart racing. I had hardly crossed the threshold when I caught a movement from the corner of my eye. Instinctively I froze and watched as figures, dressed in the flowing white robes of the tribesmen less than a hundred metres away crept steadily towards me.

Until that moment I had directed my fears towards an unseen, unknown enemy, one that might never confront me but here was the reality, shocking me to my core. My heartbeat ticked up with a vengeance and I slid back into the hollow, a large rock at its edge giving some cover and from behind it I watched the white-clad figures.

Annoyed I had not seen them earlier I wondered if I still had time to reach the relative safety of the house undetected. It did not seem possible and in a fit of panic I pressed my body close to the rock. A dangerous and volatile situation was rapidly developing and I reasoned that in an instant I could find myself at the mercy of these tribesmen. I gripped my rifle hard and I wondered just how to use it because our training was so lacking, I had never even fired it. I worried that it might jam, I worried that my aim would not be true, and I worried the tribesmen might see me.

Keeping my head low I prepared myself for whatever might come my way but after what seemed an eternity nothing happened. Still, I dare not raise my head to see what the tribesmen were doing but then real fear gripped me. Blood-curdling sounds filled the air and turning my head slightly from side to side I tried to judge from where the sound was coming, an inescapable joy engulfing me in the knowledge that the Riffians had bypassed my hideout.

Finally, I did dare to look over the shallow ridge and saw the tribesmen attacking the tiny house. My fellow soldiers had removed some stones from the walls in a desperate attempt at defence. They had created gaps from where their rifle barrels protruded and I could see from the muzzle flashes that they were putting up a brave fight. I saw white-clad figures fall to the ground as bullets from the house tore into them. Yet it did not seem to deter those following and as they approached ever closer to the small house the shooting died away as the defenders used the last of their ammunition.

Then a group of Spanish soldiers appeared in panic. They had come from the direction of the town and were in full flight, their weapons discarded in the belief that their best hope of escape was speed. A forlorn hope because the tribesmen soon had them in their sights and redirected their efforts towards the fleeing infantrymen. The soldiers had little chance of escape and as a witness I shall never forget the horror of the ensuing slaughter. A few escaped the first flurry off the flashing blades but their pleas for mercy went unheeded and the runners fell one by one.

These were young men just like me and they were dying a horrible death before my eyes, their uniforms spattered in blood and it forced me to wondered what fate awaited me. I did not want to die but I had just a dozen rounds of ammunition to put up some sort of fight, my rifle was heavy, cumbersome and, like those unfortunates out on the road I believed travelling light was my best bet too but above all else, I knew that I must remain unseen. In trepidation, I raised my head to survey my surroundings and was relieved to note that the immediate area was devoid of tribesmen. As far as I could make out, they were too busy chasing the runners and attacking the house but still, I dare not make a move and for the next few hours I hugged the ground, praying constantly to the Virgin of the Macarena until finally, the sun began to sink towards the horizon and the sounds of conflict eased. I believed that lengthening shadows would conceal me and that I could wait no longer. Carefully I removed the firing pin from my weapon and discarded it, for I did not relish the thought of dying by my own rifle. Keeping low I emerged from my hiding place and immediately found myself confronted with my first obstacle. Which way should I go? I could not return to Annual nor in the direction of the house where my comrades were still under attack. The only obvious escape route lay to the east, along the road to Ben Taieb and Dar Druis, the route we'd taken just a few weeks earlier on our way to this godforsaken place.

    The situation for my comrades was looking hopeless and I decided that I must get away as quickly as possible. Slowly I climbed from my hideout and I had not gone more than a few metres when I heard screams from the house forcing me to run as fast as I could in search of safety in another depression where I flung myself to the ground. Gasping for breath I dared to look over the shallow mound, I needed to take stock because to keep going like this would soon tire me. I felt that I should take my time, have a good look around, find a safe route of escape and after a few minutes, believing the way was clear I got to my knees ready to make a second dash for freedom. But as I stood up, a tribesman appeared from nowhere, his eyes wide with the blood lust and he was grinning hideously in the anticipation of my demise.

My mouth was dry and I regretted leaving the rifle behind but it was too late for regrets. With a pounding heart, I faced him, watching as he lifted his ancient rifle to his shoulder and levelled it at me but before he had chance to pull the trigger, I lunged at him and forced him to take a step back. Immediately he let go of his rifle, opting instead for the wicked-looking blade stuffed in his waistband and as his fingers closed around the hilt of the curved dagger a sneer crossing his face and as if playing a game, he began passing the weapon from hand to hand.

'Come on, Spanish, come on, I kill you. I kill you quick, come on,' he said in broken Spanish.

I was an easy target, his eyes told me he knew it, and time was running out for me. But then something happened. Call it inspiration, I don't know. I found myself back in the bullring and this time I was the bull, the hunted. Should I charge, thrust my horns at the matador's cape or stand my ground and let him make the first move? Time seemed to stand still as we looked at each other and then he made to move towards me. I felt a role reversal and now he was the bull and I the bullfighter.

Unarmed, not even in possession of the capote to deflect his charge I improvised. Watching his eyes, I grasped the rim of my chambergo and anticipated his move. As he thrust his dagger towards my stomach, I swept the hat from my head and waved it across his face. Timing was everything, in that split second his concentration was solely upon the chambergo and I sidestepped out of his way. Not quite a classic *remate* but enough to throw him off balance. He had lost the advantage. We were side by side and he would have to turn fully around to thrust his dagger home but I was quicker, driving my clenched fist hard into his left ear, stunning him. That gave me the time to kick him hard in the groin and as he recoiled, I wrestled the knife from his grip. I hit him again in the face and as he dropped to one knee, I thrust the knife deep into his neck, the way to kill a bull quickly and in those few seconds of life he had left, his eyes rolled in disbelief and his legs gave way.

    I thanked God that I had prevailed but I was exhausted and I needed to rest, a drink from my water bottle. Night was falling, I was alone in the dark, and I had little choice but to follow the road. I dared not risk becoming lost in open country where the danger of discovery by skirmishers was very real, the road seemed the safest bet. I estimated that it was about twenty kilometres to Ben Taieb and travelling during the hours of darkness, keeping to the road, I could be there by the time the sun returned.

And so, with an air of trepidation, I set out on my journey, the sound of sporadic gunfire reminding me to tread carefully. For hours I trudged over the broken ground, stumbling occasionally when misjudging my footing. I heard noises in the dark, undecipherable mostly but once

I did hear the unmistakable sound horses' hooves and they did not seem so far away.

Friend or foe I had no idea but I was taking no chances and as the dull glow in the east grew, I decided to get off the road. I would need to find cover, remain undiscovered and to a point, the ground aided me. Dry and broken, steep gullies cut through, the landscape helping conceal me but it also made for slow and difficult progress but I did not believe it was cavalry country. No self-respecting horseman would risk his steed over such treacherous ground, and because of that I felt safe enough and then, as the sun rose, I had an uninterrupted view of Ben Taieb.

In the distance, I could see movement and decided to take the risk of heading straight for the settlement but after trekking for half an hour I saw a large group of tribesmen. I had believed that the Riffians had attacked Annual from the west and that there would be few hostile tribesmen to the east of the town but I was wrong. I had been on the move for many hours and I was feeling the strain of my flight. I was hungry, thirsty, and tired and now I found the route to the town blocked. I still had my canteen half full, my only sustenance, and sitting on a large rock I took a drink. I remember rubbing my eyes, the headache, the blurred vision, I needed a rest for a few minutes at least but I dare not. Instead, I looked towards the rising sun for a landmark to guide me and for the next few hours I made a detour over rough ground to avoid detection.

My plan was to find a safe place to rest and then, as night fell, I would return to the easier walking the road provided. Then I heard and at first, I could not make out from where it was coming, then I heard galloping hooves and my attention focused towards a series of gullies running down the hillside. I searched for shelter but there was none; nothing could hide me. I prepared for the worst and feeling for the dagger I crouched down to diminish my bulk. I scanned the near distance and caught sight of a group of riders and struggled to focus my tired eyes. It soon became obvious that whoever it was they were heading in my direction and I began to look for somewhere to hide but to my overwhelming relief I finally saw that they were not Riffians but Spanish cavalry. For a few moments I believed myself saved, however, my relief was short-lived because from the same ravine a large group of mounted tribesmen emerged, riding fast, firing their guns indiscriminately and then a second troop of cavalry appeared. They were moving at speed along an intersecting path with the Riffians, their aim far more accurate than that of the tribesmen.

I had a grandstand view of the action and saw several native riders tumble to the ground. The group pulled up to turn and face the new threat but the momentum was with the cavalry. I watched the Spanish soldiers draw their sabres and charge the Riffians and silently I cheered them on, their sabres a blur as they cut the natives to shreds. The natives could not withstand the onslaught and found themselves driven back, many of their number killed leaving startled and riderless horses to run loose. One came my way and I clutched at the chance to escape, running alongside it, reaching for the reins, and grasping them at the first attempt.

The horse seemed relieved to find someone to take charge, coming to an abrupt halt and allowing me time to hoist myself up into the saddle. From my new vantage point, I looked around only for my heart to miss a beat as I saw a Berber horseman riding towards me. He had seen me mount the horse and held his dagger menacingly as he rode, a skilful rider, confident enough to reach out with his free hand to grab hold of my horse's bridle. I watched, hypnotized almost, I could do little, the last of my strength was ebbing away and as I had not managed to slip my feet into the stirrups. My position was precarious, I had reached a low point and seemed defenceless but in such a fluid situation it was no real surprise when another rider appeared, this time a Spanish cavalryman in dark green. His sword drawn and standing high in his saddle, the moustachioed cavalryman swung his sabre to slash at the native, consigning him to the dust.

Stunned by my sudden reprieve my relief was overwhelming but the danger was still real. A group of the enemy were riding towards us kicking their horses' flanks, yelling, and cursing, murder on their minds and they outnumbered just the two of us by ten to one.

My rescuer looked worried but again providence intervened. A group of Spanish cavalrymen appeared to our right galloping towards the tribesmen and before the natives reached us Spanish sabres were doing their bloody work. With a terrible efficiency the cavalrymen dispatched half the Riffians, those tribesmen still alive disengaging to retreat into the hills.

'Are you all right, soldier?' said a trooper riding alongside me.

'Yes, thank God. You are my saviour, sir.'

'Never mind the compliments; we are not out of trouble yet. What regiment?'

'The Seville infantry.'

'You have come from Annual.'

'Yes,' I said and the memory of that awful time resurfaced in my mind. 'It's a disaster. General Silvestre ordered a fighting retreat but we panicked and ran.'

Well, our orders are to try to save as many of you as we can. You had better stay with us.'

'What regiment are you?'

'We are the riders of the Alcantara.'

'Well, thank you for getting me out of that hole.'

'What's your name, soldier?'

'Francisco Martinez but everyone calls me Paco.'

'Well, Paco, I am Emilio Perez. I see you can ride. We need all the help we can get; we have lost a lot of our men. We fight for the honour of Spain. It is the price we pay.'

Brave words, I thought as I followed my new friend towards a group of mounted men gathered around an officer addressing them and as we neared, I caught some of his words.

'The enemy is everywhere,' he said, 'the disaster at Annual has rallied them. Survivors of General Silvestre's force tell how what should have been an orderly retreat turned into a rout. Those soldiers who escaped are following this route and it is our job to help them reach safety. We are the Alcantara and we have a job to do. We must try to save the army of Africa. Long live Spain.'

'Long live Spain,' chorused the men.

I was fascinated, these men were real soldiers, very different to the infantry regiment I had known. We were poorly trained and poorly led and it struck me that the state of the army invited disaster. It was evident that these soldiers were different, possessing camaraderie, something I had not experienced before and I could not help but feel respect for them.

'Paco, our ranks are depleted and I can see that you are comfortable on horseback. Can you use a sword; I know it's not a weapon used by the infantry?'

It was Emilio.

'If it is too much for you, I understand but the situation is desperate. Perhaps a rifle, could you manage to use a rifle on horseback?'

'I was a bullfighter, Emilio; I can handle a sword I think.'

'A bullfighter, were you famous?'

'No, I was just beginning my career in the ring, mostly I fought in minor corridas, in the country, small towns and villages but I did fight in Málaga and once in the Real Maestranza.'

'Impressive, let's find you a sword and you can stay by me.'

Neither of us was much interested in bullfighting at that time, we had a more important situation to contend with and finding a sword from a wounded comrade, he handed it to me.

'Try it; see if you can use it. We will be in action again shortly that is for certain. The teniente has informed us that a column of soldiers escaping from Annual are crossing the dry riverbed near Ben Taieb and a party of mounted Riffians are closing in on them.'

I took the sword from him and proceeded to swing it from side to side just as I had seen the cavalrymen do as they fought the mounted Berbers. I felt I could cope; I was glad to be able to do something to avenge my lost friends.

Following and the cavalrymen and without a scabbard to

hand I had little choice but to carry the sword across my saddle. It was not an easy manoeuvre and knowing little of the regiment's way of fighting I stayed at the rear of the column with Emilio. It was good to ride a horse instead of slogging it out across the rough Moroccan terrain and for the next two hours we rode westwards. Eventually, we caught sight of the river and very soon afterwards we heard gunshots. The teniente raised his hand to signal an increase in pace and at a fast trot, we rode towards the river crossing. I could see the enemy spaced out across the countryside harassing stragglers attempting to make their way to safety, and at the teniente's command, the bugler sounded the charge. Immediately the well-disciplined force spread out in skirmishing order and at the gallop, we rode towards the multitude of white-clad figures swarming over the remnants of the army crossing the river, a forlorn sight, a mass of men exhausted by their flight and to a man, they appeared unarmed.

'Stay with me and do as I do, Paco,' said Emilio, urging on his horse forward and drawing his sabre, holding it outstretched.

I did the same, holding my sword as I did at the conclusion of the bullfight and I held the reins tight. I stood in the stirrups, balancing the weight of the weapon and together with Emilio rode at the rear of the main body. We were picking up speed, surging forward to engage with the enemy, many of the retreating soldiers watching us. The exhausted soldiers somehow took heart at our charge, gathering discarded weapons, rocks from the desert to hurl at the tribesmen in an act of defiance, and then we were into the shallows and splashing our way towards the enemy. I saw the first of the Alcantara hit the mass of white and black-robed natives, their sabres exacting a heavy toll, and I too swept in amongst them, my sword swinging wildly. Whether or not I made much contact, I have little idea for the blood-and-guts action lasted mere minutes before the bugle sounded and Emilio shouted to me.

'Turn, we are charging them again.'

Pulling up his horse, he turned its head and I followed suit, bringing the horse about, preparing to charge and as we did a native sprang at us. I saw him first and shouted a warning but I was too late to prevent the man from stabbing Emilio in the leg who yelled out in pain, a signal for a second tribesman to rise from his hiding place. Reaching up he grasped hold of the hapless cavalryman's uniform and dragged him from his horse. He was in mortal danger, already wounded and struggling to fight off his assailants and I had little choice but to kick hard at my horse, driving it towards the stricken cavalryman. The natives were intent on killing Emilio and did not notice me until my horse crashed into them, the first falling under the galloping hooves. However, the second man reacted and had the wit to jump out of the way and forcing me to turn. By then Emilio was free of the grasping hands, able to defend himself and, taking a vicious swipe at the second man's head, he cut deep into the skull, killing the man instantly.

'Emilio!'

He raised his hand and with some effort managed to stand unaided long enough for his well-trained horse to return to him.

'How are you?' I asked as he remounted.

'I'm okay. Come on, we have more work to do.'

Although injured and wounded as he was, he was tough, insisting on following through with the charge leading me into a mêlée of horses and men. After just seconds I lost sight of him, my concentration centred solely upon my own struggle. I had killed bulls but never a man yet today it was a necessary evil to drive off the horde. Then, as I had seen them before, the Riffian tribesmen suddenly disengaged and ran. It was a triumph of sorts but amongst the dead and dying tribesmen lying scattered across the battlefield so were the green uniforms of the Alcantara. We had killed many of them but our losses were not so few.

As I rode back across the shallows tired, frightened eyes looked up at me, soldiers who had survived and were thankful for their salvation. They looked worn out and I was no less exhausted from my ordeals, my horse was panting heavily and I knew that she would be unable to go on much longer. But still we had to see these soldiers to safety, bedraggled exhausted men but for the time being at least the fighting was over and I was still alive.

I heard my name called, 'Paco!' said the voice, and I twisted in my saddle. 'Paco, it's me, Miguel.'

I hardly recognised him. His uniform was in rags, his hair matted, and his face blackened by exposure.

'Miguel, what are you doing here, what happened?'

Dejected eyes looked up at me and he struggled to speak.

'Miguel, what happened?'

His face seemed devoid of personality, the ordeal he had endured changing him forever.

'They are all dead.'

'How did you get here?'

'We ran as fast as we could for as long as we could. They were everywhere, killing us, showing no mercy. I saw Sergeant Pasqual take on two of them at once and he shot both until the rest of them overwhelmed him. They cut his throat in front of me; they killed the entire platoon except Enrique and me.'

'How did you escape?' I had to ask.

'I found a store cupboard built into the wall, just big enough for me and luckily they did not try the door. I think they were preoccupied with those running away.'

'Enrique, how did he escape?'

'I found him underneath two of our comrades. They must have fallen on him when they died and he had the presence of mind to play dead until we thought it was safe to move and then we just ran. Everyone was running, throwing away their guns to run faster but the natives were all around us and all they wanted to do was...'

He began sobbing as the memory of his ordeal returned and giving him a moment to compose himself, I took the water bottle from my belt and offered it to him.

'Thanks, Paco, I needed that.'

'You had better fall in with the column, then you will make it to Melilla, my friend,' I said, offering encouragement because that was all I had left.

As I left him, I felt a weight straddle my shoulders; although not a complete surprise, the news had hit me with an unexpected force. I had witnessed the beginnings of the massacre but nothing had prepared me for his description. The whole of our platoon was dead except for three of us. I'd known that the situation was bad but never in my wildest dreams did I imagine just how bad it was and in those few quiet moments after I left Miguel, I reflected on my own predicament. I had not slept for more than thirty hours but there was little chance of sleep. The Alcantara regiment who had impressed me so with their discipline and their fighting ability had suffered many casualties and as the remnants of the army trudged past them, their commanding officer addressed his men.

'Riders of the Alcantara, you have acquitted yourselves well today. You have fought to the highest standards of the regiment but we have more to do. These soldiers,' he said making a sweeping gesture with his outstretched arm, 'these men still need our protection until they reach safety. Come, we have work to do. Long live Spain.'

They were stirring words and they elicited a positive response from the brave cavalrymen who were still ready to fight; hope amid an unfolding disaster. I wished I could go with them but my horse could not and no amount of rhetoric would lift her spirits. Then I spotted Emilio leaning against his horse's hindquarters, his thigh wrapped in a blood-soaked bandage and leaving my horse I walked over to him.

'Emilio, how are you?'

'I am unhappy to say the least. My officer is sending me to Melilla with the rest of the army because my wound will reopen if I attempt to ride with the regiment. He says I have played my part and would be a burden if I went with them. He says it's better to recover and re-join the regiment later when I am in a fit condition.'

'Isn't that a good thing?'

'I cannot, in all honesty, leave my comrades when they are under such heavy pressure. The enemy is in no way defeated; the regiment needs every able-bodied man.'

'But you are not able bodied, that's the point,' I said

trying to placate him.

His face contorted in pain and I could see the wisdom in leaving him behind yet I could understand his frustration. At least his horse was still in decent condition, unlike my nag and returning to sit at its feet I tried to close my eyes for a few precious moments until just minutes later I was shocked awake. The enemy was mounting an attack, firing wildly as was their way and although most bullets whizzed harmlessly overhead a few found their mark. Then a bugle sounded and the remnants of the Alcantara cavalry mounted their horses and amongst them, I saw Emilio. He was defying orders, a brave man amongst a band of brave men but I was on my own again.

Although my nag was of little use, I climbed into the saddle in the hope that I could at least put some distance between myself and the fearsome Riffians. I could feel she was on her last legs and I struggled to keep her moving but at least her pace was enough to escape the immediate danger. I reasoned that I might avoid the tribesmen if I left the road, crossed the low hills, and re-joined the road further on; even then it could be dangerous but it seemed my best bet. I found the route east filled with stragglers from the massacre of Annual, men worn down by fear and exertion, conscripts and volunteers running away from certain death and I knew they would be a target for the Riffians. Again, I made a fateful decision and pulling away from the column I left the road and made my way towards a shallow ridge from where I hoped to see the way forward. My horse stumbled but, coaxing her forward, we finally made it and from the low vantage point, I had a view of several kilometres. Away towards the far side of the river, I could see the swirling cloaks of the tribesmen swarming like ants towards the ragged column and racing towards them the riders of the Alcantara were prominent as they charged.

It appeared that I had escaped the worst and I turned to make my way towards the coast but before I had gone very far a Riffian confronted me. I had not seen him but he had seen me and stood with his ancient, long-barrelled gun pointing straight at me. I still had the sword but I was too far away and could do nothing but kick at the horse's flanks, hoping she had at least enough energy left to overrun the man.

When I finally opened my eyes, it was dark and for several minutes I lay immobilised, a thumping pain in my head obscuring all other thoughts. I did not know where I was or what had happened to me nor for how long I lay there. I touched my head, felt the stickiness of congealing blood in my hair, and I guessed that I could not have been unconscious for long.

Gradually my senses returned, though I lay still, moving only my eyeballs, exploring my body for injury and then, by the faint moonlight, I made out the shape of my horse lying on her side. I concentrated, focusing my eyes and from the lack of movement I guessed she was dead and then the memory of what had taken place began to return. I began to go over what I could remember and just as I made the last connection, I noticed a leg protruding from under the horse's belly. The sight shook me into action, forcing me to sit up, the effort causing me to wince with pain and I felt my shoulder. There was the same stickiness on my tunic, the same congealing blood, and I realised that I had taken a bullet in my arm. I lifted it, testing it and was mildly delighted that it was little more than a flesh wound, and I was still alive.

    I strained my ears for any sound of danger and, hearing nothing, I summoned enough strength to get to my knees and finally I was able to stand. The first thing I did was to examine the carcass of the horse and the cadaver underneath. The last thing I could remember was the native pointing his gun at me and I guessed that I must have rushed him. He had obviously managed to get a shot off but it looked as if the horse had felled him. I was lucky, if the horse had not pinned him down so securely, he might still have managed to kill me.

Chapter 2

The only sign of life in the narrow street was an old cart with a sad-looking donkey motionless in its traces. That was until a figure appeared, hands stuffed into his trouser pockets, shoulders hunched as he hurried along the pavement. Francisco was sixteen years old, a free spirit, a teenager who filled his time dreaming of bulls and bullfighters because one day he hoped to follow in the steps of Triana's most famous son. He was just a poor boy dressed in grubby clothes the signs of many repairs only too apparent and his shoes were starting to come apart. His education was rudimentary, his prospects in life were few, but he had his dream.

    He lived in the poor district of Triana, home to the workers and artisans of Seville but it was a vibrant and lively place, famous throughout Spain for its flamenco and tonight was fiesta. The start of Easter week was a time when the people of the barrio could let their hair down, a chance to socialise with friends and neighbours. Tonight, the courtyard, surrounded by the crowded dwellings of the poor would come alive and for Francisco's mother it was particularly important she was one of the best dancers in Triana and she expected her youngest son to be there but Francisco was late.

    Hurrying along the near deserted street he knew he

was late and would be in trouble, the sound of the castanets warning him. Their syncopated, staccato rhythm grew louder as he neared the square, he could hear the guitars, the stamping feet of the dancers and he quickened his pace. Turning the corner, the sight of friends and neighbours filling the brightly lit square confronted him and at the centre of it all was his mother. She was taking centre stage, her back arched, her hands held high above her jet-black hair as she showed just how good a dancer she was and from the shadows, Francisco watched her throw back her head and effect the exaggerated gestures of the Flamenco.
The guitar's rapid tempo reverberated through the air, she stamped her thick-heeled shoes with speed and precision and as she advanced across the temporary wooden floor calls from the audience encouraged her.

Then the rhythm changed, the tempo slowed almost to a stop, she lifted her brightly coloured dress with both hands, exposing shapely legs and provocatively she stamped her feet. All eyes were upon her, the guitar ceased it's resonant outpouring and Carmen stood motionless as a hush descended over the small square. People paused their drinking, several men rose to their feet in expectation, and slowly Carmen began to dance. Click click clack clack went the heavy black heels of her shoes on the hard floor, the tempo slowly increasing, a sound that could not help but cut through to the Andalusian psyche, and it inspired others to join her.

The audience began the syncopated clapping synonymous with flamenco, a counterpoint to Carmen's steady feet beating out the classic rhythm of the fandango. From the shadows her son watched her and could not but admire her elegant moves, how she carried herself, the dramatic turn of her head. It was thrilling but suddenly she turned her head and her eyes alighted upon him. Taken aback he froze with apprehension but instead of the scowl he expected a smile crossed her lips and then she turned away leaving the boy relieved to know he was not in trouble.

Francisco watched her for a few minutes more before he searched the square for his father, eventually spotted him with his friends at a table several meters away deep in conversation. His father worked hard enough but was a man who preferred to spend his wages on drink rather than feed his family and the rest of Francisco's family had suffered because of it. If it was not for his mother then he and his siblings might go hungry. Carmen was the one who held them all together, finding money to pay the rent, feeding them and spending hours making clothes for her children and when there was no material left she would stitch together the rents and holes in the clothes they stood up in.

'Paco, where have you been? asked his father as he approached the table. 'Fetch me another pitcher of wine. Here, some money.'

'He is already drunk,' thought Francisco and by the end of the night, he expected that he would be carrying him home.

The boy took the coins, sighing inwardly, hoping that by the end of the evening his father would not be too much of a burden as he set off towards the makeshift bar selling pitchers of wine. He passed his mother her dancing not yet at an end and from the crowd a man he recognised, a tall gypsy, appeared. The guitars changed to the ternary rhythm of the Fandango and the gypsy began a series of *tacons*, stamping his heels as danced his way towards Carmen. In response she lifted her arms high, bent her hands towards her scalp and slowly began to work her castanets. The audience took her lead, clapping slowly at first, encouraging the gypsy to raise himself up onto the balls of his feet from where he pirouetted with a master's elegance. His dark eyes admired Carmen, teased her and as the tempo increased, he turned his back on her. She responded, stamping her feet indignantly and holding up her brightly coloured dress, exposing her shapely legs and as she swept the hem from side to side a roar filled the square. The atmosphere was electric, the two dancers looked at each other with bright sexually charged eyes and coming together, they put on a dazzling performance.

The gypsy circled Carmen like a matador testing a bull and she, in turn, provocatively spread the bright dress, dancing slowly, defiantly as the gypsy postured arrogantly, his head stiff and proud. He curved his arms towards her, his fingers snapping out the rhythm and for several minutes Francisco forget he was on an errand for his father and could not help feeling they were a match, her black oiled hair contrasting with the bright colours of her dress, he slim and with the dark Moorish features of Andalusia and as his boots drilled the rhythm on hard flooring Carmen responded. She articulated her body, twisting, turning, her arms held high, her dark provocative eyes staring straight at the gypsy. She was magnificent and Francisco felt proud yet wondered what his father was making of it. He looked back towards him and saw him in conversation with his friends and not showing the least interest in his wife's dancing.

'Paco, Paco, are we going to the country tonight?' called out a voice.

'Hi, Luis, not tonight maybe sometime in the week,' Francisco said to the boy who had accosted him.

'Yes, when?'

'I don't know, Luis, after Easter week. I must fetch my father a pitcher of wine. I will see you later,' he said waving a hand to cut short their conversation. 'I'm sorry but I have to fetch my father's wine.'

The boy gave Francisco a dejected look and he felt a twinge of guilt. He had had grown up with Luis, they had played the young bulls in the pastures of Tablada together with their friends and he could see Luis was es eager as he was to go there again. They had a routine. In the dead of night, they would venture into the countryside several kilometres from Triana where each of them would take their turn with a makeshift cape to provoke young bulls. But Luis had a deformed leg, an accident of birth and he never gained the ability to walk like the other boys, was less agile and yet that did not prevent them from accepting him as one of them. For his part Luis tried hard to be as normal as he could be and as true friends the rest of the boys looked out for him.

Leaving Luis Francisco bought the jug of wine and pushed on through the crowd back to his father who, for once, heaped praise on his youngest son.

'Good boy, Paco, here fill our glasses, will you. You have met my son?' Francisco's father said to his friends.

Of course, they had met the boy, most of the men had seen Francisco and his siblings grow up, it wasn't the first time Francisco's father had introduced him to them during an episode of drinking. 'He is going to be a famous bullfighter one day aren't you, son.'

'Yes, Papa,' said Francisco filling the empty glasses and then finding himself ignored.

Feeling dejected he decided to leave, go and look for Luis and as he made his way around the square, he met his mother.

'Were you buying drink for your father, Francisco?'

'Yes, Mama, he gave me money to buy a pitcher.'

'Spending the rent money on wine again,' she said, a look of resignation on her face. 'Where are your sisters?'

'Over there with the other girls,' said Francisco pointing towards the far end of the square.

'I'm glad you saw me dance; it has been one of the best nights I have ever danced. Did you see the gypsy? He is such a good dancer, so passionate. Now, don't you or any of your friends get yourselves into trouble and no disappearing all night looking for bulls. You're a good boy I know, Francisco. Enjoy yourself while I look for your sisters.'

She patted him on his head and he watched her go, past tables filled from where more than one man gave her an admiring look.

'Papa must be mad,' he mumbled to himself.

The light was already fading as the boys tramped across the dry, scrub-strewn ground. It was more than a week since the fiesta and the boys of Triana were up to their usual mischief. Following a well-trodden path, probably the exact same path along which their hero had walked not so many years before and the boys were excited to think they would soon be imitating Juan Belmonte.

'Have you the cape, Paco?' asked Manolito, at twelve years old, the youngest of the group.

'Look, I have made this muleta,' said Francisco, holding it up for the youngster to see. 'Tonight, I will fight like Juan Belmonte. Tonight, I will show you what I can do.'

'Bravo,' said Luis, just as keen as Paco to become a famous bullfighter, but he knew that could never be, to be a part of the group was enough, just to join them on their adventures made him feel whole.

As well as Francisco, Luis, and Manolito, there were the brothers Manuel and José. As the eldest and the most developed physically, Francisco was the de facto leader of the group, the most confident, the one the other boys looked up to. His shirt was torn, his socks non-existent and his shoes needed repair but his spirit was strong and the ambition to become a bullfighter as intense as ever.

'With an education, you can find work that pays a decent wage. You might get a job in a bank or with the government,' said Luis out of nowhere.

'What made you say that?' asked José.

'My mother told me that today, she said it's a pity we can't get more schooling.'

'Schooling! That's for girls.'

'He's right, José,' said Francisco. 'My mother is always telling me that. But I must find work when I can to help the family. My father doesn't give us enough. Me and my brother often must find the money to pay our rent. Come on, hurry, it's getting dark. We will be struggling when we pass through the trees.'

The small wood always proved problematic. The darkness concealed protruding branches that could easily hit you in the face and exposed tree roots could trip the unwary leaving them with a badly sprained ankle. Nevertheless, if they were to find the bulls, then they had little alternative but to negotiate these natural obstacles, a dangerous occupation and added to that they were trespassing and if caught then the Guardia might become involved.

Apart from Francisco, none of the others had really thought about it; he was their leader and so they left any thinking to him and on this night in particular Francisco had decided they should head for the pasture abutting the river after leaving the wood. There was a place he knew where the bulls could find water, a place where he guessed young bulls could be grazing and feeling confident in his decision, he led his little gang forward. Then from behind, the brothers began to argue, discussing the merits of fishing, one insisting the best bait was simply dry bread while the other preferred maggots.

'Where will you get a supply of maggots from?' said an indignant Manuel.

'Shh... we don't want anyone to know we are here,' said Francisco, agitated by the disturbance. 'They sometimes have a man out at night looking for the likes of us. If anyone catches us, we might take a beating or they could take us to the police. Be quiet.'

He couldn't see the boys' faces in the gloom but he knew his message had got through as silence descended and for the next ten minutes the only sound was that of the boys' feet trampling over the dry grass.

'Here, this gate, come on over it as quick as you like,' said Francisco climbing up, his stick and makeshift muleta clutched under his arm. It was a prized possession, one he would use for the first time during the night, to prove to his friends what a great torero he was and with spirits rising he led them across the field using the light of the moon to locate the dirt track he was looking for.

Nothing more than a pair of ruts impressed into the earth, the track led through the pasture and towards the river and after walking several hundred metres, Francisco called a halt. Standing perfectly still he tilted his head and sniffed at the air. He was sure they were in the right place and turning slightly he inhaled and caught the unmistakable bovine scent.

'Can you see them, Paco?' asked Luis.

'I think they are over there. Can you smell them, Luis?'

Luis angled his head and he sampled the air.

'Yes, I think so, over there. What sport we will have,' he said, pointing and hardly able to contain himself. Without a word he took the lead, limping through the knee-high grass, stopping to whisper, 'there I think.'

He was right. As they crept forwards four bulls became visible, two sitting peacefully chewing slowly on their cud, the others standing. Perfect, thought Francisco they were three-year-olds, too young for the bullring but just right for him and his friends to practise on.

'Manuel, José, take Manolito with you to stop them escaping. Luis and me will cut one out for our fun.'

'Okay,' said Manuel leading the others.

Creeping after him the boys followed on a curved path towards the bulls, still unaware of their presence. Of the three of them Manuel was particularly good at stalking; he understood the animals and was aware that their eyesight was not good but he also knew that an unfamiliar scent could spook them. Carefully he crept forward, signalling to his brother and Manolito to take up their positions and, with his eyes firmly on the black shapes, he came to a standstill while from the opposite direction Francisco and Luis made their move. Luis, unable to move fast, hung back while Francisco let the muleta unfurl almost to the ground, and gradually he introduced it to the unsuspecting bulls who while not totally wild and used to some human activity, were still dangerous.

It didn't take much to tip the scales from relaxed chewing to a full-blown charge and feeling a little uncertain, Francisco held out his stick and took several more steps towards the nearest bull. It sensed his presence and, catching his scent, raised its head, at first showing little interest in him until it finally recognised the intruder as a stranger. It let out a grunt and stroked the ground with a forehoof. The game was on. Francisco let the cloth of the muleta fall away from the stick holding it in a classic bullfighter pose, and feeling his throat dry with anticipation, he flicked the cape. The animal snorted with indignation at having its peace disturbed and took a tentative step forward, then another. Francisco had the bull's full attention and now it was time to play it.

'Go, Paco, go,' hissed Luis, encouraging his friend and stimulating the bull's aggressive nature.

As it began to trot towards Francisco its instinct to charge became overwhelming. Then, for no apparent reason, it stopped dead in its tracks.

'Come on, *ven a mi encantador*,' whispered Francisco under his breath and, almost as if the animal really did understand his words, it charged.

Francisco was ready, his stick laid across his chest, the

makeshift cape hung against his body, and as the bull drew close, he swept it into the path of the onrushing beast with perfect timing. It had to be perfect because the bull was moving towards him at such speed that he had very little time to perform his move. Turning his body to present a small target and spreading the cape out across the bull's path he drew in his stomach and arched his back. His heart rate increased so much that he felt his chest would burst open at any moment, but he had done everything with precision and as the bull swept past its horns caught nothing but the flimsy cloth.

Several metres away the boys watched, excited and fearful and as the bull cleared Francisco they shouted in unison, 'Olé' and just metres away Luis joined in with 'Bravo, Paco.'

Francisco was unaware because the encounter was far from over; the agitated bull was not about to give up. Skidding to a halt, it turned and charged, again its horns connecting with nothing more than the flimsy cloth, the experience serving only to increase its confusion. A third charge was dangerous for Francisco, the bull would learn and the mound of black muscle seemed to have grown larger. Francisco's courage was beginning to desert him and as it headed towards him, he felt panic rise in his breast and not far away Luis seemed to understand his predicament.

'Paco, run,' he shouted, compounding Francisco's fear, but a voice of reason told him to hold steady, told him not to be afraid for he would know what to do. It was the first experience Francisco had of what seemed an unworldly voice, but it would not be the last and, guided by the mysterious force, he stepped quickly to one side, spread the cape, and for several minutes performed a series of *verónicas*, turning the bull at will, and finally feeling that he was the master. One last time he held the cape out with both hands, full in the bull's face and as it charged past, he turned to run for the shelter of some trees followed closely by Luis.

'Phew, that was a close one, Paco, let me have a go.'

'This one will be too much for you, Luis, let's see if one of the other bulls is a little less aggressive.'

'What! I can handle any bull.'

Francisco grinned, amused by Luis's confidence but he knew that his friend's disability would see him hurt if he tried to fight the bull and the last thing he wanted was for the bull to inflict an injury on his friend. Luis was not proficient as a torero, though he was first class at bravado and the fact that his friends held him back would earn him kudos.

The other boys were able bodied and they too wanted their turn facing a bull; Francisco had shown the way, now it was their turn. Manuel was the better of the three, moving not unlike Francisco, and then it was the turn of the younger brother, José, who lacked experience and was lucky not to finish up on the bull's horns but in the end, they all took a turn and all survived in one piece.

'I want a go, why will you not let me have a go?' said Luis sounding miserable.

'We will, Luis, but not here, let's see if we can find a younger, smaller animal for you,' said Francisco to placate him. 'I know, I bet there are younger bulls somewhere nearby. We will find you a two-year-old to fight on our way home but first I want to fight one more bull before we leave.'

The animals had returned to grazing when the boys decided to interrupt their peace and prise a second bull from the small herd. Circling, Francisco singled out a second bull, one as aggressive looking as the first and it occurred to him that they had stumbled upon some of the finest bulls the produced on the estate and, for a second time that night, Francisco faced a formidable opponent. Again, he held the attention of his friends and Manolito, bursting with excitement, was unable to contain himself.

'Olé,' he shouted, his young voice clear and penetrating. Again, and again, he called out, his concentration on Francisco's performance absolute. However, the shrill calls of the adolescent boy carried far into the night and not so far away, a man's ears pricked up.

Carlos Luca, or to give him his full name Carlos Antonio Luca Viera de Mendoza, was the eldest son of ganadería's owner. It was not an uncommon sight to find boys and young men from Triana wandering the estate during the hours of darkness, generally appearing at the time of the full moon when the light was stronger. But their antics were costing Señor de Mendoza money. Fighting bulls are intelligent and never allowed to experience a man on foot in case they learn who the real enemy is. If they do, and take that knowledge into the bullring, the matador could be in mortal danger.

Carlos was acting as night watchman, patrolling the estate, on the lookout for trespassers. His mission was to catch any trespassers in the act and take them to the police to stamp out the practice. Hearing the calls, Carlos dismounted and leaving his trained horse standing quietly he took a pitchfork in one hand, his revolver in the other, and tried to determine from where the calls had come.

He skirted around some bushes, quickened his pace as shadowy figures came into view, then he halted, watching. So, there were four of them he mused. He would have just one chance, for as soon as they were aware of his presence, they would no doubt scatter into the night. Then a shaft of moonlight cut through the clouds and one figure stood out, a boy making cursory sweeps of a cape, taunting one of the bulls and Carlos decided that he was the one he should try to catch. Taking a few more steps, he heard the animal snort and as the bull charged, he heard encouragement from the shadows. The boy was a trespasser and as such should receive some punishment yet he was in danger of injury and that concerned Carlos. He considered intervening, use the pitchfork to ward off the bull but before he could do anything the bull was tearing through the cape leaving him amazed at how expertly the boy dealt with the animal. Standing perfectly still, he allowed the bull to pass and as it turned back, he turned to meet it using his cape as if an extension to his body and again the bull found itself charging at nothing more than thin air. Carlos was impressed, an urchin from Triana, a mere slip of a boy, performing as if he was a natural-born torero.

The bull turned and charged for a third time without warning and Carlos for a second time feared for the lad's safety, but to his relief the figure did no more than confuse the animal, causing it to pass harmlessly by and at that moment Carlos decided to call a halt to the proceedings. The boy had already reduced the potential of a good fighting bull and was costing the estate money.

'Stop!' he shouted, stepping from the shadows, gun

held in one hand, the pitchfork in the other. 'Stop what you're doing and come here.'

As expected, Carlos's command had the opposite effect. The two bigger boys grabbed hold of a younger one and dragged him away into the darkness followed closely by a fourth, less agile, stumbling, and the young torero suddenly found himself alone with the angry bull.

'Hold,' said Carlos, 'hold steady, hold steady. Don't antagonise the bull anymore.'

Not daring to move, Francisco kept his eyes firmly the bull, other than a quick sideways glance to see that there was no escape but Carlos's words had their effect. With nothing to disturb it, the bull paused and allowed him to approach with the extended pitchfork ready to coax it away.

'Come with me, boy. We have had enough of your sort causing trouble,' he said, switching the pitchfork to hold it menacingly at Francisco. 'Move.'

Francisco had little choice, Carlos mounted his horse, the pitchfork firmly in his grip and for maybe half an hour forced the boy to walk in front of him until several buildings loomed out of the darkness.

'In there,' said Carlos as they reached the first of them.

Francisco did not resist, entering an interior so dark, even with eyes accustomed to the night, he could see nothing and he began to feel very much alone.

Chapter 3

I must admit I was afraid. Alone in the darkness and surrounded by bloodthirsty tribesmen, my chances of survival were slim. At least I didn't have to worry about my assailant, he was dead, his body crushed, twisted into an unnatural position beneath the carcass of the horse. Yes, the horse was dead too and I was on foot again and still with some distance to go before I might reach safety but I realised that I could not stay where I was for much longer. What if the man under the horse was not alone, what chance would I have in my condition? My head was throbbing and the pain from the gunshot wound was almost overpowering. I was desperate, I must leave, make my way east towards the coast, if I could figure out where east was, and then I caught sight of shadowy figures, lots of them, and it seemed my nightmare would not end and my blood ran cold. I had nowhere to run to and with misplaced bravado decided I would not let them take me alive. I still had the knife and the sword both lying on the ground not far away. I picked them up and stared into the gloom, preparing myself, but there was something about the manner of those shadows that puzzled me, the way they carried themselves and I looked more carefully. The greyness of the dawn aided me, spreading some little light across the landscape and then I realised what I was seeing. Stooped, desperate-looking men, the remnants of the army, strung out in an uneven line for several hundred metres.

At least they were not the Riffian tribesmen but they were in a sorry state, dragging themselves along the road. I was surprised that I was so close to the road and took the chance to join the retreating soldiers and hoping the Alcantara cavalry was still somewhere around. With their help we might repel a native attack but it was a gamble, the last throw of the dice. My strength was fast ebbing away; the combination of exhaustion and my wounds had left me in a desperate state and so, taking one last look around I set off towards the retreating column.

I noticed the sun had swung to my left and I had the wit to realise that I was at last heading north, I must have skirted the settlement of Monte Arruit during the night and now I was relieved to know we were heading towards Melilla. For hours I trudged along, it was a hard slog, the few kilometres still to negotiate to the town was physically draining. Not only were my injuries a problem but the heat of the day was adding to my discomfort, but at least we saw nothing of the Riffians.

Why they would leave us alone I have no idea. Perhaps they had tired of the killing or maybe they needed some rest themselves and would return in due course. I did not know but I was grateful and as the sun began to set, we finally reached the outskirts of Melilla. News of the defeat at Annual had reached the town and though they were helpful, giving us comfort and sustenance, I learned that the towns people were living in fear of a Riffian onslaught and I learned also that the garrison, as at Annual, was unprepared. It seemed that my hope of deliverance was a false one, yet with so many soldiers returning there was some belief that salvation was at hand.

'You will fight?' queried a woman handing me some bread and olives.

I could do no more than give her a blank look, I was exhausted and the thought of having to take on the fierce tribesmen did nothing for my recovery.

'They will come for us,' she said, her voice breaking with worry. 'They kill everyone, they are savages.'

She began to sob until one of the other women put an arm around her and pulled her away.

'These men have been through a lot, don't expect too much yet, let them rest,' she said.

I wondered what these people did expect of us as I leaned back against the wall to take a drink from my water bottle, refilled by some kind soul and I ate some food for the first time in several days. Around me all that remained of the depleted regiments were either sat eating or slumped on the ground in deep and troubled sleep. We truly were in no fit state to fight.

I must have joined those in slumber and I have no real idea of how long I slept but when I finally awoke it was to another day. I had slipped from the support of the wall and found myself sprawled on the ground amongst the sleeping soldiers. My head was throbbing, and my mouth was bone dry but once I could drink some water, I became fully awake and my faculties returned. The pain in my arm was a misery and when I tried to stand, I found it all but impossible, my legs giving way at the first attempt, and so I leaned back against the wall to gather my strength. Finally, I did make it to my feet and I looked about me for a familiar face but there were none, just the faces of sad and beaten men. Then an officer appeared to wake those still asleep and he began to address us,

'Soldiers, we are expecting the Riffians to attack at any moment and so you are all ordered to report to the parade ground where you will be processed and re-equipped. Do you understand?'

'Yes,' a few of the men managed to mumble.

'Yes, sir! Have you still not learned how to address your superiors?'

I felt like hitting him, rubbing his tailored uniform into the dust together with his superior attitude. For all his perfection he was probably just as cowardly as those officers who had abandoned us to our fate in Annual. No wonder those simple tribesmen had routed us. If it had not been for the Alcantara with their fine horses, their discipline, and their bravery we would not be here today. Instead, we might all be lying out in the desert, nothing more than food for carrion. Yes, I thought, those men of the Alcantara were true soldiers and I wondered what had become of Emilio.

A second officer arrived and ordered us to assemble the parade ground where the commanding officer appeared riding a white horse, his perfectly turned-out uniform in stark contrast to our rags.

'You men are welcome reinforcements to the garrison here in Melilla,' he began. 'We are expecting an attack at any time and we need you for the defence of the town. I know most of you left your guns for the Riffians,' he said almost sneeringly. 'There are some spare armaments we can issue but this time don't go throwing them away because some tribesman is chasing you.'

His comments did not go down well after all we had been through. I felt we had more than one enemy, officers like him were supposed to lead us but if all they were capable of was strutting around in their fancy uniforms, we would have little chance against those tribesmen. It was officers like these who had let us down, run away at the first sign of trouble.

'*Sargento Primero*, take over will you,' ordered the general who seemed impatient to get away.

The sergeant major stepped forward to dismiss the parade and, still muttering amongst ourselves, as we made our way to a line of desks to give our details, names, regiments, and the like for a reorganisation of the remnants of the army.

'Are you wounded, soldier?' asked the officer when it was my turn. 'There is blood on your tunic.'

'Yes, sir, I think I caught a bullet,' I said, touching my arm.

'Well give me your details and then you can find a medical orderly and have it attended to.'

'Thank you, sir,' I said, relieved that at least one officer appeared human.

'Were you with the Seville Rifles?' asked a soldier standing a metre or two away.

'Yes, I was, still am I suppose. Do I know you?'

'Probably, I was in the Cartagena regiment. We were in the line with you.'

'How did you get here?'

For a moment his eyes looked vacant, reliving his ordeal no doubt and then he looked at me.

'It was hard, so very hard. When the attack began, we

fell back to defend the perimeter of the base losing only two men, but then things became desperate. We knew that the Riffians outnumbered us and surrounded we did not stand much of a chance. The general ordered us to form a defensive column; he wanted to make for an orderly retreat but it didn't work out very well. Some of the native troops shot their officers and deserted, left to join the Riffians. It caused panic, we simply broke ranks and ran. That was the signal for the natives to press home their attack. They shot many of our men and put others to the knife, the road ran red with blood. It was horrific.'

'But you are safe now.'

'For now! What happens if they attack us here, can we withstand them?'

'I don't know but it's all we can do. Have many of your company survived?'

'I don't know, I hope so. You, how did you escape?'

I related as much as I could remember and he noticed the dried blood on my tunic.

'You were wounded?'

'Yes, it doesn't seem as bad as I first thought though. I have to find a medical orderly to attend to it.'

'I know where the hospital is, come on, I will accompany you. I'm Raul by the way.'

'Pleased to meet you, Raul, my name is Francisco but everyone calls me Paco.'

We walked across the parade ground and I learned a little of my new friend. A rifleman like me, he told how he came from a large family with six brothers and three sisters, living on the outskirts of Alicante. They were poor, barely enough food coming into the household for them to live on. There was little chance of earning a proper living so when the recruiting sergeant came to town he decided to join up.

'That was a fateful mistake. I am lucky to be alive.'

'And how old are you, Raul?'

'They tell me I am nineteen, and you?

'The same.'

'Why did you join up?'

'It's a long story, a way of escape, and like yours a fateful decision.'

He was right, a fateful decision and on refection I could see Seville again, the bullring, the crowds and I felt decidedly uncomfortable wondering if I would ever go home again.

'Do you want to talk about it, what was your line of work before you joined up?'

'I was a bullfighter.'

'Wow, really?'

'Yes, really.'

'Why are you here then? Surely bullfighters earn good money, you did not need to join the army, did you?'

I sighed; I did not want to trawl over old memories, one still too raw to contemplate.

'I don't want to talk about it, Raul, maybe one day but not now.'

'This is the hospital. Shall I leave you here?'

'Yes, thanks for your help,' I said.

He gave a half salute and I wandered inside the building to look for a doctor.

'The more it stings, the better it is,' said the doctor after working on the wound, dabbing the stitches with some foul looking green liquid.

I did not believe him. In fact, I didn't believe anything

the army told me any longer, but at least the doctor was somewhat truthful and in time the sting did wear off. The stitches to my head wound were the more painful, the wound in my arm not so serious according to the doctor. I left the first aid post feeling much better than when I went in, rotating the arm a little to test it, and as I walked into the sunshine, I saw Raul talking to a group of soldiers. Looking up he gave me a wave and I decided to walk over to the group wondering if some of them might have an idea of our immediate future.

'Hey, Paco, come over here and listen to this. Tell him what you just told me,' said Raul ushering me towards a thick-set man.

'Hello,' I said, 'what's the news?'

'The army is defeated; we've lost most of the ground gained over the past year and the worry is that we are vulnerable to attack here. The situation is grim but I did hear that the Legión is coming from Ceuta.'

'They docked just an hour ago,' said another of the men.

The Legión, I had heard about them. A new force under Colonel Millán Astray formed not so long ago and already renowned for their fighting prowess. Maybe we did have a chance.

'We should go to the docks to see them.'

'I'm for that,' said one of the soldiers.

'They won't let us off the base. If we wait a bit, they will be coming here,' said a thoughtful looking soldier.

'Come on, let's give it a try,' said Raul, 'they can only turn us back.'

It was infectious; we all wanted to see the Legión and in the event, nobody seemed that interested in us, nobody prevented us from leaving the base. It was just a short walk to the docks and when we reached the ship a large crowd of citizens had already gathered and the troops had already. A military band was playing and overseeing it all a military figure with a black patch over one eye stood high on the ship's superstructure.

'I'm guessing that is Millán Astray,' said the knowledgeable member of the group. 'He's the commanding officer.'

'A few more like him and we will have those Riffians on the run,' said Raul.

I had to admit the Legión was certainly instilling confidence in everyone, the townspeople in particular, the relief on the faces unmistakable, and I began to believe we had a real chance.

The Legión themselves were a tough-looking lot and after a few barked commands they formed up into ranks and as marched away to their new positions. We too left the dock and returned to the military camp where staff officers had assigned us to new regiments and for me, it was the Extremadura regiment under Teniente Antonio Aranda Lopez. He was a young officer with little respect for his new recruits and after an initial lecture about salvaging Spain's honour before assigning us to defensive positions at the town's perimeter.

It was a chance to rest, get a decent meal and re-equip ourselves. We didn't talk much of our experiences of the past few days, the traumas still to vivid, though the regular troops who had only heard of the rout were eager to learn of our experiences. There were moments of contemplation, I could see soldiers standing alone, quiet, reflective no doubt remembering fallen comrades and counting their blessings. I tried not to dwell on the experience for like the rest of my new comrades I had survived. We were young, and we were thankful we were still alive, the boredom of sentry duty coming as a welcome interlude.

'Any movement out there, Paco?' asked Manuel come to relieve me.

I didn't hear him at first, I had inadvertently fallen asleep, the boredom too much for me, and it was only when he shook me that I realised he was there.

'No, I have watched that same area of ground for the whole night and I have seen absolutely nothing.'

'You should be careful, Paco; you could be shot for being asleep on duty.'

It was not easy staring into the darkness for hours on end, particularly after all I had gone through, and my day dreaming must have morphed into the real thing. Thank goodness it was Manuel who'd found me.

'There is a rumour that the Riffians have dispersed back into the mountains, gone back to their farms or whatever it is they do, and I hear the Legión is looking for recruits.'

'Really!' My ears pricked up. 'That's interesting.'

'Yes, why, do you fancy joining up? They say a transfer from a regular infantry regiment will be easy.'

I had no idea if I would join the Legión but the thought of it intrigued me. Since they'd arrived, I had learned something of this new fighting force, disciplined, tough, like the cavalrymen of the Alcantara

Then I heard my name called.

'Martinez, on your feet.'

I looked up to see Teniente Aranda Lopez walking towards me. Two men of the platoon followed him and he seemed agitated.

'Martinez, you have been asleep on duty. That is an offence.'

'Shit,' I thought, how had he found out? 'I'm sorry, sir, you are mistaken.'

'I don't think so, soldier. We are in a war situation and sleeping on duty carries a severe sentence.'

I protested my innocence but to no avail. He was adamant that I had fallen asleep on duty and was determined to punish me. But there were no witnesses except Manuel. Had he informed on me? Why would he? Had someone else seen me?

'I am placing you under arrest until I can decide what to do with you. You two, take him to the command post.'

I felt physically sick, stunned. I was still suffering from my ordeal, and night duty hadn't helped. I was exhausted.

'Give me your weapon,' said one of the guards.

I had no choice and passed it to him; I was not stupid, I wasn't going anywhere, where could I go? The rest of the company looked on with grim expressions, silent as the teniente ordered me taken to the command post.

'Sir, I found this man sleeping on duty,'

The officer looked at me, his expression neutral.

'What do you propose I do Teniente? We are in a war situation; we need all the able-bodied men we can muster.'

'Discipline is important, sir, an army demands loyalty and discipline from its soldiers.'

'Yes, I tend to agree. What do you propose we do with him?'

'A court martial, make an example of him.'

'If that is what you want to do then I suggest you fill out the formal paperwork and I will forward it to the general's office. In the meantime, I think perhaps we can lock him up.'

'Yes, sir, I will fill out the paperwork right away.'

'What's your name, soldier?' said the adjutant.

'Martinez, sir.'

'What regiment?'

'The Seville Rifles, sir, well it was.'

'You were at Annual?'

'Yes sir.'

'A harrowing experience by all accounts.'

'Yes sir.'

'This man has been through a lot, Teniente, do you really think a court martial is the way to handle it?'

'Yes, sir, I do, the men need to understand that they have responsibilities to their regiment and to Spain.'

'Very well, carry on.'

The teniente saluted as if he was simply on parade, a game, and at that moment I felt the urge to kill. I could not do that, could I? However, I needed to find a way out of the predicament I was in, and quickly. I felt angry, very angry, I was in danger of losing my freedom and possibly my life because of this officer. I would have bet all I had on the certainty that he had never seen action. I despised him and all those officers like him, officers who could not lead, men interested only in their comfort and self-advancement.

They took me to the prison block where I remained incarcerated for two days, time enough for Teniente

Aranda Lopez to submit his paperwork, time enough for the general to order my court martial. They would find me guilty, of that I had no doubt, and if the teniente had his way it would be the firing squad for me unless I could escape.

The thought of escape was at the forefront of my mind but I was no artisan, I did not know very much of metal and wood. My father would have known of any weakness in the cell's construction and understood how to get out, but my only chance was to overcome the guard and the thought obsessed me. How had it come to this? Why were they treating me so badly? Time was running out, I had to think of something.

I noticed the guard had a routine each time he brought my meagre rations; he would instruct me to stand well away and he would inspect the cell through a small sliding partition before he unlocked the door. I reasoned that this was the only time I could attempt an escape with a realistic chance of success and early the next morning, I decided to act.

Breakfast was not long after sunrise and having slept no more than a few hours, I was awake and alert. I heard the guard's footsteps, the small aperture in the door slid open and a pair of eyes peered into the tiny cell. He growled at me to stand back against the wall. It was always the same. Once I did as he ordered he turned the key but he could not look through the aperture at the same time. For just a short space of time I was invisible to him.

I had rehearsed the move in my mind repeatedly. The moment to act had arrived and as the eyes disappeared, the scrape of the key in the lock loud and clear, I took several steps towards the door, careful to remain out of the line of sight should he break the habit of the past few days and peer through the still open aperture but he did not. The key turned in the lock and my heartbeat increased to a point where I thought my chest would burst. But in a way the situation was no different from the bullfight, man against bull, a skilful mind against raw power.

The stout cell door began to swing open, and I made my move, it opened outwards because of the cell's tiny area and pushing hard against it I unbalanced the guard. In surprise he cried out and I pushed harder, knocking him off his feet and I rushed into the passageway to overpower him. My intention was to knock him out, steal a weapon if he had one and run as fast as I could as far as I could. What could go wrong?

Everything it seemed! The guard, for the first time, was not alone. As I pushed on the door knocking him to the floor and ran into the passage, I found myself confronted by a second soldier. I swung my fist, more in panic than with any force and he not only reacted quickly but he was skilful. Before I realised what had happened, I found myself pinned face down on the floor, his knee in the small of my back and my injured arm half way up my back screaming out in pain.

'Good try, soldier, you have spirit,' he said, hauling me to my feet, my arm still pinned painfully against my back. 'Well, you have saved me the trouble of testing you Martinez; I can see that you are no slouch. I guess you are more afraid of the firing squad than a few guards. Where were you going to run to if you had escaped?'

'Get stuffed,' I said through gritted teeth and was

surprised to hear him laugh.

'All right, let's get you out of here. I have a proposition for you, soldier.'

'Who the hell are you?' I asked in puzzlement.

'I am Caballero Legionario Ramón García of the First Bandera of the Legión.'

'What do you want of me?'

'You are in trouble, my friend, but I know a little of your history and we are looking for recruits.'

I was surprised, to say the least. Here I was on the verge of a court martial and more likely than not an encounter with the firing squad, but if I'd understood him correctly, this soldier was offering me a way out of my predicament.

'Recruits?'

'Yes, my job is to liaise with the army units already here in Melilla to find suitable recruits to strengthen our ranks.'

'And that includes me?'

'Possibly, very possibly. I can see though the fighting skills you possess leave a lot to be desired, but not to worry we can sort that out. A few weeks under my supervision and we will have you up to the standard of the Legión. What do you say, is it the Legión or the firing squad?'

He knew my answer; he'd known even before asking.

'Well then, we had better see the officer in charge and get hold of your release papers and then you can sign on with us, and when you do, you are expected to give your life to the Legión, to be prepared to die for the Legión and the glory of Spain.'

Chapter 4

Francisco had tried to find a way out of his prison but in the almost total darkness, it had proved an impossible task. When fatigue finally overwhelmed him, he lay down on a covering of straw and fell into a fitful sleep. For how long he lay on his makeshift bed he did not know, waking only when a shaft of light from the opening door penetrated his slumber. For several seconds he had no idea where he was until a voice brought him back into the world.

'Hey, boy, get up, follow me.'

Suddenly aware of the silhouette filling the open doorway he stood up, instinctively searching for a chance of escape. However, no clear route out of his predicament presented itself and the man appeared twice his size. So, instead of making a dash for freedom, he fell into step with his jailor, following him towards the impressive looking estate house.

'Wait here and don't even think of running away. I doubt you can outrun a horse and I need a spot of lassoing practice.'

Francisco looked at the floor. In this new and strange environment, he felt completely out of his depth; he had no idea of what was happening to him nor how to handle the situation but instinct demanded he remain calm. Were they going to beat him, he wondered? Perhaps they might take him to the police in Triana? It would not be the first time, he wasn't afraid of the local police, after a good telling off they usually let him go.

'In there,' said the man.

Francisco had little choice and after a powerful push to his back he stumbled up the few steps and through the open door, and into a spacious room. A man with the dark features begotten of Moorish blood, swarthy-skinned and with jet-black hair stood by the window.

'So, this is one of the hooligans who came to disrupt our prize fighting bulls, is he? What have you got to say for yourself, lad, why do you come here in the dead of night worrying our prize bulls?'

Francisco had no answer. He had entered a world of which he knew little, the world of the rich and powerful and he had no defence. The man looked him up and down, walked over to a wide, heavy desk and sat down, pushing a ledger to one side, and clasped his hands under his chin.

'You hungry boy? I do not suppose you slept too well either. Well, are you hungry?'

'Y... yes, sir,' stammered Francisco.

'Fetch the boy some olives and bread, Carlos.'

His son nodded and disappeared from the room leaving Francisco alone with his father.

'Carlos tells me you have a talent for the bulls. Tell me about yourself, I suppose you come from Triana, most of you do. What does your father do for a living?'

Francisco began to relax a little; they were treating him far kindlier than he expected and the old man seemed genuinely interested in him.

'I do, I come from Triana, where Juan Belmonte comes from.'

'You are a fan?'

'Oh yes, I dream of nothing more than to follow his example.'

'That's a tall order for one so young. You know it takes years to reach his standard or anywhere near it for that matter, it takes talent and courage. Do you have courage, lad?'

Francisco did not know how to answer and before he could even attempt to, Carlos appeared with a plate of food and a glass of water.

'Sit here with me and eat. I want to know more about you,' said the father gesturing to a chair.

Francisco took it, his stomach rumbling at the sight of the bread and sausage, he was ravenous and he cleared the plate in a very short time.

'So, Juan Belmonte, what do you know about him?'

'He is the greatest bullfighter in the whole of Spain.'

'Is he, and what is it that makes him so famous?'

'You don't know Belmonte? I thought everyone knew of him.'

The man's eyes closed as he controlled the urge to laugh aloud, amused by the boy's innocence.

'I have heard of him, tell me more.'

'He is daring. He stands so still when the bull charges, uses the muleta in such a way that he becomes invisible to a charging bull.'

'Bravo, you understand. When have you seen Belmonte fight?'

'I haven't, I learn about him from the aficionados who

congregate in the bars of Triana. I sometimes sit on a wall and listen to them.'

Laying his hands on his desk the man nodded slowly.

'I am impressed. Carlos tells me that you have his mannerisms, a little rough around the edges but a budding Belmonte nonetheless.'

Francisco's bewildered, sleep-deprived eyes lit up, fear and apprehension falling away.

'I cannot think of a better compliment. Thank you, sir.'

'We have not been introduced. I am José de Mendoza, the owner of this estate, and you are?'

'Francisco Martinez but everyone calls me Paco.'

'Ah... Paco, Paco Martinez, the bullfighter. How does that sound?'

Francisco's cheeks blushed red under the grime. It sounded great but what was the catch?

'Come with me, lad, let us find a bull, I want to see what you can do, see if you can live up to Carlos's description of you.'

Francisco's newly found confidence suddenly ebbed away. The man's expectations of him were great and he was not sure he could fulfil them.

'Come let us have a look in the pens, see what we can find,' said José getting up from behind his desk.

This time Carlos did not manhandle him; instead, he brought up the rear as his father led the way.

'There look, that bull in the corner of the pen, do you think you can work him?' said José leaning on the fence.

Francisco eyed the bull; it did not yet appear fully grown, a three-year-old perhaps. He had only ever fought bulls in open pasture in the dead of night, never in an enclosed pen and never with strangers looking on. He should have felt unnerved but the desire to take on the bull was overwhelming and with a steady voice he said, 'I will need to take a closer look.'

'By all means. Carlos, take the boy to have a look at that bull. Find him a muleta and a stout stick, let him play it for a while so that I can see what he can do.'

Carlos gestured to one of the farmhands, gave an instruction, and by the time Francisco was standing astride the fence the muleta had appeared and although Carlos had bullied him, his father had shown civility and kindness and for some reason, he wanted to impress the old man, reinforce his belief in him. However, what Francisco could not yet know was that he was not the first trespasser to undergo such an initiation. Father and son were always on the lookout for capable boys to work with their bulls. The urchins from Triana could be a nuisance, the animals were valuable and were never supposed to see a man on foot until the day of their death so the estate made every effort to keep intruders at bay, sometimes employing watchmen to chase the boys away and sometimes Carlos took on those duties.

When Carlos had watched Francisco and the other boys it was obvious to him that Francisco was the ringleader and although he could not deny the lad's skill they had decided to humiliate the boy, frighten him, prevent him and his little gang ever returning to the estate's pastures.

'Go on then, get into the pen, let my father see how good you are,' said Carlos, handing over the muleta and a stout stick. 'It is up to you now, boy. Off you go.'

Francisco was too innocent to understand the real nature of what was really happening, all he could see was the bull and a chance to fight it. Taking the muleta and stick, he cleared the fence and dropped to the floor several metres from the patient bull.

'Do you think we've done the right thing letting the lad fight that bull, Carlos?'

'Yes, of course, we have Father. It will teach him a lesson he will never forget and, with luck, we will not see any of those boys from Triana for quite some time. Frighten them I say, let this boy go home to lick his wounds and tell his friends. They won't be bothering us for a while, I don't think.'

José nodded yet he had reservations and signalled to one of his herdsmen.

'I don't want this to get out of hand, Pablo. Keep an eye on the boy and distract the bull if things look like he is getting into any real danger. I don't want him badly hurt.'

'Don't worry, Father, he is a capable lad, just a small goring will do I think,' said Carlos.

Unaware of the conversation taking place, Francisco took a deep breath and eyed the bull. It seemed uninterested in him and so he began walking slowly towards it. He flicked the muleta, attracting its attention and was almost upon it when suddenly the animal threw back its head and snorted. A bull's eyesight is not so good but there is nothing wrong with their sense of smell and Francisco's scent was beginning to permeate the bull's nostrils.

It turned its head, its eyes focused, and it picked out the shape coming towards it. Taking another step forward Francisco let the muleta unfurl fully, held it out in front of him, and paused. Sitting on the wall outside the bar listening to the older men he had learned that part of

Belmonte's success in the bullring was that he always tried to understand the bull's intentions and so, for a few seconds, Francisco watched his adversary as it lowered its head and pawed the ground. It was a strong signal and Francisco knew the charge was imminent.

He must judge the bull's path and time his move well because they were not in an expansive bullring simply a large pen, a corral and sweeping the muleta across his chest he waited. It was a trigger, the bull reacted and immediately charged towards him and as the horns came within striking distance of his chest Francisco stepped adroitly out of danger. Only the cloth of the muleta remained an obstacle to the charging bull and crashing through the flimsy fabric the sharp horns passed harmlessly by.

Francisco raised himself up on the balls of his feet and spun round ready to meet the next charge, arching his back in the way of the great bullfighters of the day and, watching from the safety of the fence, José de Mendoza pursed his lips. He could already see the boy's moves were skilful and well executed, the boy did have a real talent.

Several more times the bewildered young bull, charged Francisco, each occasion without success and José became alarmed. The prospect of the bull learning how to deal with a matador was a problem for if it did not charge fearlessly in the bullring it would be valueless and if it learned the bullfighter was the real target and not the muleta cape then it could cause real injury or even death.

'Enough, get him out of there, Pedro,' he called to his herdsman. 'I'm not sure your idea has worked, Carlos; the boy is a natural and we might have lost twenty thousand pesetas if that bull has learned anything today.'

Carlos looked glum. In the pen, Francisco noticed the herdsman climbing the corral fence, a pole in his hands and he knew his fun was about to come to an end.

'The boss says to stop. Get out while I keep this fellow away from you.'

Francisco understood and obeyed, running for the fence with the agitated bull hard on his heels. He could feel the breath of the bull on his back as with no more than a few millimetres between his rump and the scything horns, he scaled the fence to safety watched by José and Carlos. José stroked his chin in thought, beginning to realise that perhaps frightening Francisco away was not in his interest. The boy had worked the bull with skill and determination but he could see that the animal was becoming resistant and it was time to put a stop to the proceedings.

'Bravo, Paco. For one so young, you have style and you are brave. I have a proposition for you. Carlos told me that he watched you draw the bull last night, said you had an inborn skill, one we do not see very often and today I saw it for myself. We are breeders of fighting bulls but occasionally we produce a torero, a bullfighter to promote the estate and its bulls. Carlos is one and I, as a young man, fought bulls in Seville, Toledo, Córdoba even, and when my fighting days were over, I decided to become a breeder. With our help, you could become a matador but first, you need to learn about the bulls. I am offering you a job on the estate, what do you say?'

Francisco was surprised, confused and yet flattered, but how should he reply? He did not know and so remained silent.

'Well, what do you say, boy?'

'Th… thank you, sir,' he said, finally. 'I am honoured that you think I can become a bullfighter, of course, I will work for you.'

'Good, you can start tomorrow. Carlos, find him a place in the bunkhouse and set him to work.'

Carlos frowned, not pleased his plan to throw the boy out with his tail between his legs had fallen flat and now, adding insult to injury, his father had offered him a job.

For Francisco his night in Tablada had turned out well. Apart from his night locked up in the barn, the offer a job on the estate was a dream come true. He could go home to collect a few things and taking the opportunity he set off for Triana unable to think of anything else but the bulls. But he had not been home all night and it was early afternoon before he arrived home. He was tired from his ordeal, the excitement of fighting the bull and the hours cooped up in the lightless barn. But he cast all that aside as he burst through the door, eager to tell his mother of his luck. But his enthusiasm wilted and he came to a standstill under the gaze of his mother's dark, angry eyes and before he knew it a heavy shoe came flying across the room, hitting the wall just a few centimetres from his head.

'Where have you been? What have you been doing? shouted Carmen. 'Your friends told us they left you in Tablada with someone chasing you. Your father was worried gypsies had kidnapped you or worse. What have you been up to this time?'

Francisco's mother's hostile reception was nothing new; he had run the gauntlet of her wrath many times and once he was over the initial shock, he was unfazed.

'I'm hungry, is there anything to eat?'

'Is that all you can say when I have worried myself sick over you? You could be... you've been out chasing bulls again, haven't you? You were pretending to be Juan Belmonte and you were caught, I know it.'

Shaken by the accuracy of his mother's words, he paused. Not for the first time had her gypsy intuition caught him out. She seen through his falsehoods so many times, but at least this time he did intend to tell her the truth.

'Mama, I have a job,' he blurted out.

'What job, where?'

'On the de Mendoza estate in Tablada. I will be working with the bulls.'

'De Mendoza, José de Mendoza?'

'*Sí,* Mama.'

'Hm... I know of him. What have you been doing to become involved with José de Mendoza?'

'We went out looking for bulls to fight and a man chased us. The others got away.'

His mother's eyes narrowed and he knew she had guessed he was fighting a bull, a dangerous occupation in her eyes and, not wishing to antagonise her further, he carried on. The man, he locked me up in the barn.'

'Who is this man who wrongfully imprisons my son, I will give him a piece of my mind, who is he?'

'Mama, that doesn't matter because he was the one who helped me get the job. There isn't much work here, and it's a chance to earn some money, make it easier for you and Papa.'

Carmen looked thoughtful for a moment.

'Here, have some bread and cheese, and we will see

what Papa has to say when he comes home.'

'I can't stay, Mama, I have just a few hours. I decided to walk home to tell you about my job. If I can get some time off on Sunday, I will come home then,' he said picking up the bread.

'You were lucky. I have heard of the Guardia locking boys up for doing what you have done. Why didn't they take you to the Guardia?'

Francisco was beginning to feel cornered but had the wit to tell the whole truth for once and as he spoke his story began to unfold until it came to the episode in the corral with the bull. He knew his mother would scold him if she thought he had put himself in danger, but clearing his throat he decided to take the plunge.

'I... er, they asked me to...'

He didn't manage to finish; the door opened and his two sisters appeared, a welcome distraction.

'Paco, Paco is back,' exclaimed Juanita as soon as she saw him. 'Where have you been?'

'I have been fighting bulls, I am a torero now,' he said with some exaggeration.

'Now you tell me you are a bullfighter. You are a stupid boy, Francisco, you could get yourself injured, gored, even killed. I forbid it, you will not go back to that place. Your father will have none of it either,' said Carmen reaching for her other shoe.

'A torero!' said Juanita in wonder.

'Not a real bullfighter, I have found a job on an estate and I will be helping to look after the young bulls,' he said, quickly, backtracking on his boasting.

'So you say. I don't believe you,' said his mother. 'If you go back to the estate, don't you go putting yourself into danger.'

'No don't, Paco, Mama is right,' said the younger sister, Maria.

Juanita looked at her brother with wide eyes. She had never set eyes on a bullring and now her brother was telling her that he was a torero. How exciting.

Francisco looked at her and smiled. 'Don't worry, I am not yet a torero, just a farmhand.'

Pouting with disappointment, Juanita went to stand at her mother's side, all the time gazing at her brother. She knew the boys at school all wanted to be bullfighters and to have one in her family would be something to tell them.

'I must go now,' said Francisco. 'I will get my things and leave. I have to be back on the estate to start work first thing in the morning.'

'I will help you,' said Maria rushing to his side.

'Thank you, little sister, I would love you to help me.'

There was not much to do, his meagre belongings consisting of little more than a change of clothes and an old bullfighting magazine but Maria still fussed him and with his belongings wrapped in a cloth, he kissed his mother and his two sisters farewell. He was happy, he had a spring in his step as he walked along the street dreaming of the day when he would indeed enter La Maestranza as a bullfighter and began to whistle the paso doble, imagining himself at the head of his cuadrilla, raising his matador's hat to the crowd but instead of cheers all he heard was someone calling out his name.

'Paco, where have you been? Are you all right? We didn't know what happened to you.'

Francisco turned to see Manolito on the opposite side of the street and crossed over to him.

'I am fine. What about you four, did you get home all right or was anybody else on the prowl?'

'We saw no one, we just ran and when we felt safe, we crept back to see what had happened to you. We saw you with that man, but there was nothing we could do so we went home. But you did not come home and we thought he might have killed you.'

'*Madre de Dios*, I don't think that was going to happen. You can tell the rest of them I am fine and the man, he's called Carlos, he took me to see his father, the owner of the estate. He gave me a job on the estate; he thinks I could be a torero one day. By the way, where are Luis and the others?'

'Gone fishing, down by the stream, do you want me to take you to them?

'No thanks, not now, I have to go back to work. Tell them I'll see them sometime.'

'A job, a bullfighter, yes I will tell them,' said an astonished Manolito.

Working on the estate was a turning point in young Francisco's life. For over a year he worked diligently looking after the calves, eventually progressing to look after the older fighting bulls out in the pastures. The estate workers accepted him and he made friends easily. He learned to ride horses, grew taller, stronger, and then, one day, while he was keeping an eye on bulls grazing, he caught sight of two women. They looked the same age and were riding in his direction, two dark-haired, true Andalusian-looking girls dressed for riding, tight breeches and embroidered paseo jackets, their features obscured under black Sevillano hats.

'Who are they?' Francisco asked one of the older men.
'They are related to the family, cousins I believe.'
'What are their names?'

'I don't know. One of the hands tried to talk to them, showed off a bit when they came here earlier in the year. He finished up losing his job so if you want my advice steer clear of them, forget them they are not for the likes of us.'

But Francisco could not forget them. He had little experience of women, just the girls he grew up with, friends of his sisters but these two seemed from another planet and in the bunkhouse that evening he could not resist trying to discover more about them.

'They are related to the de Mendozas and they come here now and then to ride the horses. They sometimes stay for a few days,' said Luque, an experienced vaquero. 'They will be back I think, young Paco. Plenty of time to get a good look at them.'

Chapter 5

They were undoubtably the hardest four weeks of my life and when they were finally at an end, my arms and legs ached, my feet had blisters and the regimental barber had shorn my hair tight to my skull and yet I was in the best physical condition of my life. The constant physical exertion, the drills, the unannounced forced marches in the blazing sun had left my leg muscles as hard as iron. I could run for a kilometre with my rifle held high above my head and at the end of the run, I could still accurately. I had never felt as fit, so full of energy. I suppose it was a credit to the instructors who had worked us so hard but for most of the time, myself and the rest of the recruits cursed them under our breath. In addition to the physical aspect of my training, I learned to strip and clean my weapon, how to use the bayonet and at the end of it all, I was ready to join the Legión.

I had little choice as the alternative to volunteering did not bear thinking about and on the completion of our training, smartly dressed in our new uniforms, we paraded before the general. I found it hard to believe looking at my new comrades in arms that the army could have turned us into the new and impressive fighting force I was now part of. Other than the survivors of that terrible time at the hands of the Riffians there were amongst us, volunteers from home and, as befitting a Foreign Legion, recruits from abroad. Many had come from the Americas, Spain's lost colonies, and in my case, the military prison.

We were central to the army's plan to push back against the Riffian tribesmen who had overrun vast swathes of the country. Spain's gains over the past ten years had gone and the tribesmen were intent on driving us out of Morocco completely and so, to stem the tide, two new banderas had come into existence and the army was preparing to fight back. The third bandera was central to the plan, trained and fully fitted out, the four rifle companies and four machine gun companies were under the command of Major Villegas and our first deployment was escorting a supply column of pack horses and mules to the besieged hill forts.

All previous attempts had failed, the beleaguered garrisons were becoming desperate, and so the Legión's newly formed bandera was taking on the job. We left Melilla for the first of the forts well before dawn, the column of mules and pack horses stretching for easily two hundred metres along the road winding its way up into the Riff mountains. I remember shivering in the cold morning air, more through apprehension than the cold but before long the North African sun was beating down and lifting our spirits.

The long grey line of pack animals stretched almost endlessly, plodding steadily across a landscape of ravines and gullies, into the foothills before the unrelenting climb into the mountains. Our immediate objective was to reach the high plateau before nightfall and try to remain unseen by the enemy. At least there we could rest a while a defendable area the officer told us yet once we stopped for the night, I struggled to manage even a few hours' sleep my night sentry duty robbing me of half the night.

It was hard to keep myself alert as I searched for sight of an invisible enemy, the arid mountain air making it difficult to focus my eyes. We had entered the, realm of the Riffian, a hardy mountain tribe of cruel and unforgiving fighters. They were somewhere out there we knew, but in the event, we did not come under attack and as the sun returned, we once more set off on our trek and by early afternoon of the second day, we were climbing a steep winding path high into the mountains. Ahead of me, the column of mules and pack horses entered the narrow mountain path, disappearing at times as they negotiated the steep curving bends.

'Damn hot out here, Paco,' said Juan, a fellow recruit.

'It is, but not as hot as down there,' I replied pointing to the flat landscape a thousand metres below. 'It will probably get hotter; in this dry air someone with fair skin like you should be careful.'

'My English ancestry, I suppose.'

'English?'

'My mother reckons my great-great-great-grandfather was a British sailor.'

'How does she know that?' asked another soldier.

'I don't know, her mother told her I suppose and her mother before her. There were a lot of British sailors captured over the years.'

'We have the same in Cadiz,' said Miguel, another newfound friend walking alongside us.

'You still live in Cadiz?' I asked.

'Yes, in the hills overlooking the port.'

'You don't fancy a seafarer's life?'

'Well with little chance of a decent job I did consider finding a ship but then the army came to town and here I am. At least I have the chance to earn some sort of a living and to get back at the swine that killed our soldiers.'

Juan and I looked at him with some sympathy. Defeated and humiliated by the Riffian tribesmen it had proved a difficult time for Spain, though, conversely, the incident had become the army's best recruiting sergeant.

'Well, we might not have to wait too long before you can kill a few,' I said sarcastically.

The irony seemed lost on him; he had not seen the Riffians at first hand. He was in for a shock. The order to move came and, marching ever higher into the barren unforgiving mountains the mules began to struggle. Never really having considered a mule's lot, apart from the annoyance I felt at their braying, I realised how stoical the animals were, taking hardship in their stride and I was beginning to believe that we might reach the outpost trouble free. But it was not to be, my complacency interrupted by the sound of gunfire and from the head of the column, the sound of a bugle reached me and high above birds of prey began circling. The gunshots echoed round the steep rocky and I tried to determine from where the sound was coming but my ears were confused, echoes ricocheting amongst the rocky cliffs making it an impossible task.

'Take cover,' shouted the sergeant, running up the narrow path.

I did not need this advice; I was already behind the nearest boulder priming my rifle and searching for a target amongst the lofty cliffs. Around me the other legionaries were finding their own cover, their eyes looking skywards, and along the narrow mountain path the column came to a halt. An eerie silence fell upon us, broken only by the occasional braying of mules and sporadic gunfire and we waited. The natives were trying to pick us off, I could hear legionaries and native regulares ahead returning fire and I could see small figures moving up the sides of the ravine.

'It's a diversion, they want to stop us moving. They will be taking shots at us back here soon enough, lads. Let us get as high as we can before they show,' said the sergeant. 'Legionaries to me,' he yelled, the rallying call of the Legión, a call I would hear many more times during my service, the spark to light our fires.

Today was our first taste of combat and I think all our hearts beat fiercely within our chests yet we began climbing the steep slope, a dangerous manoeuvre under the eyes of the enemy but the Legión was of a different calibre to the rest of the army and with a confidence borne of the rigorous training, we went on the offensive.

'There!' exclaimed Juan. 'Over there, I can see them.'

I followed his outstretched arm; white-robed figures were creeping through the gullies towards us compelling us to duck behind the scattered boulders from where we prepared to fight. The sergeant ordered us to fix bayonets and on his signal, we renewed the charge. He left the cover of the rocks, running up the shallow incline with his rifle held out in front of him and his bravery was a catalyst for the rest of us. It was almost as if an invisible force was driving us, one that did not allow us to think of what we were doing and as soon as the Riffians saw us they began shooting. Two legionaries fell but I hardly noticed; my blood was up and I had nowhere else to go.

I had no real idea of how many of them there were, maybe twenty, concealed amongst rocks and sparse foliage and shooting in our direction. I heard the buzz of a bullet a little too close for comfort and beside me one of our number fell to a lucky shot. In general, the shooting was inaccurate and that gave us a chance to close on them. They did not seem to give much consideration as to the setting of their sights, simply pointing their guns in our general direction and pulling the triggers.

Once we were fifty or so meters away from them, we found cover and for a period we traded shot with them until the sergeant ran out of patience.

'Legionaries, bayonets at the ready.'

Around me, I could hear the metallic clicks as the legionnaires checked their weapons and we were ready for the lunacy of a full-frontal attack. We were mad to try it but the training had made us mad and without hesitation we followed the sergeant. Leaping forward and screaming profanities we rushed the Riffian position with an unstoppable momentum, our bayonets at the ready. The first of us overrunning the Riffians' position in short order, our bayonets inflicting terrible wounds, and yet the tribesmen were unperturbed by the mayhem, coming to meet us with daggers drawn. They were brave fighters but the dagger is no match for a well-aimed bayonet yet their eyes held a belief that they were more than equal to us.

It all happened so quickly; a Riffian rose to attack me with his curved dagger but I had the advantage of reach. Making full use of my rifle I drove the bayonet deep into his chest to send him sprawling and not far away I heard men screaming but we were winning, driving them from their defences, killing them and leaving the few survivors to escape the mayhem by disappearing into the ravines and gullies from where they had come.

It was a hard fight; two legionaries were dead and a further three wounded but we had killed a dozen or more of them and had driven them off but we knew they would be back. However, the engagement with such a fierce enemy had given us our first real chance to show what we could do and wreak at least some retribution for Annual was immensely satisfying. For the immediate future, we were free of their harassment and below us I could see the mules beginning to move, the shouts of the drovers echoing of the steep canyon walls.

'Don't for one minute think this is over,' said the sergeant as we descended and began to fan out alongside the column. 'Keep a sharp lookout and make every shot count. The mules make easy targets and we cannot afford to lose any of them.'

The platoon took up a position on the flank and in silence we moved with the mules and the pack horses, the only sounds those of their hooves and the jangling of tack. Progress was slow yet uninterrupted and within an hour we had passed over the high point of the trail to begin a shallow descent, squeezing between a steep, rock-strewn slope on one side and a sheer drop on the other. Nevertheless, the column progressed, the sure-footed mules negotiating the torturous route but, as the trail narrowed further, we had little choice but to take up positions between the pack animals and suddenly we were in a difficult situation. Because of the hold-up we had fallen behind schedule and a second night in the open was in prospect, and we had entered ideal ambush territory.

As night fell, progress along the mountain path slowed markedly, the increasing difficulty of negotiating the undulations and potholes in the fleeting moonlight had made the mules wary. To make matters worse, high above the enemy were watching, calling out to us, their insults echoing through the increasing darkness. They informed us that we did not have long to live and that we would die most horrible deaths. It was unnerving but nevertheless, there were no gunshots; reassuring as it seemed to indicate that they could not see us plainly enough to shoot. Although they refrained from taking pot-shots during the hours of darkness, a different story would emerge once daylight returned. They were at home in the mountains, they would know the best places for an ambush, the arrival of the dawn would bring fresh anxieties.

At about three o'clock in the morning, the order came to halt and for pickets to take up positions so that the animals could rest a while. For now though, we were safe enough and the commander believed a chance to rest and recover our strength would be of benefit to us.

'Where do you think they are, Paco.'

I was lying against a rock, dozing, annoyed at his disturbance but I understood Miguel's concern. The natives' unrelenting calls were echoing through the night, annoying and they were beginning to unnerve him.

'I don't know but I guess we will find out soon enough,' I said, losing the will to sleep, and it struck me that we would soon be sitting ducks.

'Right, you lot,' said the sergeant kicking several boots. 'On your feet, scouts have pinpointed those bastards. We have a good idea where they are hiding and we are going after them.'

The events of the following two hours will never leave me, the experience burned indelibly into my brain. Out of sight of the column, the Riffians had climbed the rock pinnacles and, from those vantage points, could observe completely the column's progress and once daylight did return, they renewed their sniping. The forward part of the column became trapped and the drovers dare not move the mules and pack horses from the relative safety of the overhanging rocky outcrops fearing the enemy could pick them off at random. The situation appeared untenable but our commander had a plan, one in which we would play the enemy at his own game. Unseen from above we would find a route up the ravine's steep side to their positions and make a surprise attack, but that was easier said than done.

On his signal we followed the sergeant in single file, our eyes wide open, searching the moonlit path for obstacles and for a time we made good progress but then the route became impassable and for an hour we searched for a break in the cliff face that would allow us to progress.

'We have to get closer,' said the sergeant. We have no choice but to climb the rock face to reach them, take them out. There is a steep ravine cutting into the mountain back along the trail. We can outflank them by climbing up there, I think. It will be difficult and I hope none of you have vertigo.'

We had little alternative, we had to follow him if we expected to emerge alive from what was becoming a desperate situation. The sergeant was one of the toughest men I ever met, afraid of no one and as strong as an ox and with a wave of his hand, he led us towards a deep cut in the rock face. With his rifle slung over his shoulder he began to climb the lower section of the rock face, where the slope was not particularly steep and the ascent proved easy enough. A plurality of protruding rocks offered hand and footholds and I gratefully reached out for them, pulling myself ever higher but as we climbed, the rock face became very steep, sheer almost and our progress slowed dramatically. Climbing was not easy for me but a few of the South Americans amongst us had grown up in the mountains and to them, climbing was second nature and like mountain goats the led the way.

I made the ascent close behind a Cuban called Alfonso. He encouraged me, pointing to the best hand and footholds and, in silence and by the light of the moon, we climbed ever higher. I could see no further than a few metres; if I had then maybe I would not have felt so brave but eventually the sheer face gave way to a gentler slope and, as the dawn began to break, we emerged onto a small plateau.

After our exertions, a rest would have been welcome but the sound of gunfire had returned, the daylight affording the Riffians sight of part of the column and they began to harass it. Judging by the sound of their guns, I guessed they were not far away and to reinforce that view, word came that those legionaries ahead had found the enemy position and that we had indeed outflanked them.

A few metres more and we reached the edge of the plateau and, gingerly looking over the edge, we could see fifty or more shapes in the early morning sun, their stark outlines a shadow against the rocks and most were standing in the open, confident. I watched them, some leaning on their rifles, chatting as if they were still in their home village, others leaning over to shoot at the mules and pack horses a hundred metres below and all were blissfully unaware of our presence.

The sergeant lifted his rifle and set his sights, signalled to the rest of us to follow suit, and a minute later, we were ready. Amazingly, not one tribesman turned to look our way, not one of them had any idea of what was about to transpire. Miguel gave me a wry smile and took aim; I picked my target, and at the sergeant's command I squeezed the trigger. A white-clad figure slumped forward, my first kill. I found another target and let off a shot but by now we had lost the element of surprise and for the next hour or more a fierce firefight ensued no one, not even the wounded remained alive. We hated these men who had performed such barbaric acts on Spain's young men and the satisfaction of knowing we had extracted at least some revenge was welcome.

'Well done, lads, anyone hurt?'

'I stubbed my toe on a rock, sarge,' said some wag, breaking the tension.

It was not really a laughing matter, but we could not resist sniggering, a release of the tension we had all been under. We had succeeded in removing the immediate threat with minimal losses, just two troopers with flesh wounds, and for the time being, we commanded the heights. The sergeant took out his mirror and flashed a signal to the men below and for a further two hours we remained in position to watch over the column then it was time to descend the way we had come.

Slumped to the ground after our hair-raising descent I turned to Alfonso as he mentioned my name. 'Cigarette, Paco?' he said offering me one and like the rest of us, he looked tired. I took the cigarette although I was not a smoker but after the night's excitement.

'Thanks,' I said taking one and as I did, I noticed his look.

He tilted his chambergo to the back of his head and wide eyed he exclaimed, 'where did he get that!'

I turned to see a passing legionary and impaled on his bayonet was a lifeless head, its eyes staring into space. As I said I was not normally one for the tobacco but the sight of the severed head left my stomach churning and with my eyes focused on the legionnaire's trophy I took the offered match. It was obvious the South Americans believed in an eye for an eye.

'We gave them what for didn't we?' said Alfonso, recovering from the shock, his face stern as we watched the soldier walk past with his trophy.

I nodded, struck the match, and lit the cigarette, coughing to the amusement of my comrades. It had been a difficult time for us, the bandera's first engagement but we knew we had performed well and, as we buried our dead, we knew this was just the beginning.

In the first year since the bandera's inception, we lost almost half our strength killed or wounded, so many faces I would never see again but those men who lived through those early days learned to survive and developed a camaraderie that was something to behold. It was the glue that bound us together, a spirit that saw us win through against adversity, against the unfathomable Riffians a constant source of worry. Annual was just the beginning of their trail of destruction and murder and for almost three years, I undertook to honour my pledge to the Legión, to avenge the fallen and to serve Spain.

    We marched the length and breadth of the Protectorate, wrestling back control of lost territory, fighting pitched battles, attacking Riffian strongholds, and destroying their villages; a violent time that changed me. I knew I had become a different person, no longer the heartbroken youth who had joined the Seville Rifles out of desperation. I had become leaner, tougher, a real soldier taking hardship in my stride yet there were still times when memories of home filled my mind, times when an uncertain future presented itself.

Chapter 6

Francisco slipped out of the house into an almost deserted street. Triana was just waking up, the sun had barely risen, dull orange rays cascading off grey-tiled rooftops like a liqueur of Seville oranges poured into a glass. Halfway along the street stood an ancient woman dressed in black a basket of homemade pegs slung over her arm as she made ready for her daily slog across the bridge in search of a few centimos to feed herself for another day. Further along the narrow street the first workers emerged from battered doorways but Francisco was too preoccupied to notice any of them. Tragedy had struck the family. They said it was an accident, said the roof beam had looked secure enough but the rope holding it had given way and his father was not quick enough to avoid it the falling beam. It had crushed him and he had taken almost a week to die.

Francisco had learned of the accident from a stern-faced José de Mendoza while he was spreading hay and had known it was bad news even before he spoke.

'Francisco, I have some bad news. Your father has had an accident. One of his friends has just left the house; he came to ask me to inform you. Francisco, I think it is a bad accident and you should go home.'

'Bad, how bad?' asked a worried Francisco.

'I don't know but I understand that he may not recover.'

Francisco felt his stomach churn and catching his breath he looked at José.

'What happened?' he asked the older man.

'I don't know exactly, only that a heavy beam fell on him. They were lifting roof beams and something went wrong. I'm sorry, you had better go home, support your mother, and see what needs to doing. Come back when you are ready.'

Arriving home a few hours later he had found the doctor with his father who lay prone on his bed, his face as pale as death. He looked as peaceful as if his life was already over and, standing beside the bed, his mother listened tearfully to the doctor.

'He has broken ribs and there is internal bleeding. All you can do is to make him comfortable, Señora Martinez.'

'Thank you, doctor,' was all she could say.

'I will call again in a few days to see how he is and I will present my bill.'

He did not dwell as he closed his Gladstone bag; the family were grief-stricken enough and to add his fee to their woes was not something he particularly enjoyed, but it was his living after all.

Francisco looked at his father, his pale unshaven face, the dark rings around his eyes, and for all his father's faults, he felt a love for him and a surge of emotion in the belief that he might not survive began to engulf him.

'Is there anything I should do, Mama? Where are Juan and the girls?'

'They have gone to the church to pray for your father.

Oh, Paco, what are we to do?'

Francisco reached out to touch his mother's shoulder, comfort her if he could.

'Mama, the doctor mentioned his bill. How much will it be, can you pay it?'

'I don't know. I, we, Papa has just a few pesetas saved, not enough for the doctor, I don't think. Let's not worry about that now,' she said, looking at her husband. 'Oh, I am so worried, so worried.'

'I know, Mama. I am, me and the girls and Juan, we are here for you. He will recover, he's a strong man, you will see.'

But Juan Martinez Senior managed to hang on just long enough for the doctor to present his bill, dying the very next day and his funeral was two days later. Through all the trauma it was Francisco who was the strong one and he did what he could to help and to comfort his mother as much as possible but after the funeral he began to worry. There were bills to pay and if he did not return to the hacienda quite soon there might not still be a job for him. Without the job he could not help support his mother and sisters and so, early the following morning he left home.

Hunching his shoulders against the morning chill, he walked along the street, deserted save for the old peg seller and her basket and for a second time he hardly noticed her, his mind preoccupied. How would they manage without his father's wages? His elder brother was there of course, and working, but for a pittance in the market; his money would hardly cover the rent.

'I am sorry to hear about your father,' said a voice as he reached the street corner.

'Mm… who?'

'It's all right, son, it's me, Jorge, a friend of your father's, you remember. We played pétanque, your father and me. I am sorry he died, he was a good man, a good carpenter.'

'Oh yes, I remember you.'

'I was at the funeral, at the back with the others.'

'Oh, good, thank you for that,' he said as memories came flooding back. He remembered the old man, the Sunday mornings playing pétanque with his father but he was in no mood to stop and talk. 'I must be off, back to work, I don't want to lose my job,' he said, wary that old men were partial to talking about nothing and if he stopped, he might never get away.

The old man said nothing, perhaps he understood, and Francisco took his cue, striding away towards the outskirts and the road to Tablada. At least the old man had snapped him out of his melancholy and, feeling a little more positive, he lengthened his stride. For Him, the drovers' road was a place to daydream, alone, without fear of interruption, a place where he might imagine himself in the bullring.

He could almost hear the calls of Olé as he walked, he could almost see the crowd waving their white handkerchiefs in appreciation of his performance and he began acting as if he was working a bull, turning, walking backwards holding the invisible cape in his outstretched arms. He heard the shrill call of an aficionado, no, a magpie circling above him, warning of a predator's approach and he searched the sky. Shielding his eyes, he caught sight of the falcon, its yellow underbelly glowing bright in the low morning sun as it commanded the sky.

He followed its flight, watching as it wheeled back and forth and he wished that he too could soar like a bird, to go wherever he pleased and look down on the world, but then birds did not fight bulls, did they.

Still daydreaming he followed the track away from the river and through the pasture, on the lookout for any bulls he could find. 'There,' he said to himself spotting several young bulls under a lone oak tree. The animals were chewing methodically without a care in the world and he was alone with them.

'I can, I will, this is for you, Papa,' he muttered as he vaulted the rough wooden fencing.

He had neither cape nor *espada*, just the shirt on his back, a nearby broken branch having to substitute for the sword. He set about stripping the branch of redundant foliage, slipped off his shirt, and pushed the rod through the armholes. He was ready, he had a muleta and an *espada*, and sweeping them from side to side, he stood erect, proud, and ready for the fight.

Since his arrival at the hacienda, he had learned a lot, learned from the more experienced vaqueros. The first rule of bullfighting they said was to have a means of escape. Normally a bullfighter would expect the picadors or his banderillos to help him if he was in trouble but today, Francisco was on his own. He looked around, made a mental note of where he might find sanctuary; a limited choice in the open pasture but after a flick of the muleta, he felt ready.

'Hey, you, come to me,' he said to the nearest bull, but it was more interested in chewing grass than in him.

'Hey, you, bull, come to me.'

Still, it did not move and Francisco stood with a hand

on his hip, the muleta outstretched, and he began to wonder why the bull was so uninterested. Perhaps he should get closer, prod it into action with the stick.

'Hey,' he said again, this time waving his shirt-cum-muleta in front of its face.

A reaction, at last, the animal's dark eyes stared straight at him and Francisco waved the muleta full in its face. At last, he had its attention. The eyes narrowed, and with a snort, the bull took a step forward.

'Come on, my friend, come on,' he said, sweeping the muleta from side to side.

It was enough. The bull raised its head and snorted again, louder and, as if someone had thrown a switch, it suddenly charged at the young bullfighter. Francisco remained calm, holding out his makeshift muleta in the path of the onrushing animal and, aware of its power, shifted his position to hold his body erect, the cloth of his shirt the only protection against the onrushing beast. He felt alive, his senses heightened by the proximity of the animal's horns and he avoided them by a whisker. Arching his back to let the bull past he felt the roughness of its hide scrape his naked torso and, as it passed him by, he pivoted on his heels, turned, and readied himself for the next charge.

It was exhilarating, he felt that he really was in the Plaza de Toros surrounded by the crowd cheering, calling out his name and Olé, Olé, cheering him on. Except that there was no audience save the two riders watching from the cover of overgrown heath.

The bull turned, snorted, and angry at finding itself duped, charged at Francisco. He stood his ground, his torso glistening with the sweat of his exertions and holding the makeshift cape in both hands he swept it across the path of the onrushing bull in an almost perfect *verónica*. Now he was at close quarters with the bull, which decided not to charge past him but to try to gore him with those wicked horns. The animal twisted and turned to catch him, but he was too quick, too skilful for it and in a cloud of rising dust the two of them performed the ballet of the bullfight.

'Who is he?' asked Jimena, leaning forward in her saddle.

'He's a worker on the estate. I'm sure I have seen him there.'

'He acts like a proper torero.'

'Yes, he is good, I'll give him that.'

'And he's good-looking.'

Isabella nodded, afraid of her thoughts, for there was something about that sweat covered semi-naked body that disturbed her.

'Come, Jimena, we do not want to be seen here, what would Uncle say if we are caught watching him?'

Jimena frowned, boys were nothing but trouble and she believed the one they were watching could do with a wash as she turned her horse and before Francisco had finished teasing the young bull, the two women were out of sight. Francisco had not the slightest inkling that anyone was watching, his concentration was solely on the bull and, satisfied with the encounter, he left the animal grazing before he pulled on his shirt, and regained the drover's road. He noticed a movement from the corner of his eye and looking up noticed two riders in the distance. He had no idea who they were and putting them to the back of his mind he walked towards the estate where he found the courtyard deserted except for several women washing clothes in the small stream.

'Where is Rodrigo?' he asked one of the women.

'He is with the boss, over in the big house.'

Francisco didn't relish looking for Rodrigo in the big house. Since his first encounter with the owner, he had not been inside but he had to let Rodrigo know he had returned to work. He wondered what to do but before he could make any decision the door of the house swung open. He thought it might be Rodrigo but instead, he saw an attractive young woman dressed in riding clothes, wide black campero riding trousers and a light blue paseo jacket over a white blouse and on her head, she still wore a wide brimmed cordobes hat. To a young man's eyes, she was stunning and, noticing him looking at her, she said, 'You, you are the one who fights my uncle's bulls. I saw you. Carlos will not be happy if he knows you torment his fighting bulls.'

Francisco was dumbstruck. How did she know?

'Y... you will say nothing, please, I beg of you. I cannot afford to lose my job. My mother...'

'What about your mother?'

'My mother relies upon my wage now my father has died.'

'I'm sorry but that is not my problem.'

'Please.'

'I'll think about it. If I say nothing, what will you do to repay me?' said the girl, a mischievous look in her eye.

'I cannot pay you. If you must report me there is nothing that I can do to stop you, but if you must act as if you are the Guardia then do it,' he said angrily with a toss of his head.

'I have never been spoken to like that before, I will tell my cousin what you have done,' she said, a hint of red rising in her cheeks as she lifted her riding crop as if to strike but he was too quick for her, reaching out to grasp her wrist.

'Get off me, oaf.'

'So, I am an oaf, am I? Is this how you see me, an oaf?'

She struggled to free herself from his grip.

'You are hurting me, let me go. You will pay for this I can promise you.'

'If I do have to pay, I will never forget, never, even when I am a famous torero, I will not forget this moment.'

'Ha, stupid boy, you will never be famous, never a famous torero.'

'Oh yes I will,' he said with conviction and after holding her gaze a moment longer he released her wrist. 'You are a wild filly, what is your name?'

'I am Isabella María Teresa García Ramírez de López. Who are you?'

'I do not have such an impressive name as you. I am simply Francisco Martinez, Paco to my friends.'

'Then I will call you Francisco,' she said. 'Now get out of my way.'

Isabella had mixed emotions as she pushed past him, no one had spoken to her as he had done, yet the image of him playing the bull, his bare chest, his elegance, would not leave her. His behaviour incensed and her anger had still not abated even when her sister caught up with her.

'Where do you want to ride this afternoon, Isabella?'

'I don't care so long as it is away from here.'

Jimena was younger but she had a wiser head on her shoulders and her eyes narrowed as she looked at her sister.

'Something has happened, Isabella, what is it?'

'Nothing, er... that boy we saw this morning. He has just insulted me.'

'Oh, how?'

'He thinks that he will one day become a famous torero and I told him he was just a stupid oaf.'

'And he accepted that I suppose?'

'I do not care whether he accepts it or not. He is just a common oaf. Come, let's attend to our horses.'

'Maybe we could ride along the riverbank, towards the city. We could take a picnic with us and find a place to rest, look out over the city. I like to see the towers and spires,' said the younger girl changing the subject.

'No, I don't think so. We will ride towards Triana. I want to see the gypsies; see how they live.'

'We can't do that, it's dangerous for us to go there, we will be robbed. Mother always tells us to keep away from the working people's barrios. They are full of thieves. We should ride along the river. It will be cooler.'

Isabella deferred to her sister, confused feelings overriding her natural bossiness and without speaking she followed Jimena to the stables. The heat of the day had almost passed, they could look forward to a comfortable ride and after ordering the stable boys to saddle their horses the staccato beat of hooves across the cobbles announced their departure. Once out on the roadway the two grey Andalusian horses needed little coaxing and the girls were only too happy to let them follow the well-worn trail. It was a chance for the girls sit back and enjoy the ride, catch up on the gossip and Jimena wanted to know what her sister was really thinking.

'Papa and Mama are back from Madrid in a few days, it will be good to hear of their trip. I imagine Mama will have presents for us. What would you like them to bring you, Isabella?'

Their father was a promoter of bullfighting, a manager of several well-known matadors and a well-respected pillar of Sevillian society, and more than that he doted on his daughters.

'A dress, a fashionable dress like those worn by the women of Madrid; one I can be seen in that no one else possesses. What about you, sister, what would you like?'

'I don't really mind so long as I see them. I suppose a dress or maybe earrings. I like bold earrings, made from gold like the gypsies wear.'

'Don't let Papa hear you say that. He will think you a trollop.'

Jimena frowned. Everyone wore big earrings at fiesta time, didn't they? Her friends competed to look the best, to show off, and she did not want leaving behind.

'We will go towards Triana, along the path leading past the Mauro estate; we haven't been that way, have we?'

Miguel saw them first, silhouetted, unidentified riders and turned to Francisco riding beside him.

'Hey, Paco,' he said squinting his eyes. 'Look over there, company, female company and they are coming our way.'

Francisco looked up from coaxing a group of heifers towards an open gate, followed Miguel's outstretched arm, and felt his heart miss a beat as he recognised the Cordovan hats and the blue jacket, he was sure it was the sisters. He tapped the lead heifer's rump with his stick to encourage it towards the gate and from the corner of his eye watched the riders' approach.

As the girls drew near and Jimena saw him, her attention drawn first to the frisky heifers and then to the handsome young vaquero.

'Oh, look at the calves, so pretty, aren't they?' she said.

'Where, oh yes I see them,' said Isabella. 'Isn't that my friend the oaf?'

'Oh, he's your friend now, is he?'

'No stupid, I meant to say isn't it that boy we saw fighting a bull?'

Jimena's eyes rolled. Isabella had called him her friend and then she noticed their way blocked.

'Those animals are preventing us passing,' she said.

'Then they will have to get out of our way.'

Francisco could see what was about to happen, either the riders would have to leave the track or his charges would and that gave him a problem, and seeing one was the girl he had crossed swords with only added to his trouble. He watched the horses' approach; something had to give and hoped that they would understand. Either they must wait or take a detour but, by the look his antagonists' eye, he expected trouble.

'You, move these cows, we want to get past.'

Francisco was not in the mood to fight her for she had the ear of the estate's owner and he could not afford to lose his job, but he had some gypsy genes and they burst into life.

'A little politeness would not go astray.'

'Don't lecture me; get out of our way if you know what's good for you.'

Miguel, working alongside Francisco stepped forward, alarmed at Francisco's stance.

'Yes, señora,' he said, physically pushing on the lead animal's rump. 'Give me a hand, Paco,' he said, frowning.

'I am not señora,' she said, I am Señorita de Lopez but unlike this one here, you show me respect,' she said, meeting Francisco's angry look.

'Move, come on, move,' Miguel said to the heifers, clipping the one nearest to him with his stick, and with a self-satisfied look, Isabella urged her horse forward purposely avoiding Francisco's eyes.

'She can get you the sack, Paco. She did it with Carlo Pissarro. He upset her one day, showed no respect, and just a few days later he was out of a job. You don't want that do you? I certainly do not, jobs are hard enough to come by as it is.'

Francisco knew that it was true. There was little he could really do about the situation; he needed to keep his job, his family relied upon him, and so he relented, vowing to get even one day with the stuck-up bitch.

Chapter 7

By the middle of nineteen twenty-five, I had seen three years' service with the Legión and I had changed. I had no choice; it was the way of the Legión, the relentless routine of marches and fighting had toughened me and made me resilient. If we were not marching the length and breadth of the Protectorate, we were fighting in the mountains or training hard. We never let up, that was our strength, and it was working. After the disaster of Annual, we were finally overcoming our enemy, instilling fear in the camps of the Riffians and restoring the honour of Spain.

Nevertheless, there were times, just a few, when we earned some respite and by June of that year, we were with two of the other banderas and the regulares at the main encampment at Ben Taieb. The weather was wet, too wet for campaigning, even for the Riffians so for a time we could rest and recuperate. We spent time training, discussing tactics, and generally preparing for the next phase which we expected to begin when the rains passed so with a few hours off duty I took the time to clean my rifle. I was sitting under the awning of a tent when Miguel appeared.

'Hey, Paco, the quartermaster has some letters from home. I hear they will be distributing the mail at ten this morning. We might be lucky.'

'Thank goodness the rain has stopped, my clothes are soaked,' said Miguel looking up into the clear blue sky. 'At least the sun is coming out and they might get dry.'

'I know, I'm the same,' I said. 'Let me put the gun back together and we can walk over to the fort, see if there is any mail for us. Are you expecting anything? Fernán and Huberto are just over there, maybe we should tell them.'

Fernán and Huberto were two Cubans, volunteers from the New World who had taken the chance to escape a life of poverty by joining the Legión. They were big men, Cuban mestizos with the swarthy dark looks of the island's natives; both tough and capable fighters. I lay my rifle to one side and together with Miguel went over to them.

'Letters from home have just arrived. We are going to see if there is anything for us. Do you want to come with us?' asked Miguel.

Huberto looked up, his expression subdued.

'I doubt there will be anything for me. That is why I am here, I've got no one. The Legión is my only family, just the same as Huberto here.'

I found that sad and my expectations of receiving a letter were low but to my surprise I did have a letter. It was from Juanita, who else. She had gone to the army office in Seville and with their help tracked down my regiment and took a chance that her letter would find me eventually. She asked how I was, scolded me for not getting in touch, and then proceeded to relate all the news from home. The greatest surprise was that she had married José, my friend. That brought back memories, our times together roaming Tablada on the lookout for bulls to fight and then of course as part of my cuadrilla.

Why had I thrown it all away? Why had I succumbed to that moment of madness? I had lost contact with my family, had not been home for almost three years. Suddenly I felt homesick and looking back, I believe that was the start of my problems.

Let me explain. During my time in the Legión, I had remained single-minded, disciplined, loyal to the Legión and I had cut myself off from my previous life but after reading my sister's letter my mind inescapably turned to thoughts of home and from that moment on those thoughts rarely left me, dogging my every move and on occasion, a lack of concentration left me making stupid mistakes.

Miguel had received his own letter and after reading it through several times he came to see me.

'Good news?' he asked.

'Yes,' I said, folding my sister's letter and placing it in my tunic pocket. 'They are all well and my sister has married one of my friends. How about you?'

'Not so good, my mother is ill. My aunt has written to tell me, said that my mother read in the paper how difficult things are out here and did not want to worry me but Aunt Lucia thought that I should know. She says maybe I could get some leave to go home and see my mother.'

'You could, why not? It would be a good reason to take some leave if ever there was one.'

'I haven't been back to the peninsula for two years. It would be something if I could,' he said.

Two years, two years, I had not been home in three years. I touched my tunic, felt for the folded letter, and wondered when, if ever, I would next make that journey.

For several hours I was reasonably content, thoughts of home filling my mind and then came the news that Riffian and Djebalan fighters were close to overrunning the Tetuán-Xauen road and our rest and recuperation ended abruptly. It wasn't long before the order came to leave the relative tranquillity of the military encampment for the mountain town of Xauen. It was early November; the weather was changing and the job of escorting the relief convoys to the besieged outposts would become more difficult.

To begin with the escort duty was no more than a mundane slog into the hills with hardly a sight of the enemy but before long their attacks began to increase. The weather began to deteriorate further and gradually it became clear that there was a need to evacuate the outposts and over the next couple of weeks we did just that and then, inevitably, the order came for the total evacuation of Xauen.

Assigned as the rear guard the Bandera found itself in a difficult position. Outnumbered by a watchful enemy we would have to leave the town under duress and that meant a breakout with the risk of ambush. The command took the decision for the main body of men and materials to leave late in the afternoon and we would follow soon afterwards to protect the rear. At six o'clock the same day we assembled on parade for an address by our commander. We were not exactly in the best of condition, dishevelled, our uniforms torn and dirty after weeks of fighting but our moral was high and after just a few minutes standing at ease Lieutenant Colonel Franco appeared. Such was our discipline and fitness we snapped to attention as if we were fresh troops and I remember thinking that he looked every bit the field commander. Unlike the rest of us he was smartly dress as if he had just arrived from headquarters, his shoulder holster strapped tight to his chest, the red bobble of his forage cap swinging freely.

'Soldiers of the Legión, he said, pausing for effect. 'You have upheld the honour of Spain, upheld the tradition of the Legión and I am to tell you that your service has not gone unnoticed. Bridegrooms of death, the king is proud of you, proud of your efforts, but we have not yet finished our work here. The garrison has left for Tetuán and our duty is to protect the column. I know you will fight to the last man should the situation demand it. Your officers have their orders so now I wish you well. Long live the Legión.'

'Long live the Legión,' we chorused, our voices strong, our arms raised in salute. We were ready for the fight and in good spirits we dispersed to prepare for the evacuation.

'You men find as much straw as you can and bring it back,' ordered the teniente. 'Search the stables, anywhere, just bring as much as you can find.'

'Funny, what're we supposed to do with straw, there are hardly any horses left in the town,' said a puzzled Manuel.

I had no idea either but the officer had not finished, ordering some of the platoon to go to visit the store to find as many surplus uniforms as they could. It seemed a rather silly order under the circumstances but when we returned with our load of straw all became clear. For several hours we stuffed the uniforms full of straw, stuffing it tight to make the dummies sit or stand on their own, those that insisted on flopping we supported with broom handles.

'Do you think it will work?' asked Miguel.

'I don't know, it might, it could give us time to get away,' I said, unconvinced.

'Yours looks like the corporal,' said Miguel.

I could not see the resemblance but his joviality helped to lower the tension and we needed something to lighten the mood because we were in a tight spot. Those tribesmen in the hills knew it too and they were waiting for us. They knew that we would eventually have to attempt to break out and when we did, they would try to kill us.

'I hardly think the corporal's face looks like that,' I said, stuffing a tunic with straw.

'Maybe not but he has the same body shape. See if he will sit up on his own.'

Of course, the straw-filled dummy didn't, and after a few unsuccessful attempts, we did manage to prop it up against a window frame. There must have been a hundred by the time we had finished stuffing all the uniforms and, looking at them from a distance, I could see we had created a semblance of reality. A strange-looking assembly, more tailors' dummies in my eyes, but I suppose to the untrained eye in the coming darkness they would possess a passing likeness to real legionaries.

It was a daring plan but if our luck held it might just work and at midnight when the order came to begin the evacuation, it began to rain. It was almost pitch black and by the time we emerged from the fortifications I was wet through. I remember my feelings at the time, apprehension yet I was unafraid for we were heading into the unknown and as we left the safety of the town, I was unable to resist taking a backwards glance feeling a strange delight at seeing the shadowy figures watching us go.

Men or simply scarecrows, it didn't matter so long as they fooled the Riffians and I could believe they would be because the stuffed uniforms did have a realistic look. With good fortune the enemy would believe they were real soldiers on sentry duty and that we were still within the fort's perimeter. The situation felt positive enough, we could escape and inadvertently I touched my tunic breast pocket, the one holding my sister's letter, and I suddenly felt homesick.

Ahead of us, the lead bandera had already disappeared into the blackness, the shadows swallowing them up, two thousand men and yet the fort appeared fully manned. In silence, we made our way down the mountain, a solitary time for us all, marching quietly in the rain. I knew the game would be up once the sun rose, when the Riffians would realise then that we had left and they would come after us.

We descended from the mountain and in the distance caught sight of enemy horsemen as we entered a narrow valley. For once we had command of the topography, a natural ambush location and our officers were intent on taking full advantage.

'C company follow me,' ordered the teniente, drawing his pistol.

Rapidly we slipped into a well-rehearsed drill, one platoon spreading to the left and another to the right while the remainder ran up the incline in search of concealed positions. The valley floor was a natural route and sure enough the Riffian horsemen followed it. Seemingly unaware of our presence and presuming no doubt that we were further ahead and were intent upon catching us. But our cover was little more than withered mountain vegetation and it was not long before a cry of discovery went up and they turned their horses to charge up the incline. But we were ready for them and all at once rapid rifle fire disturbed the stillness of the morning air.

'Got him,' said Miguel in triumph.

Their charge was reckless making them easy targets. I fired my rifle and a rider fell and then another but there were so many of them that they were quickly upon us and the fighting became hand to hand. Not far from me Huberto the big Cuban lunged at a passing rider. The man was too close for a shot and so the Huberto reached out to grip the flowing robes, dragging the man from his horse and together the two combatants fell from view. I had little time to dwell upon Huberto's fate, I had my own survival to consider as yet another rider headed straight at me screaming profanities. I took a hurried yet careful aim, shooting him in the chest just as natives on foot caught up with their mounted comrades and the situation rapidly became desperate.

'Fix bayonets,' shouted the sergeant as he shot a native at close range.

It was the only way; the native tribesmen were too numerous and too close to ward off with gunshots; we had to fight with fixed bayonets. It seemed to turn the tide, we had a reach advantage over their cruelly shaped daggers and killing so many of them disheartened the others. Adding to the mayhem were the riderless horses but our discipline held and eventually we broke them, their retreat accompanied by a hail of lead.

Then I remembered Huberto and turned back to look for him. Dead and dying littered the ground and I was beginning to believe the Cuban was amongst them until a movement caught my eye and he crawled from the hollow into which he had fallen.

'Huberto, are you alright?' I called to him.

I needn't have worried the grin on his face and the severed ear held in his hand told me all I needed to know. It was not pleasant but the act of mutilation seemed to give the South Americans some satisfaction.

'You like your little trophies don't you, Huberto?'

'*Sí*, is my reward. Is no different from the bullfight.'

I couldn't argue with that and was about to say something when the teniente shouted for us to follow him.' He was intent upon reaching the next vantage point before the Riffians had time to regroup and so, as fast as we could, we made our way towards the crest of the next hill, not a particularly elevated position and with only sparse cover but it would have to do. Reaching the crest ahead of us, the teniente paused to survey the ground ahead, but because he was in an exposed position the sun silhouetted him and he was an easy target.

For once the native's shooting was accurate, within seconds of lifting his hat to shield his eyes from the sun a bullet struck him. He fell like a rag his body motionless on the ground and immediately two legionaries leapt forward to drag him back to relative safety. It was a shock but we reacted quickly and began shooting at a large group of Riffians who appeared and were running over the wet ground towards us. Then from our rear, a machine gun began firing and the native ranks quickly thinned, they had miscalculated believing they would cut us off, close their trap. We had gained the initiative but even so, that was not the end of it; their attack had a tenacity that was hard to contain and driven back for a time they regrouped to return in force and for the rest of the day we fought them, gaining some respite only when darkness fell.

We had been on the go for over twenty hours and after catching just an hour's sleep we were back on the road to Tetuán and not long after sunrise we found the column. The rain had softened the ground to such an extent that the long line of vehicles, men and horses had turned the road into a quagmire.

'I hear the teniente is going to survive,' said Miguel, joining me as I trudged up a muddy incline.

'I'm glad about that, he's a decent man. Unlike some I could name.'

Miguel laughed.

'Yes, remember that Madrileño who commanded us last year, do you remember him?

'Do I!' I replied.

Even now I can see his face, a face I want to forget. Teniente Ramón Burgos, a brave and resourceful soldier whose sole aim in life seemed to be a desire to make our lives a misery, and to my shame, I was not sad at his passing. I was tired, exhausted and should not have wished death on a fellow soldier but my mind was becoming tangled in a myriad of diverse thoughts. I touched my pocket, the letter from home, I could see my mother as if she was standing in front of me and what of my siblings?

'How far do you think it is to Tetuán from here?' asked Huberto.

'I have no idea,' I said, looking out across the desolate landscape. I did not believe distance was the problem; the rain and the mud and the thousands of tribesmen intent on destroying us were the problem.

I was in no mood for conversation, I could see the enemy, appearing and then disappearing on either side of the road as they looked for advantage. Abd-el-Krim's Riffians were not going to let us off lightly. Ahead, the column was moving again, the mules straining, braying in protest as they dragged the wagons through mud that came halfway up a man's shin. God knows how they managed but they did, and the drovers deserved credit for keeping them moving.

Then gunfire broke out, the crack of rifles, bullets whizzing overhead and again the Riffians attacked. A mule collapsed in front of me, its painful bellow echoing across the muddy landscape.

'Cover the flank you men,' shouted the sergeant ducking low to move towards the enemy's perceived position. The platoon fanned out, Vicente, a recent recruit, and I together at the extreme right of the advance. From bitter experience, we had learned of the Riffians' likely moves and we were aware they could be lying in wait for us, ready to spring up at the last moment. It was dangerous work and I needed all my wits about me.

True to form a white-cloaked figure appeared from his hiding place, followed by several more as we began to cross the uneven terrain and suddenly, I found myself a target. Bullets missed me by centimetres but Vicente was not so lucky, clutching his chest as the bullet struck him. He had been with us for no more than a month, such a waste, but there was little I could do to help him. I had seen enough men die in the past three years; it was the way of things of course but that did not make it any easier.

We now had an overwhelming force of Riffians to contend with and death was as distinct a possibility for me as it was for the rest of the platoon but at least the weather was clearing, giving us a better view. But we were still in a desperate situation, snipers hidden amongst the rocks began harassing the column, they had taken control of some high ground with a good view of the column and they were causing a problem. Two companies received the order to attack them, a risky strategy that depended primarily upon speed and agility which we possessed in abundance and without further ado we set off up the incline.

'There are two of them there, look,' said Miguel, pointing to a ridge.

'Come on, Paco, next time they drop behind that ridge we'll run for those bushes,' said Huberto, eager to take the snipers on. 'Miguel, give us some cover in case the bastards show their heads.'

Miguel gave a brief salute and lifted his rifle while Huberto and myself fixed bayonets and, on his signal, we leapt from our position, running as fast as we could to land in a shower of stones and mud amongst the next clump of vegetation. The plan was to let our native friends take another shot and when they slipped back into their hiding place, we would hit them hard. We did not have long to wait. First one then a second head appeared, then their rifles and after two quick shots they were gone again.

'Come on,' hissed Huberto, now's our chance.' And

before I knew it the pair of us were charging up the last of the gradient, bayonets at the ready.

We caught the snipers unawares and the first man I came across, I ran my bayonet full into his chest. Beside me, Huberto made short work of the second sniper, but then all hell broke loose. Hidden from our view as we charged the ridge were more tribesmen and now it appeared, we had run straight into them. We were in mortal danger.

'Legionnaires to me,' I called out. We had taken them by surprise but that advantage was now gone and we needed help, they outnumbered us by a large margin and just the two of us stood little chance of survival but our luck held, they seemed uninterested in shooting us, which would be the easiest way to kill us but they were more intent on killing us with their knives. That gave us a slim chance. I stabbed one in the chest, and then I caught another full in the stomach I had no time to collect my thoughts as more tribesmen appeared.

A fierce looking Riffian confronted me, his dagger held towards my face and with an almost animal growl he lunged at me. I don't know why, perhaps it was the dagger, its similarity to the horns of a fighting bull but strangely I felt as if I was in the bullring and intuitively I stepped back, drawing him on to me. It was as I would a bull and turning at the last moment, I caught him with the bayonet.

I don't recall exactly what happened but once I had killed him, I dropped my guard for a second and in that moment, I felt as if someone had hit me with a hammer. Involuntarily I fell sideways, my rifle slipping from my grasp and I felt a searing pain shoot through my shoulder.

I reached out for support but could find no more than thin air and then I felt a strong arm around my waist.

'I've got you, force yourself, Paco. Come on, back down the hill,' said a voice.

I tried to speak but I could not manage more than a few jumbled words. My mouth was dry, I felt dizzy, and my legs were not working as they should but the fear of finding myself at the mercy of the Riffians was a powerful motivator for me to make them work and if it was not for Huberto, I do not think I would have survived.

Chapter 8

The warmth of the sun took hold of the timeless waters of the Guadalquivir, melting the lace curtain of early morning mist, and revealing the full beauty of the waterway. Acacia trees silhouetted against a rising tide of orange light stood as a stark backdrop, wild birds foraging amongst the reeds and in the pasture nearby black shapes stood knee deep in the disappearing haze. Not far away two vaqueros sat on their motionless horses, their task to watch over the small herd until the Mendozas and several important customers arrived.

'Have you ever been to the Plaza de Toros, Paco?'

'Not inside. I crossed the river and walked past it many times when I lived at home. It was wonderful to see on the day of the corrida but the Guardia Civil always chased us away. Have you been there?'

'Only with the bulls.'

'Did you get to see inside? The bullring?'

'We are allowed in the yard, and the pens of course when we deliver the bulls. If we can find somewhere out of the way then we can watch.'

'And did you see any bullfights?'

'No, I always returned to the ranch before the start of the corrida.

'I want to see inside the bullring, I want to see a fight

for myself.'

Luque looked at him and frowned.

'Vaqueros are not normally allowed into the ring, only the stables and the pens when we deliver the bulls. They do not want us disturbing the sand. You might manage a look through the door. Look out, here comes the boss and his friends.'

Francisco looked across the pasture as the stout wooden gate opened and riders dressed in expensive-looking clothes approached. At their head was José de Mendoza.

'We had better get ready,' said Luque.'

Francisco gripped the shaft of the *garrocha* and followed Luque at a steady trot towards the grazing bulls, ready to release them one by one to test their fighting spirit.

'Let us see what we have this year,' said José de Mendoza to his son.

'Some of these are top class, I think you will be pleased,' said Carlos.

'I hope so. Don Artiles, Don Antonio, my son tells me that you will not be disappointed with our bulls.'

'It is to be hoped he is right, José. There is always a market for a good fighting bull and you have proved over the years that your bulls are the finest in Tablada,' said Don Artiles. 'We look forward to an interesting day.'

Together with Don Antonio, he was a cattle dealer of some importance, a man whose business was to source the bulls for corridas across the whole of Andalusia and was an important contact for José de Mendoza.

'They are ready, Father,' said Carlos keeping an eye on the vaqueros busy rounding up the bulls, a twinge of regret that he was not joining them.

The trialling of young bulls was a chance for the young bloods to demonstrate their skill, their bravery, and in the past, he had prided himself on his skill. But with age came responsibility; his father was slowly but surely handing him the reins and he could not risk injury. As the eldest son, he was to stay at his father's side, entertain the important guests, and learn something of the art of cattle dealing.

'That one,' said Luque, pointing to a bull with his lance. 'Cut it out, Paco.'

Francisco nudged his horse forward, riding up to the animal to prod it with the point of his lance. He caught it in its ribs, then another prod at its rump and the bull broke free of the herd. Trotting across the pasture, the animal just wanted to be free of Francisco's lance, but ahead of it two other vaqueros were waiting and as the bull approached, they closed in, one to each side of it.

Francisco watched the lead horse come within just a metre of the bull and then, judging time and distance, a vaquero thrust his blunt ended lance hard against the animal's flank to unbalance it, a second thrust and the black mass fell, rolling onto its back with its legs flailing thin air.

This was the moment for the second rider to intervene. His lance had a more pointed tip and as the bull rose to its feet, he made himself a target. Instinctively the bull charged, only to feel the point of his *garrocha*. The sudden sharp, unexpected pain triggered an uncontrollable anger in the animal and, lowering its head it charged.

'Bravo,' declared José. 'That one has spirit. What do

you say, Don Antonio?'

'If your other bulls are as brave you will have a successful season, my friend, and I am sure that we can do business.'

All morning the vaqueros worked the bulls with Carlos and his father watching over the proceedings. Many of the young bulls showed the promise of true fighting bulls. At almost five hundred kilograms each they would surely carry the honour of the ganadería into the bullrings of Andalusia and by late morning, there were just two bulls left to scrutinise.

'I think it's our turn, Paco. What do you say?'

'Oh yes,' said a delighted Francisco.

He had learned the technique with yearlings and two-year-olds and he wanted very much to take on the older bulls, the bigger and more aggressive animals that not only would he have a chance to test, but it was also a chance to find out how well he would cope with the bigger animals.

Luque put his fingers to his lips and blew, his shrill whistle reaching the ears of the two outlying vaqueros. One raised his hand in acknowledgement and the two riders returned to the herd.

'You can goad the first one into the charge. You know what I want Paco. Come, let's go,' Luque said, spurring on his horse.

Francisco needed little encouragement and trotting alongside Luque the two vaqueros rode across the flower covered pasture towards one of the untried bulls separated from the herd. Gaining temporary freedom, the bull began to run, its blackness contrasting with the green pasture grass and Luque signalled Francisco into action. Galloping at full speed they chased the bull. Luque lowered his lance in readiness, leaning forward in his saddle for better balance while Francisco held his vertically as the two raced alongside the bull. Picking his moment, Luque thrust the lance at the racing bull's hindquarters, unbalancing it and after a second thrust the animal lost its footing.

As the bull writhed and kicked on the ground Francisco pulled up his horse, ready, and as it rose to its feet, he stabbed at its shoulder. The pain of the wound was enough to shock the bull into a state of fury and with angry eyes, it turned on him. Holding his nerve, he waited and as the bull charged, he steered his horse from its path. The bull raced past, turned quickly, and charged again, its aggression obvious, the attribute Señor de Mendoza was looking for. A bull with the right spirit would fight to the death and any bull of that calibre was valuable.

Francisco turned his horse to meet the bull again and again for the next few minutes until Carlos signalled that they had seen enough.

'Bravo,' José called out. 'We have another true fighting bull. That's at least a dozen that will perform well in the corridas, Carlos.'

'Yes, Father, he's the best one we have seen today. The lad Francisco has style, would you say?'

'Yes, I had noticed, perhaps he should try his hand in the next *tienta.* '

The news that he could fight in the next tienta came as a welcome surprise to Francisco as he was beginning to believe that Carlos's promise was beginning to ring hollow. True, he had learned to ride and he had acquired the skills needed to manage the estate's cattle but he had not taken part in a *tienta* and Carlos seemed to have forgotten his promise but today all that changed.

'The *tienta*,' said Francisco, 'they are letting me fight in the tienta.'

'Join the club,' said Luque. 'It's your first time?'

'Yes.'

'It could be your big chance. If someone of influence notices you then you might fight in one of the lesser corridas, that's how every matador starts. You want to be a matador?

'Oh yes, it's my dream.'

'There is a lot of competition, you will be lucky if you get past just our little affair here on the estate.'

'I know.'

'Look, over there.'

Francisco turned to see Isabella and her sister passing on horseback and could not help prolonging his gaze.

'Come on, Paco, Carlos doesn't like us staring at them. You don't want to lose your job, do you?'

That was certainly a possibility, yet Francisco found it difficult to take his eyes off the women, particularly the elder girl.

Will the be at the tienta?'

'Probably, but I shouldn't count on it.'

Testing the fighting spirit of four-year-old bulls in the *tienta* was an important event in the life of the estate. They were always noisy affairs; everyone would be there and it occurred to Francisco that it would present an opportunity for him to show the stuck-up girl how good a bullfighter he was.

On the day of the *tienta,* Francisco was leaning on the corral fence looking at the bulls when Carlos came up to him. 'So, you fancy your chances today do you, young Paco?'

'I hope I do well. I have never been in the ring with a bull before but I am sure I can handle it.'

'I am sure you will. You handle the cattle with skill and I know you want to get in a real bullring. Well, today is your chance. Good luck.'

'Thank you, I will try my best.'

Carlos nodded, a confirmation to himself almost that he was a good judge of character and as he walked away Luque appeared.

'Hey, Luque, I hear you're to test the first bull.'

'Yes, a privilege I think.'

'Well, I will be watching.'

'And I you Paco, be sure I will be watching you when it's your turn,' he said leaning against the fence and as the two of them cast their eyes over the bulls selected for the day's trial a female voice interrupted their thoughts.

'So, it's the boy with no name.' Francisco turned, surprised to see the sister who had tormented him. 'What are you doing here. Aren't you supposed to be out in the pasture looking after the cattle?'

'Not today.'

'Oh, and why not today?' she said knowing full well that almost everyone on the estate would be at the *tienta*.

'I am fighting one of the bulls.'

'You are a brave torero are you. Well, we shall see I suppose,' she said leaving Francisco nonplussed.

'A fine filly, don't you think?' said Luque grinning. 'I wouldn't mind breaking her in.'

Before Francisco could respond, several estate workers passing by were unable to resist a few taunts

'Hey, Paco, we will be watching you,' said one.

'Are you the new Belmonte, Paco, and you, Luque, the new Josélito maybe,' said another.

Luque waved them away but Francisco just looked thoughtful. To hear his name mentioned in the same sentence as Belmonte was an honour. Was it possible he could emulate his hero in front of a real crowd instead of an illicit performance for his friends in the dead of night?

'I had better get ready. Good luck with your bull Paco.'

'Thanks, and the same to you.' Said Francisco as Luque jumped from the fence.

Not far away, Carlos and his father were engaged in conversation with people Francisco recognised, cattle dealers and agents who had visited the ranch on occasion and others whom he did not recognise. Then a roar from the gathered spectators stole his attention. The first bull, a fully grown four-year-old appeared through the red door and facing it at the far side of the arena was Luque. He lifted his muleta to the level of his chest before waving the red and yellow cloth from side to side and almost immediately elicited a response from the bull which did not hesitate to charge.

Luque swept his muleta forcefully into the bull's path, and swivelling his body at the last possible moment, stepped back to avoid the horns and the bull passed by harmlessly. To Francisco, it appeared pure magic and as Luque pirouetted to meet the charge a second time, and several more times until Carlos called a halt. It was enough for him to make his judgement, experience told him the animal would make the grade as a fighting bull and not wanting to spoil it he signalled an end. He could not let the fight go on; if the bull were to learn the way of the matador its aggression would dilute and reduce its value. Today was for testing the bulls, the real fighting reserved for the paying public in the numerous bullrings of Andalusia.

Carlos lowered his hand and Luque's fight was at an end and turned towards a young man sitting beside him.

'You would like to try your hand today, César?' he said.

César López Aguilar, the son of one of Seville's most prominent families was a promising young matador with a glittering future because his father was rich, a shareholder in the Plaza de Toros and was keen to promote his son as the next Juan Belmonte. Already he had had arranged for César to fight in several lesser corridas and showing an early promise he was to fight in the famous Seville bullring. Today, however, he was simply an honoured guest invited to inspect the new season's fighting bulls.

'Yes, Carlos, I would like to fight one of your bulls,' said César.

'Good, I will arrange it. My father will be pleased to see you in the ring. Your reputation precedes you; it will be an endorsement for us.'

César smiled, his eyes flitting in the direction of the two sisters sitting not far away.

'Come, César, we should have a look at the rest of the bulls, you can choose which one to fight,' said Carlos rising to his feet. 'Are you ready?'

'I am ready,' said César, glancing again at Isabella as

he too rose to his feet.

She looked his way, raising her fan to conceal all but her eyes to tease César. She was a beautiful young woman and from that moment on he was determined that she would be his.

The news that César, an up-and-coming matador, was to fight in the hacienda's humble *tienta* created a stir. Although not yet a fully-fledged matador, one who had not yet fought in a first-rate bullring, César would not normally risk either his reputation or injury in a purely local *tienta*. Without promise of reward he would not normally fight but today his reward might just be Isabella and with that thought in mind he looked over the corral fence at the bulls.

'Which one do you fancy?' said Carlos.

César placed his arms on the top of the enclosure, weighing them up and choosing the one he assumed the least aggressive.

'That one, Carlos, I'll try that one,' he said pointing.

'Good, that's settled. Prepare this one for César, will you,' Carlos said to the stockman. 'You happy with that, César?'

'Yes, I will need a muleta and a sword.'

'I will bring them.'

Sitting alongside her uncle and her sister Isabella watched the proceedings but of the two amateur matadors who fought next, she showed little interest. César was the one she was eager to see. Not far away, leaning on the fence with some of the estate workers Francisco noticed Isabella and José de Mendoza. She was attractive, of that there could be no argument, her clothes smart, tailored, a flowing black skirt and white shirt, a light grey Cordovan hat on hair tied with a black ribbon created a sight no red-blooded male could resist.

Watching her for longer than a casual glance allowed she sensed Francisco's stare and turned her head towards him. With some embarrassment Francisco felt compelled to look away, the desire he had to engage with her was not going well. Calls of 'Olé' took his attention and he looked towards the gate for a sight of the bull. It was César's fight and leaning against the wall of the protective *burladero* in readiness he raised an arm. The gate swung open to reveal his chosen bull and Francisco could not help a smile for he knew that the one with the white stripe across its shoulder was not the fiercest of bulls. Working with the bulls' day in and day out had taught him something of their nature and César's bull, although big and powerful looking, its horns menacing, the consensus amongst the vaqueros was that it would not prove to be the best of fighting bulls.

César waited, confident, his body erect, the capote hanging loose at his side and for a few moments the bull seemed unsettled. In unfamiliar surroundings it took just a few tentative steps before coming to a halt. Still unaware of César it sniffed while he remained perfectly still until he felt the time right. Lifting the cape and sweeping to his left, the bull finally sensed him. A second sweep to the right and the bull raised its head, but instead of charging, it simply trotted towards him. A docile bull was no sport and César knew he must do something to provoke it.

With the cape held outstretched between both hands, he ran straight at the animal, startling it into action and once he had its full attention, he was able to perform a series of *verónicas*. Skilfully he turned the bull back and forth, yet still it showed little sign of real aggression. He had expected it to be easy but not this easy. He was beginning to look foolish and needed to do something quickly and so, as the bull turned again, he swept the cape over its head, blinding it, and gave it a sharp kick with his foot. The bull reacted, shaking itself free of the cape and this time César used the short stick to stab at its neck and finally it crossed the line. Lowering its head, it let out a great snort of indignation and charged.

The reaction pleased the crowd who roared approval at his ability to turn what appeared a timid and useless bull into an angry mass of muscle and bone. The fight was becoming a real one and from the side of the bullring Carlos watched with interest. He knew the bull was timid but was thankful that at last it was showing signs of hostility. He knew little of César, had not seen him fight until today but admired the way in which the young torero had handled the bull but he had seen enough. With proper handling the bull would do for a corrida and he signalled an end to the encounter.

From her vantage point Isabella watched the performance with interest and as César turned to leave the arena, his arm raised in salute, his eyes searched for her and she let the fan slip from her face.

'Isn't he good, Isabella?' said Carlos, re-joining her and his father.

'Yes, he looks to have a future as a matador. Perhaps we will get to see him one day in the Real Maestranza.'

'You will soon, he is fighting in the corrida during the April fiesta. We are providing some of the bulls. I'm sure you will get to see him fight.'

Some distance away, at the side of the arena, Francisco was watching the herdsmen struggling to persuade the bull to re-enter the pens when Luque appeared, smiling, ready to offer his verdict on the fight.

'He is destined for greatness that one, Paco. Did you see how he turned the bull?'

'Good for him. Yes, he handled the bull well. I didn't believe it would put up much of a fight but he did get it to perform.'

'Some of his moves were interesting. His final passes were good I thought. I expect we will be providing a bull or two for him to fight in future. His father has influence and is a good friend of the Mendozas. No doubt that will help his career.'

Francisco remained quiet, his concentration apparently on the bulls, but he was thinking. Had César chosen a weaker bull on purpose, one he could control and so appear to be a better torero than he really was?

'How are you feeling, Paco, it is your turn soon. That one looks a bad boy, there look,' said Luque interrupting his thoughts, pointing to a bull taking its frustration out on the fencing.

'I don't mind, I'll take it as it comes, Luque, you did.'

'Yes, I didn't get to choose. Come on, we'll watch Sergio fight his bull and then you can get ready. It will be interesting to see how you get on. I heard about your night-time escapade. Carlos was impressed I hear.'

'I gather so. He said he would give me a chance at a *tienta* and now he has.'

'Well, let's see what you can do then.'

Francisco grinned. Feeling apprehensive yet more than

happy have a chance to show what he could do it was something he had dreamed of for a long time. He would fight as well as he could, to show not only Carlos but also that girl.

'Paco,' two of the herdsmen called out in unison, waving to let him know that he should get ready to enter the ring.

Unlike César, clothed in a traditional campero jacket, tight black trousers and fine embossed boots, Francisco stood in just his working clothes; shirt sleeves and trousers tucked into his riding boots. Not the most endearing sight a bullfighter should make but it was all he could manage.

'Don't damage the bull, he is one of the best,' said Luque. 'He will make a good fighting bull and will be worth a lot of money. The boss will not be happy if you injure him. Take care of yourself *and* the bull, Paco.'

Francisco began to feel pressure, a weight resting unexpectedly on his shoulders and, crossing himself, he mumbled a prayer to the Virgin of Macarena to ask for her protection and then he walked purposefully towards the door. He was apprehensive, not knowing quite what to expect from the crowd because apart from César, they had greeted the toreros with a mixture of light applause and good-humoured banter but he was unknown.

With his colourful cape hanging loose at his side he avoided eye contact with anyone, instead he focused his mind and alone he faced the gateway to the bull pens. Unusually he did not sweep his cape for effect as others had done, instead, he simply turned his body to present just his profile to the bull, the bad boy Luque had called it. The bull's silky black coat shone in the afternoon sun a magnificent animal with menacing horns that trotted purposefully across the sand-covered floor. It did not immediately see Francisco as it made a circuit of the wooden wall until it suddenly stopped and held its head high. It had caught a faint aroma and it realised that it was not alone.

Francisco watched, standing perfectly still he waited; He knew the animal was aware of him, and turning its head it tasted the air picking up his scent and it looked straight at him. He took a step forward and spread the cape, enticing the animal to him. The bull reacted, tilting its head, letting out a primeval grunt and from the spectators there was a sharp intake of breath. All was still on the sunny Andalusian day, peaceful, until suddenly, powerful leg muscles propelled the bull in Francisco's direction.

The boy, for he was still just eighteen, turned to face it and shaking the cape he swept it over his hip, focusing the bull's attention. The sound of its thundering hooves, the ground vibrate beneath him, focused Francisco's mind and standing fully in the path of the charging bull he outstretched the cape and as the bull closed, he performed an expert *verónica*. The bull swept through the cloth of the capote, he turned on the balls of his feet, balanced, in readiness for the next charge and the crowd loved it, shouts of 'Olé' reverberating around the enclosure yet Francisco, lost in his own world, heard none of it.

It was pure theatre, the magnificent fighting bull, and the scruffy urchin, who only a short time ago had prowled the night time pastures in search of just such a confrontation. This was Francisco's chance to show he was a man, to play the bull with skill and self-confidence in front of a real crowd. With a flourish, he whirled the cape and, at the last moment deliberately stepped into the path of the onrushing bull. His eyes focused, his nostrils flared with anticipation and, leaving it to the last possible second turned away from the outstretched cape and felt an undeniable pleasure as the bull brushed against his undefended back.

'That was magnificent. The boy is everything you said, Carlos.'

'Better, I think father. He showed a rare talent the night I found him in the pasture but that move was top class I must admit. What do you think, Isabella, do you think he is any good?' he said leaning forward to catch her reply.

She hesitated, there was something earthy about him, his skill by the river had left her in no doubt that he was talented. Having seen him shirtless, his chest wet with perspiration had left a lasting impression and she could not get him out of her mind but then there was César, refined, well connected and rich.

'Is he any good? She said repeating the question. 'I know little of the finer points of bullfighting I'm afraid,' she lied.

'Yes, the boy has talent,' said her uncle raising his hand to signal the stockman to halt the fight.

He knew he had a first-class bull and it would do well in the corrida though it would do no good for it to become used to a man on foot. Francisco caught sight of the signal, but before anyone could stop him he decided to perform one last move. The bull was already charging and tantalizingly he waved the cape, enticing the rapier-like horns towards him. The bull took the bait and charging at speed, missed him by a fraction, passing so close he could feel its breath and falling against the animal with his back arched and his hands held high above his head he allowed it to scrape along his body just as he remained rooted to the spot. He held his position, draped the cape across his buttocks and waited. With his back to the bull, he was exposed, a sharp intake of breath from the crowd his only warning that the bull had turned and was charging again. He listened to the thundering hooves, judged his move with precision and as the cape fluttered across his exposed back the bull lowered its head ready to connect but in that instant Francisco deftly stepped aside to leave the bull racing harmlessly past.

Captivated by the move the audience exploded with delight and yet Francisco hardly noticed, his concentration fully on the bull which had skidded to a halt and was ready to charge again. However, Carlos had seen enough and by now was waving frantically at the stockman to take control and return the bull to the pens. His father had allowed the fight to go on longer than it should have, but the older man was witnessing a raw talent and he was sure his bull's fighting spirit was still intact and beside him Isabella raised her fan.

Weeks later Francisco was sitting astride his horse admiring the colourful spring flowers, the low grey shapes of the Sierra Morena Mountains in the distance and the fighting bulls spread grazing for the last. He turned in his saddle towards the drover's road and then back towards the bulls.

'They seem happy enough,' said Luque, pulling up his horse and then to the two riders with him, 'Manuel, you and Fernando get round the far side of the herd and drive them this way.'

The two vaqueros turned their horses and trotted towards the bulls, standing, sitting, content as they chewed on the lush grass and amongst them, brown bodied, long horned steers whose calming influence was necessary to render the bulls manageable for the journey about to begin.

'You did well at the *tienta,* Paco,' said Luque. 'I understand this is your reward, to help take the bulls to Seville.'

'Carlos said I could accompany you, yes, I suppose you could say it was a reward of sorts. By the way, what did you, think of César? I didn't get the chance to ask you before, what did you make of his style?'

'I had forgotten about him. Oh yes, he put on a decent show.'

'So, what did you think of him?'

'Why do you ask?'

'Oh…I am just interested. He is fighting at the *feria*; I wonder if we might get to see him.'

'I believe he is. He must have good connections; it's not that easy to get a fight at this time. He seemed capable enough and some of his moves were good.'

'What about his bull, I didn't think it was particularly aggressive.'

'Now that you mention it, I was of the same opinion on the day but, heck, that was what it was all about, sort out the fighters from the also-rans.'

'Will we get the chance to watch a fight?'

'Maybe, the boss doesn't usually let us, but maybe we will. Take the side will you, I don't want any of them straying for too long,' said Luque as the bulls began to move.

Francisco touched his hat in acknowledgement and nudged his horse out to the flank to keep the animals in line. It was slow work; the bulls had grown heavy and were content to plod along at a steady pace, a false representation of their true condition because they were literally fighting fit and their real capabilities revealed only in the bullring

All morning the bulls, their new friends the steers and the four vaqueros travelled the drovers' road until by mid-morning Luque called a halt. The sun was high in the sky, the heat of the day was building, and they were amongst the last of the lush grasses. Soon the landscape would give way to less productive ground with little decent grass for the beasts to eat and there could be no stopping if they intended to reach the city before nightfall.

On the way they would pass Triana, Francisco's home and he wondered what his family were doing at that moment. He guessed it would not be long before the girls finished school for the day and he smiled to himself as he thought of his youngest sister, Maria. She was exceptionally bright and would no doubt spend the cool of the evening studying. She always had her nose in a book and he began to wish he had paid more attention during the few hours of schooling he had endured, but school wasn't for the boys of Triana; no, their interests lay elsewhere, bulls and bullfighting.

He was still wondering about her as he felt inside his

shirt for his lunch, the piece of bread and some cured ham, not much but enough to sustain him. Taking a bite he sat back in his saddle he cast his eyes over the herd, content enough, all of them chewing happily on the grass. For an hour they rested, Luque letting the drovers relax while the cattle rested, their methodical chewing almost hypnotic and when he was ready; he ordered the drive to resume.

Francisco rode his horse close to the first of the steers, coaxing it forward, encouraging the bulls to follow. It would be their last journey; the bulls were destined to die in the temple of bullfighting that was the Real Maestranza. He felt excited, although he had never walked that hallowed ground, only stood outside as a youth listening to the roars of the crowd, he could imagine his charges fighting the matadors dressed in their suits of lights. He imagined the noise from the *alto tendidos*, the cheapest seats high above the arena, and he could see the picadors on their horses, the banderillos and soon he would see it all for himself.

A movement distracted him, a shadow racing across the ground and he looked up to see a dark shape high in the sky. Hovering to begin with the bird of prey spread its wings as it began to wheel, suddenly pulling those wings tight to its body before hurtling towards the ground. So quick, so precise was its dive that Francisco could not help feeling some sympathy for the rodent in its sights.

The bird disappeared from his view and he turned back to watch over the bulls and to re-live his performance at the *tienta*, see himself in the Real Maestranza rather than the small bullring of the ganadería. He had relived the fight many times, cherishing the compliments of the ranch hands because they knew about bulls and bullfighting and praise from them was praise indeed. Would he, he wondered, ever get the chance to fight at the April fair. He knew that César was to fight there and felt more than a little jealous of him and for a while he daydreamed until whitewashed buildings began appearing.

'Look, Triana, what's it like to come home, Paco?' said Luque.

'We're only passing through; no one knows I'm here. I don't suppose I can call in to see my mother, can I?'

'Ha, no I don't think so but we might meet someone you know; you can tell them any news you want to pass on to your family.'

'That's a possibility; the youngsters will be out in force once they know we are here. I used to do it, chase after the bulls, believing that one day I would become a torero.'

'You are a torero from what I can see.'

Francisco grinned and looked up at the sky again, the hawk was gone, the sky empty. He looked towards the river, a barge, low in the water, weighed down by a cargo of boxes and hessian-wrapped bales was in full view and on the far bank the city of Seville, its old Moorish fortifications standing out in the strong sunlight. Beyond them and the riverside buildings lay the tall mediaeval spires, like a hand with fingers outstretched as they reached for God's abode.

'We should be crossing the bridge soon,' said Luque.'

'We should look out for trouble; a dog or some rogue kids,' said Francisco snapping out of his day dream.

Luque laughed, aware of the urchins' reputation and even more so of his responsibilities. Passing through any built-up area with the herd could be tricky and Triana was no exception, particularly so if the waifs and strays of the barrios decided to pester them. Gypsy children were a particular problem and it soon became clear that they had not escaped alert young eyes. A group of children, thin and dressed in ill-fitting clothes appeared from the back streets. At first, they stood in wonderment, watching the lumbering animals but soon found their voices, shattering the peace with their shouting and laughter.

'Hey, get away,' Luque called out to one who was venturing too close.

The boy took little notice, forcing Luque to nudge his horse forward to deter the interloper and when the urchin failed to budge, he resorted to whipping him with the trailing ends of his reins. At last, the boy retreated but it was not the end of his interference, a torrent of abuse flowing freely from his mouth and then his friends joined in. Francisco could hardly restrain a laugh, the whole charade was part of growing up in Tirana, a ritual, a highlight, and he remembered the days when he had done the same and dodged lashing reins.

'Get away before I take a real whip to you,' shouted Luque. 'The little devils, they were lucky none of the bulls took offence. I would hate to think what the consequences might be if one turned on them.'

'Don't worry, Luque, I have never yet seen a bull turn on the kids, and anyway, did you see how fast they can run?' said Francisco in sympathy. 'They can take care of themselves.'

Sure enough, after gawking at the bulls in wonder and playing at bullfighters for a while, the boys gave up on their pursuit and as the herd began to cross the bridge pedestrians replaced them. The lumbering bulls were a formidable sight, a force not to tangle with and in their way horse-drawn carts and motor vehicles made detours. Finally, the vaqueros directed the herd along the wide Christopher Columbus Avenue and from bars and cafés, from open windows and narrow balconies, people looked on. The spirit of the April carnival was growing and as the edifice of the Real Maestranza came into sight, Francisco could hardly contain his eagerness to see the bullring in all its glory.

Chapter 9

The tired bulls, accompanied by their new friends the docile steers, offered little resistance as the vaqueros herded them into their pens. Francisco spread hay for the animals while the others took care of the horses and Luque went to report to the stockyard foreman while for Francisco to be so close to one of the shrines of bullfighting and yet unable to see it was hard. But his wish to set eyes on the bullring became a reality when Luque returned.

'I have spoken with the foreman and he says we can look through the gate from the pens if we want but we must not stand on the sand of the bullring. Do you want to?' he asked knowing full well what the answer would be.

'Is it the first time you have laid eyes on the bullring, Paco?' asked Fernando they stood looking through the half open gate.

'Me too,' said Manuel.

'Yes, it's the first time I have been so close. It's wondrous.'

The three vaqueros stood in silence until Fernando pulled the gate shut and the three weary cowboys returned to the stables to find Luque missing.

'He will be at the pens,' said Francisco. 'I know he worries about the bulls. He told me he cannot afford to let the de Mendozas down. They pay us well; he is so appreciative of his job and for the next few hours the reputation of the estate rests on his shoulders.'

The others understood and nodded a silent acknowledgement before they quietly began bedding down for the night. Conditions were primitive, just straw to sleep on and a shared a bucket of cold water for ablutions but after such a long day none of that mattered.

Rising early and washing away the last sleep still in his eyes, Francisco turned to the task of feeding his horse. Manuel and Fernando followed suit before saddling their horses ready for the return journey this time minus the fighting bulls. Their job was to return the steers to the ganadería, leaving Luque and Francisco to look after the bulls until the start of the corrida. As they readied themselves, Luque and Francisco returned to the pens to separate the steers where they noticed a stranger looking intently at the pen's occupants.

The man hardly seeming to notice them, but Francisco was intrigued and noticed how intently the man examined the bulls and the man himself, his features those of a true Andalusian a mixture of the Moor and the Roma and he was someone who knew bulls.

'They are fine animals, I hope they are good fighting bulls,' he said finally.

'Ah… you are El Gitano, no?' said Luque.

'Yes, I am and I want to see what kind of animals these are.'

'I think you will find them all capable of giving good entertainment, the bulls are in the best of condition. You will not be disappointed.'

'I can see they are,' he said, moving around the yard to look at the remaining bulls. Well, until this evening. We will see then how good your bulls are,' he said, and with a curt nod of his head he left.

'Who was that?' whispered Francisco having missed the earlier exchange.

'El Gitano, he will be fighting today.'

'Will we be allowed to watch him?'

'I think so, if we can find a place behind the barrier. Once the *paseíllo* starts there will be no need for us, the stockmen will handle the bulls and we will be free to find a suitable viewpoint.'

'Enrique de Justo, El Gitano, yes, I saw it on the posters. He has top billing along with Rodriguez Pallister, and then there is César.'

Luque did not say more, instead he let out a sigh and lowered his head onto his folded arms atop the wall.

'What is it, Luque? Is something wrong?'

'Yes, someone has tampered with two of the bulls during the night.'

'What do you mean?'

'The horns. Look closely at that bull there, the horns, tell me what you see.'

Francisco studied the bull's horns and at first did not notice anything unusual.

'What am I supposed to be looking at?'

'The horns, the tips, notice their shape. Someone has tampered with them, shortened them and blunted them.'

'Oh... I see,' said Francisco, understanding.

The change was barely noticeable but a closer inspection revealed the angle of the tips was not quite right and there was some sort of paint on them.

'*Afeitado*, someone has cut the ends and reshaped them.'

'Making the bull less dangerous? Yes, I have heard about it.'

'Not only are they blunted but the bull's ability to gauge distance is affected making him more likely to miss his target and that leaves me with a problem.'

'What, surely no one will see once a fight starts, the bull will be too far away from those watching.'

'That is the idea but if anyone does get close enough to notice, someone who doesn't like the de Mendozas, then it could spell trouble and I will be the one to take the blame. I should have spent the night out here then I might have prevented it.'

'Is it El Gitano you think?'

'I don't know. The draw for the bulls isn't until later today and it seems strange that only two bulls are affected.'

The two men fell silent until Francisco said, 'What if the draw is crooked as well?

'It could be and that would mean a few people know about this. Paco, promise me you will say nothing. This happens a lot but it can destroy the ganadería's reputation and that will reflect badly on me. Promise me.'

'Of course.'

'We should have an idea later today who is cheating. We must watch everyone. I don't like being used like this.'

Sitting on the low wall, Francisco picked up the last of his bread and took a bite, his eyes looking blankly into space. The vaqueros work had ended, Manuel and Fernando had left with the steers hours earlier, he had tended to the bulls for the last time, and now alone he dared to imagine. His eyes turned to the big red door through which the fighting bulls would enter and he dared to imagine that he would be the one facing them. In his imagination the situation unfolded, the bull charged, his skill avoiding those scything horns cheered by an appreciative crowd of aficionados. Exciting, so exciting until a familiar voice interrupted his thoughts. Luque had come looking for him.

'You shouldn't be out here, Paco. I need to check on the bulls one last time. These stockmen don't know them as I do, come on, you can help me' he said.

A chastened Francisco followed Luque into the stock yard and together they leaned over the wall of the nearest holding pen.

'Hey, Antonio,' Luque called out to a man spreading hay. 'Don't give them so much of that, a full stomach makes them lazy. If they do not fight like the bulls I know they are, then Señor de Mendoza will be angry. The reputation of the ranch rests upon these bulls.'

'Don't worry, Luque; we know what we are doing. Come back later, before the first fight. I guarantee your bulls will be fine.'

'I want them in the best of condition,' said Luque beginning to show a hint of irritation.

'What's wrong, Luque, are you worrying about the horns?'

'Of course, I don't like it but there is a lot of money at stake. A lot of money changes hands on the outcome of a fight. It happens.'

'Gambling?'

'Sometimes, but usually it is for the benefit of the

matador, a chance to enhance earnings for him and his promotors. If he appears to be taking risks that excite the crowd then the bullrings are more likely to be full and the prices increase. Everyone wins, in the know that is.'

Francisco wondered and took a closer look at the reshaped horns, the oil, blackened to disguise the fix.

'None of the others have been touched, just these two. I can do nothing about it so let us find a bar where we can eat and relax a little. Have you any money?'

'Five pesetas,' answered Francisco feeling in his pocket.

'That's enough for some wine and tapas, I have a few pesetas, come on, I know of a bar on Sierpes where the bull-fighting fraternity hang out. The Bar Tivoli, do you know it?'

'I have heard of it but I can't say I have ever been there.'

'Tivoli is a good place to go if you want to make your way as a matador but, be warned, some shady characters get in there.'

Just a short walk from the bullring, the bar was a mass of chatter and clinking glasses. Thick cigar smoke hung from the ceiling like the clouds over the Sierra Morena. The place was alive, Francisco's senses became more acute as he pushed through a mass of bodies, aficionados focused on the bullfight, everyone an expert. He was grinning broadly; among the bullfighting fraternity he was beginning to enjoy himself. The pictures on the walls of famous bullfighters contemporary and from an earlier age adding to the atmosphere. Then he saw someone he knew.

'Hey, Raffa,' he called out.

From his seat, a young man looked up.

'Paco, what are you doing here?'

'I'm working for the Mendozas in Tablada, I helped bring the bulls for the corrida. What are you doing here?'

'We are here for the bullfight, we saved up all year for today. You've brought the bulls, I bet you will get to watch for free, eh?'

'Maybe, I don't really know, but Luque says we can watch from behind the barrier.'

'That's the best seat in the house, lucky man.'

'We'll see, it's the first time I have helped with the bulls so I am not exactly sure, but you can bet I will try. What are you up to these days? I haven't seen you since the time we were chased across the bridge by the Guardia.'

'Ha, ha, we were lucky that day, amigo, lucky we were not locked up.'

Francisco smiled, his mind returning to the hot summer's day not so many years ago when he and a group of boys from Triana had wandered into the city in search of excitement. One of their number was a well-known thief by the name of Pablo Manzanares. Pablo could not help himself; at the least opportunity he would steal and on one day roaming the streets, the boys began pilfering bread buns from the tables of unsuspecting open-air diners. For hungry urchins, it was not an uncommon pursuit but Pablo Manzanares had higher things on his mind. He sidestepped into a jeweller's shop and when he came running out again the cry of 'Stop thief!' followed and the natural reaction of the boys was to scatter. Unfortunately, a member of the Guardia Civil was patrolling and seeing Francisco and Raffa running away assumed that they were the thieves.

'I thought that we were in real trouble that day, Raffa, we were lucky to get away. So, what are you doing now, are you working?'

'Sort of, I do a few jobs with Pablo here,' he said, turning sideways and Francisco instantly recognised the thief.

'*Madre de Dios*, Pablo, how are you?'

Gone was the thin and felonious looking wastrel Francisco had known from his youth, replaced by a young man, well dressed, his face fatter and sporting a pencil-thin moustache, yet to Francisco he still possessed the eyes of a thief.

'Good, very good. I hear you are involved in the corrida.'

'Yes, I helped to bring the bulls here.'

'So, you will have some idea of their fighting spirit. Tell me, which ones do you think will last the longest?'

'What do you mean?'

'I am an aficionado and I like to know as much about the bulls as I can. You must know which one will put up the best fight.'

'Hardly, it will depend on the matador I think.'

'Perhaps,' he said appearing to lose interest, and Francisco took the opportunity to disengage.

'Well, I hope you have a good day, I see Luque is calling me,' he lied and, relieved to pull himself away, found Luque talking a tall man with a conquistador style moustache.

'Ah… Paco, let me introduce Emilio Romero. He is a manager and promoter. You might want to have a few words with him.'

'Hello.'

'Your friend tells me you want to be a bullfighter?'

'Well yes, some day if it's possible.'

'What experience have you, how many bulls have you fought?'

Francisco could only tell him about the bulls of Tablada and it soon became clear he had done very little real bullfighting.

'I don't think very many promoters would risk taking you on, not with such limited experience.'

'Yes, but I can fight. Everyone who has seen me fight says that I have style and will go far with the right manager. You are a manager?'

'Erm… yes,' said the man, stroking the end of his moustache with a nicotine yellowed finger. 'I can arrange for you to meet with a promoter, put you forward as a potential addition to his programme, but only as a banderillo. Everyone starts from the bottom. I might be able to help you. Would you mind filling my glass and I will tell you how.'

Before Francisco could answer, Luque took him by the arm and led him away.

'Save your money, Paco. Save your money for your dinner, we might not eat again until we return to the ranch.' Then, lowering his voice, he said, 'This place is full of hustlers. They come here to prey on aspiring bullfighters. Look, over there, the grey-haired man, Sergio Gonzales, a minor promoter. Granted, he does have his finger in a few pies, but the corridas he is involved in are truly small-time, villages out in the country, affairs where the bulls are on their last legs. He makes a living I guess but at the toreros' expense. Never work for the likes of him unless you get paid before a fight or you will never be paid.'

Francisco looked back at Emilio Romero. Already his attention had turned to another young hopeful and just past him, Rafael and Pablo Manzanares were both deep in conversation with two other men. It seemed to him that deals were in progress all over the place and he wondered if he might ever get the chance to meet a promoter who really could help him.

'Time we were going, Paco,' said Luque, finishing his drink.

Luque waited just long enough for Francisco to down the last of his beer before heading for the open door, followed closely by Francisco. Pushing their way through the crowd of promoters, agents, and hopefuls, the two of them emerged into the *feria,* a street party in full swing. Laughter and noise filled the air, crowds of carriages, horses, and automobiles all jostling for position on the crowded roadway. The carnival atmosphere was infectious and as Francisco made his way along the path his gaze fell upon a pretty girl. For a moment she returned his smile before her fan obscured her face and she turned away. Nearby, four women in brightly coloured dresses were dancing the Sevillana, skirts spread provocatively as their bodies swayed to the rhythmic clapping of onlookers and Francisco thought of his mother. She could put all these women to shame with her dancing he thought.

From an early age, he accompanied his mother as she aired her dancing skills at the fiestas of Triana and from no more than eight years of age he had accompanied the older boys on their excursions into the city, he was no stranger to the goings on but this time was different.

Having driven the bulls from Tablada for the corrida he considered himself part of the celebrations, not simply an onlooker. A disturbance caught his attention, a group of boys, lively and mischievous reminding him of his youth and of his adventures at the various fiestas.

For a time, he stood and watched them make their noisy way along the street. An argument began, a distraction something Francisco was familiar with and he guessed the outcome. Sure enough, the boys arguing was diverting the open-air diners' attention and that was when bread rolls began disappearing from their plates. He could not help but chuckle at the boys' audacity for how many times had he and his friends done the same.

He pushed past the dancers and followed Luque towards the wide waterfront road filled with horse-drawn carriages carrying the well-to-do of Seville. A tram carrying the less affluent thundered past, pedestrians thronged the walkway and barges sat immobile on the Guadalquivir's still waters. Francisco could see that the tempo of the fiesta had noticeably increased since they had left for the bar Tivoli. Time was moving on; the start of the bullfight could not be not far away and they needed to be in the bullring before the start of the corrida.

When they finally arrived outside the bullring it seemed that everything had changed, the place was buzzing with an activity he had not seen earlier, a large crowd gathering, ticket holders eager to take their seats. The matadors and their entourages would have arrived earlier, resplendent in their fabulously sequined and colourful suits and now Luque must make one last visit to the bulls. Passing the open door to the arena Francisco gazed in wonder at the freshly raked yellow sand before joining Luque already leaning over the wall of the first pen.

'They look fine Paco, the stockmen will look after the bulls now, the performers do not want us getting in their way so let us see if we can find a good place to watch.

Francisco grinned, pleased at the prospect of being able to watch the bull fights, it was an unexpected bonus. Footsteps sounded along the corridor and coming into view, dressed in his suit of lights, was El Gitano. He seemed not to notice the two vaqueros as he entered the small chapel. The opening ceremony was not far off and he was following the time-honoured ritual of praying to the Virgin of Macarena, the patron saint of bullfighters. Every bullfighter did the same, to ask her to watch over them and protect them in their encounter with the fighting bull.

Respectfully Luque and Francisco remained silent as they passed the chapel and made their way into the arena to find a place behind the *barrera*. For half an hour nothing happened, they waited and Francisco took the opportunity to look around, up at the highest seats where people were leaning on the barriers, chatting, and enjoying the afternoon.

The *areneros* made one last rake of the yellow sand and all was ready. A trumpet sounded, Francisco's heart raced with excitement and a hush of expectation spread through the crowd their eyes turning as one towards the red doors just beginning to open. It opened wider and the band began playing the paso doble, the signal for the start of the parade.

First to appear were the sheriffs, two horsemen dressed in the clothes of an earlier time, tall plumes of red feathers sprouting from their hats. Circling the arena in contra rotation they symbolically checked that all was as it should be and, returning to the gate, they turned towards the president's balcony and raised their hats.

The President of the corrida raised his hand holding a white handkerchief, the signal for the start of the bullfight and replacing their hats the two sheriffs galloped back to the big red doors to lead the *paseíllo*, the opening parade. First came the three matadors marching through the gate line abreast followed by their entourages. The picadors on their heavily padded horses came first and then the banderillos, their capes hung loosely over their shoulders and, last of all, the sword carriers. The audience rose to the occasion, the spectacle of the toreros inducing a crescendo of noise until eventually the three matadors positioned themselves in front of the president's balcony. The mood of the audience changed, a hush descended and the band ceased playing and solemnly the president waved his handkerchief to give his permission for the fight to begin.

For a time, the picadors rode back and forth to put their horses through their paces and the banderillos spread their yellow and red capes in a show of competence. For several minutes, the cuadrillas of the three matadors entertained the audience until a trumpet heralded the arrival of the senior matador. The picadors, banderillos and all the other players in the spectacle dispersed and to a cheer, El Gitano appeared through the matador's entrance to walked majestically towards the centre of the ring, his cape slung over his shoulder where he bowed to the spectators before making his way to the *burladero* to await the first bull, leaving the preliminaries to his banderillos.

The *toril* gate opened and a magnificent black form burst into the waning sunlight to a roar from the crowd. Bewildered by the novelty of its new surroundings the bull raised its head, sniffing the air as it trotted out into the open space of the bullring. The animal had known nothing other than the tranquillity of the lush green pastures, nothing of man other than the mounted vaqueros and noise of the people shouting annoyed it. El Gitano remained behind the burladero, his dark eyes watching as his banderillos ran at the bull, swinging their capes to goad it.

He would soon have to fight the animal, alone, he must learn quickly the bull's characteristics, its temperament, how it might charge.

The three banderillos worked as a team, approaching the bull from different directions to confuse it and as the animal turned to gore one or other of them, they used their capes to avoid injury yet to demonstrate the bull's fighting qualities and in those few minutes they laid bare the bull's fighting qualities, its turn of speed, its agility and most of all its aggression and El Gitano was ready to face it for the first time.

Emerging from burladero he walked towards his adversary. At first, the bull was not aware of him, its poor eyesight an impediment, and it had not yet picked up his sent. Slowly he spread the red and yellow *capote*, the smaller of his capes and shook it until finally the bull did notice him. Lifting its head, it sampled the air and turned and moved towards him, slowly at first, inquisitive, until its powerful neck muscles flexed and it charged.

Each time the bullfighter raised his cape and each time

the bull charged Francisco was on his feet, anticipating El Gitano's every move. As the matador swept his cape in front of the charging bull Francisco mirrored his actions with an invisible cape.

'You enjoy his style, Paco; different do you think?' said Luque as El Gitano withdrew to the safety of the barrier.

'Yes, his passes, the way he turned. I want to see César fight; see how he compares.'

'You will. Look, the picadors.'

Francisco turned his head towards the entrance gate just as the trumpet announced the arrival of the picadors. Galloping out onto the soft yellow sand they rode towards the bull with their pikes held out in readiness. The first of them approached the bull from behind, stabbing at the great mass of neck muscle and forcing the bull to turn. Angered, it began to chase the horse but before it had gone very far the second picador caught up with it and stabbed the neck muscle angering the bull further, their actions having the desired effect of enraging the bull.

'Now there will be some fun Paco, these banderillos are good I hear.'

'They will need to be, the bull is strong and I think a little crafty.'

'Ha, they all are. You should know that from your work.'

'I suppose so,' said Francisco resting his arms on the barrier in front of him.

'If our other bulls perform as well as this one then I think the ganadería will have a very successful corrida.

El Gitano performed well during the rest of his fight, the banderillos extracting gasps of delight from the audience at their tricks and daring and at the end of the final act the bullfighter raised his arms in triumph to a sea of white handkerchiefs and calls of "Olé". The second matador did equally as well to leave Francisco feeling envious of César who would fight next and as the trumpet sounded to announce his arrival, he looked towards the gate.

César, the home-grown torero looked tremendous in his blue and gold suit of lights, his cape over his shoulder and a black montera tight on his head. The crowd immediately warmed to him and Francisco could not help feeling envious. He watched him cross the arena, waving to his supporters and it was not until the *toril* gate opened that it dawned on Francisco that César's bull was one with the shaved horns.

Initially it was a shock to know that he was cheating. This was a man who would not fight the bull on equal terms, who would have the advantage of knowing that there was much less chance of injury and then when César's second bull appeared it was clear that bull also had cut back horns and Francisco felt nothing but distaste. Yet César fought well he could not deny it, but it rankled that César was fighting bulls to a large extent restricted in their ability to judge distance and if ever the horns did come close to catching him, then the damage would be minimal.

Francisco had enjoyed his first experience of the bullfight, witnessed several passes he did not know existed and he was learning something of the shadier side of bullfighting. Someone had tampered with the horns and how was it that César had drawn both bulls? Francisco struggled to come to terms with the exposé; for him bullfighting was an art, man against bull and not despoiled by disfiguring the bull. He was seeing César in a new light and for the rest of the fight he watched his every move to discover how he was exploiting his advantage.

Lacking the experience of the other two matadors Francisco could expected César to fight to the same standard as the more experienced matadors. Nevertheless, for him to be fighting in this bullring should mean he was still a very capable bullfighter. Francisco leaned forwards, his elbows resting on the barrier and he watched César perform his first passes. They were passable, good enough but he did not let the bull come too close.

Then Francisco began to understand. César's style was to lean into the bull a fraction of a second late, to make it seem the horns were closer than they were and of course, altered just enough, the bull was misjudging distances and the young matador was in far less danger than it would appear. Clever, very clever thought Francisco, an almost imperceptible advantage that was paying dividends. The small advantage fooled the audience and although he was performing most of the same passes as El Gitano, his timing was not so accurate. But that did not seem to matter because each time the bull attempted to gore César its sharp horns were just short enough of their target to avoid injuring him.

It was fascinating to watch. If Luque had not drawn his attention to the alteration then he would never have known and would be cheering César's skill and bravery just like ten thousand or more other souls who had come to watch him and deciding to keep his own council he remained in his position for the rest of the corrida to watch the two senior bullfighters who did not disappoint.

However, when it was time for César to face his second bull, he left his place.

'Where are you going?' asked Luque as he began to leave.

'I need a leak. I'll go into the stock yard. It will be empty now will it not.'

'I suppose so but be careful, we've been granted special permission to watch today so don't go spoiling it for the future.'

Francisco nodded, gave a suitably compliant look, and slipped away. Where he was going, he did not really know but he was determined to get as close to César and his men as he could, to see if there was anything else going on. He had noticed how the picadors had sapped the bull's strength, weakened it. Perhaps the lances were not of the correct length. What if they were longer than they should be, what if they were injuring the bull so much it could not fight as well as it could? He didn't know the answer but he was going to find out.

Instead of making his way to the gate through which the bulls entered the ring from their pens he made his way towards the *puerta de cuadrillas* through which the matador and his cuadrilla entered the ring and just as he drew near the trumpet sounded for the start of César's second fight. He rightly assumed that no one would know him and reaching the gate he stood in the shadows to watch. If anybody challenged him, he could say he had lost his way. After all, to the uninitiated the bull ring's layout could appear confusing.

The gate, just a few meters away swung open and César marched out at the head of his team. Looking straight ahead and behind him the banderillos with their small capote capes over their shoulders. He did not notice the young torero he had met just once before and the rest of his men were too preoccupied. As the men on foot passed by Francisco took several steps towards the gate and just as the picadors appeared he stopped and looked at them. Their lances looked no different to any he had seen but his inquisitiveness got the better of him and a gruff voice told him to move away, but before he did, he took one last lingering look at the man's pike and was as sure as he could be that its length was more that the regulation demanded.

Chapter 10

After the team of mules unceremoniously dragged the carcass of César's second bull from the arena and the crowd began to disperse, Luque and Francisco returned to the stables to feed and water their horses. Their work finished and as it was too late to return to the ganadería the two vaqueros had some time on their hands and they would use it to effect.

'See if you can find that bucket, Paco, at least we can try to appear respectable. We don't want to let the boss down, do we?'

Francisco grinned. He was looking forward to the *feria*, the sights and sounds, the bright lanterns, the fairground, the casetas, the little houses erected by the well-to-do to receive their friends and business associates. Years before, as a youngster wandering the streets with his friends, he had found them fascinating but had never set foot in one. Urchins were not welcome but tonight he would finally enter one. They had an invitation to visit the caseta of the de Mendozas.

'I saw you counting your money, Paco. I would not worry too much,' said Luque as he finished drying his face. 'There will be plenty of food and drink at the boss's caseta. We can eat and drink as much as we want.'

'I've never been to one of those places, you know. If we

came too close as kids someone would chase us away.'

'It will be an experience for you then, a chance to meet some of Seville's monied people. Anyone who is someone will be there so don't go making a fool of yourself, stick with me and let's keep out of the way.'

Bright lights were everywhere, the city aglow and everywhere crowds thronged the pavements. The waterfront was busier than Francisco had ever seen it, so many varieties of horse-drawn cart, carriages full of revellers and the motor vehicles of the well off. Everyone was of the same mind, making their way towards the Prado de San Sebastian and the feria. In the distance fireworks erupted with colourful light, beacons drawing them towards the fairground. Excited, Francisco felt an urge to spur his horse on but with so much traffic that was an impossibility until eventually they cleared the city limits and left the road to ride through a meadow filled with temporary cattle pens. A gypsy encampment with smouldering fires lay to one side and in front of the two riders, an iron-framed bridge draped with electric lightbulbs. It was the centrepiece of the fair and riding under it they made their way past a series of tents and towards rows of casetas spaced along on either side of a brightly lit boulevard.

'Hey, Luque, some wine, amigo,' called a man from one of the first chalets.

Luque waved and then turned to Francisco. 'He is my cousin Pedro. Let's have a drink with him.'

'You were at the bullfight today, Luque?' said the man, handing a glass up to Luque and another to Francisco.

'Yes, working. My friend here helped me bring in the

bulls.'

'You are still working at the Ganadería Mendoza?'

'Yes, three years now.'

'You will be getting a pension soon.'

'Ha… not yet, I hope. Thank you,' he said taking the offered glass. 'Good health, to you and your family. They are well?'

'Yes, my daughter is here somewhere, with her boyfriend.'

'And Maria, she is here?'

'Yes, inside, I'll get her.'

The woman, Maria, had seen them already and appeared through the caseta's drapes smiling broadly.

'Maria, how are you?'

'I am well, Luque. Who is this you have brought to see me?' she said looking Francisco over, a twinkle in her dark eyes.

'Maria, meet Paco, Paco, this is Maria. Now don't go teasing him,' he said to her.

Throwing back her head Maria laughed and then came to Francisco.

'You're a fine-looking lad, where are you from?'

'Triana, I work with Luque.'

'Triana, hey, you must have gypsy blood, I like gypsy blood especially in a young man like you.'

Francisco felt himself blushing, unsure, until Luque intervened.

'He's already spoken for Maria. We must go I'm afraid. Come on, Paco, time to enjoy some tapas with the boss. Adiós, Pedro, Maria, thanks for the drinks,' he said, nudging his horse forward.

'Why did you tell her I was spoken for?'

'You needed rescuing; she's a real man-eater Maria. She would swallow you whole if she has a mind to.'

'What about her husband, doesn't he get jealous?'

'Naw, she was just teasing you, she does it all the time and she knows if she does step out of line, Pedro will give her a clip. It was good to have a few words with him about the family,' said Luque encouraging his horse to move.

The roadway stretched as far as Francisco could see, bustling with activity, a spectacle to enjoy. Families walked together, the little girls dressed in brightly coloured flamenco dresses, the boys in waistcoats, half-sized córdobes on their heads. And there were the courting couples, pretty girls in bright dresses sitting sideways on their lovers' horses, arms wrapped tight around their waists.

'There, look,' called Luque pointing. 'Over there, I can see Carlos.'

'I see him,' said Francisco.

Luque crossed the street followed by Francisco and, after making their way through the crowd, they dismounted and tethered their horses to a rail. Francisco was awestruck at the caseta's size and stood back for a better look. The structure a far more lavish affair than the one belonging to Luque's cousin. Not just a simple chalet, it looked a full-blown villa with an extravagantly decorated veranda, red and white striped curtains hanging everywhere and it even had its own staff. Francisco could smell food; he had eaten almost nothing all day and could see a chef busy carving a ham leaving his stomach remind him how empty it was.

'This is a really impressive affair Luque.'

'It is, and look, over there, Carlos is talking to César. I

wonder what their conversation is about.'

'The horns?'

'Not a word Paco. Say nothing or we might get the sack.'

Luque gestured to Francisco to follow him, away from the boss and the matador, inside where the air was thick with tobacco smoke and rowdy conversation. A guitar was playing a well-known flamenco tune as they entered and looking nervously around Francisco was relieved that nobody seemed to notice them.

'It looks like the party is going well. Do you know any of these people, Luque?'

'Some, not all. There is Santiago Moncada Sánchez over there. I do not know him personally but I do know that he is a prominent personality in the bullfighting world. He has his finger in many pies, a rich man I think.'

Francisco looked towards two well-dressed men deep in conversation. One a bit older than the other, maybe forty or fifty, Francisco guessed, the only clue that he had greying hair. The other was more his own age, slim with jet-black hair.

'Señor de Mendoza told me to bring wine for you and to tell you to help yourselves to some food,' said a waitress to Luque. 'What would you like, I can bring the wine now and if you see the chef to choose what you want to eat, I will bring it to you.'

'That would be just fine,' said Luque. 'Some wine to begin with thanks. Well, Paco, it's our turn to party. Are you hungry?'

'Hungry, my stomach thinks my throat has been cut.'

'Me too,' he said looking at the girl. 'We will get some food and you can bring the wine there,' he said pointing to some tables.

'No problem, señor, follow me and I will introduce you to the chef.'

The girl was about to lead the way when Carlos appeared through a group of people and came towards them.

'Luque, I'm glad you have made it, the girl is looking after you?'

'Oh yes, thank you.'

'The bulls, they performed well today. There is something I need to tell you about them, I will see you later.'

Luque nodded and Carlos turned back towards César who had become the centre of attention.

'What was all that about?' Francisco asked,

'Nothing, I don't suppose. Did you see César bending his ear? I bet a céntimo to a pile of horse manure it is something to do with him and those bulls with the shortened horns.'

'I'm not keen on César.'

'Me neither but we had better not say too much.'

'Mm... you're right, maybe I am just hungry and talking out of turn. I'm sorry.'

Luque seemed not to hear, turning instead to get his hands on some food.

'I have some very nice beef taken from one of the bulls César fought, or perhaps you prefer a little fish,' teased the chef.

'Beef.'

'Beef.'

'I thought so, you guys always want beef on a day like today.'

'It's one of ours,' said Luque. 'It would be rude not to.'

'It's good,' said Francisco, a trickle of grease oozing from the corner of his mouth after he had sat down and attacked the steak, the last thing he said for several minutes.

'You soon polished that off, Paco.'

'I'm hungry,' he said, mopping his plate with a piece of bread.

Finally satisfied he wiped his mouth on a napkin and took a sip of wine, at the same time casting his eye around the caseta. Some faces he recognised, cattle dealers who he had seen on the estate, and of course there was Carlos and César but apart from two others he knew no one. He looked again at César, careful not to appear too inquisitive. He had renewed his conversation with Carlos, his gestures animated, describing his passes at the corrida Francisco guessed.

'I wonder if he's telling Carlos how he faked some of his moves,' he thought. Still, what was it to him, he was not a bullfighter like César, what harm was it doing him? He took another drink of wine and turned away unable to look any more. It should not have mattered to him that César was cheating but somehow it did. There is an art to bullfighting, the torero risking serious injury or perhaps his life in the pursuit of perfection and here was César playing games. It disgusted him.

When he looked again they parted company, was with his this father and two well-dressed men. He had no idea who they were but they looked to be men of importance. Then from the corner of his eye, he recognised the girl who had tormented him. Dressed in a blue and yellow dress she carried a fan black, a contrast to her dress and she looked stunning. Her entrance had something of the theatrical about it, her fan flicking back and forth as she passed amongst the guests. Men's heads turned and they eyed her enviously, and to Francisco's dismay, she made straight for César.

He stretched out an arm in greeting and for several minutes the two of them engaged in an enthusiastic conversation, the beautiful girl, and the celebrated matador. All Francisco could do was watch, as a poor vaquero and had little chance of getting to know her and taking his half empty glass he walked outside the caseta to watch the world go by.

'Hello again, you were the one playing the bull down by the river. You were very good,' said a voice.

Turning towards the woman Francisco did not recognise her to begin with until it dawned that she was younger of the two sisters.

'Er… that would be a month ago I think.'

'Yes, we were out for a ride. You didn't see us but we saw you, we watched as you fought the bull all on your own.'

'Mm… yes, I did, you haven't told anyone have you?'

'No, why?'

'We are not supposed to play the bulls, especially on foot. They are never to see a man on foot until the day they enter the bullring.'

'Don't worry, your secret is safe with me.'

'You are Carlos's cousin; I have seen you around the estate. You were at the bullfight today?'

'Oh yes, we would not miss it for anything. Isabella wanted to see César perform. By the way, I am Jimena,' she said holding out her hand. 'What is your name?

'Francisco, but everyone calls me Paco.'

'Well, Paco, pleased to meet you,' she said, her dark eyes looking him over. 'Oh, there is my friend Camila. I was looking for her. Nice to meet you, Paco,' she said with a smile.

'You are favoured there, Paco,' said Luque. 'It's not often they mix with the likes of us. Come back inside and let me introduce you to a couple of friends. They have contacts and you might find them useful, that is if you are still keen on trying your hand in the ring. Maybe they can help you.'

Inside the caseta Luque ushered Francisco towards Two men stood talking near the bar and made the introduction.

'Fernando, Santiago, this is Paco, a budding torero. I have seen him perform and I must admit he has something.'

The two men nodded a greeting.

'Luque gives you a good introduction, Paco. What makes you think you are better than all the others?' said the one called Santiago.

'I cannot say, it is not for me to puff out my chest and boast, to see me fight is the only way you can judge me.'

'Bravo, a good answer but where can I see you fight? Not in the Plaza de Toros, that is for sure. Do you fight in any of the *novilladas*?'

'I have nothing planned.'

'You must if you are to progress in this profession. You will need a manager like me, but first you need to make a good impression. As you so rightly say, the best way to know how good you are is to see you fight, the only real way to judge your skill. There are several novilladas planned next month, the annual novillada of La Rinconada for instance. It will be a good test for you if you are serious.'

'Thank you, I will think about that.'

'What did your boss have to say about his bulls today, Luque?' he said turning away from Francisco and feeling excluded from the conversation, Francisco left them to wander around the caseta and was surprised to see Isabella standing alone.

'Hello, it's the budding torero.' she said as he approached. 'What are you doing so alone?'

'Oh, just mingling, talking. I met two men who manage up-and-coming bullfighters and they want to see me fight.'

'I want to see you fight, Paco, but first I want to look round the fair. Where is your horse?'

'Just there,' he said pointing to the row of horses.

'Take me round the fair.'

'What, on my horse?' he said with surprise.

'Of course. All the girls are riding on horses and I want to.'

'Maybe I shouldn't...'

'Nonsense, if I want to ride on your horse with you then I will. Come on, show me,' she said grabbing his arm.

The contact surprised him and unable to resist he willingly led her to his horse, climbing into the saddle before reaching down to help her scramble up behind him. She was an expert horsewoman and had little difficulty sitting side-saddle behind him, her arms wrapped around his waist.

'Oh, you are a strong man Paco, you will not let me fall will you?'

'Of course not, how could I let such a beautiful girl fall from my horse?'

She giggled.

'Where are you from, Paco?'

'Triana.'

'Oh really. I have never been there. You must take me one day, I want to see the gypsies. Have you family there?'

'My mother, sisters and my older brother. My father died not long ago.'

'I'm sorry. Look there, the bridge with all the lights, take me there.'

Francisco nudged his horse forward.

'Your parents, they are still alive?' he asked.

'Why yes, Mama and Papa will be at the caseta later. Papa is very well connected and the *feria* is a good time for him to do business.'

'What business is he in?'

'Bullfighting,' she said in a matter-of-fact manner.

'Oh, how?'

'He provides bulls for most of the large bullrings in the country and he is a promoter of bullfights. He knows everybody. He works closely with the de Mendozas. José is my uncle.'

'And Carlos is your cousin?'

'Yes, obviously. Papa manages some of the best bullfighters in Spain and Mexico. He manages César. You know César?'

'Yes, he was fighting today.'

'Didn't he fight well? I had one of the best seats and I saw both his fights.' The vision of Francisco playing the bull beside the river was still in her mind. 'Would you like to be a matador, Paco?' I bet you would like to fight in the

Real Maestranza. You could probably make it as a torero.'

'A matador?'

'A banderillo maybe,' she teased.

'Not a bullfighter then?'

'Oh yes, I am sure you could,' she said tightening her grip. 'Down there, take me down there.'

It was past midnight and the youngsters of Seville were making the most of the feria, calling out as they rode past each other, and Francisco was beginning to feel that he had not a care in the world.

'You are stopping in Seville tonight?' said Isabella, her lips close to his ear.

'No, we ride back to the estate when we are finished here.'

'And when do you think you will be finished here?'

'Daybreak I guess.'

'It will have been a long day for you, will you not sleep?'

'I might catch some sleep while I'm riding back, a few minutes here and there,' he said.

'I do not want to wear you out, take me back, Mama will arrive soon and I don't think she will be happy finding out I have been riding around with you.'

'What's wrong with me?'

'You're a boy,' she said her arms tightening further.

Francisco grinned and turned his horse around, his mind firmly on the girl's body pressing against his. But all too soon the experience came to an end, within just a few minutes she would leave him but for the short time they'd been alone together he had experienced something he wished would not end. He jumped from his saddle and reached up to help her down, moved closer to her only for her to step away.

'Thank you for the ride, adiós,' she said, brushing him aside and his world came tumbling down. It was as if she had smashed his heart into smithereens. How could she be so dismissive? How could her mood of fun and togetherness have changed so quickly? He had been with some girls in Triana but at the worst of times, they had never left him feeling like this.

Isabella was from the opposite side of the social divide he knew and maybe he should be thankful for the little time they had spent together, but that didn't help his feelings.

Isabella leaving him like that was a disappointment to and his experience of the *feria* left him with mixed feelings. Riding alongside Luque he cast his mind over the past few hours, remembered every detail of the ride with her sitting behind him and his time herding the bulls. To witness the bullfights at close quarters had been a wonderful experience, one that had left him wanting more.

Unquestionably he had the ambition to become a matador and he had learned that he needed to show what he could do on a bigger stage. At the first opportunity he had returned to the bar to search out Sergio Gonzales, the minor promotor to try to convince him that he was worthy of a chance to fight in one of his corridas. After buying the man a few drinks he had come away with a promise. Sergio said that he could fight in the local corrida at the sleepy pueblo of La Rinconada just a few kilometres to the north of Seville and now he was walking there with his friends.

'How much further, we've been walking for hours.'

We're nearly there I think.'

'How do you know?' asked Manolito.

'I was told that the road has a long sweeping bend not far from the town and this looks like it.'

'I hope you are right, my hip hurts,' said Luis, dragging his foot.

'Do you want to stop for a while?'

'No, I don't want to hold you back, Paco, I don't want you to miss your big chance.'

'Thanks, Luis, look there is a man and a donkey coming our way, we can ask him how far it is.'

The man was a water seller leading a donkey weighed down with his wares and once the boys realised this they could not help but lick their lips. Luis took the initiative.

'Señor, how much for a cup of your water and tell me, do you know the whereabouts of today's corrida?'

The man's sleepy eyes blinked several times.

'At La Rinconada?'

'Yes,' said Francisco, I want to fight today but we are new to your beautiful town and do not know where the bullring is.'

'Beautiful town, ha. You must come from a poor place if you think La Rinconada is a beautiful town.'

'Well, perhaps not so beautiful then. Your water, *señor*, how much for a drink of your water?'

'One or one each?'

'Thwone eaff,' said Manolito unable to contain himself, his tongue so dry he could hardly get his words out.

The water seller looked over the little group, weighing them up, for his mind was not so sleepy.

'Twenty céntimos, each, one peseta for all of you.'

'One peseta!' exclaimed Francisco. 'That sounds a lot.'

'It is but if you are thirsty and if you still want to know the way to La Rinconada then one peseta is cheap enough.'

Francisco licked his parched lips and looked at his little band. 'Very well,' he said reaching into his pocket. 'Five cups.'

The man's face fashioned something resembling a smile but to Francisco, it was more a look of triumph.

'The town, where is it?'

'Over there,' he said pointing. 'About an hour's walk.'

A drink of water and half an hour sprawled out on the ground rejuvenated the band of adventurers and once they sighted the first of the whitewashed buildings their spirits began to rise.

'Luque told me not to expect too much, there is no proper bullring here, just the town square. They make a barrier of farm wagons to close it off. That is their bullring.'

'Chances are we will fit in for once eh, Paco,' said Luis.

'I expect so, we will make it a spectacle, make it a day they will not forget, the day the four musketeers of Triana came to town.'

Laughing and excited by the prospect, the boys quickened their pace, even Luis with his injured leg kept up and entering the town they noticed the atmosphere change. Gone was the quiet of the countryside, replaced instead by a buzz of excitement as the townspeople and country folk from far and wide gathered for the annual event.

'We just made it I think, Paco,' said Manolito looking at all the people. 'Where do we go?'

'I have no idea but I will ask around. That man there on the black horse, he seems to have some authority.'

Francisco went up to him.

'Señor, I have come to fight today, Sergio Gonzales has engaged me to fight in this corrida. Do you know where I should go?'

'Who?'

'Sergio Gonzales, the promotor. He told me he had arranged the fights today and I gave him a deposit of five pesetas to secure my place.'

'Sergio Gonzales, never heard of him. This is just a local affair, anyone who thinks they can fight can take part. You will need to give your name to that man in the straw hat,' he said pointing. 'He will tell you what you should do.'

For a few moments Francisco felt stunned. He had parted with five pesetas in good faith and now realisation dawned that the man had swindled him, but his disappointment did not last as the man in the straw hat added his name to the list of hopefuls.

'Good luck, Paco,' said Manolito with a grin. 'This is a big chance for you I think.'

'I hope so,' said Francisco wondering what he had let himself in for.

The small-town corrida was certainly different. The arena was simply the main square fenced-off with farm carts and bales of straw, quite small, and he had little idea as to the fighting qualities of the bulls. He needed to see those bulls, find out what he would be up against and walking up to the man in the straw hat he asked.

'The bulls, where are the bulls we will be fighting? I would like to see them.'

'We have a mixed bag, there are not many animals around here that could grace a corrida in Seville or Córdoba but you can see them if you want, they are penned round that corner. I will call your name out when the fights start. You will have to take what comes I am afraid. This isn't the big city you know.'

The man finished scribbling on his piece of paper and with a sigh of resignation tipped his straw hat to the back of his head and left Francisco to his own devices.

'The one with the white streak on its neck looks a bad one,' said a young man of about Francisco's age leaning on a farm cart.

'You have come to fight?'

'Of course. What's your name?'

'Paco.'

'Well, Paco, I'm Felipe. Do you know which bull you will be fighting?'

'No, I was told we have to take what comes. I think you are right though that one does look dangerous, those uneven horns, I think they will be a problem.'

'Well, we will see,' said Francisco's new-found friend, thoughtfully stroking his chin. 'Look, the first fight must be getting under way, they are getting the brown bull out.'

Francisco watched as a local man began prodding the brown bull while two other men with poles looked on. The first would-be matador was already at the centre of the square, his posture telling Francisco he was inexperienced. At the edge of the square, sitting upon yet another farm wagon, the president for the corrida signalled the fight to start and from the side street, the brown bull entered the ring. The youngster intending to fight it moved his cape and the bull stopped dead in its tracks and the would-be matador swept the cape across his body. Francisco could see that his nerve was beginning to fail.

'Stay still,' he found himself saying, but it was too late.

Taking a step towards the bull the novice bullfighter swept his cape in an arc, and immediately the bull charged at him and the novice bravely stood his ground. The bull was too quick for him and before anybody realised what was happening the lad found himself thrown into the air and landing awkwardly, he tried to regain his footing but the bull had already turned and was ready to charge again.

Instinctively Francisco leapt to his feet and vaulting the protective barrier he raced towards the injured youth. He had not managed to regain his feet and was in real danger of serious injury and Francisco was not alone in seeing the danger. From around the square other men were also coming to the novice's aid, one using his hat to distract the animal, another trying to pull on its tail, and Francisco began to drag the unfortunate victim to the safety of the barrier.

However, throwing off the unwanted attention the bull changed tack. Twisting its body round, it looked for a new target, but Francisco had his wits about him and aware that the bull was fast approaching the injured youth turned to face it. Standing on the balls of his feet he stretched out his arm and waved it furiously, a target, enough for the bull to focus its effort on him. The audience gasped with anticipation, thrilled by the sight of some real drama, and Francisco did not disappoint.

Lowering his arm at the very last second, he sidestepped out of the bull's path and as it thundered past, he ran towards the fallen cape, diving to the ground to retrieve it.

With the cape in his possession, Francisco jumped to his feet and stood motionless to confuse the bull. He was in his element, felt alive, cool and in control, it was the moment he had been waiting for, to be in the ring with an aggressive fighting bull and surrounded by an appreciative audience. He hardly heard the calls of 'Olé', the encouragement of the crowd because his concentration lay solely with the bull. The beast was big and powerfully built but it was no thoroughbred and Francisco guessed God had not blessed the animal with a great deal of intelligence.

A series of classic verónicas soon had the audience's attention and he began to feel as if he was in the bullring with just a playful puppy dog. He guided the bull around his body, a *tanda*, turning with it, performing every move he could think of and before long the people of the little town were euphoric. Never, they said, had a novice bullfighter performed so skilfully nor so bravely at their humble *novillada* and when it was over, they lifted Francisco to their shoulders to paraded him around the square.

'*Madre de Dios,* Paco, that was brilliant.'

'Everyone thinks you are the best *novillero* to fight here,' said Manolito wearing a huge grin.

'Francisco, you remember me,' said a voice.

'Ah, Señor Romero, yes, I remember you, the bar Tivoli.'

'We spoke at length about your desire to become a matador if you remember. Well, you have certainly proved yourself a capable bullfighter. Your performance was impressive, so much so that I want to make you an offer. Can we speak privately?'

Chapter 11

During their first meeting, Emilio Romero had told Francisco that he was a promoter of bullfights, a manager of matadors but just like Sergio Gonzales he was a liar. His manner was persuasive and the naïve Francisco was receptive to his lies.

'I am arranging a bullfight in Lebrija in two weeks' time. It is a small, local affair without picadors. I need a matador and his cuadrilla so if you can muster a competent cuadrilla then I can offer you the job. What do you say?'

Francisco thought for a few moments, excitement overruling his better judgement. He did remember the conversation with Emilio in the Bar Tivoli and yet seemed to have all too easily forgotten Luque's advice.

'It sounds good, señor, the kind of opportunity I am looking for, but there is the matter of the fee. I will have to pay the cuadrilla and there will be my own expenses. To reach Lebrija we will need to travel by train and that will cost money.'

'Money is not a problem. I can offer fifty pesetas for both you and your cuadrilla. That should more than cover expenses and you will have the chance to show what you can do to a bigger audience. I predict that you will have a glorious future. Now, what will you call yourself?'

'Call myself?'

'Yes, for the posters, I must have posters to advertise the event.'

When Francisco broke the news Luis's eyes sparkled with joy. 'Lebrija, when, where is it?'

'It is on the fourteenth of next month, three weeks' time and I want you all to be in my cuadrilla,' he said to his friends. 'What's the matter, Luis, you don't look as if you want to do it.'

'It's not that, Paco, it's my leg. I don't think I can be a banderillo. I can't move fast enough.'

'Who said you are to be a banderillo? I want you to be the *mozo de espada*, my sword carrier. It is just as important as being a banderillo but it saves you having to dodge the bull.'

Luis's eyes sparkled, pleased that Francisco had singled him out for the special job.

'Thank you, Paco, thank you.'

'So, it's settled then. Manolito and the others I am sure will be happy to act as banderillos. Come on, let's go and tell them.'

Although pleased with the offer to take part, Francisco was aware of the need to dress according to custom and his friends had little more than the clothes they stood up in. The cost of new bullfighters' clothes would be beyond them and that was a problem.

'I haven't any money to spend on clothes,' said José when Francisco told him.

'Me neither,' said his brother.

'But maybe we could borrow some just for the one fight,' said José

'You all know my mother died. She was a good seamstress. She could have made us the clothes if she were still here,' said Manolito.

'I'm sorry, Mano, but she's not,' said Luis. 'My mother can sew a bit. What about your sisters, did your mother teach them anything?'

'They made these clothes I'm wearing.'

'Not bad,' said Francisco pulling at an exposed fold in his friend's shirt. 'You could ask them couldn't you.'

Since the death of his mother, Manolito's two sisters had taken on the task of looking after him and his father. It was true that both were skilled seamstresses but they had other jobs, repairing, and washing clothes for more well-to-do families in the city, helping in the market, anything to make ends meet and Manolito was not sure they would be willing to help

However, as the word spread so did the enthusiasm to become involved and a day later Manolito was proud to announce, 'they will do it, Paco. Bridgit says she asked. Florencia and she will help but we have no money for the materials. She says she will make our clothes for the bullfight so long as we provide the materials.'

'Where will we get the cloth?' said Francisco looking puzzled.

Bridget says we will have to do what they do, beg steal, or borrow. She said that they can sometimes get hold of the off-cuts and second-rate material from the Jewish tailor on San Jacinto, you know the small workshop near the junction with Rodrigo.'

'Yes, I know it. We will try there in the morning and we can tell the others to start looking, maybe they can find old clothes we can use, get your sisters to alter them.'

'Bridget says she has some sequins and coloured thread but nowhere near enough. She says we might have to buy some.'

'I have my wages. It's not much and I give most of it to my mother. She is a good seamstress though, I bet she will help us.'

From somewhere the boys did beg, steal, and borrow. Coloured cloth, sequins, ribbon, and cotton thread, enough for Manolito's sisters and Francisco's mother to turn out a set of passable costumes for the newly formed cuadrilla. Carmen's skill in making her flamenco dresses came in useful, and by the end of it all, Francisco had a passing resemblance to a real matador and his friends were realistically looking banderillos. It had been a struggle and some of the clothes were not a particularly good fit but the unruly youths of Triana saw themselves only as brave toreros when they looked in the mirror and two days later, they set off for the sleepy town of Lebrija.

'Don't forget your costume when we leave the train, Mano,' Francisco joked as he jumped from the running board, his newly fashioned suit of lights tucked under his arm.

His friends followed him and he paused for a moment to look across the rusty steel tracks towards the town's low buildings. Lebrija was no less sleepy than a hundred such towns, consisting of buildings bleached by the hot summer and packed tightly streets but it did have its very own bullring, a circular structure rising above the rooftops. Even before Francisco could declare that he had seen it, Luis said, 'That will be the bullring over there.'

'Well spotted,' said Francisco sarcastically. 'We are in good time, let's have a look round, see if we can find Señor Romero.'

The boys gathered and began to walk towards the buildings when José, striding ahead of the others called out, 'Look, a poster with today's bullfight on it.'

The other boys rushed to him to examine the primitive artwork, expressions of wonder on their faces.

'It has today's date but who is El Caballito? It says he has one of the finest cuadrillas in Seville with him. Who's that, Francisco?

'That's us.'

'Us, and El Vaquerito, where did you get that name from?' asked Manuel.

'I am the little vaquero, am I not? I ride a horse. What else could I call myself?'

'El Vaquerito. It sounds authentic,' said Luis examining the poster. 'And we are the finest cuadrilla to come out of Seville this season it says. Wow, not much to live up to then.'

As they stared at the poster, a figure approached; the moustachioed and self-styled impresario Enrique Romero.

'Ah, you are here I see,' he said. 'You like the poster; I think it will draw a good crowd today. Have you managed to get hold of the right clothes, Francisco? It is important you know; the people around here are pretty stupid but if you are not dressed in the right clothes, they will start to think I have swindled them.'

Francisco bit his lip. 'Where are the bulls?'

'Come, I will show you. There are four bulls and you must kill two of them.'

It sounded a strange request, thought Francisco, but as this was an out of the way arena, perhaps the bullfights here were a little different. In a poor farming community, money would be in short supply, he understood that, and when he finally set eyes on the bulls, he realised just how little money there was. Two were no more than three-year-olds, small in stature and with underdeveloped horns. Hardly the stuff for a proper corrida. The other two were bigger and older, how old Francisco did not know, but at least one of them had the makings of a fighting bull.

'The two smaller ones are for sport, to begin with, get the crowd in the mood. The other two you are to fight like a real matador, and kill.'

It looked easy enough thought Francisco, except for the black Miura, a powerful-looking animal with a white streak running down the middle of its face and it had deformed horns, gangly and angled that could make it unpredictable and dangerous.

'What do you think, can you handle them?'

'I expect so. This one here could be difficult but I will not know until I am in the ring with it.'

Enrique seemed satisfied or maybe just relieved that the show would go on.

'It is two hours until the first fight. You will need to get ready in the stable, no fancy changing rooms here and no chapel. If you want to pray before you fight there is a church just around the corner.'

Francisco did want to pray, it was normal. Any matador who knew his job prayed, prayed to the Virgin of Macarena to ask that he might emerge from the fight alive.

'He doesn't look an easy bull, Paco,' said Luis resting his weaker leg against a bale of straw.

'No, that bull is the one to watch, the young ones are no more fighting bulls than the ones we used to chase during our excursions to Tablada, but I will need to be careful with that one. Let's have a look inside the bullring, see what kind of place it is.'

Lebrija was not a rich town and it showed. The bullring was a small affair with whitewash peeling from the walls and seating minimal, just three rows very close to the sand-covered floor and anyone not lucky enough to claim one would have to stand. Though it was a backwater, the locals were no less bullfighting aficionados than the citizens of Seville and he knew he must fight well.

'Right, let's find the others Luis, get ready. Have you got your suit?'

'Yes, it's here,' said a proud Luis holding up a small bundle tied with string. 'I can't wait to put it on.'

Francisco smiled at his friend, encouraged by his enthusiasm. A localised affair like this, full of noisy spectators needed an enthusiastic cuadrilla because judging by the bulls they would know little of the finer points of the bullfight.

A single trumpet blasted out a none too melodic paso doble to introduce the fledgling bullfighters; not the parade a first rank bullring might expect but the trumpeter made the best of it and proudly Francisco strode out at the head of his cuadrilla. Manolito, Manuel and José in line abreast, marched behind him and Luis brought up the rear, his disability overcome by pride and his limp hardly noticeable.

Francisco worried that their costumes might not appear authentic but to the unsophisticated audience they seemed genuine enough and, with his first hurdle cleared, he turned his attention to the real purpose of the afternoon. Within just a few minutes the first bull would appear and when it did, he watched from the side-lines. Manolito, Manuel and José took it in turns to torment the animal, running at it placing their long darts neatly in its neck.

So far they were holding their own, the crowd was enjoying the spectacle with plenty of encouraging calls and the young bulls behaved respectably until they tired and were withdrawn from the arena. The undersized bulls had served their purpose but now the time for the main event had arrived.

Francisco took a moment to look at his audience. Simple farming people, most of them wide-eyed and with vacant grins on their faces, but amongst them, he could see more serious eyes and hoped there would be at least some aficionados out there. The lone trumpet sounded and with his *capote* draped over his shoulder, Francisco walked towards the president who made much of his permission, waving the white handkerchief as if carrying the standard at the battle of Bairén.

Francisco took up a position near the far barrier and waited. Within seconds, the first of the bulls appeared; a different proposition to those that had gone before. The animal looked powerful, its brown and white hide covering hard muscle and swinging its head from side to side, it circumnavigated the perimeter of the bullring.

It was not yet time for him to confront it, his assistants would take care of the preliminaries and taking his cue,

Manolito ran towards the bull with his cape held wide. The bull was just halfway around the ring when it became aware of him, sniffing at the air it came to an abrupt halt and instinctively lowered its head. Manolito stopped and visibly stiffened, fixated by the horns, the crowd gasped in anticipation of a goring and the bull charged. Manolito recovered his composure and holding out his cape he let the tip of a horn rip through the cloth before turning to run towards the safety barrier. The bull followed close on his heels forcing him to leap spectacularly over the rim of the barrier and not more than half a meter behind him the bull crashed into the barrier with an almighty bang.

Then it was the turn of the brothers Manuel and José who appeared from behind the barrier with their capes spread. Parting company they approached the bull from opposing ends of the bullring and began enticing it to charge. Confused to begin with the bull turned back and forth finally deciding upon Manuel. He knew he was the target and he waited, bravely standing his ground with his cape held wide, and with some dexterity he turned the animal towards his brother, who took up the challenge. Playing the angry brute was no easy task but between the two of them they expertly controlled the angry bull and all the while the waiting Francisco took note of the bull's disposition.

The first real fight for Francisco and his cuadrilla of one-time ragamuffins proved a success. In the eyes true aficionados their performance probably left much to be desired but it convinced the present audience that they were watching true toreros, and it was Francisco's despatch of the bull with the wicked horns that left the locals in no doubt that they had witnessed a real bullfight.

'Where is Romero, Luis, have you seen him?' asked Francisco, as he left the arena.

'No, the last I saw of him he was talking to the stockman. That was just before we fought the last bull.'

Francisco's eyes narrowed and remembering Luque's words heard alarm bells ringing; Luque had warned him that Emilio was less than honest but he had believed him and there was no sign of the fee promised.

'Shit. Search for him, he has our money. Luis, go and have a look in the street, the rest of you search the stables and the *torils*. Find him,' he said angrily.

For twenty minutes or more they searched the square and the surrounding streets pushing through the departing crowd until finally they had to concede defeat. The crooked impresario Emilio Romero had disappeared into thin air, there was no sign of him and the realisation that he had swindled them left Francisco distraught and he could do no more than hold his head in his hands.

'You seem upset, young man.'

Francisco spread his fingers, to see who was speaking and was surprised to see a face he recognised.

'Señor, hello, I hope you enjoyed the corrida,' he said in a half-hearted attempt to come to his senses.

'Hardly a corrida, but you made it a success. Your style impressed me. Come and have a drink with me.'

'I cannot now. We are looking for Emilio Romero. He has our money.'

'You will need to look very hard, my friend.'

'Why?' quizzed Francisco, knowing the answer.

'Emilio Romero is not the most honest individual to emerge from Seville. He will be long gone and will have taken your money with him I have no doubt.'

Francisco's lowered his eyes, hurt spreading across his face.

'You are not the first torero to be duped by a promoter and you will not be the last. Do not be too downhearted,' said Santiago, 'I have a proposition for you. Join me for a glass of wine and I will tell you something to your advantage.'

Francisco looked unconvinced.

'How much did he offer you for the fight?'

'Fifty pesetas.'

'How about if I reimburse you the fifty pesetas, will that convince you of my sincerity?'

Chapter 12

The bullring of the Andalusian town of Cáceres was small compared to Seville's Real Maestranza but it did have a fervour all its own, an atmosphere that its larger relatives found hard to match. The seats were filling up and the hot afternoon sun had begun to wane, a hum of excitement filled the air and, waiting by the *puerta de cuadrillas,* Francisco was beginning to feel the pressure. Although he had finally achieved his ambition of fighting in a real corrida, it was a daunting task to walk out in front of a such an audience.

The afternoon was the result of his meeting with Santiago Moncada Sánchez, the time when the promotor had given him the opportunity he had been waiting so long for, a chance to fight in a corrida with established bullfighters.

'Hey, Luis, what do you think?' he said, as his cuadrilla came towards him.

'It looks great, Paco,' said Luis gazing over the wide-open area of yellow sand.

'Yes, and you certainly look the part,' Manuel said to Francisco.

'Rafael Ortega and David Muñoz are two top matadors; I only hope I can live up to their standard. Fighting alongside them will lift our profile. This could be the start of something.'

'I hope so, you deserve it.'

'We, Luis, we deserve it. I cannot manage without a cuadrilla I can trust.'

Luis nodded, a smile creasing his lips. He had seen Francisco perform in the moonlit meadows of Tablada, and he had known all along that his friend had what it took to become a matador. Today would be a test for him, for him as a matador and for the three banderillos performing together for the first time in an established bullring, and as the sword carrier, he was determined to play his part.

'Are you all right, Luis, you are looking rather thoughtful?

'Yes, I'm fine, Paco. I just worry about my leg. I don't want to let you down.'

'Don't be silly, we know you can't keep up with the rest of us but you are not expected to. Just do your best in the parade and then keep behind the barrier during the fights. You do not need to do more,' said Francisco, reaching out to ruffle his friend's hair. 'Promise me you will keep out of the way, Luis.'

The trumpet sounded announcing the start of the preliminaries, Rafael Ortega, David Muñoz, and Francisco came together line abreast and led by the mounted sheriffs they led their entourages out to the strains of a paso doble, not a single tuneless trumpet this time but a full-blown band.

The scene was set, Rafael Ortega and his cuadrilla took their positions, the trumpet announced the first bull and the big red door swung open and for the two experienced matadors, the fights were little more than routine. Their cuadrillas were competent and they played the bulls with a panache that only came with experience. Performing with the artistry expected of them they raised cheer after cheer from the crowd and then Rafael Ortega walked out fight. David Muñoz followed with a similar performance and all the time, Francisco watched and learned and then it was time for him and his cuadrilla to enter the ring.

'Good luck, Paco,' whispered Luis.
Purposefully, Francisco walked out into the wide-open space, his heart beating fast and to the president's balcony he went to receive permission to fight. A wave of the hand and a blast from the trumpet was all it took to thrust him and his cuadrilla into the fight. Luque and another of the vaqueros from the ganadería had joined him as his picadors and they rode out to begin proceedings while Francisco watched the animal's every move.

Finally, he appeared from behind the barrier, his cape held loose at his side and the men of the cuadrilla withdrew to the perimeter. Now he held centre stage he was, for the first time, experiencing the excitement of a real bullfight and it inspired him. He had to come to terms with his opponent, understand the half tonne black mass eyeing him suspiciously from just a few metres away. Extending his cape with both hands, he coaxed the bull into action, standing his ground as it charged, he performed a series of *verónicas,* playing the bull, judging its strengths and weaknesses at close quarters and when he was satisfied, he retired to the barrier.

Luis could not restrain his enthusiasm, moving as fast as his disability would allow.

'Paco, what a day we have had. I think we pleased

them. Did you hear them shouting El Vaquerito?'

'At the end, yes, I heard nothing during the fight. I needed all my concentration for the bull. I tried to read its intentions; a distraction could have seen me on the end of its horns.'

'Francisco,' a voice called from the passageway. 'Francisco I would like a word.'

It was Santiago, beckoning, a serious look on his face.

'Is something wrong?'

'No, nothing is wrong, quite the contrary, I congratulate you on a job well done. Rafael and David Muñoz performed as I would expect them to but you are new and unknown. You have an individualistic style, Francisco, one that sets you apart. You are a very capable bullfighter and I would like you to fight for me for the rest of the season. Come to my office on Tuesday morning and we can discuss a contract. What do you say?'

Francisco was speechless yet pleased and when Santiago handed him a wad of banknotes his eyes lit up.

'Here is your fee, you have earned it,' said Santiago with a smile.

Watching Francisco fight had convinced Santiago of his potential and he knew that with his connections, it would be a simple matter to find Francisco more fights and if he fought as he knew he could, then they would both make money, a lot of money.

By the end of August, Santiago was offering even bigger fights to his protégé. The young torero's skill and bravery was getting him noticed and Santiago decided to give him the chance to fight in Málaga, one of the best bullrings in Spain. On the bill that afternoon was a matador from

Valencia, Antonio Ordóñez, the senior matador for the day, and the other, César.

'Have you seen the poster, Paco?' said Manuel.

Francisco had, at almost the same time, but it was Isabella who sprang to mind. He had not seen her for quite some time though he had heard that she was close to César.

'There look, César is on the same bill,' said José, adding to his disquiet.

'Yes, I can read,' he snapped back.

This would be no ordinary corrida. He was becoming a minor attraction on the bullfighting circuit and today his stage was one of the foremost bullrings in Spain. Málaga was the biggest bullring so far in his fledgeling career, one where practically everyone who mattered in the bullfighting world would be and with confidence in his ability, Francisco raised his arm to acknowledge the cheers of the crowd.

He turned to face the president's balcony and a sea of faces looked back at him and he noticed a woman staring at him, a face instantly recognisable as Isabella and in a moment of inspiration, he called out to her.

'Señorita, I dedicate my bull to you.'

She did not reply, instead her fan slowly passed across her face and her eyelids fluttered. Francisco held his breath until finally she graciously bowed her head in acceptance and Francisco's heart leapt. He swept his cape from her shoulder and spread it theatrically, doffing his montera in salute and he was ready.

His emotions ran high that afternoon and his performance was inspirational. His *verónicas*, *gaoneras*, and *molinetes* were skilful and precise and at the end of it all he killed the bull cleanly. The afternoon was a triumph and in the end his cuadrilla held him aloft, parading him around the arena to finally deposit him in front of the president's balcony.

Raising his hat, he saluted the president who awarded him an ear for his performance, the first time it had happened to him and in response he turned towards Isabella.

'Señorita, please accept this gift from me.'

In response, she rose from her seat and came to the barrier her cheeks flushed and a smile upon her lips. She looked even more beautiful than he remembered and without hesitation he said 'you must dine with me tonight,' the boldness of his proposal surprising even him. 'Where is your hotel? At eleven o'clock tonight I will come for you.'

She accepted the bull's ear and in a sign of surrender her fan closed and quietly she said, 'Hotel Alhambra, I will be waiting in the lobby.'

She looked lovely dressed in a red satin dress a black lace shawl hanging loose over her shoulders and in her hair, she wore a red rose.

'Where shall we eat, have you a restaurant in mind?' she asked.

He had to admit that he had little idea of where they should dine. The rush of blood that had led him to this moment had not extended much further and he had not thought through the consequences. He had never been to Málaga and dining out in style was a new experience for the boy from Triana.

'Er... I have not given it a lot of thought. We usually

find a bar; tapas are normally good enough for us.'

'Tapas! I thought you wanted to eat in a proper restaurant, not a cheap tapas bar.'

The young matador looked down at his feet, this was not a good start. Then, shrugging off embarrassment, he took the initiative.

'Perhaps living the way you do has spoiled you. How about roughing it a little. You saw me as no more than a simple farmhand and now I can afford the finest of restaurants. It is true, I can, but an evening amongst aficionados, drinking wine and eating tapas, discussing the state of bullfighting is an enjoyable pastime. Come, let's try the Bar Mahon, we ate there yesterday.'

'How far is this bar?'

'See the square at the end of the street, well it is just off there, towards the waterfront.'

Sensing a weakening of her resolve he pressed home his advantage.

'How often do you come to Málaga?'

'Two or three times a year. We come for the Feria de Málaga in August every year. Papa likes to do business here, meet people he rarely sees during the year, important people for his business. The April fair in Sevilla is the other big event for us.'

'So why are you here now?'

'We came to see César fight but I have heard so much about you lately and when I heard you were fighting in Málaga in the same corrida I decided to come and see you as well.'

'I'm flattered, did you enjoy the corrida?'

'It was good, yes. I particularly liked Rafael Ortega's performance, he has a class all of his own, his *faenas* were awe-inspiring.'

Francisco was delighted by her knowledge but what did she think of his performance he wondered?

She said nothing.

'Here, the bar. It looks busy,' he said, guiding her through a crowd of people.

'Señor, señora, I will find you a table if you will follow me,' said a waiter.

'Would you like some wine, what would you like?'

'Papa always drinks Rufina when he is in Málaga.'

'Rufina?'

'Yes please,' she said staring past him. 'I'm hungry and that food does look tasty.'

'You look lovely by the way; I like the way you arrange your hair.'

'Thank you, sir. I have to say you looked pretty good yourself this afternoon in the ring.'

Now was his chance he thought. 'Did you enjoy my fights?'

Her eyes flickered a little and he held his breath until she finally released him from his torment.

'You were quite brilliant, Paco. I knew you would be a matador of substance one day, ever since we watched you fighting down by the river.'

'Oh… yes, your sister mentioned that you had watched me'

'You were quite a sight, your bare chest, not something we ladies should be exposed to for very long.'

'Long enough though from what I heard.'

Isabella lowered her eyes for a moment before tilting back her head, a wry smile spreading across her lips.

'Come on, let us eat, I'm starving,' she said, changing

the subject. 'You are hungry, Paco, when did you last eat?'

'This morning, I had some bread and olive oil. I cannot eat much before a fight. For one thing, I feel sick and can hardly swallow.'

'Are you ill?'

Francisco wished he had not said anything.

'Er… not really, it is just that I never eat much for breakfast and with the corrida, I have been too busy. It does not do to fight on a full stomach.'

She seemed to understand and as she lifted her glass, her eyes teased him and he realised just how beautiful she was.

'You are not yet married,' he said in a matter-of-fact manner.

'No, I am not.'

'Is there no one special?'

'N… no, no one special,' she teased.

'I find that hard to believe, what about César?' he said, probing.

She pursed her lips and drained the last of the wine.

'César, it is true I have been seeing him and he is good company. I go to watch him sometimes when he is fighting. He is a good bullfighter and will do well with my father's help.'

'Is that why he wants to be with you?'

'César is attractive, successful and fun to be with most of the time but he is possessive; he sometimes thinks he owns me.'

'You don't like that.'

'I do not. I am my own woman; I don't need a man telling me what I can or cannot do.'

'Is tonight a problem?'

'It could be,' she said with a mischievous look in her eye that Francisco did not understand.

'When we finish here would you like a walk down by the waterfront? I've never seen the sea before and I promised myself that today I would go and look at it.'

'You won't see much now, it's too dark.'

'There will be some light, I'm sure.'

'Okay, it's usually cooler near the sea and that would be nice,' she said. 'Have you girlfriends, Paco?'

'Girlfriends! Hell, I don't even have one,' he said getting to his feet.

'You must have admirers now you are becoming a famous torero,' she said as they left the bar.

'I am not particularly famous and I do not have time for girlfriends, I spend time with a few of the girls in Triana now and then but nothing serious, I am always too busy or out of town.'

'So, there is no one.'

'No, no one I'm afraid.'

'Look over there, the sky, the moon is changing. The moon on the water look how beautiful it is,' she said, slipping her arm in his.

The move felt so natural and for the next ten minutes they walked arm in arm towards Isabella's hotel. Francisco felt good, happy, and relaxed the day's tensions melted away and as they reached the hotel entrance, he made to say goodnight. Before he could speak though, she reached up and kissed him on the lips. Her nearness, her perfume combined with the wine played heavily upon his emotions and in the true style of the bullfighter, he began to play her. A peck on her nose, then he kissed her flickering eyelids one by one until she pushed him away.

'Not here, someone might see us, my room.'
'What about your sister?'

'We have single rooms, don't worry,' she said taking him by the hand and in what seemed just seconds they were falling onto her bed.

Ripping at each other's clothes with passion they had a hunger for each other that could only end one way and when it was over Francisco lay still. Dawn was not far away, the birds outside the window were waking up and their song reminded him that no one should see him leave. He looked at Isabella, her eyes closed and her breathing steady. He must go and slipping from the bed, he gathered his clothes and as he struggled into his pants he looked down at her determined that this one night should not be the end of the affair. He had to see her again and as if reading his mind, she opened her eyes.

'You are leaving me so soon, abandoning me now that you have had your way with me. Kiss me.'

'You were sleeping; I didn't want to disturb you.'

'So, you would creep away like a common criminal without even a goodbye kiss.'

'Now that you mention it,' he said leaning over her, inhaling her perfume, feeling the softness of her lips again. 'Perhaps we can meet some other time.'

'I would like that, Paco, when we are again in Seville, let us arrange to meet. I will not see you at the Mendoza *ganadería* will I?'

'No, I have left my job. I can earn a living fighting bulls. That is what I want to do. Santiago Moncada has given me a contract to fight and he pays me well. I have no need to work as a vaquero anymore. Give me your address, maybe I can visit your house.'

Francisco did not catch her look, his infatuation for her blinding him.

'Er... no I think it better if we meet elsewhere. What about the stables near the Golden Tower? It is where we keep our horses. I will be there two or three days during the week and Jimena and I always take a ride together on Saturday mornings.'

'I know it well; I will look for you.'

'We could ride along the riverbank. I know a few trails. You have a horse?'

'No, not any more. When I left the estate, I had to give up my horse and I have no need of one now.'

'I'm sure one can be found for you,' she said, stretching her arms above her head and he could not resist gathering her up and kissing her one last time.

'Be off with you, young sir,' she said pulling the bed sheet to her chin. 'Until we meet again.'

Francisco touched her lips with outstretched fingers and finally pulled himself away.

The train journey home was a quiet affair, Francisco, fatigued from the corrida and his night of passion could not sleep, Isabella's image filling his mind. For the whole journey back to Seville, he thought of nothing else and determined that he would see her again. But they moved in different circles and it was unlikely their paths would cross and so, after torturing himself for two days, he decided to pay a visit to the stables.

For more than two hours he watched the comings and goings but of Isabella there was no sign. What if she did not intend to visit the stable today, should he ask someone where she might be. He felt dejected, and finally realising he was on a fool's errand he decided to leave and go to the Bar Tivoli. At least he could have a drink and could catch up on the latest gossip.

The sun was still warm and made for a pleasant walk but he hardly noticed, his mind preoccupied but when he did reach the bar, he ordered a cool beer to drown his sorrows. He found a deserted table and leaned back in his seat wondering what to do about her when a shadow swept across him and he looked up to see one of César's cuadrilla, Victor Lopez, an outsized man, a bully.

'Ah, El Vaquerito, the famous torero, what are you doing here?'

'Oh, just taking a beer, why what do you know?'

'Buy me a beer and I will tell you all I know.'

Francisco did not like him very much but it might be a good chance for him to learn something of César's plans. It was becoming plain to him that he and César were becoming rivals not only in the bullring but also in love.

'You did well in Málaga last Sunday,' said Victor, pulling up a chair.

'Nice of you to say so, thanks.'

A faint sneer appeared on the picador's face, he was playing the same game, fishing for advantage. It was the way of things; competition was fierce for places on the billboards and Francisco was learning that money and fame did not necessarily depend upon ability.

'What about César, the crowd seemed to like him. Where is he fighting this weekend?'

'We are contracted to fight in Madrid, a feather in César's cap. The king could well be there, it will be a full house. How about you, do you have any plans to fight in Madrid?'

'No, my fights are all in this part of the world. I'm not famous like César.'

That seemed to satisfy the picador and after a short and inconsequential conversation, he made ready to leave when the young Manolito appeared.

'Hi, Paco, didn't we have a good day in Málaga?' he said, delighted to see Francisco.

The picador turned and looked Manolito up and down. 'Who's this? Oh, yes, one of your banderillos.'

'Victor, meet Manolito, Manolito this is Victor. He's part of César's cuadrilla, one of the picadors.'

'Yes, I know I recognise him. Pleased to meet you.'

Victor seemed unmoved, simply nodding an acknowledgement.

'Málaga was a good corrido don't you think, Victor? Didn't Paco do well… er… and César. He put on a good performance.'

Victor's face changed imperceptibly from neutral to one of mild annoyance causing Manolito to retreat to the bar.

'He's too weak to make a good banderillo. I watched him. You need to up your game if you think you can replace César's cuadrilla. We are the best in Seville.'

'Sorry, if we have offended you,' said Francisco holding up both hands in a sign of contrition. Why Victor would make such a comment. Manolito was simply trying to be friendly.

'He's quick on his feet and good enough for me, thank you.'

The big man shrugged his shoulders, slammed down his empty glass, rose to his feet and walked away without a word, leaving Francisco feeling more than a little irritated.

'I do not like him, Paco. Does he see us as a threat or something? Why would he?' said Manolito returning with his drink.

'He is a good picador, I'll give him that, but he's not a very nice person, I think. I have heard stories about him.'

'You don't think. Hey, I do not think either. So, what are these stories, Paco?'

'Nothing much. I hear he is a debt collector when he is not working as a picador.'

'Oh, I see what you mean. Another beer?' he said.

'No thanks, Manolito, I have to go to Santiago's office before siesta; find out the arrangements for Córdoba this weekend.'

'That should be something special, Córdoba. Wow, we really are moving up in the world.'

'Maybe, but we still have a lot to learn, not least to find out how to deal with the likes of him.'

'Perhaps, but we are doing well enough right now.'

'I suppose so. Hey, I am thinking of purchasing a horse. I hear there are some fine horses for sale at the stables on Castellar Street. Do you know anything about that?'

'No, not much. Where will you keep it?'

'I'll find somewhere. That is if I buy one,' said Francisco wondering if owning a horse might help him get closer to Isabella.

'Well, good luck, I am off, I'll see you later when you know the arrangements for Sunday.'

'Yeah, okay, Mano, adiós.'

Francisco watched his young friend leave and, alone again, his mind returned to his failed sighting of Isabella.

Perhaps he might see her if he returned to the stables, he thought about that and, making up his mind, drank the last of his beer.

The stables looked little different as he peered into the gloomy interior, quieter if anything, and this time he plucked up the courage to step inside. As his eyes adjusted, he managed to make out a row of stalls on each side of him and taking a few steps further he could see a figure grooming a horse and was convinced it was Isabella.

'Isabella, is that you?'
There was no reply, just a rustling of straw underfoot.
'Where are you?' he said staring into the gloom.
'Here,' she said.
'It is you, show yourself.'
'You will have to find me.'

She was teasing him and Francisco was not in the mood for playing games. Searching for her in the gloom his eyes finally focused on a pair of riding boots beneath the horse's belly. He was sure it was her and scrambled between the horse's legs he grabbed the first boot he could get his hands on and took Isabella completely by surprise. She squealed in fright and before she could pull free, he rolled her into the straw. She struck out at him, catching him with a glancing blow on the side of his face and in retaliation he smothered her with his body and pinned her down and for several long seconds their lips made contact.

'You frightened me then. Don't do that again,' she said finally pushing him away.

'Ha, ha, serves you right for hiding.'

'How did you find me?'

'Oh, just on the off chance I thought I might see you,' he lied. 'How about a walk?'

'Okay, I am finished here for today. We can take a walk over the bridge to Triana and I can see where you come from.'

'I'm not sure that is such a good idea.'

'Why?'

'Well, there is not a lot to see and if the kids spot us, they will make our lives hell. Ever since I became a little bit famous, they've pestered me.'

'You are more than a little famous Paco. All right then, how about the river, we could go along the riverbank and find a quiet place, somewhere to sit and talk, watch the world go by.'

'I know a place. I sometimes sit there and dream about bullfighting.'

'You don't need to dream any more,' she said gathering her hair and deftly pinning the black filaments into a bun at the back of her head.

In the low light she looked every bit as beautiful as the last time he had seen her. The gold earrings stark against the blackness of her hair, an Andalusian princess he thought and as they left the stables, so besotted he hardly noticed his surroundings.

'Shall we sit a while, watch the river traffic?' he said.

'Yes, I would like that but I must not stop for very long because I am going out to dinner tonight and I need to get ready,' she said, glancing at her watch.

'Oh, somewhere nice?' he asked.

'Yes, a restaurant in Santa Catalina,' she said and catching the look in his eyes, 'César is taking me to meet his business manager.'

'Oh... how interesting,' was all Francisco could say, his mouth suddenly feeling as dry as the sandy floor of a bullring.

'It's just dinner, nothing more,' she said dismissively. 'I think he hopes I can influence my father in his favour.'

Chapter 13

I did not lose my arm, though at times I felt that might be the outcome. The motorised ambulance did not help as it seemed not to have even one spring to lessen the banging and shaking that was causing me so much discomfort. All night I endured that crazy ride, the worst journey of my life when I lay on the stretcher in the company of other wounded soldiers. Some were in a far worse condition than me, moaning and screaming in pain as we bumped over what seemed like every pothole in Morocco and we were still not out of danger.

Not until after first light did I feel safe, not until the column reached the relative safety of Tetuán, a well-fortified town where we could gain some respite. It was there I received some basic first aid but the doctor was fearful that gangrene might set in and advised that I should go to the military hospital in Ceuta. Someone in authority took the same view, there were too many wounded and so the order came to evacuate the town, the third bandera and some Moroccan regulares to accompany the column of ambulances and supply vehicles.

If I believed the army was acting for the good of our health then I did not know the army very well. there was an acute shortage of ammunition and food and as the wagons would be empty for the drive north to pick up supplies it was an opportune time to evacuate the wounded.

We left at midnight, travelling the coastal route of forty or so kilometres to Ceuta across a flat landscape alien to the mountain tribes and thankfully they stayed away and for the first time in almost four years I would be out of the war zone. I was thankful for that though the injury was serious enough to exclude me from further involvement in the fighting and what did the future hold? Maybe I would use the use of it and then where would I be?

Stories of the army's poor medical facilities had filtered through to us and that left me more than a little apprehensive. I expected little more than a tent, perhaps the odd volunteer nurse, and I hoped they would know what they were doing. However, it was not long before the reality of the situation became apparent. The doors of the ambulance swung open, the bright sunlight almost blinding me and I did not know what to expect.

A silhouette filled my view and a voice boomed out 'Right, welcome to Ceuta. We'll soon have you out of here,' and then I must have passed out because I do not remember anything after that until I heard a voice not far away.

'He's back with us.'

I managed to turn my head just enough to see a young woman's head poking through a curtain.

'Hello,' she said smiling. 'How are you feeling?'

Was I with the angels? She was so calm and reassuring and I could do no more than mumble a few unintelligible words.

'The doctor will look at you soon. We didn't want to

disturb you when they brought you in. Would you like a drink of water?'

I licked my lips, dry and cracked and the next thing I remember was the cool water trickling into my mouth. It was so good, like my first beer after the bullfight.

'Good afternoon, soldier, how are you feeling?' said a man's voice.

'I feel like I have been hit with a sledgehammer.'

He did not laugh, instead he just watched me for a few seconds and then he reached out to touch my arm.

'You have a bullet wound in the shoulder. The bullet is still in you and I believe you have a broken bone. That is where you will be feeling most of the pain. First, we need to clean your wound. The nurse will attend to that and then I will come back to see you. I'm Doctor Juan Garcia Giménez, what is your name, soldier?'

'Francisco Martinez, private, third bandera sir.'

'Okay, we're not so formal here Francisco. The nurse will dress your wound and I will call back in an hour or so.'

'Francisco, is it?' asked the nurse.

'Yes,' I said rather weakly. 'Paco to my friends.'

'You are among friends here, Paco. Now let me see what I can do with this wound of yours.'

She began to probe and the pain increased; sweat rolled off my forehead and into my eyes and I felt helpless. I felt her soft touch as she gently wiped away the wetness and I was able to focus my eyes again and could not take my eyes off her until the curtain opened and the doctor returned.

'Yes, I can see the problem more clearly now,' he said probing the wound. 'You have extensive lacerations and

I'm sure you have a broken bone. I need to reset it and I need to find the bullet. We will get you into the operating theatre as soon as we can.'

I must have slept the clock round. I had no real idea of time, not that it mattered, time was unimportant. When I opened my eyes, I was aware of sunlight streaming in through the high, narrow windows of the ward and I was conscious of pain in my shoulder. Closing my eyes again I mentally explored my body, the pain across my chest and in my arm and it did not feel good, there was a strange feeling but before I could explore further a nurse spoke to me.

'Would you like some water?'

I turned my head, slowly, carefully, to look at the her, a different nurse this time, equally caring and gentle and she lifted the drinking vessel to my lips.

'Doctor says the operation was a great success. I'm not supposed to tell you, that's his prerogative, but I'm sure you will feel better knowing.'

'Mm... I do,' I said, trying to sit up but I could not because they had encased the broken bone in plaster and strapped my arm securely to my chest. That was the cause of the strange feeling and I was going nowhere soon.

'What's your name?' I found myself asking her.

'Isabella.'

I thought I had escaped Isabella but for a fleeting moment I was not sure that I had.

'And where are you from, the peninsula?'

'Yes, Madrid as are many of us, we volunteered together.'

'From what I can see you are doing a good job,

Isabella.'

'Thank you, Francisco, you are too kind.'

'How do you know my name?'

She smiled.

'It is on your record card. Now enough talking, you are still weak and need your rest. You know to call out if you need anything. There will be a nurse in the ward most of the day and night. Are you hungry, do you think you can manage some soup?'

How long was it since I had eaten? I found it difficult to remember and the bowl of chicken soup and bread she brought to me was very welcome. She fed me one spoonful at a time and I could not help but cast my mind back to Isabella. I had not heard her name spoken for three long years though her memory returned periodically to torment me. The fighting and the will to remain alive had filled my waking hours, overriding any thoughts of her but now I had time to reflect. Feelings and memories long suppressed began to surface, Mama, my brother and sisters, Seville, the bullfighting and my cuadrilla. What had become of them in almost four years? In all that time, I had received just two letters, Juanita's letters, my only contact with home and to my discredit, I had singularly failed to reply to either one.

The nurse, Isabella, sat beside my bed and began spoon feeding me the soup. It was tricky exercise but she managed without spilling and I began to feel a lot better.

'Good, you managed to eat all of it. Is there anything else I can bring you, some olives perhaps?'

'Yes, some olives would be nice.'

A week passed, a week in which I received the best care

and attention I could have expected, a week in which I began to heal. The bullet was just a memory and inside the plaster cast my broken bone was healing, and the sun was shining. I felt the happiest I had in a long time and perhaps the time had come for me to write the letter home that had evaded me for so long. Christmas was almost upon us; the nurses had told me they were looking forward to a simple celebration and it occurred to me that a letter from me was the only Christmas present I could give my family.

'Nurse can you find me some paper and a pen, I need to write a letter.'

'Are you sure, you are not left-handed, are you?'

'Oh, I forgot the cast,' I said flexing my fingers, holding a pen might be a little more problematical than I had realised.

In the event, nurse Isabella proved helpful, she found me the writing materials I needed and sat with me as I attempted to put pen to paper. At first, I could hardly form the letters but with her encouragement, I managed to create a passable piece of writing.

'There, I knew you could do it. Your writing is good enough, I am sure your mother will be able to read it.'

'I don't think she will. My sister will have to read it to her. Mama can't read or write because I don't think she ever went to school.'

'Oh, that's sad.'

'Not really, she manages well enough and she is one of the best flamenco dancers in Seville. I think that's what she was doing instead of going to school, dancing.'

'We are all different, Paco. Remember that it is not what you have but who you are.'

A simple statement that caused me to reflect, her soft, kind eyes nullifying my normal recourse to flippancy. I had gained much respect for her and her fellow nurses, learned that all were volunteers and mostly they were from Madrid. They had come out to Morocco through a strong sense of duty after learning of the disaster at Annual and the lack of provision for the wounded. I was grateful to her and her colleagues, their care and understanding as much a component in my recovery as the skill of the doctor.

'Would you like to sit in the sun, just for a while, until it starts to cool?' she said. 'I have to change the sheets so it would help if you got up from the bed. If you sit outside, I can get my work over a little sooner and then I could come and sit with you. Would you like that?'

Would I like that, of course I would? 'Er...yes, thank you.'

'Can you get up off the bed?'

'I can try. I have managed it once or twice. My arm is the problem not my legs,' I said, as I carefully swung my legs over the threshold, leaning on my good arm to push myself upright.

It was difficult and I almost managed unaided until nurse Isabella stepped forward to help. She was stronger than she looked, and as I got to my feet her hair brushed against my face, her natural perfume confusing my senses so much so that I couldn't help but stumble.

'I've got you, don't worry, Francisco.'

'Paco, call me Paco, all my friends do.'

'You consider me a friend?'

'Of course,' I said our eyes meeting for the first time.

'Can you manage on your own?'

Unfortunately, I could and the moment passed.

'Sit here while I change your sheets. I will come back and see you soon. Don't go away,' she chuckled as she left me in the garden.

Laughter, how long was it since I had heard laughter like that. The only laughter I had heard for a long time was the alcohol-fuelled laughter of legionaries usually directed at some unfortunate who was the butt of a joke, but her laughter was different, innocent.

'How are you, Paco, have you managed by yourself?'

'I'm fine thanks,' I said pleased to see her return.

'You seem to be on the mend. I have just seen Doctor Juan Garcia and he told me he is satisfied with your progress. Has he mentioned anything about your discharge?'

'No,' I said, slightly alarmed.

If I left the hospital, where would I go? I understood it would take at least a month for me to recover and I had been there no more than fifteen or sixteen days.

'If he has not said anything, I would just forget about it, for the time being anyway. Don't worry about the immediate future. So, tell me about yourself, Paco, where are you from, Seville isn't it?'

'Where is it you are from?'

'Er... yes, Seville.'

'Ah, bullfighting country, do you like bullfighting? My father used to take me to the Fuente Del Berro in Madrid. So exciting though the result never appealed.'

'Fuente Del Berro, fantastic, I used to fight the bulls.'

'No, really?

'Yes, I should be fighting them now,' I said regretfully.

'Why so sad, what happened?'

I could not help my feelings and I looked down at the floor.

'Something happened didn't it; do you want to talk about it?'

'No, not now. Just tell me what is it like, a bullfight at Fuente Del Berro?' I said to deflect her questioning. 'Seville is impressive but they say Madrid is even better. I have fought in the Real Maestranza.'

'Really, you must be special, Paco, to fight there.'

'Maybe, but I am not so sure. Tell me about Madrid, are your family rich?'

'What kind of a question is that?'

'I... I'm sorry. You seem well educated, as if you come from a good family. Not like me, the poorest of the poor.'

'Don't say that. I can see you have talent; you are intelligent and maybe you had a hard beginning. Life moves on you know, there are opportunities out there and if you can, you should take them. Yes, my family are well off, we have a big house in Salamanca. You know Salamanca?'

'No, but I bet it's nothing like Triana.'

'I have heard of Triana, some soldiers we treated came from Triana. It's near the river, isn't it?'

'Yes, and to the south are the great estates where the fighting bulls are reared.'

'You know the ganaderías?'

'Yes, most of them, I worked for two years at the ganadería de Mendoza, for José de Mendoza and his scheming son,' I said with an intensity I soon regretted.

Isabella's eyelids flickered. She was opening my heart almost against my will and exposing feelings I had kept secret for so long.

'Is that why you joined the army, because of something he did to you?'

'I... er, I.'

Her eyes captivated me and I could not resist.

'I ran away I guess, but not because of Carlos.'

'From what then?' she said reaching out to touch my sleeve.

'From everything, from bullfighting, from the thugs, from...'

Those eyes, they never left mine, they had a quality that penetrated my soul.

'Was there a girl?'

The following day I received a visitor, a staff officer, and even before he began to speak, I felt a feeling of foreboding sweep over me.

'Private Martinez, good morning,' he said taking a seat beside my bed. 'I see you are recovering well from your wounds. I am here to see what progress you are making. The doctor is of the opinion that you are unfit for active duty and unlikely to be for the near future. Therefore, it is the army's decision that you receive an honourable discharge.'

It was an unexpected turn of events, one of mild shock mixed with relief I suppose. Nevertheless, a discharge from the Legión was a daunting prospect.

'Thank you, sir.'

'I will write the order when I return to my office and make arrangements for your repatriation. There will be a release payment of one hundred pesetas plus your army pay and any accrued debt will, of course, be deducted.'

Of course, with deductions for uniforms and broken

equipment, our pay was always much less than we expected. It was small wonder the army did not charge for ammunition.

'So, you have a ticket home, Paco?' said Sebastian, a soldier in the next bed. It seemed that he had overheard everything.

'It looks that way. I suppose you will be heading the same way soon.'

'I expect so, can't say I'm sorry. We lost many good men, even the general died in the fighting. I am lucky to be alive even though I have lost a leg. Do you know when you will get your discharge?'

'The doctor says I should be fit enough to leave for the peninsula in a week or so, he says my wounds are healing well. Look, the nurse is back with our medication, I believe she is the reason I am getting better. I wouldn't mind taking her home with me.'

'Morning, nurse,' said Sebastian as Isabella pushed her trolley past his bed.

'Morning, Sebastian, and good morning to you, Paco,' she said as she deposited a pill on his bedside table.

'Looks like you're the one in favour,' laughed Sebastian.

I wish, I thought and then I began to wonder about the other Isabella, the one back in Seville. Even though they had the same name they were very different people. Nurse Isabella was gentle and caring and she had worked wonders on me whereas Isabella was not so easy. Although our conversations had reminded me of a few upsets she had at least helped me come to terms with them.

'It happens to everyone eventually, Paco,' she said. 'It's

God's way of making us better people, teaching us that other people have their own feelings even though we might not like them.'

'Señor Martinez,' she said, stopping her trolley at the end of my bed and snapping me out of my thoughts. 'Time for your medication.'

'Ugh, not molasses again?' I said pulling a face.

'Come on, open wide, look at Sebastian, he doesn't complain and see how well he's looking. It is all due to his daily dose of molasses.'

Sebastian pulled a face too.

'There, that wasn't so bad, was it?'

'I guess not,' I said trying to rid my mouth of the pungent-smelling goo.

'I'll help you take a walk this afternoon; doctor says you need to get more exercise.'

'Thanks.'

Sebastian looked at me from his bed and I knew what he was thinking.

Eventually the day arrived for the removal of the plaster cast. It was a simple task for the doctor to cut it away to leave me feeling elated though a little apprehensive. I still had to find out how well it had healed and was I able to use it as I had before. Under the supervision of the doctor, I carefully rotated the limb. It was stiff and I could not raise my elbow to the vertical.

'Francisco, I think we can call it a success. There is some restriction to your movement but that is normal, with exercise and rest you could be back to full health eventually. The skin is in good enough condition, we will apply an ointment for a few days and that should get rid of the flakiness. I am pleased with your progress and I think we can let you go soon.'

He looked at me thoughtfully, stroked his chin and picked up my record card from the end of the bed.

'I advised your commanding officer that I did not believe you would be fit to return to active duty.'

'I know, they are giving me a medical discharge.'

'You are happy with that.'

'Yes, why?'

'You seem to have recovered better than I would have imagined. You have no desire to go back to your regiment?'

Again, he gave me an inquisitive look.

'Thank you for that, doctor, I just hope I can regain all my strength but you know I feel my grip is nothing like it should be.'

My honourable discharge was a relief to say the least, a reprieve almost. The weeks I had spent at the hospital and the treatment I had received had helped me recover more than my physical health. I had joined the army as an angry and inexperienced young man running away from what now seemed a triviality and for the past three and a half years I had risked my life in the service of Spain. I had had enough of soldiering; I had served my country and I had nothing to be ashamed of, except perhaps that I had left my friends at home in the lurch.

'I hear you will be leaving us soon, Paco,' said Nurse Isabella later that same day when she came to sit beside me in the garden.

'The news travels fast around here.'

'As it should, it's good to know how our patients are

progressing wouldn't you say?'

'It's very pleasant here, I shall miss the view across the bay and I shall miss these interludes. Thank you for looking after me.'

'Not just you, Paco, I care for all patients just the same.'

'I know, but I feel we have got to know each other a little and I will miss you.'

I dared to look into her eyes and she returned that look, her clear blue eyes steady and then, to my surprise, she asked about Isabella.

'Will you see her when you return home, what is her name? You never did tell me.'

'Isabella.'

'Oh, it's the same as mine.'

'Yes, a coincidence.'

'Not really, there are thousands of Spanish women called Isabella. It is Queen Isabella's fault; we're named for her.'

'Yes, I know and I am Francisco because of Saint Francis, or so my mother told me.'

'Will you see your Isabella again?'

'Who knows? I must admit that I would like to see her but what good it will do me? I have no idea.'

She reached out to touch my hand.

'You will overcome any bad feelings, Paco, I am sure. Now I think you should try some exercises, get that arm of yours moving. I have other patients to attend to so I will leave you. Arm up, arm down,' she laughed as she walked away and I felt a strange lump in my throat.

Under the early spring sun, the blue waters of the bay

sparkled, in the distance grey mountains filled the horizon and I remember my feelings. Excitement, trepidation because very soon I would cross that stretch of water and return home. At long last I was leaving Morocco and the seemingly never-ending war. I was worried about my reception when I finally reached Seville but at least I would never have to face the fierce Riffian tribesmen again and I would not have to endure the forced marches or live on the worst of food. Even so I had become accustomed to life in the Legión, the comradeship of men whom I would never see again. I was one of the lucky ones I said to myself as I leaned against the back of my seat and moved my arm in a slow arc. It was a lasting memento of my time with Miguel, Pedro, Fernán and Alfonso and I remembered Huberto the big Cuban and felt sad for he would never return home. There were others too, their faces already fading from memory, young soldiers who would never go home, and I thanked the Lord for sparing me. It was time, and as the vibrations of the ship's engines shook the deck I did not look back.

Chapter 14

It was a milestone, to fight in Córdoba's Cabra bullring was a big step forward in Francisco's career. Although he was the junior matador his name was becoming familiar to the bullfighting public and today the aficionados had come not to see just El Cazador, the senior matador or César the other rising star but Francisco himself and Santiago knew that the extra pressure could be dangerous.

'You are prepared?' he asked Francisco as he emerged from the chapel.

'Yes, I have made my peace with God; and I am now in the hands of the Virgin of Macarena. Whatever she wills for me then I will accept.'

Santiago nodded briefly, satisfied that Francisco looked relaxed and not over confident. He had seen too many young men wilt at this point, to perform in front of a very large crowd was a daunting experience and that could lead to mistakes, fatal mistakes.

'Good luck.'

Francisco raised his head, a look of determination on his face and the older man could not help but smile. The boy had talent, of that there was no doubt but in those few moments he had seen something more, something only the great bullfighters had, a serenity and a confidence possessed by just a select few.

Behind *the puerta de cuadrillas* the matadors and their cuadrillas were assembling ready for the start of the parade and joying his own, he looked briefly across at César. A rivalry was developing between them, natural competition with the added pursuit of the hand of Isabella and she, sitting next to her father waited for the start of the corrida.

'You are seeing César still?'

'Occasionally, sometimes he takes me to dinner and of course I see him at the corrida.'

Isabella was embarrassed by her father's question. She knew he favoured César as a suiter, he had hinted that he would like to her marry him more than once and although she liked César she was not ready to settle down and as the parade began to unfold, her eyes settled first on Francisco in his suit of gold and blue and striding out alongside El Cazador César. No, she was not ready just yet.

'César looks good. We are expecting great things from him today, he has improved under my tutelage and his prospects are good. I have arranged for him to fight in Madrid at the end of the season. We must all go and stay in the capital for a few days.'

'Yes, Papa, I would like that.'

'They have some lovely shops in Madrid,' said her sister.

'I expect your mother will want to spend time shopping, but I will be going for the corrida. What about you Isabella, shopping, or bulls?' said her father, teasing her.

Gaspar de Lopez loved his daughters but he had always

yearned for a son, a boy to bring up in his own image but it was not to be. Jimena's birth had proved difficult, the doctors advised against more children and although disappointed at the lack of a son he had nevertheless lavished time and money on his daughters. From an early age, they learned to ride, to appreciate the finer points of the bullfight and to dance the Sevillana. Now in their late teens and early twenties, accomplished in all things Spanish society demanded, the time had come for Isabella, at least, to find a suitable young man to marry. To reinforce the family's place in Sevillian society he had decided upon César. The young man came from a respectable family, his father was a banker with connections and that could only improve the family's standing. However, he had no real idea how full a life eldest daughter was living.

'What about César, Isabella? He's a good catch.'

'Please, Papa, I'm not ready for marrying just yet.'

Gaspar's eyebrows rose slightly and he refrained from saying more knowing Isabella's temperament, she was one to handle carefully.

Jimena listened, aware of the pressure her father was putting on her sister. For her marriage was a more distant prospect and like her sister, she had a thirst for the freedom marriage had the habit of curtailing. Sitting back in her seat she looked across the arena, her eyes following the brightly dressed performers, the matadors, their cuadrillas, focusing finally on Francisco. She had met him briefly at the Mendoza ranch and seen him fight in Málaga and liked what she saw. He was good-looking and his style of fighting was certainly attractive. She remembered seeing him play the bull beside the river and she remembered seeing Isabella ride off with him during the *feria*. At the time it seemed no more than light-hearted frivolity but she knew how Isabella could treat men, spin them around her little finger. On its own, riding round the fair with him was nothing, but there were other moments, enough for her to suspect there was more than just a causal relationship between them. César on the other hand was well known to her and more than once she had found herself subjected to his oppressive charm. But her father had decided Isabella should marry into Sevillian society and it appeared that he was the chosen one. How would that play out, she wondered?

Francisco was the junior bullfighter and would not fight until El Cazador and César killed their first bulls and for a time his position was that of a spectator.

'His *molinete*, how quickly he turned, Paco. How graceful his *estocada*. The bull died well,' said Luis absorbed in El Cazador's fight.

'I know, Luis, his *molinete* was as good as I have seen. He knows how to play a bull with skill and passion. Look the aficionados are showing their approval.'

'I think they will award him both ears for that,' said Luis.

El Cazador bowed to the crowd cheering him and waving their white handkerchiefs as the team of mules dragged away the bull he had just slain and then he turned to the President who waved the white cloth as a sign that the bullfighter had earned his reward of the dead bull's ears.

The trumpet sounded and all heads turned to the cuadrilla's gate.

'It's César,' said Luis excitedly.

César walked forth and raised, strutting across the sandy floor to the cheers of his growing band of followers and for the next twenty minutes, he and his cuadrilla worked the powerful black bull until the inevitable end.

'He's good Paco.'

'Not that good Luis. I've told you to watch carefully how he leans into the bull, how he makes it look as if he's taking chances when he isn't. Is it just me who sees it?'

Luis did not have time to answer, it was time for their first bull and as the paso doble echoed around the bull ring Francisco proudly led out his cuadrilla for their first fight of the corrida.

Three magnificent bulls were already dead when El Cazador faced his second bull and he did not disappoint, playing the animal with consummate skill. Then it was the turn of César to face his second bull and straight backed, oozing with confidence, he strutted to the president's balcony to show his respects.

'Mister President, I wish to dedicate my next bull to the fair lady Isabella Maria Teresa García Ramírez de Lopez.'

In her seat Jimena sat up. 'Oh, did you hear that, Isabella? César is dedicating the bull to you. How exciting.'

Isabella smiled, and spread her fan gently wafting the warm air from her face. All eyes were upon her as she stood to bow her head in a gesture of acceptance and César lifted his hat in salute. It was the perfect gesture and the crowd agreed, a ripple of applause greeting him. But for Francisco it was disturbing, his emotions were running high as they always did when he was fighting but now, to see César almost steal Isabella from under his nose, he was beside himself with fury. He was in love with Isabella, of that he was sure, and had believed she felt the same, but now, as the trumpet announced César's second bull and he remembered how she had avoided him he felt the curtain of doubt descending.

The bull entered the ring as normal, trotting around and absorbing its unfamiliar surroundings until it found its way blocked by the picadors. Victor took the initiative, cantering past it, prodding it with his lance to test its resolve and for a time the second picador took to enticing the bull to charge. He skilfully turned his horse as it came at him, the horns missing by a whisker. He turned again and raced alongside the bull, stabbing it with his lance.

Francisco looked on with interest. He was not so proud to think he could not learn anything, even from a picador and as he watched it seemed to him that the bull was exceptionally aggressive and the sharp pike stabbing at its neck was making it very angry. Victor returned to the fray, guiding his horse alongside and prodding at the bull's loins with his lance, the deep incisions drawing blood and intensifying further the bull's rage and then the animal paused, apparently unsure. It turned its head towards the second picador who was approaching and without warning it charged his horse. The rider was too slow in avoiding the onslaught and the bull drove low into the horses unprotected belly, skewering it with its horns and toppling it.

The horse squealed in terror as it fell and the picador rolled clear, attempting to scramble to his feet but the bull had not finished with him and charged again. The crowd roared with excitement. This was what they had come to see, the unpredictability of the bulls, the bravery of the toreros and the danger.

It was not an uncommon outcome and Victor was alert to the danger, skilfully urging his horse forward to put it between his fellow picador and the enraged bull. Skilfully he stabbed the bull's neck, distracting it long enough to give the unseated man a chance to regain his saddle. But with his horse hurt, the pair could not carry on without risking more severe injury and he withdrew leaving Victor and the three banderillos to take care of the bull

'That was a lucky escape, Paco.'

Francisco simply nodded; his eyes set firmly on Victor whose rapid response to the dangerous situation, he had to admit, deserved some respect.

Then César appeared, walking across the fine yellow sand with an indifference that seemed at odds with the mêlée taking place. His cape hung casually from his shoulder and when he was ready to check the angry bull, he let it slip.

Victor controlled the bull, turning his horse left and right, avoiding the scything horns, coaxing it towards the centre of the bullring where César was waiting and with a sharp twist of his wrist, he made the folds of the capote rippled violently to gain the bull's attention and then he turned his back on it.

'What is he doing?'

'Showing off I think, Mano,' said Francisco. 'It's a bit early to be trying those tricks.'

César had purposely made the risky move, an offering to his followers. Turning on his heels at the last moment he presented the cape to the charging bull and to a chorus of 'Ole' he deftly side stepped. He had pulled it off but it was close, the trick had worked and he knew that in her seat, Isabella would be watching.

'Phew, that was close. That was no false move,' said Francisco believing that César was being reckless.

Isabella and her father did not see it that way. Caught up in the excitement they and Jimena joined in the chorus of 'Olé' rising to their feet to applaud.

'Did you see that, Isabella? He will soon be known as one of the best matadors of Seville, the boy has a great future.'

'Yes, Papa, he fights well. What do you think Jimena?'

'Oh yes, bravo,' she said watching César make his way to the small barrier as the second act of the got under way. The banderillos made their moves, running at the bull in spectacular fashion to plunge the colourful darts into the bull's enormous neck muscles to weaken it and then the trumpet sounded for the final act and César entered the ring in an arrogant manner. His confidence was high and his audience sensed a special performance. Roaring approval they urged him on and César responded, playing the bull to perfection, the magenta and yellow of the muleta contrasting with the black hide of the bull. He was fighting as well as he had ever fought, the knowledge that Isabella was watching driving him to risk far more than he would normally but he was getting away with it.

It would soon be Francisco's turn to take to the ring but for now, César was receiving the plaudits and Paco could not deny that he deserved them. He glanced towards Isabella to see her with her sister and father and he could not help feeling some dismay at how enthusiastically she was applauding César. soon it would be his turn and he had something to prove.

Until the third act the fight had gone as many others had before it, the picadors and the banderillos taking part in most of the action but the third act was Francisco's alone. With a determination to outshine his rival he stood purposefully at the centre of the bullring, alone, his capote hanging loose over his sword. At first, the wounded bull did not notice him until the cape fluttered and the animal's inbred instinct to charge took control. The flimsy cape was Francisco's only protection but that was how it always was and as the bull came within a smidgen of his unprotected body he span away from it and out of danger. A series of passes had the crowd cheering him and at the end he finished with a spectacular spinning of the cape and as one the crowd rose to their feet to shout for more.

Francisco had the measure of the bull and he was confident that his performance was better than that of César and like César he began to take chances. The bull was unaware of human frailty as Francisco turned it, controlled it, and bent it to his will. It had learned, in those few short minutes that the cape was not its enemy and gradually it began to change its approach.

The man, a mere fifty kilograms against its more than four hundred kilograms should be easy to kill. Although the picadors and the banderillos had done their job the weakened warrior, breathless and blood-soaked was not yet finished and with mucus streaming from its snout it eyed its antagonist. Facing it the matador, proud, resolute made ready for the final thrust of his sword, and at that moment glanced in the direction of Isabella

It happened so fast, he had taken his eye off the bull and he had paid the price. If it was not for the quick thinking of Manuel and Manolito, it could have been so much worse.

'What happened out there, Paco?' said Manuel, a puzzled expression upon his face. 'What were you thinking of?' he said as between himself and his brother they carried Francisco from the arena.

'I'm all right,' snapped Francisco, 'It's only a nick.'

'A bit more than a nick, you need stitches in that. Let's get him to the infirmary, get the doctor to have a look at him,' said Manuel.

'What caused it? He seemed to lose concentration; and looked away from the bull when he should have been watching its every move,' said José.

With a subdued Francisco supported between them José and Manuel followed Manolito and Luis reached the infirmary where the doctor was waiting for them.

'I've never seen him like this. Something isn't right,' said Luis. 'I think maybe he wasn't happy about César fighting so well. There is a rivalry building up between those two and I don't like it.'

'Leave him with me,' said the doctor once they had him on the bench.

Luis was first to leave, walking into the corridor and wanting some time to reflect he made his way out into the stock yard. He worried for his friend, nothing like this had happened before. Francisco was normally too quick and athletic for a bull to catch him but he had put himself in danger.

'Your man did not do so well, did he? '

Luis turned around to see Victor, César's bullying picador with a sneer on his face. Was he trying to cause trouble?

'What's it to do with you, go away.'

'I think your Vaquerito is not the star you all believe he is. César put on a much better show, didn't he?'

Luis turned away, upset, concerned at Francisco's unfortunate lapse of concentration did not need Victor's criticism. His comments had only added to the belief that an unpleasant rivalry was building up between the two camps.

'I don't like him, I don't like him one bit,' he muttered to himself.

At the same time Francisco was lying flat on the doctor's table, his face contorted in pain.

'You have taken quite a goring,' said the doctor as he cut away Francisco's trousers and began to clean the wound. 'It's bad but not too bad, half a dozen stitches should do it. Here, bite on this,' he said offering his patient a piece of thick leather. 'It will make it easier for you.'

Francisco wondered where he had got that idea from because the pain was almost unbearable but at least the doctor was a quick worker.

'Why are you all looking so worried, it's just a scratch,' said Francisco as Luis returned, his face pale and sombre.

'A bit more than a scratch but I'm pleased to say he will live,' said the doctor.

'Well, that's reassuring. When can I fight again?'

'You're a tough bunch you toreros, and it isn't such a

bad wound. Provided you don't move much for two or three days you could be fit enough in a couple of weeks.'

'Two weeks, I can't leave it that long; we are supposed to fight at Ayamonte next Sunday.'

'Well, it's on your own head. I think a two-week rest is better.'

'Are you sure you will be fit for next Sunday's corrida?' said Luis.

'Don't worry, I'm sure I will be healed up by then.'

Luis wasn't so sure but he wasn't the one with the injury and decided to remain quiet.

'Can you get to your feet,' said the doctor.

'I'll try,' said Francisco beginning to lever himself into an upright position.

'That hurt,' he said taking a first tentative step, 'but I think I can manage.'

'The horn has penetrated the muscle on the outside of your leg, but no major blood vessels were damaged, you were lucky.'

'It dragged you quite a way, before we could draw it off,' added Luis. 'I will tell the others to come and help you Paco.'

La Bodega Tarantino was popular with Córdoban society, and Gaspar de Lopez was especially keen to dine there after the corrida. It was a routine he followed each time he came to the city. The corrida of *la Nuestra Señora de la Salud* was an important event in the bullfighting calendar, a time when young up-and-coming matadors could show their mettle, a time for Gaspar to meet old friends, do some business. He had taken on the management of César's bullfighting career some time ago and was more than satisfied with his performance that afternoon. He expected that his business associates would be impressed too, men who controlled much of the bullfighting industry and tonight would be a chance to further the young man's career.

'For you, señor, your favourite table,' said the smartly turned-out waiter. 'I will take your food order when you are ready. Would you like some wine?'

'A bottle of your finest Rufina and some iced water,' he said as Isabella and Jimena followed, taking their seats.

'Have you girls a preference? The fish is especially good here.'

'Yes, fish is fine for me,' said Jimena picking up her menu.

'I have asked César to join us, Isabella, he will be here soon. I think it will give you a chance to get to know him better.'

'I know him well enough.'

César had arrived just a minute after them and recognised by the diners was basking in the limelight, one or two men had stood and were congratulating him on his performance and the women were all eyes.

'César, welcome, I'm glad you could join us. Please take a seat,' said Gaspar rising to greet him.

'Thank you, Isabella, Jimena, good evening,' he said taking the hand of each to kiss. 'Señor de Lopez, it is a pleasure to join you and your daughters.'

Isabella's father inclined his head, and beside him, Isabella gave a weak smile of welcome and to pour some cold water on his exuberance asked, 'do you know how Francisco is have you heard anything?'

'No, I haven't, other than that he was taken to the

infirmary. I don't think his injury was so bad, otherwise, he would not have finished the bull.'

'That was a brave thing to do considering what happened to him,' said Jimena.

'Yes, a brave thing,' said César taking the vacant seat next to Isabella. 'I missed the goring he took; I was behind the barrier with my cuadrilla and only looked up when I heard the crowd. It sounded serious by the way they reacted and that is when I went to his aid but I wasn't needed in the end, his men had got him to safety and one of the picadors was taking care of the bull.'

Jimena had witnessed the incident and was horrified to see Francisco tossed like a rag doll.

'He was lucky his men reacted so quickly. I saw it all,' she said. 'They dragged him to the barrier in no time at all while the picador kept the bull at bay.'

'I saw that too,' said her sister. 'I saw him limp back into the bullring. He was in obvious pain but he faced the bull again.'

'He deserves respect for that.' said their father. 'Now, let us order some food, I am hungry after such a busy day. I hear the langoustines are excellent César.'

'What about you, Isabella?' said César turning to her.

The return to Seville proved difficult for Francisco, the incessant lurching of the ancient carriage exacerbated an already throbbing pain. He tried to rest but no matter how he moved his body he could find only temporary relief and leaning back in his seat he closed his eyes. Why had he done it, why had he taken his eyes off the bull and why had Isabella not mentioned that she was coming to Córdoba?

For an hour he put up with the discomfort, drifting between the pain in his leg and a growing pain in his breast as he probed everything that had happened for answers. He knew that he was at fault for losing concentration, for looking for her when he should have concentrated solely on the bull and through it all he could almost see Isabella laughing at him for being so stupid.

'We are here, Seville Paco?' said Luis shaking him out of his melancholy. 'What are you going to do?'

'Nothing much, I could do with a strong coffee to help reduce this bloody throbbing.'

'Me too, let's find a bar.'

Francisco stared into the almost hypnotic blackness of his coffee, his thoughts still bouncing back and forth.

'How's the leg,' asked Manolito taking the seat opposite.

'Er... mano, hi... better.'

'Should you really be fighting at the weekend?'

'I will make sure I can fight. Why, don't you think I am up to it?'

'I didn't say that. I am just looking out for you, Paco, we all are. You were out of sorts, that is all, but the bull gored you pretty badly.'

'I don't feel so bad, I'm healing already.'

'Get me a coffee, black,' Manolito called to the waiter.

'I hear we might be fighting in Madrid next season. Is it true?' asked Luis.

'Could be. Santiago is already negotiating fights for us for next season; he has mentioned Madrid and Barcelona.'

'What good is that if you are disabled by going back in

the ring too soon,' said Manolito. Get serious about this weekend Paco, do not fight if you are not fully fit. If you aggravate the injury and make it worse you can forget Madrid or anywhere else for that matter.'

Francisco did not answer, next season was too far away for him to consider seriously and he was brooding over his poor performance rather than worrying about his injury.

'I'll be fine. Trust me.'

Luis and Manolito looked at each other and said nothing.

'What time is it, Mano?'

'Half past eleven.'

'Right, I must go. I'll see you and the rest of the boys later in the week.'

Luis looked at Francisco, he felt pushed aside and was concerned at his friend's uncharacteristic mood until it dawned upon him, he may have unwittingly unlocked the puzzle of the mood change. He had sensed something on the train back to Seville, watched Francisco from the corner of his eye and he had cast his mind back to the moment the bull had caught him. He had looked away at a critical moment? Why had he had taken more risks than usual and why did he look away at the worst possible time?

For three days, Francisco stayed in his rented room, leaving only to buy food at the small bar just along the street and during that time his wound began to heal but his broken heart did not. He could not get Isabella out of his mind no matter how hard he tried, lying on his bed he tried to understand why she was rejecting him.

By the middle of the week, he felt ready to properly test his leg, make sure he could cope because he was more determined than ever to fight in the corrida at Ayamonte. If he could not win Isabella through status and money then he would do it by becoming the most famous bullfighter in Seville. No, more than that, the whole of Spain he told himself and decided that now was the time to properly test his leg.

Walking at a steady pace, he explored his leg, the stiffness was wearing off and he hoped that it would hold up for the corrida. Gradually he increased his pace, striding through the narrow streets on what was a beautiful warm day with a clear blue sky. He was feeling good, perhaps a walk along the riverbank would be nice, take coffee outside a little café he knew and watch the barges on the canal. And there was Isabella. What was he to do about her?

The thought occupied him for a while and eventually he reached the bridge leading to Triana and the sound of military music filling the air. Inquisitive and increasingly pain free he walked towards a circular tent with a proud Spanish flag flying from its conical roof and a military band playing to an audience of passers-by and in front of the tent stood two officers resplendent in their uniforms.

'What's going on?' Francisco asked an elderly man standing to one side.

'Recruiting, they have come to recruit for the army of Africa.'

'Africa?'

'Yes, haven't you heard? There is fighting in Morocco. The tribes are rebelling.'

'Oh yes, I had heard something.'

'Now then, young man, how would you like to join this man's army? We are recruiting all week,' said one of the soldiers spotting his approach. 'You look as if you could do with a regular job with regular pay. You will get to see some of the world if you join up. Come with me and I will explain everything, you can sign up right away and we'll make a man of you.'

'The army? I don't think so, I have work.'

'Well never mind, perhaps not this time but remember, if you ever come upon hard times there is always a job for you in the army.'

Francisco thanked him and remained for a time listening to the band before deciding finally that he had had enough and continued his walk. He was near the stables and decided to make a detour. He had no idea whether he might find Isabella there and if he did what he might say but a force seemed to be propelling him in that direction.

'Paco, what are you doing here?' said a woman's voice from behind him and spinning round he was surprised to see Jimena.

'I thought I might see Isabella.'

'She's not here, she is out riding with César.'

César! Francisco's heart seemed to stop in mid-beat.

'Are you all right, Paco, you don't seem too well. Is your wound hurting you? I saw what happened, I'm sorry.'

'Oh really, that is nice. I thought I might see Isabella,' he said feeling disappointed

'No, she isn't. Is there something you want to tell her, perhaps if you tell me, I can pass it on?'

'I... I just wanted to talk to her, she was at the corrida, I didn't know.'

Jimena raised her hand.

'You are upset, Paco; I can see that, I know about you and my sister, it's no secret to me. I know you have been seeing each other and I can see now that you are jealous of César.'

'What... no I'm not jealous of that cheat.'

'Cheat! That's a bit strong, isn't it?'

'Not if you had seen what I saw.'

'What do you mean?'

'He cheats, that's all I will say.'

'That's a serious thing to say, Paco. Are you sure?'

'Look I have said too much already. Things go on under the surface in bullfighting. Let us just say I have seen things that perhaps I really should leave alone. Forget what I said... please.'

Jimena's expression of compassion looked genuine enough but she was amusing herself by tormenting him.

'I thought you knew about César and Isabella. She will marry him you know. I am sorry, Paco, but you must see the logic. César comes from a good family; his father is a powerful banker and Papa can help make him famous. He will be a good catch for my sister. You can't compete with that, the best thing you can do is forget her.'

Francisco was crestfallen as the logic of Jimena's words hit home. What of his career, where was that going after his disastrous performance in Córdoba?
He felt that the whole world had suddenly turned against him.

'Listen, that could be them returning from their ride.'

Francisco turned towards the road and caught sight of Isabella and César riding towards the stables. He felt he had no choice but to face them and stood square in front of her horse.

'Oh, Paco, what are you doing here?'

'I came to see you. We need to talk.'

'Talk? I... I...'

'She doesn't want to talk to you, leave her alone,' said César pulling up his horse.

'This is nothing to do with you. Isabella, I want to know what is going on?'

'I said leave her.'

'César you might think you are the greatest torero in all of Spain but to me, you are nothing more than a lapdog. I saw the horns of your bulls. You are not the brave matador you want everyone to believe.'

'Liar,' shouted César raising his riding whip.

'Come on; let's see what you are really made of,' said an angry Francisco.

Before César could dismount Isabella let out a scream.

'No, no fighting. Stay on your horse, César.

Jimena heard her sister and came running to find Francisco facing César's and his horse with clenched fists.

'Come on if you think you can beat me,' said Francisco beginning to circle.

'Stop it, both of you,' said Jimena taking the initiative and stepping in front of Francisco 'César, back off and you, Paco, come with me and calm down. Can you not see that whatever it was you thought you had with my sister is over? Move on, she does not want to talk with you right now and who can blame her. Come on, away from here,' she said, glowering up at her sister.

Francisco felt caught in a dilemma. On one hand, Jimena was trying to pull him away and on the other

César ready was to fight him.

'Come on, Paco, it's best if you go. She has done it before more than once. You are not the first beau she has scorned. She is not worth it. I know she is my sister and I love her dearly but she is with men as a cat is playing with mice. Take my advice, Paco, forget her, find someone else and concentrate on your career in the bullring for I know that one day you will make a great torero.'

Francisco hardly heard her. Distraught and humiliated there was little more he could do than leave and without looking back, he strode towards the river. Confused and hurt, his mind was in a whirl. Why was Isabella so negative towards him, why would she not even speak to him? And that César, well he could kill him, that was for sure.

Half an hour later he was still brooding when a familiar voice broke into his thoughts.

'Hey, Paco, Paco, wait.'

Turning, he saw Luis hurrying towards him in his own inimitable way.

'Didn't you hear me?'

'What, no, why?'

'I want to know about your wound, are we still going to Ayamonte, can you fight?'

'Questions, questions, nothing but questions, Luis. Yes, I will fight at Ayamonte.'

'Your wound is healing?'

'Sort of, it's not so stiff now and the pain has gone.'

'Good, we were worried about you.'

'No need to worry about me, Luis.'

Luis was not so sure. Francisco's eyes were not as

bright as usual and his face had a pallor he had not seen before.

'Are you sure you are all right, you seem a bit vacant?'

'Vacant!' snapped Francisco.

'I'm sorry, I didn't mean to offend you. Come on let me buy you a coffee, and something to eat, you look half starved. You can tell me of your plans for Ayamonte.'

If nothing else Luis was a therapist. Well, of sorts, chatting incessantly, deflecting Francisco's mind away from his immediate discomfort and calming him.

'Did you see the soldiers by the bridge? I could hear the band from miles away, which is why I am here. I wish I could play the trumpet.'

'Ha, ha, you are a comic, Luis. Why would you want to play the trumpet? You can't even march like a soldier.'

Luis's eyes changed, a hint of sorrow in them leaving Francisco feeling uncomfortable.

'I'm sorry, Luis, I didn't mean anything by that. Hey, you and I are alike now; look I can't walk straight after the goring I took in Córdoba.' And as if to demonstrate the point he hobbled along beside him.

'Your wound will get better, mine will not.'

'Aw, I really am sorry, Luis, come on let's find a bar and have that coffee you promised. How is my sword by the way? I hope you are looking after it properly?'

'I polish it every day.'

Francisco put his arm over Luis's shoulder.

'You are a good *mozo de espada*, the best, Luis. You march with dignity in the bullring my friend; you are truly a part of the cuadrilla.'

César was annoyed with Isabella, the look on her face left

him wondering if she still had a fondness for Francisco and decided he must act.

'That lowlife we have just chased away, I don't want you seeing him ever again. I will speak with your father to make sure we never fight at the same corrida again so you will have no excuse.'

Isabella's eyes flashed angrily. It was true she did feel something for Francisco, but apart from his success in the bullring, he had nothing much else to offer her. She was approaching marriageable age and it was a man's ability to give her the life she expected that mattered most to her. Francisco was still nothing more than an aspiring matador. Her father understood this well, suggesting she choose César and for her to go against his wishes would be, in the end, unthinkable.

'Isabella, are you listening to me?'

'Yes,' she answered, avoiding his eyes. 'I will do as you say, Francisco means nothing to me.'

César grinned and reached out to kiss her cheek, satisfied that she was bending to his will. Francisco though was another matter, a threat to his plans if he remained a bullfighter. He needed to deal with him.

Francisco was unaware of the danger César posed. Perhaps if he could see Isabella alone then he might convince her to come back to him and re-live the exciting times they had shared. It seemed a real possibility until the quiet voice of reason advised him that it was not possible. A product of the poorest of Seville's barrios, he had come to realise that he was out of his depth. To Isabella he was simply a plaything and that made him angry and his anger transferred itself into a loud thump on the table.

'Are you alright? Do you want a drink, Paco; you look a bit funny.'

'Funny! What do you mean?'

'Look, you are my best friend. We've known each other a long time and something is wrong. What is bothering you, you haven't been yourself ever since we got back from Córdoba?'

'Oh, nothing I can't handle.'

'So, there is something. Is it your leg, do you think you will not be able to fight on Sunday?'

'No, not that.'

'What then?'

'I don't want to talk about it.'

You've got woman trouble, haven't you?'

Francisco stiffened, his eyes focused on some distant nothingness and Luis's words struck his heart like an arrow.

'It's that stuck-up bitch from San Vicente, isn't it?'

'How do you know about her?'

'Come on, Paco, we all know about the wonderful Isabella. She's a good-looker, I'll give you that.'

Francisco looked crestfallen and now it was Luis's turn to console *him*.

'Hey, I didn't know it was so serious.'

'How did you know about us?'

'Easy, you were seen sneaking back to our lodgings in Málaga and once Manolito saw her leaving your lodgings. Luque knows too, he said she used to ride around the estate where you worked and that you had gone off with her at the *feria*.'

'*Madre de Dios*, is nothing sacred? Yes, I suppose I

have woman trouble.'

'Do you want to talk about it?'

'No.'

An awkward silence descended, Francisco peered into his half empty glass and Luis stared out of the window.

'Come on, my friend; let's go home, I've had enough for today.'

'Home, you mean your real home, Triana?'

'Yes, I haven't seen my family for a while. It might do me good.'

'I am sure it will,' said Luis grinning, happy that his friend's dark mood was beginning to lift and as they made their way towards the bridge their conversation turned to bulls.

'The Miura you fought, the one that gored you, it was some animal, Paco, those horns were as dangerous as I have ever seen.'

Francisco did not need reminding and was about to tell Luis so when there was an interruption to their conversation.

'Francisco Martinez, well, well, we meet again.'

Surprised, Francisco turned to see César and his picador Victor together with a third man.

'I want a word with you. This afternoon was only the start, now it's time to give you a proper warning.'

'What do you want?' said Francisco. 'Don't be throwing your weight around here you jumped-up prick. I would have given you a good hiding earlier if it wasn't for Jimena.'

That was the catalyst, Victor was first, running across the narrow street and landing a blow on Francisco's shoulder, knocking him into a doorway. Francisco tried to fight back but when César joined him, landing several blows to his face and abdomen he fell to the ground gasping for breath.

'Let this be a warning, my friend,' said César as Victor grabbed hold of Luis and pinned him against the wall. Then a knife appeared in the hand of the third man and holding it at the throat of a fearful Luis, César gave his final warning.

'I'm sure you don't want your friend here to have an accident but be warned, if I see you hanging around or even speaking to Isabella then your crippled friend will never walk again and you will never fight another bull.'

'Leave him alone, you bastards,' Francisco managed to say through swelling lips. 'If you want to hurt anyone then you can try me.'

'Ha, you can hardly stand up. No, just remember what will happen if you so much as look at Isabella again. Leave them, come on boys.'

Luis was shaking uncontrollably as he slid from Victor's grasp and as if to reinforce the warning Victor gave him a vicious jab in his ribs leaving him sobbing with fear. Francisco felt around his mouth for damage to his teeth as hewatched their assailants walk away. There was nothing he could do except console Luis and vow that one day he would get even.

Francisco had wiped most of the blood from his face by the time he stepped into his mother's house and from her initial look of pleasure at seeing him her face changed to one of concern.

'What happened, you look terrible Francisco.'
'Some trouble with robbers. It's nothing, Mama, but

they hurt Luis, he became too frightened to leave on his own so I helped him home. Can I stay here tonight?'

Before his mother could answer his sisters appeared, alerted by the sound of the door.

'Paco, your face, what happened?' asked Juanita.

'He's been attacked by thieves,' said her mother.

'I will fetch a bowl of water, we need to clean the blood from his face,' said Maria, dashing away.

'Of course, you can sleep here tonight, there is always a bed here. You know that.'

'Thank you, Mama,' he said, lowering his weary body onto a chair. 'I'm fine, it hurts a bit but nothing is broken, I will heal. Look, I heal quickly,' he said pointing to his thigh.

'What?'

'I was gored last weekend in Córdoba.'

'Oh, Francisco, I have been expecting something like that. All the bullfighters I know of finish with an injury. You were lucky I think.'

'What's that about a goring, Paco?' said Maria returning with the bowl of water. 'I did hear that you had an accident last weekend. Are you all right, can I clean that wound?'

'No, stop fussing, sister, my leg is healing well enough, just attend to my face please.'

The three women fell silent and Maria began to dab Francisco's face, his mother and sister anxiously looking on.

'Your hair is matted with blood; it might be easier just to cut it off.'

'Do what you want, I don't really care.'

'Paco, that's not like you. They must have shocked you,

those robbers. Did they steal much?'

'Nothing, it was a warning.'

'A warning?' said his mother, her eyes narrowing.

'I don't want to talk about it.'

'It might help if you did. Now, are you hungry? We have some bread, cheese, and a little olive oil. Fetch him something to eat, Juanita. I think there is some sausage as well, left over from dinner. You must eat, son; you must keep up your strength.'

'Thanks,' said Francisco, puffing out his cheeks.

'Perhaps after a good night's sleep, you will feel better. First, though, you need to eat. Bring him some wine Juanita.'

'Where is Juan?' Francisco managed to ask in between his sister's none too gentle swipes with the wet cloth.

'I don't know. Your brother comes and goes. At least he is working,' she paused, 'I think.'

'There, that's better but there is swelling and a lot of bruising,' said Maria, admiring her handiwork. 'Does it hurt, Paco?'

'Of course, it hurts.'

'We hear a lot about you, Francisco, you are becoming famous,' said his mother.

'I am not so famous now, Mama.'

'Why, has something happened?'

'I think I am losing my touch. I made a mistake in Córdoba. If I don't do better in Ayamonte in two days, I could well be out of a job.'

'But you will do better, brother,' said Juanita, coming to his rescue. 'I have heard that you are one of the best new toreros in all of Andalusia and I know that you are a fighter. Don't give up just yet, we have not had the chance to come and see you fight the bulls.'

'Thank you, sister, thank you for your support.'

Exhaustion may have been the root cause but more likely, being at home with his family, relaxed and feeling safe caused Francisco to sleep for so long on the simple straw mattress on the floor of his mother's room. He slept all through the hours of darkness, his mother watching over him and when the dawn broke, she quietly left him to wake her daughters.

'We should leave him alone until he wakes naturally, girls, why don't we go for a walk down by the river as we used to do with your father, let him sleep in peace?'

The girls dressed quickly, joined their mother, and the three of them walked together through the narrow streets.

'He seemed in better spirits when he lay down to sleep. He mixes with some strange people these days.'

'No stranger than half of Triana, Mama,' said Juanita.

'I suppose not but you hear all sorts of stories about the bullfighters. There is too much money, everyone wants it.'

'Do you think Paco is rich now, Mama?' said Maria.

'Not really, I think he earns a lot of pesetas every time he fights but he told me months ago that most of it goes on paying his cuadrilla and now that they fight in the bigger cities, he has hotel bills to pay. I don't think there is so much left for him, but he is a lot better off than working on the estate and he is generous towards us.'

'Oh, I thought he was becoming very rich like Belmonte and the other famous bullfighters.'

'Maybe one day, Maria, but not yet I think.'

Chatting as they walked, they discussed what

Francisco, storing up questions for their return. However, when Francisco finally rose from his mattress, he was in no mood for conversation. The deep, undisturbed sleep had freed his subconscious and allowed it to roam and when he finally opened his eyes, he knew what he had to do.

Chapter 15

At first, I found it difficult to account for my actions in any reasonable way but the nurse, Isabella, was understanding, her soft, kind eyes never leaving mine as I related the train of events that had led me to this point.

'I never meant to hurt my family nor let my friends down but the weight of responsibility proved too much I believe. I could not leave Luis to the mercy of those thugs. He was scared you know. I told you he has a disability, his leg, deformed at birth; it left him especially vulnerable. He has been my friend ever since I can remember and I somehow feel a responsibility towards him.'

'Those thugs, the ones who beat you up, do you know who were they?'

'They were from a rival cuadrilla, César's. He is a year or two older than I am. He was fighting in corridas before I started and I would see him at times on the ganadería where I worked. He was always full of himself.'

'Why would he attack you, was it rivalry in the ring?'

'Yes, I'm sure of that. He is a good enough torero but he cheats and I don't like that.'

'Cheats?'

'Cutting back the horns, making sure he draws the less aggressive bulls, stuff like that. I've seen it.'

I was expressing feelings I had kept hidden for years

and now I was finally telling someone. The mixture of relief and anxiety made me feel hot, sweat began to trickle into my eyes and I had to stop talking. I knew of plenty of soldiers who kept secrets, men who had done bad things, men who had run away just as I had but, in the regiment, we never enquired, always we respected the other soldiers' feelings.

'Are you all right, Paco, you have gone quiet, you seem upset? Go on, tell me more if you feel up to it, if not then we could walk a little further until you do want to talk again. It's an interesting story, you must have enjoyed your life as a bullfighter?'

I did not know what to say, how to describe the feeling of standing alone in the bullring with five hundred kilograms of angry flesh and bone bearing down on me. It was really all about earning a living and doing what I wanted to do and temporarily I felt lost for words until Isabella led me through the garden. We passed other soldiers, some covered in bandages, missing an arm or a leg and it occurred to me that I should thank my lucky stars that I had come off so lightly.

'Look at the sea, Paco, isn't it beautiful, so blue. I did not see the sea until I set sail for Morocco. I expect you didn't see much of the sea living in Seville?'

'No, the first time I saw it was when I fought in Málaga.'

I remembered Málaga only too well, Isabella, the night of passion and suddenly the sadness came over me.'

'Are you okay, you seem lost?'

'Er... I'm fine.'

'Come on, you can tell me what's bothering you, it's

part of the healing process. Some of the soldiers here have experienced traumas that a civilian would not believe. We talk to them; it helps them recover. It is not always just the physical injuries we have to heal you know.'

She was getting to me, involuntarily I was opening my heart, I couldn't help it.

'Is that woman, Isabella, your problem, was she the real reason you joined up?'

I could feel the dam beginning to give way, all those inner thoughts, those secret thoughts pushing hard against the imaginary barrier. Of course, it was true.

'It's something I do not want to talk about.'

'It might help if you do. What was she like, did she treat you badly? Was the beating you took something to do with her?'

Christ, why do you have to have the same name and how come you are so perceptive?'

'To answer your question, I read a lot, especially poetry. I like the works of Gustavo Adolfo Bécquer, his legends, sensitive works that make you think. You should read some of his stuff, maybe there is a softer side to you.'

To tell me I had a softer side was a shock. 'I read a little,' I said with some embarrassment.

I had hardly read anything, and to my relief she let the subject drop.

'I cannot stay much longer, Paco. We have new patients coming to the hospital this afternoon and I need to prepare the beds. Yours will be free soon, I think. You must be excited at going home. Can you make your way back to the ward or do you want me to come with you?'

'I'll be fine, I will sit on that bench over there for a while, watch the sea; maybe you can tell me about your poet tomorrow.'

She smiled a warm, protective sort of smile but if I thought that I was special then I only had to look around and see how she treated the other patients. On reflection, that must have been the time when I was really on the mend. I was starting to feel bored, thinking of home and what it would be like to return after so long. I had suppressed my feelings during my time in Morocco, my overriding wish was simply to stay alive. The memory of Isabella and the hurt I felt had slipped down my list of priorities but now I was going home I had time to reflect

Could I really pick up my life where I had left off? The voice of reason told me it seemed unlikely because from my recent experiences I had learned how unpredictable life's journey could be. Perhaps a fresh start should be my aim, but that posed more questions than it answered. I took a seat looking out over the waters of the Mediterranean, the mountains of home sitting darkly above the azure sea away in the distance. What would happen to me?

'Hey, Paco, Paco, it is me, Vicente.'

Snapping out of my melancholy mood I turned to see a comrade from the platoon.

'Vicente, what are you doing here? You look to be in one piece.'

'I am, I am just passing through. I came this morning with some of our wounded. Guard duty.'

'So, where did you come from? Last I heard the regiment was still in Tetuán.'

'It was until yesterday. We attacked a place called Ainyir. It was a hard fight, a few men of the bandera killed and about thirty wounded, some of them I helped escort here, to the hospital.'

'How's it going, the war?'

'It is certainly better than for some time. If I am reading the situation correctly, I think we are just mopping up now. What the future brings is anybody's guess.'

'Of course.'

'Where will you be going once you leave here Paco? A civilian if my guess is correct?'

'Yes, I have my discharge papers and they have told me I will be going home as soon as the doctor signs me off.'

'Lucky you. Did you hear Fernán died?'

'No, when? He was with us when I took the bullet. What happened?'

'We were sent out to relieve one of the blockhouses to the southwest. As usual, the bastards were waiting for us and we had a time of it throwing them off but we did. We killed a lot of them but we had our own casualties and unfortunately Fernán was one of them.

'I'm sorry. How is everyone else?'

'A couple with minor wounds, but you don't want to be worrying about us, you'll be a free man soon, Paco.'

'Yes,' I said, a twinge of guilt at leaving friends and comrades behind.

Vicente did not stay long; his mission was complete and his orders were to return to the regiment as quickly as possible. Like Huberto, and now Fernán, I would never see him again, a sad parting.

The following morning Nurse Isabella appeared on the ward earlier than normal, her smile a tonic to us all.

'I have news for you, Paco; the doctor will sign you off

when he does his rounds and tomorrow you can leave us. Isn't that good news?'

On the face of it, I suppose that it was good news but it brought my immediate future into sharp focus; what awaited me at home, could I earn a living? I had no idea but the one thing I expected I could not do was to return to the bullring. I had let Santiago and my cuadrilla down, and no doubt my last performance marked me as a failure in many people's minds.

'One last walk, Paco?'

'Yes, I would like that,' I said.

'I think the army has arranged passage for you on the next ship sailing for Cadiz. The hospital can arrange transport for you to the docks.'

I remember looking into her eyes, blue, unlike the deep brown eyes of the Andalusian girls, and I felt a pang of regret. For six weeks she had nursed me, helped me recuperate, mentally as well as physically. Nurse Isabella had begun a process that my troubled mind would have to complete alone.

'Come on then, let us make a circuit of the garden, I can't stop too long, we have more casualties arriving soon and I must help but I can spend half an hour or so with you.'

'You will not get into trouble, will you? I know you spend a lot of time with me. I feel that I am monopolising you.'

She lowered her eyes and, as the beginnings of a blush began to show on her face, she looked away.

'I told you it is all part of the healing process. You have not monopolised me so stop worrying. Now, have you thought what you will do when you get home,' she said.

'Will you become that famous torero you told me about?'

Now it was my turn to blush.

'I don't think so. After my last performance nobody will touch me, and I left my friends in the lurch. I let them down, they relied upon me for their living and I let them down.'

'Tell me about that last morning, what was your motivation to just walk out on what seemed a successful life as a bullfighter? Every boy growing up in Spain would gladly swap places with you for that chance and yet you threw it away.'

'I felt that I had lost my touch, that last fight in Córdoba really knocked me back and then Luis. I couldn't leave him to worry about César and his henchmen, I don't even know if I can face a bull again.'

'Nonsense, be positive, Paco. Isabella was your motivation and you have told me about your rivalry with César, it had nothing to do with bulls and being in the bullring but more to do with people, people who have done you wrong.'

'I was second best?'

'I'm sorry, I... I meant that you were being pushed aside, that must have hurt.'

'It did,' I sighed.

'Well, it's all in the past; you must not dwell, pastures new beckon. Look forward, be positive.'

'You like that phrase, don't you?'

'Yes, my mother always told me that. As a woman, you do not get the same chances in life as the men and my mother said I should get over those disappointments, be positive, find new opportunities.'

'She sounds a wise woman, your mother.'

'Yes, she was.'

'Was?'

'She died two years ago, tuberculosis, that's why I decided to become a nurse.'

'You're a bloody saint, do you know that?'

This time there was no hiding her blushes and reaching out she squeezed my forearm.

'Thank you for that, Paco, but you know every one of the doctors and nurses in this hospital deserves that honour.'

'I know.'

I was feeling good, as well as I could remember, and then my world seemed to tumble down.

'I have to go, there is Nurse García. She said she would let me know when the ambulances arrived and it looks as if they have. I think it must be goodbye, Paco, you are leaving us and I will not be able to see you again. Good luck and remember, be positive. I will look out for your name on the posters.'

I lifted my hand in a weak salute and I swear she had a tear in her eye as she turned away.

The ship sailed across the straits full of returning soldiers, some at the end of their service, some going on leave and amongst them a reminder of what we had sacrificed. Several amputees lined a part of the deck, their wheelchairs arranged in a neat row. Kitbags piled high on the deck waited patiently as their owners smoked and chatted and I was alone. I felt that I could not easily mix and so I found a secluded place to watch Spain grow into something more than just a hazy shape on the horizon. I was going home and running through me were mixed emotions of excitement and joy yet I was apprehensive returning home after such a long absence. I had no more than a second-hand canvas bag and three hundred pesetas to show for my years fighting for Spain, that, and a whole lot of memories both sad and happy ones and my connection with Morocco finally broke when I planted my feet on the quayside of Algeciras.

I did not look back, instead, I strode towards the railway station with Isabella's words ringing in my ears. She had told me to be positive and I had determined to be so and sitting back in my seat on the train I looked forward to returning home, to see the olive groves, the flowering Amapolas, and with my nose pressed up against the window I watched the Andalusian countryside speed past. As we neared Seville the green pastures I knew so well appeared and there they were, the black shapes of the fighting bulls, and I truly felt I was home.

Chapter 16

I walked into the tiny house unannounced. My mother was sitting at the table about to begin her evening meal and for some stupid reason I had believed that to surprise her with my homecoming would make her happy. I was wrong. Almost as soon as she saw me her face, that had at first registered shock, soon turned to one of anger.

'Francisco Martinez, what are you trying to do to me? I almost had heart failure,' she said, her gypsy eyes flashing a warning signal.

I had seen that look many times during my years growing up and I knew what to expect. I knew that she loved me, but that still would not stop her.

'You disappear without so much as a goodbye, I hear nothing for years, and here you are as if nothing has happened. I could kill you,' she said, reaching down to remove her shoe and I prepared to dodge out of its way. My reactions were good as I avoided the shoe slamming into the wall just a few centimetres from my face.

'Your aim isn't so good these days, Mama,' I said in a forlorn attempt to make light of the situation.

'Cheeky dog, my aim as good as I decide it to be. Where have you been all this time? If your father were alive, he would beat you good and hard for putting me through such torment. After more than three years I finally receive a letter from you; a letter that arrived only yesterday.'

'I know, Mama, I'm sorry. At least I had a couple of letters from Juanita so I knew you were all safe. I am hungry, is there anything to eat? I have a few pesetas if you need to buy food.'

'There is some bread,' she said, not particularly interested in feeding me, instead she held out her arms, her temper checked for the moment, and I went to hug her. 'Oh, Francisco, I have been so worried, I hear stories about the fighting in Morocco, your sister sometimes reads the newspaper for me. But you are here now.'

She let me go and pushed me away to cast her eyes over me, the dark, expressive orbs devouring me.

'You look well; do you have to go back?'

'No, Mama, I have been invalided out of the army, I do not have to return to Morocco ever again.'

Her eyes lit up and she hugged me again, tears rolling down her cheeks and she let me go.

'Where are Maria and Juanita and is Juan working, what does he do?'

'Maria works at the bank, she's a clever girl, and Juanita is married.'

'I know, José, Juanita, she told me in her letter.'

'She has a baby girl.'

'I didn't know that, she must be pleased, it's what women want isn't it, a baby.'

'Typical man, not all women want babies you know. Anyway, they seem happy enough but José cannot hold down a job for long. His excuse is that the only job he ever wanted was to be a banderillo.'

'That's my fault, I suppose?'

'You did your best for all of them.'

'What about my brother?'

'He's gone to live in Cadiz. He works on the docks unloading the ships. It's good money and he seems to like it there. I hope he can hold the job down this time.'

'So, it is just you and Maria living here now.'

'Yes, just the two of us. She has a part-time boyfriend but I do not see much of him. I think your sister is what they call a career girl, she prefers work to marriage. The way she carries on I can't see any signs of grandchildren either.'

I had no answer; in over three years their world was bound to change. Mine had for sure.

'Can I stay here for a while, until I decide what I am to do?'

'Of course, you can sleep in the girls' room; Maria can double up with me. Now, what about a glass of wine, would you like one? You can sit over there in your father's chair and tell me all about yourself since you ran away.'

'Ran away? You think I ran away?'

'Yes, from those thugs, and I have learned about that fancy woman of yours, the one that caused all the trouble.'

I felt humbled, how did my mother know about Isabella?

'You will be surprised what I know young Francisco. Not much gets past me where you are concerned. Listen, that will be Maria.

I turned to the door and seconds later my youngest sister walked in.

'Francisco, Francisco you are not dead.'

'What made you think that?' I asked in surprise.

'So many have died over there, so many that I thought

it would happen to you some time.'

'Don't be silly, here, give me a hug.'

Dropping her bag she took two steps towards me and threw her arms around my neck, hugged me tight planting kisses all over my face with such ferocity that I had to tell her to stop.

'I can't stop kissing you, Paco, I am so happy to see you,' she said starting again.

'Get off me, you are like those monkeys in Morocco that used to plague us.'

Finally, she relented and unhappy at the comparison to a monkey took a place sitting at my feet and her big brown eyes never left me for one second.

'Was it as bad as they say? I hear stories at work, I know families who have lost sons over there. I hear the tribesmen are mad.'

'Not mad exactly, uncontrollable, bloodthirsty, and very dangerous if they have a knife in their hand.'

'Have you killed many of them?'

Her words caught me by surprise, she was asking me to re-live memories I preferred to forget and my expression must have betrayed my thoughts. Mama noticed and lifted the bottle of wine.

'Let me refill your glass. Maria, he hasn't eaten yet, go and see what you can find for your brother.'

On the previous occasion I had slept at home I had woken up troubled, with only one thought on my mind and that thought had changed my life. This time was different, this time I was going nowhere.

'Ah, Francisco, you are awake,' said my mother as I walked into the tiny yard to the smell of freshly baked bread.

'I had almost forgotten about your bread. Can I have some?'

'Soon, it needs a little longer,'

'Where's Maria?'

'She's gone to work; she leaves early every morning to catch the tram. What are you going to do today?'

I had no plans, just being back home and seeing my family was enough for the time being.

'Where do Juanita and José live now?' I asked.

'Just off San Jacinto, behind the church. They rent two rooms.'

'I will look them up.'

'I'm sure Juanita will be just as pleased to see you as Maria. Here, this bread is done; there is some olive oil on the table.'

The bread was delicious, just as I remembered, very different from the offerings of the army cooks, and after washing it down with some coffee I pumped some water into a bucket to wash. I still felt a little groggy from my sleep but the cool water brought me back to life as I set off to find Juanita.

'Paco, what a surprise,' she said when she opened the door, her new baby cradled in her arm. 'When did you get back? We only received your letter a few days ago.'

'Yesterday, I sailed from Ceuta and then I caught the train from Algeciras. It's surprised me how quickly I could move from one world to another.'

'That's rather philosophical for you. Where did you learn to speak like that?'

'Oh, I learned a lot in the army.'

'It's so good to see you home safe, Paco. Are you still in

the army?'

'No, not any more, I have had a medical discharge.'

'You don't look disabled.'

'I took a bullet that broke a few bones but I'm well on the mend now.'

'You have had it rough by the sound of it but at least you survived. I know a lot of our boys were not so lucky.'

'Your baby is beautiful, she looks like you and I suppose there must be some of José in her too,' I said changing the subject.

'His nose, look.'

'Where is José, where does he work?'

'He's a porter in the market. It is a job I suppose but it does not pay much. He still talks about the cuadrilla, the times you had together and of course the money. You were good to them all, Paco, it's a pity those times have gone.'

Yes, they had gone but I was beginning to view the past from a very different perspective. I might have felt hard done by at times but I did not feel sorry for myself and the short time living at home again had shown me just how important my family was for my sanity. Whenever I had found myself either in trouble or debt Juanita had come to my rescue, an adult way before her time and she had a sensible head on her shoulders.

She invited me into her home, made some tea and we talked. She wanted to know everything that had happened to me and as we conversed memories resurfaced. I remembered the times when she would talk to me, try to explain where I was going wrong, keep me on the straight and narrow, and to a large extent she did. But she had another quality, she could read my mind. It was uncanny.

Even from a young age she seemed to know instinctively what I was thinking, always one step ahead of me, saving me before I had even begun to fall, and maybe that attribute still lingered.

'You have had a hard time, Paco, haven't you? I can see in your face how you have matured. I know about Isabella, we all do. She treated you abominably I hear and it is rumoured that she was the one to drive you away.'

The look in my eye must have given me away.

'I am sorry if I've offended you but isn't it history now Paco? A lot of water has flowed under your bridge these past three years, you have seen things no one should have to but you have come out stronger, I can tell.' Her gaze did not waver until the baby began to whimper. 'It's time for her feed. Pass me that shawl and I will spare your blushes.'

I reached out and gave her the shawl and within seconds the tender noise of the baby settling into her feeding routine was the only sound. I looked at Juanita, the mother she had become and she looked back at me with a twinkle in her eyes. It was captivating and I could not help but feel happy for her.

'I can see there is nothing fundamentally wrong with you brother, for all your trials and tribulations you are still the carefree Francisco I know and love. Now you are back home, have you any plans?'

'Not really, I suppose I will have to find work of some sort.'

'What sort of work can you do, what are your skills?

I suddenly felt cornered. I had no skills other than those of a vaquero or perhaps a soldier.

'You are going to fight bulls again, aren't you?'

I do not really know why because I did not deserve it but my friends were still my friends. My old cuadrilla came to see me one by one and we talked of the old times when we fought together in the ring and I could feel the old ambition resurfacing as we talked, laughed, and stood with our imaginary capes fighting imaginary bulls. Perhaps the most important person in my rehabilitation was Luis, always in tune with my mood and one day, out of the blue, he looked me in the eye.

'You have to go and see him, Paco. You still do not have a job and how long will your money last? In my opinion, you are a wasted talent.'

His words stung, but he was right. But how was I to convince Santiago to give me a second chance?

'We should go to his office, see him, and you can explain why you left in the first place. I'm sure he will understand.'

I felt embarrassed; to have to tell one of the most influential bullfighting impresarios in Andalusia that I had run away because of a woman might prove too much for me.

'Let's go today, after siesta when he is probably at his most receptive.'

'What makes you say that?'

'Papa. Mama always twists him around her little finger after siesta. She says that is when he most pliable and I bet Señor Moncada Sánchez is just the same.'

'I can't fault your logic, Luis,' I said scratching my head.

The elegant interior of the building at the heart of the San

Lorenzo district was as I remembered, a very different proposition to my family home. My luck was in. Santiago opened the door to my knock and contrary to my belief that he would be dismissive, he ushered me into his office, its cool interior a contrast to the heat of the day, the gloomy interior perfect for showing off the dark, expensive wood and the place had a smell all its own.

'Paco Martinez, well this is a surprise. You have returned from the dead. So, tell me, where have you been since I last saw you? How long is it, three, four years? You disappeared after the corrida in Córdoba and you left me with a problem. I had to find other toreros to take your place for the rest of the season.'

'I'm sorry about that; sorry if I put you to extra expense, perhaps I can find a way to repay you.'

'No, that isn't an issue. Some decent young bullfighters made a start in the business thanks to you, though I must confess none of them has your talent. You still have that talent?'

'I don't know, that's why I have come to see you. I was hoping I could fight in some minor bullring; find out if I can still perform.'

'And you want me to arrange it?'

I felt my heart sink at the look in his eyes, his expression, serious. Then he relaxed and smiled at me..

'Let me see,' he said opening the ledger on his desk. 'I can fit you in for a corrida in a month's time. The corrida is in Antequera.' Then his serious look returned. 'You put me to some trouble with your disappearance; I had high hopes for you.'

I just looked at him, wondering where the conversation was going. He was a businessman and they only ever thought about money.

'It will give you the chance to prove yourself, Paco, and if you can show me that you have lost none of your passion and talent for the corrida then I will look to managing you again but there is a caveat.'

'A caveat?' what is that I wondered?

'I cannot, in all honesty, pay you the amount you were used to. I know you will have expenses and so I propose to pay you just one hundred pesetas for this first bullfight. What do you say?'

What could I say? I was overjoyed; I still had a small amount of the money from my discharge so if the fee did not cover everything then I could use that money for expenses. But that would leave the cuadrilla empty handed, they would have to come along for nothing, and I would have to hire picadors. That would cost money.

'Well, do you accept my offer?'

Manolito's face lit up when I told them the news, Juan and José too had broad grins on their faces and standing apart Luis looked on with no more than a simple smile.

'Antequera, that's great,' said José.

'And you, Luis, are you happy to come along?'

'Of course, Paco, I wouldn't miss it for the world but let's do it right.'

'Of course, I know it's a chance not to miss.'

'Does your costume still fit you? You have put some weight on since you returned,' said Luis to the others' amusement.

'It probably fits him everywhere except that belly of his,' said Manuel.

It was good to hear, the banter, feel the camaraderie.

They were all keen to try to rebuild our reputation as the finest cuadrilla Triana had ever produced. That was probably not quite true, but they did not really care.

'There will be no spare money for you after I have paid the expenses.'

'Sounds like a free weekend in Antequera, what could be wrong with that?' said Manolito, his grin even wider, if that were possible.

'Paco will take them by storm and with a little bit of luck we can carry on where we left off. Isn't that right, Paco?' said Luis.

'I hope so my friend, I hope so. A beer on me, come on, let's celebrate.'

'I do hope we can make it, Paco, it's been difficult since you left,' said Luis as he lifted his glass. 'To be your sword carrier was an honour and you paid me well but since you left, I have found it hard to earn any money, a few days selling newspapers that's all.'

'How's the leg, can you manage the corrida?'

'Oh yes, I can get about well enough, well enough to carry the sword for the greatest torero in all of Spain.'

'Don't be silly. But I appreciate your confidence in me. I haven't been in the ring with a bull for more than three years and I really am not sure how I will cope.'

'Paco, how about we go to the pastures of Tablada one night, do what we always did, find some bulls and play them, at least you can get used to them again,' said Manolito. 'At least you will know in your heart of hearts if you can truly return to the bullring.'

The train from Seville arrived in Antequera just after one o'clock in the afternoon and from it we stepped, five young men with something to prove. I was not the only one on trial, my friends felt that my reputation, as it were, reflected upon them and they were determined to show the world how good they were.

'What about the picadors, have you arranged anything, Paco?' asked Manuel.

'Santiago has arranged for the picadors, but what he did not tell me until yesterday was that I was the one to have to pay for their services. I am sorry, boys, but there is going to be very little left for you.'

'We know, Paco, we are just grateful you are giving it another go,' said José.

'I'll second that,' said his brother.

By now, all four of them were looking at me and I felt deeply the trust they were placing in me and then, together we walked towards the small bullring with our bundles under our arms.

'Nice looking arena,' said Luis as we walked through an arch. 'Shall we take a look at the bulls, find out what we have to deal with?'

'Yes, good idea,' I said looking around.

'Who are you?' asked a man approaching from the shadows.

'Francisco Martinez, we're here for the corrida,' I said, turning to face him. 'Are you something to do with the bullring?'

'Ah, yes... I have heard of you, Señor Moncada Sánchez told me about you, asked me to arrange for two local picadors to join your cuadrilla. By the way, I am Pedro García; I am in charge here today. Good luck, you will need it with those bulls,' he said pointing towards the pens.

What did he mean? No matter, after our recent midnight foray back in Tablada I felt I could handle any bull in Spain.

'Come on, lads, let's have a look in the pens and then we can find these picadors who are costing me so much.'

'He looks a handful,' said Manolito pointing to an enormous bull chewing nonchalantly in the nearest pen.

He was big for sure and I stood on the bottom rail of the pen to lean over for a closer look. The bull lifted its head, its eyes picking us out and for a few seconds, nothing happened until the powerful animal snorted and then, without warning it charged, butting the side of the pen with such force that Manolito fell from the rail.

'*Madre de Dios,*' he said with a strained laugh. 'That took me by surprise. You do not want him today, Paco.'

'We'll see, the other bulls might be worse,' I said remembering Pedro García's words. Not long after I had to attend the draw for the bulls and I found myself in the company of Hernan Pérez and Miguel González two experienced bullfighters. Hernan Pérez was the senior and he had the privilege of drawing first, then it was Miguel González and finally, my turn. I drew a dark brown bull of the Vista Hermosa herd; white-faced between well-formed, symmetrical horns, a powerful-looking animal, but it was Miguel who drew the big beast.

'I'm glad you didn't draw that one, Paco,'

I ignored Luis. How could I tell how the bull would perform until I faced it in the ring? Bulls are unpredictable and it took a few passes before I had the measure of any one of them. I was more concerned about my reception in the ring. If the aficionados learned who I was and remembered my ignominious retreat then I would be under severe scrutiny. I needed to be at my best.

Two hours later dressed in our reconstituted bullfighting clothes we took to the ring. I watched the picadors hired for the day ride around the ring. They seemed competent and after prodding the bull with their lances they gave way to Manuel, Manolito and José who ran at the animal to planting their banderillas with a skill that defied a lack of practice and as the bull weakened, the trumpet announced the start of the third act. It was my time to face the bull alone.

'Don't take too many risks, Paco, keep your mind on the bull, we don't want it to end like last time, do we?' said Manolito.

I hardly heard him; I was single-minded in my quest to restore my reputation but as soon as I emerged fully into the light, a section of the crowd began to hurl abuse at me.

'Look, it is the brave torero that runs away from a woman,' called out a voice and from another, 'What kind of a bullfighter is he?' followed by laughter and unintelligible catcalls and I felt unnerved until I saw a face just a few meters away and I knew that I must go on, I must give it my best shot, and gritting my teeth, I froze out the abuse and with the bull standing the centre of the ring I approached the president's balcony.

'Señor President, I salute you; I salute all here today and I dedicate this bull to Señor Moncada Sanchez,' I said removing my hat to toss it into the sea of faces. But the response was less than I would have wished for, instead of cheers, a second section of the crowd decided to hurl abuse at me.

'Hey, Martinez, will you be running away soon? We

remember you. You're the one that could not face a bull anymore.' For a moment I felt the comments penetrate my defences. I tried to ignore them, told myself that these imbeciles would not be a barrier to my return. It seemed not to matter that I had risked my life in the service of Spain while these so-called aficionados had sat on their fat arses criticising and complaining. Then, from nowhere, a vision of that wonderful nurse filled my mind and I remembered her words, words that inspired me, and I turned from the president and Santiago towards the section of the crowd tormenting me.

I let my cape slip, spread it wide and with a flick of my wrists I enticed the bull towards me as if a mysterious force was guiding my actions. A peace descended upon me, it was as if I were deaf and working in total silence and the bull seemed to move in slow motion as I controlled it with my passes. From that moment I fought from the core of my emotions, my confidence was high, I tried new tricks. It was as if the bull was simply a puppet and I the puppet master. Finally, I spread the cape and the bull lowered its head, five hundred kilograms of angry bull intent on destroying me. However, I was ready, as ready as I had ever been and sweeping the muleta across my chest, I invited it to me. It was a brave animal, it had never once backed away but I had learned its characteristics, its tendency to favour the left, it was predictable, exhausted and time had come.

I let the muleta hang loose, held the sword, angled towards the killing zone, and I ran at it, leaping above stationary horns and plunged the sword deep into the killing zone and with hardly a blink of its eyes, the proud animal sank to its knees. It was only then I heard the crowd and felt elation as I realised how much I had turned them. As the bull died, caps, straw hats and seat cushions sailed into the air, cries of 'Olé' filled the stadium. It was a moment to savour.

After my first performance, the crowd were respectful. I handled my second bull in much the same way as the first, playing it carefully until I had the measure of its rhythm. Although the animal was less aggressive than the first it possessed a cunning nature that required more finesse on my part. I began with a series of *verónicas*, turning it to the left and to the right, wearing it down, positioning the beast where I could best show off my skill. This time I did not feel so isolated and with my confidence returned, I did hear the crowd, shouts of encouragement, roars of 'Ole' 'Ole' after each pass. I had truly laid to rest the ghost of my past failure and although it left me in a mood of celebration, I decided that I must pay a visit to the chapel.

The chapel was cool and tranquil, and kneeling in front of the altar I recited the prayer I had spoken many times. I thanked the Virgin for her protection, for the wellbeing of my cuadrilla and was about to stand when a figure entered and knelt beside me. It was Luis, eyes closed and quietly mumbling a prayer, then I noticed his knuckles were white from clasping his hands together so tightly. Finally, he crossed himself and we stood together, motionless, looking at the figure of the Virgin Mary.

'Paco, I had to make a prayer for your deliverance. Your performance today was sublime. You truly are back with us.'

'That makes two of us, my friend, you all performed as I know you can.'

It was an emotional moment for us both and with my arm around his shoulder; we emerged from the chapel. I realised then how important I was to him, the crippled boy whose chances in life were almost zero until he became my sword carrier and now, he had the added responsibility of organizing our travel and accommodation. He had found a reason to live. It was moving, and forced me to acknowledge that I had changed too. My time in Morocco had done more for my soul than I realised. The discipline, the arduous training but above all the shared comradeship had helped me through those difficult times. I had survived when many had not and for a fleeting moment, I recalled their faces, their humour, their bravery and now Luis and the cuadrilla had replaced the Legión.

'You're very quiet,' said Manolito as we changed out of our colourful suits into more sober outfits.

'Reflecting, thinking about the past that's all, and thinking about how I can improve.'

'I can't see how you could improve after that performance.'

'Thanks, but you know there is always room for improvement. I remember the death of Josélito, the greatest torero in all of Spain, a man everyone thought immortal. I remember when his body returned home to Seville after his death in Madrid and when we crossed the bridge to watch the funeral procession. I cannot ever remember seeing so many people. It looked to me as if the whole of Andalusia had turned out and now, I see it as a reminder of how easily triumph can turn to tragedy.'

'A sobering thought,' said Luis.

'Come on. I will buy you all a drink,' I said licking my

parched lips and as we emerged into the corridor, we were met by Santiago.

'Francisco, you were wonderful today. You have lost none of your magic, your verónicas were truly artistic, and I congratulate you. You must dine with me tonight. We have much to discuss.'

'Thank you, *señor,* I appreciate that,' I said, hardly able to contain my joy.

I had believed him uninterested in me but it seemed I was wrong.

Santiago was already waiting for us as we walked into the restaurant, a silent greeting on his lips and Luis, as alert as ever, gripped the sleeve of my shirt.

'Paco, you go and have dinner with Santiago, we will take another table. We should let you discuss any business with him in private.'

I understood and quietly thanked my friend for his understanding. Like me, they too relied ultimately upon Señor Moncada Sanchez for their living.

'That one, is it wise to keep him in the cuadrilla? A deformity like that could be a liability you know,' said Santiago as I sat down.

'I don't think so, he is my friend, I have known him all my life, he is loyal, he gives good advice when I need it, and he will never enter the bullring during a fight.'

'The waiter is hovering; do you know what you want for dinner?' said Santiago changing the subject. 'The steaks are very good, prime cuts from the day's bulls.'

'I'm sure, but perhaps something a little lighter this evening for me.'

He leaned back in his seat and took a small box of

cigars from his pocket.

'The finest Cuba can produce. I have them rolled especially for me. Try one.'

'Thank you, I don't smoke often but perhaps I will tonight.'

'You deserve one, you dedicated your first bull to me, a kind gesture and I appreciated it. As is tradition, I must reciprocate with a gift of my own and for that, I give you this.'

He put his hand inside his jacket and pulled out a folded piece of paper.

'It is a reward for your performance today. You are a remarkable young man, Francisco. I can see your potential and I am prepared to back you.'

I dared to believe.

'This contract is for you to fight in corridas I am arranging. It is for three seasons and all across Spain. What do you say?'

'I say thank you very much, señor, thank you.'

'You had better read it, make sure you are happy for there will be no turning back once you sign.'

My impulse was to sign there and then. If he had offered me a pen at that moment, I would have signed without question but something held me back. I have no idea why, perhaps a moment of doubt, was it Luis, his caution?

'Do you mind if I take a few minutes to read it then, see what is expected of me?'

'No,' he said, his eyelids flickering almost imperceptibly.

As we waited for the food to arrive, I scanned the text. The fees were all I had hoped for but I became concerned when I read that he would choose my cuadrilla. I could not agree. My friends and I had been together for a long time, friends who supported me in my fights and most importantly, I trusted them.

'I... I can't, I have to choose my own cuadrilla, I—'

He did not let me finish, holding up his hand to silence me.

'Francisco, perhaps I was being too presumptuous. I have already let you know that I am unhappy about your sword carrier but you have convinced me he is not a problem. I want to make sure there is continuity. After the last episode, I cannot afford for you to let me down. Look, I can see that your cuadrilla work well together, you proved that today. How about if I strike that clause out, then will you sign?'

To have sole control over the personnel in my cuadrilla was important. I had to have the confidence that they would protect me if a fight got out of hand. If a bull was able to gore me, or worse, then I had to have complete trust in the cuadrilla to recover the situation.

Santiago took the pen from his pocket and unscrewed the top.

'Here, pass me the contract,' he said striking out the offending clause. There, does that satisfy you; can I have your signature?'

'Gladly, señor,' I said, taking the offered pen and with a shake of our hands, we sealed the contract.

After snatching just two hours' sleep, I should have felt exhausted for the return to Seville but my mind was a whirl. Santiago had given me the chance to redeem myself, show what I could do and I knew that I must not let this second chance slip through my fingers. I had put on weight since my return from Africa and although my fitness level was reasonable enough, I felt that I must return to a fitness level achieved in the Legión, anything less could be a death trap in the bullring.

'Mano, Manuel, José, last night I promised you a future but there is a caveat.'

'What is that,' asked Manuel, 'what's a caveat?'

'It's something extra you must do. For more than three years I marched the length and breadth of Morocco, fighting hard and training hard with the Legión. We never rested on our laurels, always we had to be ready and that is how I want you to be, always ready.'

'What do you mean?'

'I mean, Mano, that you are to begin physical training straight away, tomorrow. If you are strong and quick-witted, we will do well. That was a lesson I learned from the Legión and so many times did I see it pay off. We will find somewhere to train, a place where we can run.'

Luis was grinning, he knew he would not be a part of any physical training regime because of his disability but I think he understood my logic.

'Tomorrow, we'll meet at the bar on San Jacinto near the market at nine o'clock. Luis, are you going home to Triana?'

'Yes, I want to see my mother, make sure she is all right.'

'Good, I will walk with you, I want to see my mother too, and you José, you will be going home to my sister and niece?'

'I will, but not straight away, Manuel and I are meeting our cousin, we'll follow you later.'

So, we dispersed, Luis and I leaving the station for Triana while the other three went their separate ways.

'I think you are right to get them running and doing press-ups, Paco. I have seen many unfit men in the bullring and they do not perform well. Some of those bulls are quick, too quick at times.'

'Yes, that's the whole point, less chance of an accident,' I said.

It felt good to be returning home and halfway across the bridge we stopped, falling silent for a few minutes as we gazed down the river, both of us lost in thought.

'How many times have we done this, Luis?'

'Hundreds, Paco, we must have stopped here to watch the boats hundreds of times.'

'Look at that one,' I said pointing to a slow-moving barge crawling its way across the flat grey waters of the canal. 'I wonder what she's carrying.'

'Gold and silver from the New World,' he said as we carried on across.

I laughed.

'Not these days, Luis, more like coal or potatoes.'

He did not respond, instead, his eyes were wide, staring.

'What's the matter?'

I followed his gaze and there, leaning against a wall, was Victor, the bully boy picador from César's cuadrilla.

I felt Luis stiffen with fear.

'It's all right, Luis, don't worry,' I said. 'Just keep walking.'

Victor had seen us, and as we approached, he dropped the butt of his cigarette, screwing it into the floor with his boot and he looked straight at us.

'So, it's the deserter. Come back to pick up where he left off. If you think you are going to outshine César then you can forget it. Give up now and go back to herding bulls instead of fighting them. If you do not, I might just have to help you on your way.'

'You and whose army?'

'Think you're clever don't you, Martinez? I am warning you to keep out of our way or you will get the same treatment we gave you last time. Take my advice and leave town while you still can.'

'Okay, I hear you, don't worry, I will.'

'Good, that's what I want to hear,' he said, his lip curling in triumph.

'Come on, Luis,' I said, leading him away from the sneering Victor who believed his warning was having the desired effect.

'Are you really going to leave Seville, Paco, stop bullfighting? What will we do, we are relying on you now?'

'Don't worry, Luis; I have no intention of leaving. *'Come mierda gilipollas*,' I hissed under my breath, sending Luis into a fit of laughter.

'If he heard that then we are in trouble,' he said.

'Naw, he's a bully and bullies only take on people they can terrorise. He doesn't frighten me. He wouldn't last five minutes in the Legión?'

'Oh, Paco, tell me about the Legión. I have heard stories.'

'Well, how about this for a tale. We were heading for a hill fort that was under siege, leading a column of mules along a treacherous mountain path....'

Chapter 17

My mother's face lit up as soon as I walked into the little house but it did not last long, replaced by the frown I knew so well.

'Francisco, let me look at you. You are not injured, thank God.'

'No, Mama, I was careful and the boys worked well together.'

'No one is injured?'

'No, Mama, we are all in good health, don't worry, no mother will be blaming me for her son's injuries.'

She visibly relaxed, her worries appeased.

'Good, I am glad of that. What is that stupid grin on your face?

'Señor Moncada Sánchez was there, he has given me a contract to fight for the next three seasons,' I blurted out.

'Three seasons! That *is* something.'

'The money is more than I could ever dream of. You will not have to worry about the rent or where the next meal is coming from, Mama.'

'I always knew you would do well, Francisco, but it will bring danger with it, no?'

'I can handle it. Is there anything to eat, I am starving?'

'Some bread and olives and a little ham perhaps. You

know your father would be proud of you.'

'I know.'

'I will bring you some food.'

'I've come home to see you and Maria and I want to visit Juanita.'

'She will be pleased to see you, I am sure. Here take this with you, a shawl I knitted for her.'

'What about Maria, will she need baby clothes?'

'I don't think that will ever happen. She is more interested in her job than getting married. She has boyfriends I think, but they do not seem to last very long.'

'Give her time, Mama, I am sure there is someone out there who is right for her.'

'I hope so, here, eat this,' she said putting the plate on the table.

I was hungry and I rapidly devoured the food while my mother watched over me and after draining the cup of water, I picked up the shawl to set off to visit my sister. I left by a small side street that led onto San Jacinto, the main thoroughfare with a few people going about their business. Some recognised me and waved, one even congratulating me on the fight at Antequera. How did he know, I wondered?

Then I smiled to myself, Luis, I bet it was Luis. I guessed that unable to contain his excitement, he was telling everyone who would listen to him and I was still grinning when I finally saw my sister.

'A present from Mama,' I said placing the shawl on the arm of her chair. 'Where is José?

'He's gone to see if he can get his shoes repaired. The cobbler stays open late. Thanks, how are Mama and Maria?' she said touching the wool.

'Mama is fine, managing well enough and Maria will be travelling home from work, I think. José will have told you about the contract?'

'Yes, it's so good to know that that there will be money coming in. Without you we would struggle to make ends meet.'

'I know, I'm glad to help and God willing, you will eat well for some time to come.'

She smiled at me and as if at a signal the baby began to stir in her cot.

'It's time for her feed; the shawl will come in handy straight away,' she said lifting her daughter from the cot.

For a moment I watched her, content as she breastfed the baby until the sound of the door opening diverted my attention.

'Paco, you have come to see our daughter? She's beautiful, don't you think?' said José, his newly repaired shoes burnished black.

'Yes, she's beautiful,' I said and for a time we talked in whispers, the only real noise in the room that of the feeding child.

'She will have a proper education, Paco, not like us, eh?'

Juanita looked up from her task, serene and happy. To see her in this way made me happy too and for a time I watched until the baby fell asleep and I knew that it was time to leave.

'Here, sister, buy Conchita something nice, something to make you happy,' I said, depositing a few pesetas on the table.

'What can make me happier than to have you still in one piece? I worried so much about you while you were in

Morocco, the stories I heard, and read in the newspapers, so many of our boys killed by those heathens.'

'Well, I think the army is on top of it now. It seems we have joined the French to finally put an end to it.'

'Maybe, the Gallardo family on Calle Peñaflor, they were informed just two days ago they have lost one of their sons. He was no more than a boy, such a shame.'

José fell silent and I said my goodbyes, stepping into the street thinking of the war. It was a shame young soldiers were still losing their lives. I was relieved that I was out of it. Sticking my hands into my trouser pockets, I could do no more than hope those I'd left behind were surviving and just as my melancholy began to deepen a cheerful voice snapped me out of it.

'Luis, what are you up to?'

'I am fetching this bread for my mother. it saves her having to come out.'

'Good for you, Luis, I will walk with you. I've just been to see my sister and her baby.'

'I hear she is like José, got his nose.'

'Oh dear, his nose,' I said bursting into laughter.

'Is his nose so bad?'

'Not particularly for him, for a girl maybe. I am just making fun, Luis, nothing meant. Heavens, I couldn't say anything against my niece, now, could I?'

'You're as bad as my father. He makes fun of my disability,' he said becoming subdued.

'Aw, forget it, and don't be downhearted because we think you are as good as the rest of us. Your limp doesn't affect anything.'

'Really.'

'Yes really, and if all Señor Moncada Sánchez's

promises come true you will be strutting your stuff all over Spain and then what would your father do? I'll tell you what, he will be boasting in every bar in Triana that his son, Luis Vicente Lopez, is the best sword carrier in the whole of Spain.'

'And getting drunk at other people's expense.'

'Yes, and getting drunk at other people's expense,' I laughed.

It brought back memories of my own father who was an expert in the art of the tall story. I had seen him captivate an audience and they in turn had plied the storyteller with drink to keep entertainment flowing.

'Come on, I will walk with you,' I said.

'Shall we have a drink; I have a few centimós left. How about the bar we used to go to just round that corner?'

'A good idea and maybe I will have a chunk of that bread.'

Five minutes later we were sitting in the bar, glasses of beer in front of us and for over an hour we put the world of bullfighting to rights.

Time to go,' I said breaking off a lump of his bread and insisting on picking up the tab.

'I said I would pay,' he protested.

'I have eaten half of your bread; you will be in trouble when you get home. What will your mother say? Let me at least pay for the drinks.'

Feigning protestation he allowed me to settle the bill and a minute later we emerged onto a deserted street. The pedestrians from earlier had gone home, the carts were idle and the donkeys were in their stables. Apart from a distant street light, it was dark, with just a few illuminated windows to guide us.

I do not know why, but I began to feel uneasy, I sensed danger. Perhaps I had spent too much time in the Legión. From the corner of my eye, I noticed something unusual in the shadows and instinctively I pushed Luis into the nearest doorway.

'Don't be alarmed, Luis,' I whispered. 'Stay here and stay still.'

I turned towards the shadows; a movement, then I saw figures approaching, more than one and they were coming towards us and in the dim light I made out the features of the bullying picador

'So, it is the runaway torero and his one-legged friend,' he said coming closer.

'You did not run me out of town, you oaf, I left of my own free will.'

'And now you are back, fighting bulls again. Well, we don't want you back in the bullring so maybe I should encourage you to leave again, *of your own free will*,' he laughed.

'Go and boil your head,' I said and then Luis began to shake.

'Looks like your friend has got the message. Now it's your turn,' he said, rolling up his sleeves.

I looked the three of them over and stood my ground. The situation was turning into a repeat performance but this time things were different. The three thugs beginning to circle me might have thought that they were tough but they bore no comparison to the ferocious tribesmen of North Africa nor the legionnaires I had spent so much time with.

Victor seemed impatient, facing me with fists

clenched, his shoulders hunched over and taking several steps forward, he struck out. I feinted to one side and deceived him enough for his fist to connect with no more than fresh air, a classic move which left him exposed. I had handled charging bulls and Victor was no different, just a charging bull. As he passed to my side, I smashed my clenched fist hard against his ear, a trick learned from the Cubans and disorientated, he paused, ready to attack me a second time. In that split second, I landed a second blow, leaving him grunting with rage. He turned and with his arms outstretched he tried to grab hold of me but I was too quick. Ducking under his swinging arm I gave him a short sharp jab, my fist connected with his nose which resulted in a flow of blood.

Bewildered, he could do no more than stagger away from me, calling on his friends for help. They answered by stepping forward to take a swing at me, the second thug crashing his fist hard into my shoulder and knocking me sideways. Now I was on the defensive, stumbling as I tried to regain my footing and then they managed to grab my jacket to grapple me to the ground. If they succeeded, I would have little chance but I remembered my training and landing several blows in quick succession, at the same time kicking out at their shins, I stopped them in their tracks. Two more swift blows of my fists and the two of them fell to the floor but Victor was recovering and enraged, with blood streaming down his face, he took a wild swing at me. He missed the side of my head by a hairs breadth and I had time to spin round to wrong-foot him and I drove my fist into his midriff. The pleasure I felt as my fist sank into his soft belly was unbelievable and as he doubled up, I put my foot against his chest and set him flying.

From the corners of my eyes, I saw the other two thugs were trying to outflank me and one jumped me from behind. He clamped his forearm around my neck and in desperation, I could do no more than stagger backwards. I seemed to be losing the battle and that made me angry. With all my strength, I twisted and turned attempting to break free from his vicelike grip. In desperation I kicked out at his shins and whether I connected or not I do not know, but the arm around my throat slackened its grip and in a moment of respite my strength returned and I kicked out a second time. This time his grip released entirely and I turned my attention to the second man who was coming at me with fists raised. A big man, almost the size of Victor and just as clumsy, a natural bully yet he did not seem to have the first idea of how to fight. Swinging his arms like a windmill, he growled like a mad dog and I dodged out of his way, a simple task that allowed me to turn and hit him squarely in his face. I pressed home my advantage, hitting him twice more with such force that he toppled to the ground and I looked again for Victor but the big picador was in no mood to carry on.

'You threatened us, you have tried to stop me entering the bullring. Well let me tell you Victor, if you ever try it again then this is what you can expect,' I said the anger in my voice controlled and menacing.

I think he got the message, nursing his broken nose, a look of defeat on his face and with both of his accomplices lying prostrate on the ground he was in no mood to argue. I had taken them on and beaten them, a good result but I could not remember flooring the last one to attack me. Then I noticed Luis standing nearby holding his boot with the extra-large heel.

'That was brave of you,' I said.

Luis grinned, his confidence sky high and from that day he carried my sword as if he were Rodrigo Díaz.

We travelled most of southern Spain: Córdoba, Badajoz, as far as Alicante during the summer months and by the end of the season I had killed almost one hundred bulls and receiving no more than a few scratches in return. My reputation was growing and the bullfighting aristocracy of Seville had begun to take notice of me and when the season finally ended, I began to receive invitations to dinners and events. One such evening was in honour of the Real Maestranza's retiring president. Manuel Ortega Diaz a man revered not only in the bullfighting world of Seville but far beyond. It was an honour to receive the invitation, a chance to meet important members of the bullfighting fraternity, and as Santiago's guest, I would meet his wife for the first time.

I wanted to impress the promoters and bullfighting impresarios who would attend and so I spent some of my newfound wealth with one of the most notable tailors in the city. For the first time in my life, I owned a fine suit of clothes that was not for use in the bullrings and posing in front of the tailor's full-length mirror I admired my reflection. I turned to the left, to the right, held my head high and walked back and forth much to the tailor's amusement.

'Even though I say it myself, Señor Martinez, you are wearing one of the best suits in the whole of Seville. I cannot remember ever having turned out such a fine suit.'

It was quite some time after that I came to realise that

he was pulling my leg with his flattery but it did earn him a substantial tip. After dressing in my new suit and preening myself in front of my much smaller mirror, I took a motorised cab to the hotel to meet just about everyone who mattered in Sevillian society.

For a time, I stood alone watching carriages and motor cars arrive, their expensively dressed passengers descending to the wonder of less affluent onlookers. Then a fine black automobile pulled up opposite me and from it, Santiago emerged followed by a woman and I raised my hand. Seeing me, he shepherded his wife in my direction, the lights of the hotel illuminating the woman and I was impressed by what I saw.

'Francisco, may I introduce Gabriella. I do not believe you have met her.'

'No, the pleasure is all mine, señora,' I said taking her outstretched hand.

The woman was, I guessed, a good five years older than my twenty-six years, elegant and stunningly beautiful in her loose-hanging silk dress and a fur stole. An impressive diamond necklace hung loose around her neck the sparkle of the diamonds attracting me and when I looked up at her she held my gaze.

'You are the up-and-coming star of the bullfighting circuit I hear Francisco. My husband speaks highly of you.'

'Thank you, señora, and please, call me Paco. Francisco is the name my mother uses and it makes me feel like a little boy.'

'And you are not a little boy, are you?' she said, her eyes giving me an unfathomable look.

'Er... no, not any more,' I said, unsure of how to

counter her line.

'Santiago tells me he is hopeful you will rise further next season Paco. I will be looking out for you, to see how high you can fly.'

She unnerved me and then Santiago turned towards me, offering a glass of champagne, rescuing me.

'Your good health, Francisco.'

I lifted my glass. 'And to you, Santiago, Gabriella.'

Gabriella smiled and I had to admit she was certainly different. I had always assumed Santiago was not a man who chased women, conservative, reserved, never more than polite to those he met, and so to see him with this woman was a real surprise. I could only assume the reason for their coupling was that opposites really did attract, or more probably it was his money.

I could not stand there all night looking at her, although I would have been perfectly happy doing just that. The foyer was filling up, spilling over into the grand reception room and, to my relief, Santiago suggested we move there.

The volume of chatter was rising and in conversation with Gabriella, I felt compelled to lean closer to hear her reply. I will never forget that moment, her perfume, an aroma I had never encountered before, her eyes, her hair, and those sparkling diamonds.

'Tell me, where is it you live now?' she asked. 'I hear you are a product of Triana. You do not still live there, do you?'

'No, I have a room at the Alameda in Macarena, not far from the Plaza de Toros.'

'Of course, a torero would naturally want to be close to the bullring. I admire you for that.'

I bowed my head in appreciation.

'Everyone who matters will be here tonight,' said Santiago. 'A good time for you to meet people who can promote your career, Francisco. Oh, look, there is Pedro Alvarez. I am glad he's here. He has contacts in Catalonia and the Zaragoza region where I am just beginning to place bullfighters. I will certainly have to have a few words with him before the night is over.'

I took a cursory glance towards Santiago's person of interest but my eyes did not get that far. Crossing the room was a face I had not set eyes on since leaving Seville for Morocco. She appeared from nowhere, dressed in a fine blue and red-layered figure-hugging dress but it was her face that drew me; the one I remembered, but now with a paler complexion and she looked thinner and she had cut her hair short in the fashion of the day yet there was no mistaking that it was Isabella. César appeared through the crowd of guests, put his arm around her and my emotions took a dive.

'Paco, that woman, you haven't stopped looking at her. Does she mean something to you?' said Gabriella.

'I... I, no she does not mean anything to me. Erm, would you like your glass refilling?' I said in a clumsy attempt to deflect her questioning.

'She is with César, I see. But she means nothing to you?'

'No,' I said reaching for her empty glass, a distraction maybe but also a chance to face down ghosts from the past.

Spaced near the entrance to the foyer, waiters stood with silver trays and at least one carried full glasses. I crossed the room passing close to Isabella and César and this time I was not about to run away.

César saw me first, alerting Isabella who turned to look in my direction as I crossed the room. César gave me a hostile stare but I ignored him, instead, I looked straight at Isabella. I do not think at first, she knew me, the look in her eyes one of confusion until finally she did recognise me and turned her head away. I said nothing to either as I passed and after swapping the empty glasses for full ones walked back to Santiago and Gabriella, not wholly sure where my feelings lay. I had laid no ghost to rest and I had irritated César.

'A full glass for you señora, and one for you, Santiago.'

'You are not having one, Francisco?'

'No, I do not like to drink much these days, it dulls the senses and I think it will be too easy to lapse on an evening like this,' I said, acutely aware of my position. The last thing I wanted was some sort of scene.

'Here's to your gallant and talented torero, Santiago,' said Gabriella touching her husband's glass with hers. 'It is admirable that he can control himself so well.'

She lifted her glass in salute, her eyes roaming the room before returning to mine.

'They are calling us to dinner, my love,' said Santiago, offering an arm to his wife. 'Francisco,' he said, leading.

Obediently I followed. The successful middle-aged impresario and his attractive wife, an enigma I thought yet I was not complaining as I found it impossible to drag my eyes away from the rhythmical swaying of Gabriella's expensive silk dress.

We took our places, I sat next to her and once I caught her watching me from the corner of her eye and thought little of it. I heard César, just a short distance away, boasting of his prowess at the April *feria*. Many of those present had seen him fight, he was a rising star and they hung on to his every word and I suppose I was more than a little jealous. He was cementing his reputation as a bullfighter, he had a following that guaranteed contracts, and he was with Isabella. In my eyes, he had achieved all that I could ever wish for. What of Isabella? I could not help wondering what might have been and feeling a little downhearted my mind drifted and then I heard César announce that he and Isabella were to be married. My ears pricked up and I strained to hear his words.

'Raise your glasses, my friends, to the girl who will make me very happy in the not-too-distant future,' he said.

'To Isabella,' I heard and then, 'to César.'

Someone said how lucky he was and I felt my stomach turn over. This really was the end; they were getting married and there would be no room for me. I was being stupid I knew, but the finality of it seemed to overwhelm me.

Suddenly I stiffened, unable to do anything but stare at my dinner plate. It felt as if a bull was goring my thigh, a small bull maybe but the pain was real, sharp yet manageable, and keeping my composure as much as I could, I turned to look at Gabriella whose eyes were wide with delight.

'Can you pass me the water jug, Paco, I think I have had enough wine for now,' she said, her grip on my inner thigh becoming more limpet-like by the second. I could do little without exposing the indiscretion, and a battle of wills ensued and with her strong fingers tight on my leg I reached for the water jug.

'There, let me fill your glass,' I said picking up the jug of water.

She looked at me in triumph but I could not let her win. She lifted her empty glass with her free hand, as I made to fill it and I took my chance, letting slip the jug to cascade water over her dress.

'Oh, forgive me,' I said, taking my napkin in one hand to dab the spillage and prising at her fingers with the other. Surprised by the suddenness of my reaction she released her grip and her eyes filled with surprised anger.

'My dress, it is ruined!'

Everyone at the table turned towards us, her husband with a puzzled expression on his face, and those who had witnessed the incident examining Gabriella's expensive dress or her ample bosom.

'I'm so sorry; it was an accident, here, my napkin,' I managed to blurt out.

'Never mind that,' she said, and lowering her voice whispered, 'You should be the one to clean my dress.'

Her response was surprising yet in a way I should have expected it. This beautiful, exciting woman seemed not to care one jot about the consequences of her flirting. For me, though, it was alarming and I think she knew that. I could not afford to alienate Santiago. How would he react if he believed I was pursuing his wife? What would that do for my career?

I tossed the napkin in front of her and turned to Santiago.

'I am so sorry; it was an accident. I will pay for a new dress for your wife.'

Santiago simply looked at me, unconcerned, smiled and reached across the table to put his hand on my forearm.

'It is of no consequence, Francisco; she has lots of dresses. I buy her at least one a week, there is no need for you to worry. I tell you what, you can escort her home for me as I will be going on to a small gathering when we finish here.' He smiled and patted me on the arm. 'Good, it is done then. Gabriella, you will have this charming young man to escort you home tonight. He will keep you safe.'

It is an understatement for me to say that I was surprised and, in my innocence, I accepted the task with good grace. Gabriella seemed satisfied and from the corner of my eye, I noticed Isabella staring at us. Perhaps I was not quite old news after all. Then I concentrated all my attention upon Gabriella who, once she had wiped away the water behaved impeccably and the incident forgotten almost immediately.

We both slipped into small talk with those around us and I counted my blessings that Santiago had not noticed his wife's indiscretion. She was an intriguing woman, attractive and with an untroubled attitude I had never seen in a woman before and I had now come to realise that she was manipulating me. How would I handle escorting her home I wondered?

Santiago spent much of the evening in conversation, no doubt doing some business and making new contacts leaving me to entertain Gabriella and as the evening ended the three of us walked out into the warm night air. Santiago raised his arm to hail a cab before turning to myself and Gabriella.

'Ah... there, my taxi. I will leave you two good people now, if you don't mind.' he said. 'I am meeting friends to play cards and to enjoy a good brandy, a fine way to finish off the evening. Don't wait up, my dear.'

'I won't, Santi, I'll see you tomorrow some time and you can replace this dress for me.'

'And some diamond earrings perhaps,' he said holding her chin in his fingers and angling her head towards him.

His eyes were loving but I thought it strange that he would abandon her and entrust her to my care while he went to play cards. But I had already seen that they were no normal couple and they seemed happy enough.

'So you are my Prince Charming tonight, Señor Paco.'

'I suppose I am. Do we need to find a taxi?'

'No, we have an apartment beside the river, it's not far.'

'Santi, I haven't heard him called that before.'

'It is my pet name for him and you are Paco but that is your name for everyone. I need a pet name for you. Let me think, Franci?'

'I don't like that very much.'

'Cisco?'

'That is too obvious and I don't like that either.'

'I know, Perroito, my little puppy dog, yes tonight you are my little puppy dog and we will begin your training straight away,' she said leaning in to me and kissing me full on the lips.

Involuntarily I recoiled and she laughed at me. I was concerned that kissing Santiago's wife in public might create a problem; it surprised me that she would even think of such a thing, yet nobody seemed to care and she simply put her arm in mine.

'Which way?'

'Over there, Perroito, it is not far.'

As we walked, she pressed against me, it felt good I have to admit, her breath on my face, her sweet perfume and I found it difficult to understand Santiago not wanting her.

'The woman, the one you say means nothing to you, tell me about her and why she means nothing. I saw your face, and noticed that she kept looking across at you. There is something between you, no?

'No.'

'I think she might still be in love with you.'

'Don't be silly, our affair is long finished and anyway, César announced tonight that they are to be married.'

'Ah yes, César, he sees himself as the next Belmonte, I think.'

I did not want to talk about Isabella or César. The wound inflicted upon me by Isabella had healed I was sure and this beautiful, sophisticated woman seemed intent on completing the process. She fell silent, leaving me with my thoughts for a while until she tugged at my arm.

'Just down here, follow that path,' she said steering me towards a terrace of well-kept dwellings.

'Here, the key, open the door, Perroito,' she said handing me a large ornate key.

'Go in, we can have a nightcap, a treat for bringing me home, A brandy perhaps. I have a bottle of the finest Andalusian brandy or maybe some Scotch whisky. Do you like whisky?'

'A brandy will do just fine,' I said looking around the spacious, well-furnished apartment.

I was impressed. Dark wooden floors and panelling in the traditional style, an expensive-looking writing desk, and a leather armchair in which she ordered me to sit. I took my place and watched as she walked across the room to fill the glasses.

'You like my little hideaway?'

'Hardly a hideaway,' I said letting my eyes settle on her.

'I was renting this place when I first met Santi and within a month, he had bought it for me. It is my private space, where I can relax when I have been shopping or when I just want to be alone. Here try this, I think you will like it,' she said handing me one of the glasses and wrapping her arm around mine.

'To your good health, Perroito, and to a successful career in the bullring.'

I slept until noon in the largest bed I have ever slept in and when I finally awoke it was to see Gabriella looking at me.

'You are ready again, my love?'

'What about Santiago? He mustn't find us like this, too much depends upon it.'

'Calm down, Santi will not come here, he will go to the villa in San Lorenzo when he decides to come home.'

'He must know what we have been doing, what will he say, what will happen to my career?'

'You are such a worrier. Can't you see?'

'See what?'

'Santi and I are married but we live separate lives. It is a fact. But some things must remain hidden from view, for his public reputation and never forget that we both rely upon him for the good life.'

I could not disagree, and what did it matter so long as I

could keep on fighting bulls?

'Now, Perroito, one more time and then you must leave because I am to go to the villa. Santi will want me with him this evening but we will meet again soon I hope.'

Chapter 18

The nineteen twenty-seven season was ending; my final fight was in Málaga where I expected to be fighting with Pablo Ruiz, known as El Lobito, and Ramón Rodríguez Verges, bullfighters from Salamanca. I was to be the second matador but when it came to the corrida, I discovered that El Lobito was not fighting after all and Santiago informed me that he was relegating me to the position of junior matador.

'Expediency, Francisco, expediency,' he said. 'Pablo was gored badly last Sunday and his injuries may take a month to heal. I am not even sure he will return to the bullring.'

'Oh, I'm sorry, I had not heard,' I said, more concerned with my position as the junior in the coming corrida. 'Why am I still junior, I would have thought now is the time for me to move up the rankings if not headline the fight?'

'A delicate situation, Francisco, Pablo was to be the senior matador and Ramón the junior but I felt it best to make him second and for this corrida, make you the junior.'

'So, Santiago, who have you brought in that is more important than me?' I said, beginning to feel angry.

'César López Aguilar.'

'What! That upstart, why?'

'Calm down, please. This is business, I must provide the matadors for the corrida and César is available. I am lucky to get him and there will be more of a draw if you two are fighting on the same bill.'

I could not look at Santiago, my mind confused.

'Look, Francisco, I know you two do not get on and what's more, the public know it. Just think what an attraction it will be, the new top matador and the challenger. You are fated to take the top position next season but consider this, you will have the chance to show the public who is the better killer of bulls. You could claim the crown as Spain's best matador, and think of the fees we can charge. You are already a wealthy young man but after this corrida, if my plans work out, your money could increase tenfold.'

I looked him in the eye.

'Tenfold, that's ridiculous.'

'Well, perhaps, but your earnings will at least double.'

I thought about that. To double my earnings was no small feat and I began to calm down, yet I could not believe that just one fight was going to make much of a difference.

'Look, if it makes you feel any better, I can offer you a thousand pesetas extra to fight, provided you perform well that is.'

'Make it fifteen hundred and I will think about it.'

'Twelve hundred?'

Twelve hundred pesetas added to my normal fee of two thousand certainly appeared a sound reason for playing a secondary role to César. Perhaps it was, but I was not happy with the idea of playing second fiddle.

The bright September sun was already sinking towards the horizon and the heat of the day beginning to cool as I walked through the *puerta de cuadrillas*. The paso doble cut through the air and I felt my heart thump. As the youngest, my place was between Ramón Rodríguez Verges to my left and César to my right. I glanced at César, resplendent in his suit of lights, proud, acting as if he were the most important person in the arena walked with purpose and for an instant, he to meet my gaze a hint of superiority showing on his face and I vowed to myself that I would do my level best outperform him. I did not like him and perhaps Santiago was right, why not profit from our rivalry.

During my first fight the Miura gave me little trouble, its size the inverse of its fighting qualities, and although it possessed aggression, I found the animal easy to control, my verónicas pleasing an already receptive audience and as I came to understand better the bull's characteristics, I performed a series of intricate passes in quick succession. But the bull lacked the true fighting spirit of the breed and it took all my skill to convince the crowd that they had seen a real bullfight. It was not a great fight but I knew I had acquitted myself well enough and as I left the arena Ramón came out to face his final bull.

The experienced bullfighter played the animal as he had the first, his passes clean, expert and he performed well but his bull had a mean streak and just before the final act it gored him badly and César, as the next senior matador, stepped in to finish the fight. It was not uncommon for the next senior matador to step in and kill the bull of an injured bullfighter. César was clinical, killing the bull cleanly but in triumph milked the situation for all it was worth throwing his hat into the crowd even as Ramón's cuadrilla carried the wounded bullfighter away.

Then it was the turn of César to fight his final bull. It appeared through the open gate and from the arch leading to the cuadrilla's gate the two picadors entered the bullring. The bull at first did not notice them, finding space to stand and wonder at the unfamiliar scent and the noise of the crowd but it did not take long for the bull to become aware of the. Trotting towards the picadors it suddenly picked up speed, lowered its head and charged. The men quickly rode out of its way, divided, and circled the bull, enticing it to them stabbing with their pikes whenever it came within range.

Victor was skilled and entertaining, controlling his horse to avoid the scything horns passing him and his horse by millimetres. To me he seemed overly aggressive towards the bull, plunging the end of the pike too deeply into the bulging muscle. There are rules and he was breaking them but what really annoyed me was that the President of the corrida did not intervene. Was this another of César's short cuts.

I knew full well that the bull would tire prematurely should the infractions continue. But nothing happened and when César strutted to meet the bull at the centre of the arena the animal was already losing blood. But the bull was brave and responded to the matador's moves, charging the cape to the roar of the crowd and grudgingly, I had to admit that he had come a long way since the day I had first seen him fight. I watched his every move. I noticed his footwork, how he avoided the horns, cleverly pulling his feet back to limit the danger of a goring. But some of what he was doing was trickery and that left me more determined than ever to best him.

From the safety of the barrera, I watched César unfurl his muleta and with his sword held behind his back out of the bull's sight he prepared for the final act. Rising on the balls of his feet, he paused, leaning back slightly in a classic pose and around him the crowd, impatient for the kill, waved their white handkerchiefs. Shouts of 'Olé' echoed around the bullring and César played to the crowd, strutting animatedly towards the wounded and exhausted animal. It could hardly lift its head and I knew then the picador's lances had done their job.

The bull had fought well, I could see that it was an intelligent animal, and when César stopped his advance, it seemed unmoved, holding its ground, motionless, its head hung low in the face of impending death. César stepped towards it and at last, the beast reacted, pawing the ground, summoning its last reserve of strength and in one last effort its powerful legs propelled it forward. I drew in my breath fearful that the bull was outwitting the matador; the animal had learned through its pain and torment that the target of its anger should really be the man and not the flimsy cloth. To attack César seemed to be its aim.

It all happened in slow motion, César was too slow and the bull caught him with its horns, tossing him into the air to a collective intake of breath from those watching. I could not help but react, racing from the safety barrier to spread my muleta in front of the bull, draw it away from César. It rushed at me and I turned it to one side, my own body turning with it and then a voice cut through to me.

'It's mine, back off, Paco. I can handle it.'

César had recovered, risen to his feet, and was showing annoyance at my intervention.

'I will kill it, move out of the way. It is my right to kill it.'

I could not argue, it is a law of the bullfight, but the way he demanded the privilege made my blood boil.

'Of course,' I said, controlling my emotions but inside I was outraged.

The bull was standing motionless but was still dangerous and now his cuadrilla had come to his aid to draw the bull off and leaving César time to face it with a free hand.

'Stay still,' he commanded me and I obeyed.

I knew as well as anyone not to compromise a matador's attention in such a dangerous situation and so I stood perfectly still. It was obvious that César had not received a serious injury and taking up from where he had left off, held out his sword and with a flourish drove it into the killing zone.

'That was a brave thing you did Paco,' said Manolito. 'You intervened at just the right time. Any longer and the bull would have done some real damage. The crowd were really cheering you.'

'I didn't hear them, too preoccupied, I guess. I wonder if that was the was the spur that drove César back into the fray.'

'I am sure it was. By the look on his face, I think he was worried you were upstaging him.'

'He thinks a lot of himself, doesn't he?' said Manolito,

coming to my side.

'Isn't he entitled to?'

'All he had to do was kill the bull but instead, he went in for theatrics and look what happened.'

'Let us not dwell on it; I did the same remember. Come, we have my second bull to fight in a few minutes,' I said.

My second fight was a success and I felt that I had at least equalled César's performance if not bettered it. I tried several moves I had practised yet never performed in a real bullfight and they seemed to go down well with the afficionados and my cuadrilla lifted me high on their shoulders to carry me from the arena to a cacophony of cheering.

'You took a chance there, Paco. I have not seen you do *revoleras* quite like that before. I didn't think you would pull it off you know,' said Luis as we passed through the gate.

'Have faith, my friend. I had to do something to take the crowd's mind off César. Did you see him strutting after he killed his second bull? It was as if I had not existed. Have you heard how Ramón is, was the goring serious?'

'I heard that he went to the infirmary and that later they took him to the hospital.'

I hoped that Ramón's injury was not serious and made a mental note to try to visit him in the hospital before we left for home. Then Manolito came up to me, his face a picture of contentment.

'Great move at the start, Paco, it really got them going. Don't worry about César and his crew; you were better today, we were better.'

'Thanks, Mano,' I said delighted by his enthusiasm.

'Let's eat,' said his brother. 'I'm starving. Where shall we try tonight?'

'The bar Mahon is good, brilliant tapas,' I said.

Was it because the tapas were the best in Málaga or had I another reason for suggesting the Bar Mahon, did I honestly expect I might see Isabella there? But they all agreed and as soon as we changed out of our bullfighting clothes we headed straight there.

'Looks busy, Paco, I can't see any tables free,' said Luis as we reached the threshold.

He was right, it appeared that we were too late for a table and I was about to suggest looking elsewhere when one of the waiters approached us.

'Señor Martinez, a pleasure to see you here at our establishment,' he said. 'Can I find you a table? We can always accommodate a torero as famous as you.'

More than a little bemused, I followed him, asking myself the question, was I famous? I had never felt famous, not until that moment, and I was slightly astonished to see him usher several diners away who seemed to have priority yet they showed no sign of ill will at losing their table once they recognised me. Quite the contrary, congratulating me on my performance and insistent upon shaking my hand.

'Wow, isn't it great to be looked after like this,' said Luis, taking the seat next to me. 'We never get treated like this in Triana, do we, boys?'

Laughter broke out, the banter started and we all began to relax after what had been quite a difficult day. I had handled my bulls well and any disappointment at seeing César take all the glory soon evaporated and my mind turned to Ramón. He'd made just one small mistake and on reflection, I knew that it could easily have been me. It is every matador's nightmare, that a singular mistake could end a career or even a life.

'Have you heard how Ramón is, Luis?' I asked.

'I spoke to one of his cuadrilla I met in the street on the way here. He told me the bull had gored Ramón badly and that they did take him to the infirmary but the doctor sent him straight to the hospital,'

'That is serious if he is in the hospital. I will see if I can visit him before we catch the train home tomorrow,' I said, then I noticed Manolito staring at something behind me.

I half turned, the same waiter who had found us our table was making a fuss of some other diners and I instantly recognised them. the waiter was seating César, Isabella, and the brutish picador Victor not far away and I turned in my seat for a better look. At that moment Isabella glanced at me and our eyes met for a fleeting moment, until Manolito said, 'look, Paco, Santiago and his wife have just walked in,'

It was reason enough to break away and I looked towards the entrance where Santiago and Gabriella were talking to a waiter, Santiago saw me and waved.

'Francisco, boys, how are you all? I heard you were here and thought it good manners to show my face,' he said coming to our table.

I stood to greet him, shaking his hand, and then I said hello to Gabriella, kissing her on both cheeks.

That may have been a for her perfume made my head spin.

'Nice to see you again, Paco,' she said.

'You attended the corrida?'

'No, unfortunately not, the train was held up, we have only been here for a couple of hours. I hear it went well for you though,' said Santiago.

'Yes,' I replied, 'as well as I could have expected. There was an incident with Ramón Verges, he was badly gored.'

'I know, we have just come from the hospital. I hear César saved the day. It is always a bad day when a matador is badly injured. I feel responsible as he is under contract to me for this corrida. His injury is quite bad and I do not think he will be fighting for quite some time,' he said pursing his lips and adding, 'I will need someone to fill his shoes until the end of the season. Perhaps we can arrange a few extra fights for you Francisco.'

I nodded my head and Gabriella looked at me.

'Paco, nice to see you again.'

'And good to see you, Señora,' I replied.

'We are staying at the same hotel as yourselves, I believe,' she said.

'We are being offered a table; we should leave you now. We can meet to talk later Francisco, perhaps a nightcap at the hotel,' said her husband.

'Of course, and thank you for letting us know about Ramón.'

Sitting back in my seat, I noticed the rest of the cuadrilla looking at me.

'What's the matter with you lot?'

'Nice to see you again, Paco,' mimicked Manolito.

I picked up a half-eaten bread bun and threw it at him.

'Cheeky so and so, look here's our tapas, I'm starving,' I said in a feeble attempt to hide my embarrassment.

The food was good, the wine flowed freely and my cuadrilla, in a state of constant chatter, was pleased at the prospect of more fights. They earned a good living supporting me and the chance to earn even more was very welcome. Eventually though, we had eaten our fill and emptied the wine bottles and the time was right for us to leave.

With my back to César's table, I had not looked around since catching Isabella's eye, but as I rose from my seat, I glanced across looking for Isabella. She was still there, beside César, stony-faced, while he chatted with passing admirers and she seemed not to notice me. I shrugged my shoulders and I was about to follow Luis and the others to the door when trouble flared.

I have no idea of the cause but Victor, the overbearing picador, stood and began pushing at a man in a small group surrounding César. It looked as if a fight was about to break out but then, to my surprise, Isabella intervened, berating the group and then César joined in, waving his arm, pointing to the door. Several waiters rushed across and began trying to defuse the situation and eventually the group began to leave.

Puzzled, I watched, saw they were coming my way and as they neared me one spoke to me.

'Paco Martinez, I recognise you. You were very good today.'

'Thanks, it is good of you to say so,' I said and unable to quell my curiosity I asked,' You were having some trouble with César's table?'

'Yes, that so-called matador and his thuggish henchman. They are no more than common thugs.'

'What did they say to you?' added Manolito who had also paused to watch.

'We simply congratulated César on his performance, said it was a shame the matador from Salamanca was injured, and then I told him I thought that you had played your second bull with real skill, skill to be admired. 'That was when the big man, the picador, threatened us.'

'Threatened you, why?'

'Because I also said I thought you were fighting in the mould of Belmonte. It seemed ridiculous that such a remark should offend him but then César himself joined in and said that you could never be as good as Belmonte, not even as good as him.'

'Honestly, he has a big head, that one,' said one of the man's companions. 'Anyway, we enjoyed your fights today. We will come to see you next time you fight at La Malagueta.'

'Thanks for your kind words. What about the woman, how come she got involved?' I asked.

'She was annoyed that the big one was attacking us, said it was not the way to behave and that you had every right to protect a fallen torero. She's feisty that one, the big one soon backed off when she tore into him.'

'She pays his wages,' said Manolito grinning. A bunch of stuck-up clowns if you ask me.'

The situation was returning to normal, César and his friends returned to their seats and Santiago was making his way towards us with Gabriella in tow.

'Francisco, we are leaving now. Shall we see you back at the hotel for a nightcap?' he said

'Yes, I look forward to it. Do you boys want a drink back at the hotel?' I asked.

'We'll catch you up, Paco,' said Manuel. 'There are some flamenco dancers in the square and we are going to have a look. We'll see you in the morning, visit Ramón, eh?'

'Yes, I would like that,' I said as I watched them go.

'You can walk with us,' said Gabriella. 'You can tell us what we missed at the corrida.'

'Yes, you must tell us how the fights went, Francisco. I have a meeting with the owners of La Malagueta tomorrow to discuss next season's programme and it is my intention that you will fight here again. If they enjoyed your performance then it makes my job easier,' he said, 'and maybe I can get a higher fee.'

I smiled to myself as I followed them both into the warm, dark night and taking a last look back at Isabella, I saw her in sombre mood, and I hoped she might look up but she did not.

Turning back, Gabriella looked at me and smiled.

'What a lovely romantic evening; the reflection of the light on the water. Do you think it's romantic, Paco?'

I blew my cheeks out, surprised yet not surprised, the wine I had consumed blunting my inhibitions and I looking at her I could not help but notice a twinkle in her eyes.

'Yes, romantic indeed.'

'What do you say, Santiago, do you see it as a romantic evening?'

He just laughed and turned his head towards his wife, the darkness obscuring them from me and their closeness left me feeling a little left out and not wanting to intrude I fell back, the reflected light the harbour amusing me and I wondered about Ramón and as we turned towards the hotel, Gabriella released her grip on Santiago, allowing me to catch up with her.

'You say you went to the hospital.'

'Yes, but only Santiago went to see Ramón. I waited outside.'

'Oh, I thought you—'

'No, I didn't want to go in there. I do not like hospitals at the best of times. Stop worrying about Ramón; Santiago said he was comfortable and the doctor thinks he will make a decent recovery. It's a lesson for you Paco, you are a big earner these days and you need to be careful. Just think of what you could loose if you are badly gored. Take a leaf out of César's book, he is careful to avoid injury because he knows how it could impact on his earnings.'

'He cheats, him and his cuadrilla will do anything it seems.'

'But he is popular and you are becoming popular with the paying public. Don't throw it away on some silly pride.'

Our discussion was becoming heated and I worried Santiago might overhear our exchange, believe that perhaps I was not such a good bet. I bit my tongue and found some relief as we entered the hotel.

'What would you like to drink, Francisco, a whisky perhaps?'

I prefer brandy if you do not mind,' I said as we walked into the bar.

'I hear there was bad blood between you and César today, Paco, tell me what happened,' said Santiago, handing me my glass.

'He performed well, his *verónicas* were impeccable

and at the end of his first fight his *remate* was of the highest standard,' I managed to say.

'Do you feel you can compete with him?'

'What… I don't understand.'

'I am wondering if you feel that you can perform as well as you say César can.'

'Of course, I can perform better than César. He cheats you know,' I said, the alcohol lowering my guard.

'Yes, I am aware of that, but the audience isn't and that's important. Listen, I have plans for next year. I may see you in the morning but if I don't, then telephone me when you get back to Seville.'

'I will,' I promised, standing to shake his hand and kiss Gabriella good night on her cheek.

'Until we meet again,' she said, turning to follow her husband.

I still had a little cognac left in my glass, and for a further ten minutes, I sat with the glass cupped in my hands, reflecting on the events of the day and Santiago's words.

I suppose it was fatigue coupled with the alcohol knocked me out. I do not know but as soon as my head hit the pillow, I was sound asleep, until that is, I heard a faint knocking on the bedroom door.

'Señor Martinez.' Then again, the light tap, tap, tap. 'Señor Martinez.'

I forced myself awake, acknowledging the interruption to my sleep, and struggled out of bed.

'Who is it?' I asked.

'Room service,' said a muffled voice.

'Room service, at this time of night.'

'Si señor.'

I switched on the light and opened the door just a little to see the porter standing in the half-light, a tray in his hand.

'What is it?'

'Excuse me, señor I have to put the tray on the table.'

'What... er, over there I suppose,' I managed to say, hardly awake and with my judgement clouded I stood aside.

I was beginning to wake and wondering what exactly was happening. Something was not quite right and I was about to challenge him as he came fully into the light. Instead, my jaw dropped and I was suddenly wide awake.

'Hello, Señor Paco, I have brought you something to help you sleep,' said Gabriella, tossing away the porter's cap as she letting her flimsy clothing slip from her shoulders.

Chapter 19

The nineteen twenty-seven season had proved very successful, my cuadrilla had a degree of security, and I had more money in the bank than I could ever have imagined. I was under contract with Santiago to fight for two more seasons and if everything went well, I would be a wealthy man. I was so busy that I did not find much time to visit my mother and during this time my younger sister had grown up. I had not noticed, shame on me, I told myself. Invariably Maria was at work whenever I paid a visit home although on one occasion, I did see her.

'About time you paid a visit, Paco, I haven't seen you more than two or three times since you left the army.'

'I'm truly sorry, Maria. Time just seems to have disappeared. Hey, it's not all my fault, you are never here when I do come to see Mama, you're always working.'

'I have a career at the bank; I have to work long hours.'

'I suppose so,' I said.

'She is doing well,' said my mother.

'What is it you do?' I asked, imagining her a teller working behind a counter.

'I work in private finance. I passed some exams and they moved me from the position of cashier into the back office. We deal with all the wealthy people of Seville and beyond. It is really interesting, I love it.'

'Good for you,' I said, rather amazed.

'I hear you are doing well, brother. Mama told me you have signed a contract with Señor Moncada Sánchez. Is that true?'

'Yes, why do you ask?'

'He is one of our clients and before you ask, I cannot tell you anything about him other than that he is a very wealthy man.'

I knew that. I had witnessed the sumptuous décor of his office in San Lorenzo and in our intimate moments, Gabriella had let slip that he was wealthy, a successful entrepreneur; the reason she had become his wife I supposed.

'You have dealings with him?'

'No, not personally, I do the figures to help clients invest their money to make more money.'

'Money makes money, eh?'

'It does.'

Having lived from hand to mouth for most of my life, I had little idea about money only that I wanted as much as I could get. I had watched my account grow but other than that I had never given it much thought.

'How much have you earned this year, Paco? I know successful bullfighters earn a lot and by all accounts you are successful.'

'I don't really know.'

'You don't know! How responsible is that?'

I could do no more than shrug my shoulders.

'What do you think, Mama, what should he do with all the money he's not sure he has?'

My mother looked just as blank as I did. Maria was sharp, educated, a far cry from my meagre education and she was leaving me trailing in her wake.

'You need someone to help you. You have a great chance, Francisco, don't waste it.'

Francisco! she used my Sunday name and that gained my attention.

'I see the amount of money that flows in and out of the bank every day, I see how the wealth of rich individuals can grow and I think you could be one of those individuals.'

I looked at my mother, saw her jaw drop.

'What do you suggest?'

'First, open an account at the bank where I work, transfer your money there and tell them you want me to oversee that account. I will make sure that we invest it wisely. If you think you are rich right now, brother, just see what can be done in a few years.'

'I need a drink,' was all I could say.

'Isn't she good?' said my mother, pouring me a glass of wine. 'I have no idea where she gets it from, certainly not me.'

Autumn came and went and I did as my sister asked, transferring the money I had accumulated into a new account at her bank. She is a clever girl, and even then, she knew far more than I realised. She looked after my money, advised me on investments, making them grow almost before my eyes. Investments! When had I ever thought of investments? Never, but under her tutelage, I was learning. I left the details to her and, feeling confident with my situation, I spent the rest of the year wandering around Andalusia visiting bull breeders. The fascination I had for the bulls growing daily as I learned of how to breed different attributes into the animals while at the same time, I made lots of connections in the world of bullfighting and in late January, Santiago sent for me.

Sitting behind the finely polished mahogany desk Santiago rested his chin on interlocked fingers, pausing for a few moments before speaking.

'Look, Francisco, I know you don't get on particularly well with César and his cuadrilla but I see it as an opportunity.'

'An opportunity, in what way?' I said, immediately on the defensive.

'In the bullring, it is man against bull, the ultimate contest. That is what everyone comes to see but also to compare the different matadors, to support their favourites. You know that, you have your own following, maybe not so many as César but you have enough. The rivalry between Belmonte and Josélito was something. They lifted the art of bullfighting to where it is today and who knows where we would be if Josélito had lived. Only Juan Belmonte remains. You know he took a bad goring in Barcelona at the end of last season?'

I nodded, everyone knew what had happened to him; he was the star of the bullfighting world, everything he did was common knowledge.

'Well, he has decided to retire.'

'No! The greatest torero, retire, no.'

'Yes, and that leaves a vacuum, I think your rivalry with César can fill that vacuum. Just think of the money we can make. There are no others I know of that could do that; we must seize the chance now. I am working to make sure both you and César fight on the same bill several times during the season. We can advertise the fights as *mano a mano*. What do you say?'

What could I say? To compete for Belmonte's crown would be an honour. Whoever came out on top would be the best bullfighter in Spain and all that would entail. I have to say it was an exciting prospect.

'Gabriella asks after you by the way. She says she has not seen you in months. You must come to dinner one evening. Do you have a lady?'

'Er... no, not now.'

'Come to the villa next Tuesday, shall we say at eight 'o'clock? You can stay the night and on Wednesday you will accompany me to your old stomping ground the Ganadería Carlos Viera de Mendoza. I am invited to look at the bulls they have bred for the coming season and I would like to see Carlos anyway.'

'Carlos de Mendoza?'

'Yes, his father died last year. Carlos is the *Ganadero* now.'

'Of course, I did know but I haven't been back there since I first entered the ring. José de Mendoza treated me well enough, a sad loss.'

'And Carlos, you get on with him?'

'Yes, I suppose so. You could say he discovered me. He caught me fighting his young bulls one night and locked me in a barn. I thought he was going to call the Guardia but instead, he gave me a job on the ranch. It was to stop me bringing my friends on his land to play his bulls, I think. Still, I had a good job, I learned about bulls, learned to ride. He did give me a chance.'

'Good, well on Wednesday you will not be Francisco the common vaquero anymore but Vaquerito the bullfighter.

A week later I went to Santiago's villa for dinner and on that occasion, I managed an uninterrupted sleep. Waking early, I dressed and decided to sit a while in the garden but as I crept down the stairs a soft voice called out to me.

'Paco, good morning.'

Gabriella, the perfect host who for once had resisted temptation stood on the landing looking down at me, a wry smile on her face and I noticed her fully dressed and ready for the day.

'Good morning.'

'You slept well,' she said as she followed me down the stairs.

'Yes, very well.'

'That's a shame, I thought I might find you wandering around unable to sleep in a strange bed.'

I just laughed.

'Breakfast, what would you like to eat? We have a servant working in the kitchen.'

'Oh, just coffee and some bread will do.'

'Coffee and bread! That's not much for a fit young man like you, although I suppose you haven't exerted yourself a great deal since you have been here.'

'No, I've been a little restrained. I need space and privacy to exercise properly.'

Now it was her turn to laugh.

'There, the breakfast room, make yourself comfortable and I will see what we can offer you. Coffee and bread indeed, what do you take me for.'

The room was not unlike the main dining room we had occupied the previous evening, full of expensive looking furniture and on the walls oil paintings of bulls and bullfighters. One drew my interest, a strange painting and I walked over to it, A collage of a bullfighter in different poses and I was not sure of what I was seeing. With his arms outstretched he held the classic *verónica*, the *molinete* but unexpectedly he was naked from head to toe. Standing back, I folded my arms and studied it when Santiago appeared.

'You like my pictures, Francisco?'

'I'm no expert, Santiago. They look fine, the bull there,' I said, a little embarrassed, 'I remember fighting a bull just like that.'

'It's good to know you are at least taking an interest in art. Ah, here comes Gabriella with your breakfast. What have we got this morning, my dear?'

'He was content with just bread and coffee. Try this ham, it's the best there is in all of Spain and these olives, the pick of the crop.'

'You spoil me,' I said.

'Nonsense, Francisco, we are not spoiling you, on the contrary, we are educating you. As a famous torero, the great and the good will want to get to know you, invite you to all manner of functions. We can't have you mixing with them and not knowing anything about food and wine and of course, there is the etiquette,' said Santiago.

'I will teach you Paco. You should come here at least once a week for dinner and I will teach you how to mix with the highest of society,' said Gabriella in an unexpectedly business-like manner. 'Now, let's eat for I know you have a busy day ahead of you.'

Santiago smiled and nodded his head.

'She is right, Francisco. You are becoming famous and

people want to be seen with you. That is for the future, for now though let us go to see Carlos and his bulls.

Santiago was not just the owner of a fine motor car but he had a chauffeur to drive it, and the driver, dressed in a smart grey uniform was waiting for us.

'We will drive over to the Mendoza *ganadería* to see Carlos this morning and once we are finished, I can drop you off in the city. Does that suit you?'

'Of course, thank you.'

I do not know what made me think it, but I felt that Gabriella had changed. She was still flirtatious but in a much more subdued way, a more professional way perhaps, and she came to the door to see us off she spent several minutes in deep conversation with Santiago. From the car I watched them and it seemed that she was the one doing the talking, Santiago nodded his head and for a moment glanced towards me.

'You have not been back to the ranch since your days as a vaquero, Paco?' said Santiago returning to the automobile.

'Er... no, there was never any need for me to,' was all I could say, wondering if I was the object of Santiago and Gabriella's conversation.

'Well, I think there is now. As you know Carlos worked with his father for many years. José was knowledgeable and he knew how to bring out the best in his bulls and, in my opinion, Carlos has inherited that skill. We will look at this year's offerings, see what kind of animals they are. You know yourself; a timid bull is no good in the ring.'

I had never travelled far in a motor car, a novel

experience for me, and I spent most of the journey looking out of the window. I marvelled at how fast we went and finally, we drove into the ganadería's courtyard, Carlos came out of the house to meet us.

'Who is this, another protégé, Santiago.'

'He is more than that, Carlos. You should know him he worked for you.'

Carlos looked again.

'*Madre de Dios*, Paco Martinez, well, well,' he said and then, 'it is a pleasure to see you again Santiago, and I have heard how Paco here is making a name for himself.'

'The pleasure is all mine, Carlos. How has the breeding season gone? Have you many calves that I might expect will grow to be *toros bravos*?'

'Yes, this is the first season we are trying something with a Miura we bought from Don Eduardo. He is a direct descendent of Murciélago. He was very expensive and his first offspring are just a year old. If we can breed the bull's aggression into our own strain then I think we will create a lineage that will become famous throughout Spain.'

'I am impressed, Carlos. I will keep an eye on the calves as they grow. Who knows, my young friend here might well be fighting them in a few years' time.'

Carlos turned towards me.

'So, the ragamuffin I caught messing with our bulls is becoming a star bullfighter, eh? I was first to see his potential, wasn't I, Paco?'

'Yes, you did and I thank you for giving me the chance.'

'What is it they call you in the corridas?'

'El Vaquerito,' said Santiago.

'Of course, I remember. You have come a long Paco.'

'I hope so.'

'I have to say you did worry me out there in the dead of night. Although it was dangerous and you were worrying our bulls, I could see how good you were. It was after I spoke to my father, we decided that we were better off giving you a job rather than have you and your friends return later to damage our investments.'

'I can see that now. I am sorry for what we did but we were young and we just wanted to fight bulls. There aren't any bulls in Triana, you know.'

'No, I don't suppose there are,' he said, beginning to laugh. The *tienta* last week gave a good indication of which bulls are good enough for this season's corridas Santiago, we will find the best of them in the north pasture. We can take a ride over there if you like.'

'That's good, Carlos. I like to take a good look at the animals before I pay out any money.'

'They tell me you ran away a few years back, Paco. What was that all about?' said Carlos catching me off guard.

'Nothing, best forgotten.'

'So, our vaquero is becoming famous, is he, Santiago?'

'He's doing well and under my tutelage, I am optimistic for him.'

'César is known as the best matador in Seville these days. He used to come here often a few years ago. He's married my cousin Isabella and they come here to ride our horses on occasion.'

'Ah yes, César López Aguilar, that is interesting. You are right Carlos, he is a famous matador these days and recognised as the best in all of Andalusia, but Francisco is equally good, if not better.'

'Is he?'

'Yes, and next season we will see who really is the best.'

'Well, I wish him luck. From what I know, César will not take kindly to anyone trying to steal his crown.'

I was astonished that they should talk like that. I had no desire to lay down any challenge to César, I simply wanted to fight bulls to the best of my ability and for my performances to speak for me but I sensed that, perhaps, something was about to happen and I was involved.

During the nineteen twenty-eight season I found myself fighting on the same bill alongside César on more than one occasion. We fought at Córdoba, Jerez, Málaga twice, and several other lesser arenas. Although our growing rivalry was not quite the war I'd anticipated, it did draw the attention of the bullfighting public and as we fought in bullrings further afield stories began to appear in the newspapers. Some were true but many others seemed concocted and a long way from the truth.

I was not so naïve when it came to newspaper stories. I had read the reports of the fighting in Morocco on those few occasions we regrouped and rested in preparation for the next campaign. I had seen then how distorted the truth could become, the successes, the failures. I had been there and seen with my own eyes that the reality was not how the newspapers reported it.

'Says here that César is looking like a successor to Belmonte, Paco,' said Manolito poring over his newspaper.

'Do you believe that?'

'I don't know. I have never seen Belmonte fight, but the reporter says he saw Belmonte and reckons César is as good.'

I did not want to argue. I had read some of the rubbish printed in that newspaper. I had never met the reporter but it seemed to me he did not know much about the finer points of bullfighting.

I leaned back in my seat as the train rumbled on across the flat countryside.

'Don't look so glum, Paco, stories like that sell newspapers, you must know that,' said Luis sitting opposite. 'This rivalry with César makes for good publicity and more circulation. Even we are benefiting. Every corrida where you and César fight on the same bill is a sell-out. It's not doing you any harm, is it?'

I had to agree, even so, it galled me to have to read of the esteem in which the public held César when I knew half of his passes were not all they seemed. He was still cheating but I had to admit he was good at it.

'When are you both fighting on the same bill next?'

'I think in a month's time. Santiago told me he has arranged a corrida in Barcelona for the twenty-sixth and told me to expect César to be on the same bill,' I said, adding, 'He will be the senior matador.'

Luis said nothing, looking at me for a few seconds to judge my mood before gazing out of the carriage window.

'I think we are about home,' he said.

Manolito looked up from his newspaper to confirm, and then looked at me.

'You get a lot of praise, Paco; it's just that César gets more.'

'Shut up before I stuff that paper where the sun doesn't shine.'

'You will need more than one newspaper to fill his arsehole,' said José drawing laughter from the rest of the cuadrilla and deflating my anger.

I turned away, looked out of the window and caught my reflection superimposed upon the moving countryside and the face looking back at me was not my face. Had I really changed, was I changing? I did not know but I could see quite clearly that I was becoming bitter; my eyes seemed hollow, the corners of my mouth turned down in a pout.

'Damn it,' I heard myself say.

The rivalry with César was beginning to consume me, I was less carefree, less inclined to take criticism and the relationship with my cuadrilla was becoming strained. I had been through a lot in the past five or six years, and when I stepped down onto the platform, I knew I needed some idea of a solution to my problems.

'Francisco,' I heard.

Looking along the platform I recognised Santiago and he was coming towards me and so I left my cuadrilla and walked towards him.

'You enjoyed the corrida?' I said, looking for some positivity because the last thing I needed at that moment was for him to heap praise upon César.

'It was a good weekend. We made a very respectable profit and that is what we really want. You must come to dinner some time; Gabriella often asks how you are. I thought she was going to teach you some table manners. Has nothing become of that?'

'No, I think she has forgotten. I have not seen her for ages. Yes, I would like that,' I said suddenly noticing the same young man whom I had seen entering his office many months before alongside Santiago.

'Ah, Pietro,' he said turning to greet his visitor.

'Francisco, meet Pietro. He is a good friend of mine, he is Italian, an artist. You saw some of his work on my wall.'

'Hello,' I said offering my hand, surprised by the strength of his grip. I suppose I had imagined artists were not particularly muscular individuals. 'I admired your paintings of the bulls Santiago has hanging on his walls, they were very good.'

'No, I don't paint bulls, I paint the matadors and dancers, the human body, not lesser animals,' he said smiling.

'We are discussing Pietro's next work; I might buy it if he can convince me it's worth having. Give Gabriella a telephone call and arrange dinner; here is my card with the number. Well, I look forward to dinner whenever that is but if you will excuse us, we have some business to attend to.'

I watched them leave, Santiago the middle-aged impresario and the boyish-looking Pietro and for a fleeting moment I wondered about his painting of the bullfighter. Then I looked at the card and wondered where I might find a telephone.

It was not quite the first time I had ever used a telephone but I had no idea where to find one until I asked Luis.

'The main post office.'

'Of course, it's obvious, isn't it? You know everything, Luis,' I said, grinning at him.

'Not quite everything. Who are you ringing?'

'Er... Santiago suggested I call a friend of his to arrange to visit a *ganadería*. Santiago says he has interesting stock I might like to see,' I lied.

'Oh, that sounds like a good idea,' lied Luis in return.

I heard the ringing tone and my heart rate picked up. It seemed to ring forever until I heard a clicking sound.

'*Digame*,' said a female voice I hardly recognised.

'This is Paco,' was all I could say, feeling more afraid of the black shape of the telephone than any bull I had ever fought.

'Paco, how nice to hear from you.'

'Is that Gabriella?' I said straining my ear.

'Of course. How was Málaga?'

'Good, good. Listen, I have just left Santiago and a friend. He says to talk to you and arrange dinner next week. So I am,' I said rather clumsily.

'A friend, who?'

'An artist, Italian, called Pietro.'

'Hello, are you still there?'

'Yes, I am still here. Dinner next week you say, oh dear, my diary, I have left it at the apartment. I tell you what Paco, why not meet me there at eight o'clock tonight and I can look in my diary, see what evening we are free. Eight o'clock, you know where it is.'

'Yes, of course, eight 'o'clock,' I said.

She hung up and left me looking at the clock on the post office wall, wondering if I could survive until eight o'clock.

On the previous occasion I had climbed those stairs darkness and expectation had obscured almost everything but today was different. I was early and the sun was still some way from setting. I had time to look around, at the flowers in a large earthenware pot adding colour to the grey architecture. The stout wooden door with ornate with reliefs was impressive and a bell pull protruded from the wall. I pulled it and for several seconds stood staring at the carving on the door until finally, a key turned in the lock and the door swung open.

'Paco, come in, it is good to see you again. It has been a while, how are you?'

'It has, I'm fine thanks,' I said stepping over the threshold and into a haze of perfume.

'A glass of wine, a brandy maybe, I know you like a brandy.'

I could not help looking at her, she was as beautiful as ever.

'Brandy.'

'Me too, helps me relax. Sit over there on the settee while I get your drink. So, you saw Santi, he was with that Italian halfwit Pietro, was he?'

'Yes. Halfwit you say?'

'He's not too bright, probably a decent artist but that's all.'

'You don't like him.'

'I put up with him,' she said, handing me my drink.

'I don't understand.'

'When he is around, Santi has eyes for no one else.'

'Not even you?'

'Not even me.'

'Is that what the painting on your wall is about?'

'Of course, they like that sort of thing.'

'I didn't like it particularly. What sane man would face a bull naked?'

'It's not the bovine variety that interests them. Anyway, we have established where your preferences lie. Drink up, we have some catching up to do.'

If Gabriella had the ability to do anything then it was to take my mind off my problems even if just for a short period of time.

'Perroito, that was wonderful, you play me just as you would play a bull in the ring.'

'Except you are not a bull, far from it,' I said, running my hand across her body, my eyes devouring her. In the half-light allowed in by the shutters I looked at her face, her skin smoothed by our passion but I could not help my anxieties resurfacing.

'Are you all right, I felt something, as if... I don't know, something.'

'I'm fine, it's just...'

Now it was my turn to pause.

'There *is* something bothering you, Perroito, what is it?'

'César.'

'What about him?'

'It's as if everyone is against me and for him. Even my own cuadrilla is beginning to believe he is better than me.'

She turned onto her back, put her hands behind her head, and stared at the ceiling.

'You don't care,' I said.

'Don't be silly, I care about you more than you know.'

'Well, that's something I suppose.'

'Listen, Paco, this is serious business. It was my idea to pit you against César. I knew it would lead to fireworks, it's what I planned.'

'Planned? You're telling me this was all planned.'

'Don't be upset, hear me out,' she said, the lines returning to her face as her voice took on a more serious tone. 'Santiago and I are going to make you a wealthy man, make us all rich. Listen to me. The golden age of bullfighting has been over for some time, ever since Josélito died. No one has replaced him. Belmonte was his foil and now even he has given up fighting bulls. Who can blame him? To my mind, that leaves a vacuum and someone must fill it. Why not you and César? I know of your feelings for Isabella, I have seen your face when she is around and I have seen hers. There is something between you, I think. No matter, this rivalry is a valuable commodity we can sell to the bullfighting public.'

'What am I supposed to do, put up with being used?' I said indignantly.

'Yes, is the straight answer. We were worried your pride might get in the way, which is why we said nothing. Look at it this way Francisco, we have started the ball rolling and the bullfighting public is beginning to notice you, and you are becoming famous. It is what you want, recognition? I'm sorry if I have hurt you, Paco, but can you see what we are trying to do?'

'I can, yes, but that doesn't change the fact that you have betrayed me.'

'I haven't betrayed you; I have always had your interests at heart. If I had spoken about it before you might not have acted as you did in trying to outperform César and then the public might not have become so interested. We needed to make sure it was a plausible rivalry. That was why Santiago took you to see Carlos de Mendoza; we knew that he would relate everything to César because he is involved with his management. He fell for it didn't he, César is as eager as you are to become the best bullfighter in all of Spain and will do his upmost to better you. I know you are better than he is so don't worry on that score. Have you ever read Shakespeare?'

'No, who is that.'

'An Englishman who wrote plays. No matter, but a famous line from a play is 'time will out' and give it time and you will be heralded as the best bullfighter in Spain.'

Her argument was convincing. It was true I did harbour ambitions to become the best bullfighter in Seville, but not like this. Yet when she mentioned the rest of Spain something stirred within me. Yes, of course, I enjoyed the appreciation of my followers, the wealth bullfighting had brought me, but I had always considered the rivalry between myself and César natural, uncontrived, and now she was telling me that she and Santiago planned to make our rivalry public property.

I lay back in the bed, my annoyance subsiding as I considered the possibilities, the money, and it occurred to me that I had some sort of power over Gabriella and Santiago and that made me reach out to her, roll my body onto hers in a gesture of domination and I looked her full in the eyes.

'I will not do it; you can forget next season.'

Initially, there was no reaction and I worried I had gone too far but then her eyes narrowed, focused on mine, and I felt her stiffen.

'You cannot walk away from this, Francisco; it's too big an opportunity. Don't walk away, please.'

I smiled inwardly. I was in the bullring and my opponent had just shown weakness, I could exploit that weakness and I began to play her.

'You have worked behind my back for your own advantage. Why should I not walk away? My honour is at stake.'

'No, don't say that. If it works as we expect, then we will make a lot of money.'

'But I am under contract, my fees are set. How will I benefit from this scheme of yours?'

'We will renegotiate your fees, a bonus every time you fight *mano a mano* with César. Santiago is prepared to pay you more, I know. If he is not then I will make him. Don't walk away, my love.'

I drew my sword and plunged it deep into the killing zone, metaphorically speaking that is, and with joy in my heart, I looked forward to the new season.

Gabriella was persuasive and determined, and not long after, believing she had convinced me to agree to her scheme, Santiago summoned me to his office.

'It is done, I have re-written your contract. Would you care to read it through?'

I picked up the several sheets of paper of the new contract and began to read. Together with Gabriella, I had verbally agreed that the terms of the original were to remain, the only real change being the fees I would earn. The numbers were impressive, the underhand tactics Santiago and his scheming wife had employed were benefiting me more than they had expected I think.

'Here, my pen. Sign it where I have indicated and I will have it witnessed,' he said handing me his pen. 'You are happy, Francisco?'

'Yes, very.'

'A glass of sherry, a drink to celebrate?' he said smiling.

By late spring I had gathered my cuadrilla, Luque had returned for another season as one of the picadors and I had invested in a motor car, a Ford Model T made in Cadiz. I kept it in a garage near where I was living and every day for the best part of a week, I went to look at it. I could do no more because I could not drive, my only experience of anything remotely mechanical was the time spent stripping and cleaning my rifle in the Legión. Then, quite unexpectedly, my brother came to the rescue.

'You seem to know your way around a motor car, Juan,' I said, showing it off to him.

'There are lots of them on the docks. I sometimes speak with the drivers and they show me things. I can change the oil, you know.'

'When are you going back to Cadiz?'

'At the end of the week, I wanted to see Mama and our sisters, and you, of course. I went to see Juanita and her baby yesterday. The little girl is growing up.'

'She is. What about you, have you a girlfriend these days?'

'One or two, nothing serious, I don't earn enough to afford a full-time woman.'

That made me laugh.

'Come on, let's go for a spin,' he said. 'Where do you fancy?'

I looked at him and puffed out my cheeks. It was one thing to own a motor car but quite another to be able to drive it.

'I don't know how,' I said with some embarrassment. 'I was hoping to find someone to show me.'

'I'll show you. I have driven some of the lorries on the docks to help speed up loading. I can drive but we need to find a quiet stretch of road, somewhere out of town. I will drive to begin with, then you can have a go. It's easy enough.'

Easy enough! It did not seem so easy when I sat in the driver's seat and put the machine into gear. The grinding noise was a little frightening and until he showed me how to use the clutch properly, we spent our time bouncing along the road like a pair of wild frogs until, after two or three hours of perseverance, I was able to steer the thing with a fair degree of competence.

'I'm not sure you should be out on your own just yet,' said Juan. 'I'm here for a few days so I can help if you want.'

I was grateful for his attention and by the time he returned to Cadiz, I was driving with a certain degree of proficiency and for the next two weeks, I spent every day driving. One day I decided to head north to Rinconada, follow the route we had walked just a few years before and I was amazed at how short a time it took. Then, with my confidence increasing, I dared to venture into the city, duelling with the traffic then I took my little motor car to Triana to visit my mother.

'Francisco, I am impressed; you will have no need of a horse anymore.'

'No, it's the modern way, Mama. I can drive anywhere in Spain whenever it suits me. Where would you like to go?'

'Me?'

'Yes, I can take you for a ride right now, if you like.'

Her face drained of colour; as a woman born of a different age and confronted by something she did not understand had made her afraid.

'Those things are not for the likes of me, Francisco. I don't want to go in it.'

I would have felt like laughing if it were not for the fact that I could see she was genuinely afraid.

'Just sit in it for a few minutes.'

Finally, I persuaded her and on that glorious Sunday afternoon, I took her for a ride across the bridge.

'I haven't been into the city for years, not since your father was alive. We would come across sometimes when we were courting. When there was a corrida we would come to sell flowers made from scraps of cloth and the girls would put them in their hair. They were good days, happy days,' she said somehow forgetting the hardships I remembered.

We'd been poor but at least my father always had a job, not like Luis's father. He was just a labourer and once the construction of the new canal ended the work dried up and they did suffer. I can remember as kids Papa would sit Luis on his knee and feed him our leftovers. But now our lives had changed, no more scraps from the table because I was becoming a rich man. Thanks to my sister I was benefiting from a boom in the world's stock markets and I had developed the habit of checking stock prices in the newspaper finance sections almost every day. It forced my grasp of numbers to improve and I and marvelled at how easy it was to make money.

Chapter 20

Nineteen twenty-eight began quietly enough but as the start of the bullfighting season approached more and more stories of the rivalry between César and myself were beginning to appear in the newspapers. There were hints that our enmity extended beyond the bullring and discussion raged over which of us would, by the end of the season be Spain's foremost bullfighter.

Córdoba was the venue for my first *mano a mano* with César, my contract dictated that I was to fight in Granada followed by Almeria a week later, then we travelled to Córdoba for the first showdown and on the morning of the corrida I sat on a row of seats overlooking the bullring reading the morning's paper.

It seemed all of Spain was now aware of my rivalry with César and the newspaper was portraying me as the antagonist. I read a little further before discarding the newspaper in disgust, annoyed that I they saw me as the villain.

'What is in the paper, Paco?' said Luis picking it up.

'There is nothing in there of any real interest. They seem to be setting me up as the loser in all this. César gets nothing but praise.'

'It's only some hack with nothing better to do. They will say anything to sell their newspapers. Here let me have a read,' he said retrieving the paper.

He was right of course; I was getting ahead of myself.

'It's nothing, Paco, just newsprint. Your performance is what matters and this season not last. I know you are better than him and we both know he is not averse to cheating. Now if that came out what would people say?'

Luis's words resonated. Yes, if it became general knowledge that César cheated then that could go against him. then again if it did come out what would be the effect on our rivalry and more importantly my fees. It was a puzzle but it was dawning on me that I needed César and he needed me.

'Pass me the paper, Luis, I didn't finish the article.'

The manner of César's approach to his first bull was no more than the public would expect, playing it with skill and perseverance and I watched him closely. He had learned new tricks, controlled the bull with a skill and dexterity I had not seen before, his every move producing cheers from his supporters.

'He looks more confident than last season,' said Manolito leaning on the barrier next to me.

'Be careful when it is your turn, Paco, we don't want you trying risky passes just to prove you are better than him,' said Luis.

'Don't worry, my friend, I know what I am doing,' I said, a little irritated at his overly protective tone. I was fighting bulls not running a kindergarten I said as César's fight came to an end and just minutes later the trumpet announced the start of my fight and after my banderillos left to take their places the heavy gate swung open to reveal my bull. A cacophony of sound greeted it overwhelming the animal and for a time it seemed reluctant to enter the ring until a hefty stab in its rump by a stockman's staff convinced it to move.

Finally overcoming its initial shock, the bull trotted into the open and from behind the barrier Manolito ran to confront it. I watched its reaction as he showed his cape, shaking it to draw the bull to him and then the brothers José and Manuel joined him and for a time they played the bull. I left them to put the bull through its paces before I made my appearance, my cape ready for the first verónica. Then, to my astonishment, a torrent of abuse emanating from a section of the crowd reached my ears, unpleasant words and all directed at me.

'Think you're the best Vaquerito? Well think again, you are no match for César,' shouted someone and then, 'You wouldn't know one end of a bull from another and then cutting comments about the time I returned to the bullring, remarks on my suitability to be where I was.

Mild insults were a standard part of my working life good humoured banter aimed at me but this section of the crowd seemed particularly vitriolic. The rivalry between César and myself had become very real. I was becoming affected by all the publicity and now the abuse and began to feel an anxiety I had never experienced before and that did not go unnoticed by the attentive Luis.

'What's wrong, Paco, you didn't seem yourself today?'

'I wish I knew,' I said as I peeled off my clothes.

'I said for you to be careful but you were practically timid. It's not like you. This thing with César is getting to you, isn't it?'

'Not really, I can handle him.'

'Maybe but you're not being straight with me, Paco. I

have known you all my life. If anyone knows what makes you tick, it's me, and I know something is wrong.'

I found it increasingly hard not to confess and taking a deep breath I looked at him.

'I've not been sleeping well and each time I read about how good he is in the newspaper I just want to throw up.'

'Hm… not unexpected, is it? You are under a lot of pressure in normal times but this thing Santiago and his woman have invented is putting you under more strain than ever to perform well. And then there's the other woman, Isabella. What are your feelings about her these days?'

'Hey, Luis, that's a bit much isn't it?'

'Not when all our livings depend upon you. We need you in a good frame of mind, we need you to stop worrying about César, that you think he is already the best matador. We need you to be positive, workmanlike, and perform as we know you can. I think the first thing is for you to do is to forget about reading any more newspapers. I will tell the others that if they find you reading about you and César to snatch the paper away from you.'

Hearing Luis talk like that was a shock. He was always quiet, reticent when it came to an argument and yet, here he was giving me a dressing down. Maybe that's what I needed. I thought of Isabella and the end of our affair, how I had felt at that time. Then I had run away but there was no running away this time.

'Alright, Luis, let's get changed and go for a beer. Tell the others, tell them the drinks are on me,' I said, my confidence returning.

Three weeks later, I again found myself subordinate to César in Alicante on a glorious weekend, and the fiesta was in full swing. Since Córdoba I had experienced success in Salamanca, Toledo, and in Seville where I was top of the bill and my following was growing. The support of the fans was important, bolstering my confidence fighting alongside César and his noisy supporters

'Brilliant, you were far better than César today, assured and positive, Paco, you are back to your old self. Getting rid of those newspapers was one of the best things you ever did,' said Luis looking up at me as the boys carried me shoulder high from the arena.

I had no answer; he was right and he certainly played a large part in my rehabilitation, if you could call it that. I had faced my demons and to a large extent I had got myself back on track. After deciding to forego my daily newspaper the biggest step was learning how to blank out the vociferous name calling and abuse certain sections of the crowd were hurling at me. In a way it was not too difficult because once I located the worst offenders, I would coax the bulls as far away from them as possible thereby nullifying their comments and depriving them of a decent view. It worked well and I certainly felt better, so much so that my performances were on a par with the best I had achieved.

'Yes, that was a great fight, better than César's by a long way,' said Manuel as the boys lowered me from their shoulders.

'Listen to them,' said Manolito. 'Get out there and take a few more bows Paco.'

I did as he said, lifting my black montera hat to acknowledge the cheers, satisfied that a large part of the crowd was sympathetic to me, there was nothing more I could do

Unusually for César he began his second fight with a *gaonera*, the cape held at his back, most of the purple and yellow cloth exposed to his left side. I remember feeling a tinge of admiration, for although I disliked him, I liked his approach. He had read the bull accurately, because when it charged it favoured his left. He had positioned his cape perfectly for the bull to pass harmlessly by, a good start that raised a cheer from his supporters and after several passes he withdrew leaving the disorientated bull to his cuadrilla for the rest of the first act.

The bull had to trust its senses and instinct, it had no experience of the environment in which it found itself, the air full of strange scents, and already aroused by César it raised its head and charged towards the first object that moved, a horse the picador spurred on to clear its path. Swinging the horse towards a more open area of the bullring the subordinate picador escaped and Victor took his cue. Riding hard with his lance outstretched he came upon the bull from behind and jabbed the tip of his lance into the bull's great neck muscle. The bull, still fresh and angered by its tormentors had an agility superior to the. Flinching from its wound it chased after Victor, driving him towards the barrier so fast that Victor could not control the horse. Although he had understood the danger his reaction was too slow and his mount took the full thrust of the charge, the bull's raw power tipping the squealing horse over. A gasp rose from the crowd in expectation of serious injury as Victor lost control but as the horse fell he managed to jump clear and within seconds, the rest of the cuadrilla had swarmed around the bull and as quickly as the incident unfolded it faded.

Victor mounted a second horse to complete the task of inflicting pain on the increasingly angered bull and as the first act ended the banderillos returned with their long darts to torment the bull further and at the end of the second act it showed signs of weakening, the colourful banderillas hanging from its thick neck muscles, rivulets of blood running down over its shiny black hide and when the men left the bull stood motionless and alone at the centre of the bullring and César's supporters called his name. then César stepped

The trumpet announced the final act and César stepped forward to attract the bull's attention. He waked purposefully towards the panting animal, his cape hanging oose by his side and when he was just a few paces away he turned to the side and lifted the cape, turned his head theatrically away from the bull. A hush filled the air, nobody moved until the bullfighter turned his head sharply and shook the cape. The bull took the bait and charged, the crowd came to like, roaring encouragement and César skilfully sidestepped.

The outsmarted bull could do little more than stand panting heavily and it was evident to any aficionado that César's confidence was high.

Sitting with my cuadrilla the following day we waited for our train to journey back to Seville and I reflected upon the corrida. I had already broken my promise to Luis and bought a newspaper keen to read if the journalist deemed the corrida a success and what did the writer have to say about myself and César.

In front of the cheering crowd we had dispatched our bulls with the assurance and composure expected of us and although the article was full of praise for César its author still had good things to say about my performance and wrote that he found it difficult to determine which one of us was *numero uno*.

'It says here that Victor was lucky not to be badly injured. What do you reckon, Mano?' I asked.

Manolito looked up from his own paper and pursed his lips.

'It's what picadors do. He handled the situation, he got out of the way quickly enough and do not forget the rest of César's cuadrilla were onto the bull before it caused any real damage and the horse survived.'

'They say you handled your bulls well, Paco, and you did,' said José looking up from his own newspaper.

'Maybe I did, but not as well as César, according to this.'

'That's rubbish,' said Luis. 'You did what you had to. As usual, César was just showing off. I wouldn't worry about him just yet; we have a long way to go until the end of the season.'

Prophetic words from Luis. The season was long and hard, we travelled the length and breadth of the peninsula, fought in the bullrings of Barcelona, the Basque country and for the first time, in Burgos. In June we fought in the newly opened bullring of Granada and later in the month, in Seville and then in early July I was again fighting on the same bill as César in Valencia. Each time we met; the arenas were full to bursting and the newspapers were in general agreement that honours were even.

'Madrid is the big one,' Manolito said as we travelled to our next corrida. 'The crowds are getting bigger all the time; did you see how many people were turned away yesterday? We could have filled the bullring twice over.'

'At least,' added Manuel. 'They were chanting your name all over town. Did you hear them as we went back to the hotel?'

'Yes,' I said leaning back in my seat.

I had replaced earlier, poor performances with a string of far better fights, my confidence had returned, and in less than a month I would fight the final *mano a mano* with César in Madrid. It would be my first fight in that noble arena and the newspapers were billing it as the final showdown. I had come a long way in just two short years and to fight in Madrid would be the pinnacle of my career. But my success had created another problem, money. I had lots of it but little idea of how to manage it, that was for Maria to do. She was looking after my savings; wealth I suppose I should call it, and she was doing an outstanding job. When I had fought in Seville, I made time to visit her at the bank and cast my mind back to our meeting

'These are were truly impressive numbers brother. Stock markets all over the world are rising and you have a considerable income from your investments. You are becoming a wealthy man, Francisco. Have you decided yet what you going to do with it all?'

'Phew, I don't know, I haven't really given it a thought. What do you suggest?'

'Land, what about a ganadería, an estate for when you retire?'

'I have told you; I have no intention of retiring. I still have years of bullfighting in me.'

'Maybe, but eventually, everything comes to an end, Francisco. You have a wonderful opportunity to secure your future, and, think about this, you will have large tax bills to pay.'

My Sunday name and what's this about tax? Suddenly I became attentive.

When we did finally arrive in Madrid, I found it noticeably cooler than Seville, the September rains had come early, the shiver running down my spine not completely because of the cold. I had not slept well for several nights, tossing, and turning as my mind tussled with the biggest fight of my career. Manolito had told me a month earlier that the fight in Madrid had already sold out. The papers were still debating whether César or I was the best torero and the pressure was getting to me. But I was a bullfighter, it was my life, I simply had to handle it and when I took my first look inside the Plaza de Toros the view astounded me and all my worries about the coming fight relegated to the back of my mind.

The Madrid bullring was not a modern structure like Barcelona's Las Arenas but at around sixty years old it had not lost its place as the foremost shrine to bullfighting.
I gazed with admiration at the wide expanse of seating, the tall arches, and the canvas awnings to protect the most affluent patrons from the sun. Already men with rakes were spreading the bright yellow sand, its significance not lost on me. During the golden age of bullfighting, Juan Belmonte and Josélito had fought *mano a mano* on that same

sand and in just two days' time myself and César would try to emulate them.

'Wow, it's impressive,' said Luis coming to stand by my side. 'This is definitely the place to fight, Paco.'

I did not need telling. To fight here in front of the king was the pinnacle of any matador's career, but for me there was an added pressure and I was nervous and two days later I was taking in that same view.

'It's about time to draw the lots,' said Luis looking at his watch. 'Over there I think, that's the way to the pens.

Luis led the way, shuffling along in his own unique way and we arrived at the stock yard to see that César, Isabella and Victor were already there.

'Ah, Francisco, you have arrived at last,' César said with a hint of sarcasm.

'Of course, why would I not?'

'Yes of course. You know my wife. Look how beautiful she is,' he said.

'Francisco, it is so nice to see you again. How are you keeping?' said Isabella.

'I'm fine,' I said, confused at such friendliness.

'César is wonderful, isn't he? Look at the diamond ring he bought me, such fine gold,' she said holding it up in front of me, almost under my nose.

I had not been so close to her since the dinner the previous winter and feeling compelled to, I looked at the ring on her finger. It was obviously very expensive but more than that, I noticed her hands. Those same hands I had held, felt explore my body, and I should have felt something but to my surprise I did not. How plain her hands looked now, her fingers thick and ugly and as I looked at her face, I could see that the beautiful girl I had spent so long adoring was not so beautiful after all.

'César is the best matador in Spain, Francisco. Of course, you should know that, and in front of the king today everyone will know,' she said, her eyes holding mine.

In that split second, I understood. César's smirk, Victor's piggy eyes and Isabella's attitude, were an attempt to use my perceived feelings against me. Only minutes earlier it might have worked, but not now for I had seen the real woman, a cunning and materialistic woman and instead of feeling upset, I felt a release. The prison cell in which my heart had resided for so long had just dissolved before my eyes.

'It's a very nice ring, now what about the draw?' I said to the watching official and from the corner of my eye noticed a look of surprise on her face.

'Which ones do we hope to have, Luis?' I said, turning to my friend, ignoring both Isabella and César.

Victor was glowering at me. What the brute expected to achieve I did not know for I had given him a good beating the last time he tried to intimidate me and I had no doubt I could do it again.

Later in the day I gazed out at a city bustling with traffic from the hotel room window and heard the noise of automobile horns drifting up from the street below. I turned away from watching Madrid's daily life and thought about my own situation. It would be several hours before I stepped into the bullring but first, I had my dressing ritual to undertake.

'When it comes to dressing me, you are the only one

who can fit my *coleta* without it dropping off, Luis,' I said good humouredly as he entered the room with my undergarments.

He smiled to himself. Every false ponytail fell off eventually; it was the nature of things.

'Red or blue today, *Jeffe*?'

'Blue, I do not anticipate any need to hide the blood,' I said with perhaps a little too much bravado.

He knew me well enough to understand that in a short time I would face the biggest test of my career. I needed to be fully prepared, the audience could be unforgiving and today I would fight in front of the king. That is an honour for any bullfighter and especially so for a poor boy from Triana. I needed to look my best and knew I must perform well.

'Francisco, you seem preoccupied. Are you worrying about César?' asked Santiago, a witness to the dressing.

'A little I think.'

Luis looked up from fastening the buttons of my shirt.

'Perhaps you should focus your energies on the bulls. Forget about César, forget about the crowd. Do not let them intimidate you, ignore them,' he said 'Here put on the waistcoat while I fetch the *chaquetilla*.'

'You have lost a bit of weight, Paco, see the slack,' he said, returning to help me on with the short jacket. 'Once the season is over, we'll have a week just eating.'

'You like your food don't you.'

'Well, some maybe.'

'Some! I remember you sitting on Papa's knee when you were a kid. You would eat anything and everything.'

'We never had enough at home. Your father was good to me,' he said lowering his eyes.

'I remember,' I said reaching out to pat him on his shoulder. 'Just my shoes and then we can leave for the bullring, eh?'

'It's a big day for you, Francisco, a big day for all of us. I wish you luck,' said Santiago standing back to admire the *traje de luces* in which Luis had so capably dressed me.

'Is there any news of Mexico?' I asked picking up my montera and putting it on my head before I took one last look in the mirror.

'Yes, it goes well but nothing is yet finalised. I will let you know when it is time to sign the contract and then we can show the New World what kind of bullfighter you are.

'Just Mexico?'

'For the first months, and then I am planning for you to visit Caracas and Cuba on the way home next spring.'

'What do you think of that, Luis, we're going to go to South America?'

Luis's jaw hung loose. I had not told anyone that Santiago was trying to arrange a tour for the winter season. I had earned a million pesetas for the season and expected to double my earnings with a winter in Mexico and Venezuela and of course, the cuadrilla would receive their share.

Luis's face lit up.

'Mexico, oh I have dreamed of going to Mexico. When will we go?'

'Not so fast, young man, I have to finalise the arrangements and I will, once tomorrow's papers come out with the story of the corrida, of how Francisco was crowned the best killer of bulls in all Spain.'

'You don't know that yet,' said Luis, his smile

beginning to wane.

'Trust me, young man, the papers will all be for Francisco, I promise you.'

Luis, trusting, innocent Luis, looked at Santiago with uncomprehending eyes but I understood finally. Quite suddenly it dawned upon me that not only had Santiago and his wife conjured up the rivalry that now gripped the bullfighting public but that he was also manipulating the newspaper stories. There seemed no end to the man's deviousness, and Gabriella, what part was she playing? Whatever it was, I had to admire them, for together they had made me wealthy, more so than I could ever have imagined.

It was two hours until the start of the corrida, the first of the crowds were already passing through the entrance as our limousine pulled up and with Luis's help, I made my way inside. Taking a moment to reflect, I looked through an open gate at the wide expanse of the sand covered arena and I felt a twinge of uneasiness. It was not unusual, I had similar feelings at every corrida I ever took part in but somehow this time was different. I could not shake off a feeling of foreboding. I usually did but the gnawing feeling in my stomach would not go away.

'Is there anything you need us to do?' asked Manolito as the cuadrilla met Luis and myself.

'No, I think I would like to spend some time in the chapel. I will catch up with you later,' I said believing that a period of calm might help my mood.

The encounter with Isabella and César had affected me more than I realised and was not what I would have wanted so close to the beginning of the corrida. The backdrop of the very public enmity whipped up by the press had served to amplify that situation and that, I knew, was dangerous.

The chapel was cool, the interior gloomy and illuminated only by light entering through a small stained-glass window. I knelt before the altar and prayed to the Virgin of Macarena, asking her to watch over me, protect both me and my cuadrilla in the coming contest and as I prayed, I felt a shiver run down my spine. Was it a portent of things to come? I did not know but even so, if that was God's will I prayed that I should die fighting in the bullring.

I had never questioned my mortality in such a way before. So far, my youth and vigour had protected me but something had changed. I did not want my death to be a lingering affair; the thought of a procession of mourners by my bedside waiting for me to leave this life was abhorrent. A morbid thought, yet it was obvious that I was beginning to doubt my ability and I felt compelled to close my eyes tight to calm my nerves. I took a deep breath and gradually the shadow of death passed. My feelings were not unusual, other matadors had confessed to the same fears and, shaking off my melancholy I left the chapel to walk along the short corridor and back into the outside world. Passing the along the white walled corridor I looked at posters announcing corridas past hanging on them, a graphic history of bullfighting that seemed to come to life and energise me.

César and his cuadrilla had already formed up near the archway leading to the main gate. The two sheriffs, on their fine white horses, were ready, and as we formed up, they rode out into the weakening afternoon sunshine and at their appearance the watching crowd exploded. Unable to contain their excitement the noise was deafening, funnelling through the arch towards me but the name I heard called out was not mine.

'They are shouting for César and not a lot for El Vaquerito,' I said.

'That means nothing, Paco, they are just excited,' said Luis coming to my side. 'It is the end of the corrida that matters. When you have shown them what you can do, I bet there will be more white handkerchiefs waving for you than César, just you wait and see.'

He was right, what was about to happen would determine which of us would emerge as the greatest bullfighter in Spain. The public were fickle, past triumphs counting for naught.

'Are you alright, Paco?'

I turned my head towards Manolito.

'Yes, why shouldn't I be?' I snapped.

'Sorreee, you seemed preoccupied that's all.'

'I'm fine, just lost in thought for a few moments. Nothing to worry about,' I said trying to convince not only them but also myself. 'Let's get ready,' I said, glancing at Luis.

'I don't think I have ever seen such a crowd,' he said.

'It's no surprise, have you read the papers? They are calling this the corrida of the century and it's still only nineteen twenty-eight,' said Manuel.

I listened to them for a few minutes more, watched César and noted him fidgeting with his cape. He too had nerves, he was apprehensive and knowing that gave me strength. I was as ready as I could be and placing my *capote* over my shoulder, I wished my team good luck and

Luque on his horse, nodded, and gave me a reassuring salute. This was it, the final showdown; today the public, the newspapers would judge which of either César or myself was the best bullfighter in Spain.

The sheriffs returned from their circuit of inspection, reported to the president and then they galloped towards us. All was in order and the white shawl appeared in the President's hand, the signal for the start of the corrida. The trumpet sounded and the band began to play and the mandatory paso doble filled the air. César looked across at me, I acknowledged him, and then, side by side, we led our cuadrillas out into a setting guaranteed to make even the most cynical rise to the occasion.

We waved to our supporters and detractors alike as we strutted like cockerels and when finally, the *paseíllo* was complete, myself and my cuadrilla retreated to the safety of the *barrera* to await the first of the bulls. It was César's privilege, as the senior matador, to fight first and for the next twenty minutes, the stage was his.

César played his bull with the degree of skill his public had come to expect, his passes were competent if not inspiring though I could see he was still playing his old tricks. His picadors had weakened the bull more than they should have, their lances' point's longer than those prescribed in the rules. Nobody seemed to notice and if they did there were no repercussions for César, only the adoration of his followers and as the bull died, they rose to their feet singing his praises.

Now it was our turn. Manolito and the brothers Manuel and José strode from their sanctuary behind the *barrera* while I waited with Luis at my side. The president raised his white shawl and the gate opened to reveal my first bull, a heavyweight of the Vistahermosa line with a fine silky black hide and horns well-shaped. A formidable opponent weighing over half a tonne and unfazed by the baying crowd, it rushed into the arena to come skidding to a standstill in a flurry of yellow sand as the unfamiliar scent of twenty thousand people unnerved it.

I wondered just what kind of animal I was fighting, so big so powerful and yet it seemed lost until finally, it raised its head, sniffed the air, its less than perfect eyes finally alighting upon Manolito and it charged, its bulk more agile and quicker than I would have expected. As it raced towards him, he turned and ran, vaulting the barrier to escape the charge, only for the bull to crash headlong into the woodwork and send splinters flying in all directions. Then, rapidly losing interest in Manolito, the bull turned to look for another target.

I had insisted upon the cuadrilla keeping fit and even after the arduous season we had endured, each of the banderillos were still capable of a good performance. Manuel was particularly adept, and as the bull charged, he ran at it, leaping spectacularly into the air and over the black hide. Outwitted, the bull turned on him and forced him to run for the safety of the *barrera* and as it rushed past, I watched the animal carefully, noting every move it made. It was important I knew something of its characteristics, its preferences during the charge for I would need to try to manage it, control it and bring it under my will.

In the event the fight was successful and my cuadrilla carried me on a lap of honour, the President awarded me both ears for my performance and to my pleasant surprise the crowd seemed to shout my name louder than they had César's and by the look on his face he was not taking my triumph lightly. Of course, today was important to us both, the day probably when the papers would hail one of us the best in Spain and whoever received that honour could name his price.

At the sound of the trumpet César's banderillos entered the arena and César's second bull, a Miura appeared at the gate. Hand-picked for its strength and aggression, like all the bulls, the animal had sharply curved horns and powerful shoulders, a dangerous combination. As the banderillos set about chasing the bull around the ring, testing its reactions, its courage, Victor sat astride his horse and watched before he and the second picador joined the fight.

'They need to be careful,' I said to Luis as the picadors approached the bull.

'I know, it looks a quick learner that one.'

'Exactly,' I said watching the bull as it turned to charge the horses.

For several minutes, the picadors guided their horses, confusing and goading the bull, their lances inflicting pain until eventually it failed to charge anymore. The tired animal simply stood in the centre of the bullring, head lowered as it caught its breath, blood-streaked mucus streaming from its nose and the crowd began to show its displeasure. I could see Victor was not happy, cantering his horse around the perimeter and then he urged it towards the bull, attempting to force the charge. But the bull looked indifferent, the crowd let out a moan of disappointment and I could see the frown on César brow.

He knew a timid bull would do him no favours with the aficionados and I wondered what he might do.

But the bull was no coward, at the very last second, it raised its head and twisted its body out of Victor's path and turning its horns almost caught the horse's rump. If it had then the power of the thrust would have tossed the horse like a feather. But Victor was aware and through his ability as a horseman he managed to escape injury and reignite the bull's fighting spirit.

'That could have been nasty,' said Manolito leaning on the barrier.

'It could have but he did very well,' I said as the picadors gave way to the banderillos and a blast of the trumpet announced the second act.

I reflected that an intelligent bull was always a danger and would learn very quickly and if it possessed a natural cunning then the matador should be wary. The picadors were and I could see they were keeping a distance between themselves and the bull until they had planted their darts in its bulging neck muscles and as it weakened, they became more adventurous. It was what the crowd wanted, expected and the three banderillos did not disappoint. After several minutes tormenting the bull they persuaded it towards the centre of the ring and with a wave of their hands, ran for the safety barrier.

The trumpet sounded for the final act and César made his appearance, strutting across the sand to the bull stood motionless at the centre of the bullring its head lowered and panting as blood streamed from its nose. and with his jaw set in determination for the word was that no one other than our individual supporters could say which of us was the best and this was his last chance before the season ended to prove himself. He started with his trick of turning his back on the bull and that drew enthusiastic applause from his fans. Yet as the fight progressed, I noticed he was still using his trick of leaning into the animal yet keeping far enough away from the horns to fooling his fans into believing he was taking a bigger risk than he really was. I could not blame him but to me it still amounted to cheating. At least today no one had shortened his bull's horns. The corrida was too important to have scandal.

He fought well enough but I had seen him perform many times and his moves, to me, were predictable and in the end he took his bow, not a brilliant performance I thought but as if to cover its mediocrity his cuadrilla made a great show of carrying him shoulder high to the President where, to my amazement, he awarded César both ears and the tail.

'He doesn't deserve them,' Luis said

I looked at him and then at José standing nearby, a look of incredulity on his face.

'Showmanship, that's all his lot can do well,' he said

As César, my second bull was also a Miura, powerfully built and harbouring a smouldering aggression as it burst into the ring, racing forward as if nothing could stop it. The bull was no *manso,* timidity not one of its attributes. It was a fine specimen of a fighting bull weighing in at well over five hundred kilograms I guessed, is jet black hide shining in the afternoon sun. Almost perfect except for one small detail, one horn angled lower than its twin.

The brothers Manuel and José began the first act working together, teasing the bull, forcing it to charge and then Manolito ran at it, confusing the animal and from behind the barrier I watched its every move. The Bull tended to paw the ground just once before launching its charge and it appeared to favour the deformed horn, slewing round at the end of its charge, preferring to use that horn to gore its opponent and I found that strange.

The bull was exceptional, giving my banderillos a hard time, a brave and dangerous bull, of that I had no doubt. Manolito survived a dangerous encounter with it and when the picadors entered the fight, they needed all their skill to keep the animal under control and unlike César's picadors they did no more damage than the regulations allowed leaving the bull capable, in control of its faculties and I believe those who really understand bullfighting realised César's cuadrilla had weakened his bull more than perhaps they should have and left it with much of the fight taken out of it. But to give César his due, he played the animal well and the crowd cheered his every move and now César's fight was over and for better or for worse it was my turn to show the world what I could do.

The trumpet announced the final act of my fight, the banderillos and picadors had done their work, now it was just me and the bull. I took my sword and the muleta. Stiffened by a short cane rod and stepped from behind the barrier to face the bull. Alone, near the centre of the ring it seemed uninterested in me, its head hung low, the pressure of its wounds beginning to tell and I knew I had to do something to revive its fighting spirit.

The animal picked up my scent, and turning in my direction, sniffed at the air, its eyes focused and I walked closer and then I turned my back on it and sank to my knees, I spread the cape over my shoulders in invitation, stimulating its instinct to attack and the bull reacted. I knew what was coming. My scent together with the fluttering of the cape was enough to trigger the charge and although I could not see the dark, angry eyes nor the flared nostrils, I heard the scraping of a hoof.

With a snort the bull launched itself at me, a simple straight attack and knowing I had little time to defend myself I rotated the muleta fully over my head and with my arm outstretched, placed it squarely in the bull's path. A dangerous move yet I executed it to perfection and as the bull swept harmlessly past, I jumped to my feet to see it skid to a halt and within just a second it turned. A roar of anticipation erupted, a noise of such magnitude I could believe that everyone in Madrid heard it. Without hesitation the bull charged, a straight and even charge, one that I could easily counter and spreading the muleta wide, I met it head on. With a twist of my left-hand wrist, I began a series of natural passes, turning the maddened animal one way and then the other, tiring it. I had the measure of the beast, I understood it, its preferences and for several minutes I worked a dangerously choreographed dance prompting the excited crowd to call my name and to calls of 'Olé' I swept the fan like shape, swirling it back and forth and the crowd loved it.

I knew the time had come for me to finish the job I was born to do. I placed the bull squarely and for a minute I left it waiting while I strutted my stuff, holding my head high, proud, turning it sharply for effect and as I passed the barrier

'Luis called to me, 'it's a strong bull this one, Paco, be careful.'

'It is, but it is also predictable,' I said through gritted teeth.

'You be careful, my friend, good luck.'

The animal was tiring yet was not quite finished and so I began to play it a little longer. This was the last fight, the last in a hard season, and more than just a bullfight; it was *the* bullfight, the one that would fix in the minds of the Spanish public the one whom they considered the best bullfighter in Spain. The newspapers had built the corrida, the *mano a mano,* into something special, an occasion and the crowd knew it and I knew in my heart that it was I and not César who was the premier bullfighter.

The bull raised its head, its imperfect eyes searching for me and it pawed the ground, I stood erect with my cape hanging at my side ready to perform the *coup de grâce*. The crowd sensed the end was near, cheers and calls spread all around and, with my sword in one hand I raised the muleta. Timing, it was all about timing... and position and when I judged the time right, I shook the cape drawing the beast closer and at that moment it seemed to mutate before my eyes, returning from the docile, beaten animal back into the fierce beast that had entered the bullring just twenty minutes earlier.

From somewhere it summoned up one last store of energy and my over confidence allowed it to catch me off guard. It came at me so quickly that I found myself having to twist my body to avoid the horns but at the same time it swerved just enough for the deformed horn to catch my inner thigh, the hard, sharp horn plunging deep into muscle. I could not escape as the bull turned me towards its bloodied, angry head and for an instant our eyes met. I swear that it had planned the move, the look in its dark eyes almost human as I found myself skewered, helpless, and then held aloft by the enormous strength of the animal.

Frantically I searched for help, screaming in pain as I looked frantically for the banderillos and yet, surprisingly, it was Luis who was the first to come to my aid. He had watched my every move from behind the *barrera* engrossed, his head constantly on the move as he copied my actions, my feints, lifting his shoulders as if he was the one playing the bull. Engrossed so deeply in my fight he had anticipated the goring and even as the bull gored me, he was leaving his place of safety. Stricken and as helpless as I was, I still witnessed his uneven gait propelling him towards me, shouting, his arms waving to draw the bull's attention. The bull turned towards him and lowered its head releasing me from the shackles of its horns and I fell onto the sandy floor unable to do anything other than watch as Luis used the scabbard of my sword, the only weapon he had to defend himself. He bravely stood his ground, waving the scabbard with a ferocity I had never seen before to try to keep the bull at bay, a puny gesture but one that saved me.

I must have passed out for I did not know where I was when I emerged from the blackness entombing me. My eyes were unable to focus, I had no idea where I was nor what had happened to me, and finding it difficult to understand the situation I searched my mind for clues.

Then it hit me, a searing pain engulfing my thigh and groin and I could do no more than cry out in pain.

'He's awake,' I heard someone say and then closer,

'how are you feeling?'

'Me?' I questioned stupidly.

'Yes, how do you feel? You have had a nasty goring.'

I opened my eyes but could make out no more than a shadow looking down at me. My mouth was dry and I tried to lick my lips but my tongue felt swollen, too big and then I felt a hand on the back of my head and a trickle of cool water eased my thirst.

'Where am I?' I finally managed to ask.

'The Hospital de la Princesa. I am Doctor Fernando Suarez Garcia.'

Finally, I managed to focus my eyes enough to recognise a white coat, and then the doctor looking at me a serious look on his face.

'You are in safe hands now.'

'Wh... what happened?'

'You were gored, badly gored, the bull you were fighting turned on you. They say you had no chance to avoid it.'

Involuntarily I licked my lips and felt the cup press against them for a second time and I gulped down more water. The liquid helped and gradually my mind began to clear. I remembered the fight in a vague and disjointed way. The noise, the bull, still I was confused but I was beginning to remember.

'What happened, what went wrong, how bad is my wound?' I said and then I remembered Luis, the memory flooding back.

The last I remembered was that he was in a dangerous position, and I knew he could not handle the bull on his own. We would never let him play even the three-year-olds in Tablada and I feared the worst.

'Paco, are you awake, are you alright?'

A familiar voice.

'Luis?' I said, confused.

'No, it's me, Manolito, we are here, me and Manuel and José. How are you feeling. We were worried.'

'Where is Luis?' I asked again.

'Er... he will not be coming Paco, er... the accident,' said Manuel, his voice husky, different somehow.

'Accident, oh yes.'

'He's dead, Paco, he tried to save you. The bull caught him square in the chest. He's gone, I'm sorry, we are all sorry.'

'Dead,' was all I could say, the shock too much for me to take in and I closed my eyes, pushing my head against the pillow as if that might ease the pain.

For several minutes no one spoke until finally I opened my eyes to see three pairs of anxious eyes looking back at me.

In the bullring, there is always the danger of a serious injury or even death, a fact of life for a bullfighter but when it happens so close and to one less equipped to deal with the situation it comes as a shock. No one was closer to me than Luis and the news of his death left me stunned, a feeling of hollowness inside and I did not know quite what to do. I looked at each of my friends and saw in their eyes the same hollowness I felt. Once the five musketeer we were now four.

'The funeral,' I said, 'when is the funeral?'

'The day after tomorrow, Santiago arranged for Luis to be taken home and we are accompanying his coffin on the last train this afternoon. Santiago and his wife are travelling by car tomorrow,' said José.

'We can only stop a little while longer Paco,' said Manolito. 'The train leaves at four o clock and we cannot miss it.'

'I know,' I said, 'I wish I could come with you.'

'There is nothing you can do; you're not fit to travel. You need to get back to full health.'

After a few words, the boys left me to catch their train. None of us mentioned the bullfight, even César did not enter the conversation, our thoughts solely for Luis. I watched them troop out of the ward and after they had gone, I lay there I trying to relive the fight, the accident, how it had happened was it my fault? I couldn't answer any of the questions and through trying I became overwhelmed with fatigue and I drifted into a deep sleep.

I must have slept for a long time for it was light when I finally woke and the doctor was already doing his rounds.

'Do you feel better today, Señor Martinez?' he said when he reached my bed.

'Yes, better, but my best friend was killed looking out for me. How do I handle that, doctor?'

'I'm sorry, yes I did know. My job is to repair your body, but for your anxieties, your mental wellbeing, then I can only offer a sympathetic ear I am afraid. We need to change your dressing,' he said placing a thermometer in my mouth and taking hold of my wrist.

'Right, your heart rate is fine though your temperature is a little high, but nothing to worry about. Now let me have a look at this wound of yours. I put rather a lot of stitches in when you arrived and I need to see just how well they are holding,' he said, peeling back the solitary sheet. 'We don't want any infection, do we?'

'No, I suppose not,' I said closing my eyes tight as the sharp pain returned to my lower body.

'The stitches are holding but the dressing needs changing. I will tell the nurse to come and take over. You are a lucky man, Señor Martinez. I will see you again tomorrow.'

I nodded, thankful at least for his attention and turning my head I noticed a nurse holding an enamel bowl.

'Señor Martinez, would you mind if I remove the sheet from your bed, I have to change the dressing.'

'Er, no,' I said, caring for nothing except Luis.

'Just relax,' she said, 'I need to peel back the dressing, okay.'

I think I looked at her and mumbled something like 'just get on with it.'

She was smart, professional looking, and wearing a white cloth mask. I could not see her face but I could see her eyes and they were looking straight at me.

'I hope you have done this before.'

'Once or twice. I think you forget I have changed your dressings before.'

'I haven't needed dressings changed, not since I was gored in Málaga a couple of years ago. Were you one of the nurses there?'

'No,' she said turning to make a start on the dressing, a pair of scissors in her hand, and as she reached over to begin, she added, 'The last time I did this for you was a few years ago.'

'Did what?' I asked, puzzled.

'The last time it was your shoulder, not your leg. I cleaned that wound several times.'

'Cl... when, what?'

I was confused and as I tried to understand what was going on, I looked more closely at those blue eyes. I didn't understand, but those eyes, what was it about them?

'Nurse Isabella!' I exclaimed, shocked, and puzzled.

'Yes, Nurse Isabella. We will have to stop meeting like this, Paco.'

'Where in heaven's name have you come from?'

I was all questions but she had her work to do and ordered me into silence.

'Wow, that hurts,' I said.

'It is supposed to, it is not doing its job if does not sting.'

'Phew, that was hard,' I said after she finished her work.

'I'm not surprised, it's a nasty wound. The doctor says you are lucky to be alive. You have lost a lot of blood so we need to make sure you drink plenty of water, tea, coffee, anything like that. Would you like some now?'

I nodded, my mouth was very dry and involuntarily I licked my lips.

'Here let me pour you some water,' she said removing her mask and turning to the small table beside my bed.

'That's better,' I said after draining the glass.

'I heard you were fighting in Madrid; I have been reading about you in the newspapers. You have caused quite a stir you know.'

'I have a rough idea that I had. It's not my fault you know.'

'How?'

'The newspapers, they have blown the rivalry between me and César up out of all proportion.'

'And you nearly lost your life in the process.'

'Isn't that a matador's lot? We run the risk of injury every time we fight, it's the job. Anyway, what are you doing here, what happened in Morocco, why did you leave?'

'Not long after you were discharged from the military hospital the army joined with the French to take on Abd el-Krim and his Riffians.'

'I know about that, I read about it in the papers. So, did it affect you in the hospital?'

'Yes, although the war dragged on for some time, we didn't see so many casualties and headquarters decided to send most of the volunteer nurses back home. I was one. I told you I came from Madrid so, of course, I returned here. After a short rest, I wondered what to do and recognised that nursing was something I enjoyed so I made enquiries. The hospital was short staffed, I told them of my time working in the military hospital and I was offered a post.'

She stopped talking, tilted her head back and the way the sunlight caught her face reminded me so much of our time in Ceuta. She was as I remembered, a natural beauty, her blue eyes, her olive skin, and most of all her radiant smile.

'I will have to go, Paco. I have another patient to see before my shift ends. I will come and see you tomorrow.'

She began to move the screening from around my bed and as I watched her walk away, memories of my time in Ceuta flooding back and after a while I must have fallen asleep because from my slumber, I heard my name called. First, I thought it was the nurse but when I opened my eyes it was to see Gabriella looking at me.

'Francisco, good you are awake, how are you feeling?'

Santiago was with her and both had a serious look on their faces.

'I am so sorry this has happened and Luis...'

She looked at Santiago for support; he hesitated before offering some consolation.

'He was a good man, Francisco, he will be sorely missed I am sure, but we must be positive.'

'Positive, what is there to be positive about? My best friend is dead. He died trying to save me. There is nothing to be positive about.'

'Don't upset yourself,' said Gabriella, touching my arm. 'We are only thinking of you and how we can rebuild for next season and the tour of Mexico later this year,' she said looking at her husband.

I could not quite take in what she was saying; any thought of next season, never mind Mexico, could not be further from my mind.

'You are going to the funeral?'

'Yes, we are driving back in the morning so we can attend. I understand you will not be coming'

'No, the doctor will not let me leave hospital for several days. The rest left yesterday. I am glad you are going. Tell everyone my thoughts are with them, will you?'

'Of course, and by the way, the newspapers are hailing Luis as a hero. The way he walked was a joke in the past, but his bravery has made people see him in a different light.'

'I suppose I should be grateful for that. He always wanted to be known for his job and not his disability. Make sure his mother gets his money, will you? They were very poor until I gave Luis the job of sword boy. It made him so proud, not just to be my favoured assistant but that he could help look after his family.'

'We made more money from this corrida than any other. You will earn a lot from it and so will the cuadrilla. I know it is little consolation but Luis's family will at least be looked after.'

I just nodded. Gabriella meant to comfort me I am sure but her words seemed callous and as I looked up, she avoided my eyes, simply patting me on my shoulder and wishing me a speedy recovery.

'César offers his wish for your speedy recovery, and Isabella, she is concerned for you also,' added Santiago. 'When you are well enough to travel come and see me at my office, your contract has come to an end and we need to talk about the future. I know now is not the time but when you are ready.'

'And what of this rivalry between me and César the two of you dreamed up. Who us top dog, César I suppose?'

'After Luis's death that did not seem so important. I made sure the newspapers I can influence printed stories about him and that your rivalry was for the good of bullfighting. True there will be fanatical supporters on both sides who proclaim their favourite the best but overall bullfighting is the winner.'

There seemed little else to discuss, I was weak, feeling tired and my mind in a whirl after all that had happened. And now Mexico, a new contract, I felt exhausted and, seeing my distress, they left me. After all I had been through, I simply wanted peace. The pain had returned and I was in no mood to do anything other than lay back on my pillow and fight it but through it all I saw Gabriella and remembered our liaison.

Had it meant anything? I did not believe so. I remembered more than the passion, the conversations and promises, they had seemed important but now I began to see that my relationship with her was about nothing more than money. She and Santiago had used me, groomed me I suppose. They had used me all along and I felt stupid, but to be honest, they had helped make me wealthy.

I do not know how long I slept but I awoke to the sound of birdsong, sunshine forcing its way through the slim partings of the window blinds and I became aware that someone was looking down at me.

'Good morning, Señor Martinez. How are you feeling this morning?'

'Good morning, doctor,' I said, coming fully awake, turning to look at him. 'I am feeling well enough,' I said, not at all sure if that were true.

'I think we might try to get you up on your feet today. Do you think you can manage?'

'I suppose so. I will give it a try.'

'I will ask the nurse to assist you after breakfast; we need to see if there are any complications.'

'Complications?'

'Stiffness mainly, but you might find that you cannot walk easily and we may need to try some physiotherapy,' he said taking a quick look at my record card before leaving me alone.

It was a shock to learn I could have problems walking and in a moment of black humour I could not help feeling that Luis had something to do with it. In my mind I saw his face and I called out, Thanks, Luis, I see you are still causing trouble. Then it struck me, what would I do if I could not walk properly, not be capable of fighting bulls anymore? I did not have time to dwell.

'Good morning.'

'Isabella,' I said.

'No need to sound so surprised,' she said, a smile lighting up her face. 'Doctor says you should try standing. Can you do that, do you think?'

'I'll try,' I said.

'Right let's sit you up, swing your legs over,' she said and gingerly I did, pausing halfway to gather my strength. 'Good, now hold my hands.'

If ever I needed an incentive to hold Isabella's hands, then this was it and, between the two of us, I managed to stand.

'I'm not a pretty sight, am I?' I said, looking down at my naked legs and the great swathe of bandages covering the wound.

'Nothing I haven't seen before,' she replied and I remember thinking that if anyone could make me walk it would be her and for maybe half an hour, guided by Isabella, I walked slowly between the rows of beds. Some of the other patients, by now aware of who I was, offered encouragement, telling me the bulls of Spain were worrying that I would soon return to the bullring.

'Will you go back to Seville, Paco? It could be a problem travelling, the wound could open,' said Isabella as I sat back on the bed.

'That was my plan. Do you think I should do something different?'

She looked at me with those wonderful blue eyes, her cheeks flushed, and I could not help myself.

'Do you have someone special?'

She did not answer immediately, her eyes simply looking at me, tracing across my face, and I knew then what I must do. Nineteen twenty-nine could wait, I had found something far more precious than bullfighting.

Author's note:

Bullfighting is a contentious issue in many quarters. Even in Spain, the home of bullfighting, attendances are declining particularly among the younger generation and the argument to ban bullfighting outright rages in the Spanish courts. Personally, I am not in favour of bullfighting but this is an account of a young man of his time. Today that same young man might aspire to become a pop star or perhaps a footballer but the narrative is the same, of ambition, flawless talent, and the luck that turns a dream into reality.

Printed in Great Britain
by Amazon